End Run on
MADISON
AVENUE

End Run on

MADISON AVENUE

Bob Goldberg

www.ivyhousebooks.com

PUBLISHED BY IVY HOUSE PUBLISHING GROUP
5122 Bur Oak Circle, Raleigh, NC 27612
United States of America
919-782-0281
www.ivyhousebooks.com

ISBN: 1-57197-354-0
Library of Congress Control Number: 2002113593

Printed in the United States of America

To Lee, Marsha, and Mark

ONE

HE SLOWLY entered the elevator, artist's portfolio tightly clutched under his right arm, fingers of his left hand bent securely around the handle. Five well-dressed men, all wearing dark winter coats that covered pinstripe navy blue suits, followed him quickly. Each coat was open wide enough to permit their broadly striped silk ties to weakly peek out from their starched white shirts. Their expressionless faces seemed to be deep in thought. *Corporate executives,* he surmised as he noticed their briefcases. These men were the "old-chum" breed from prep schools and private colleges. At an interview some weeks before, he recalled with anger a similar group of well-suited, faceless young executives. One of them, looking at his frayed French cuff, sarcastically asked, "Where did you prep before college?"

In the elevator, no one smiled, but their eyes lifted slightly when a young woman with long black hair, perhaps about twenty-five, entered. She carried a large black portfolio that contrasted sharply with her pale tan knobby turtleneck sweater and her tan wool pants. *An artist,* he thought. *Could we be going to the same place?* He quickly studied her face, her alert looking dark eyes, and a somewhat solicitous smile; she was perhaps a little nervous. Fearful of meeting her eyes, he lowered his gaze to the floor.

He knew that he was anxious. He perspired. Anxiety was something he continuously had to deal with. Beads of sweat tended to roll down from his armpits, travel along his light gray shirt, and cluster in little balls inside his French cuffs. He had concealed the frayed edge by folding it a little shorter and he now wondered if his perspiration would undo the fold. This meeting was very important to him. It was going to be an introductory presentation. Roland had been calling this particular executive for weeks just to get the appointment and then he had made it for a Wednesday morning. He always felt better in the middle of the week.

The Philip Morris lady with whom he had spoken suggested a meeting on Monday afternoon. He knew that at the start of the week, he would be unwilling to tear himself away from the magical influence of his drawing table. He would probably be annoyed if he were forced to leave his assistant alone to start an important project without his artist's eye and creative input. Sure, Madeline was a capable artist, but the growth of his business depended on his own insights and his own talents.

The elevator car stopped on the twelfth floor and Roland watched three of the faceless men exit, walk briskly into a well-illuminated wood paneled reception area, nod to a faceless receptionist, and then disappear. He thought that everyone in executive groups was always faceless. He knew that they had clean, tanned faces and that they looked so much alike. But he never could recognize any one, even if he had met with them the day before. He smiled. *Why do I hate them so much?* He thought. As the doors closed, he moved to the rear of the cab to see who would exit along with him when they reached the twenty-second floor.

Roland Levy dreaded presentations of his work, especially before executives. Not that it was bad and not that he had only a limited collection of printed samples of successfully designed packages. He had definite ideas about visual impact and instant communications that he felt were strongly personal. He always found it somewhat difficult to explain how his designs demonstrated these ideas when he himself was not exactly certain. There was always the fear that others—especially executives with lengthy careers in judging and approving all the look-alike consumer packages that crowded the dull shelves in retail stores—would not even begin to understand him when he started to talk about his theories of graphic directions.

"Just leave samples on the table or give us a collection of photographs and we'll judge whether we will call you for a project," was the response that he knew so well. He reasoned, *If the artist and his work are one, why must they be separated? Why do executives who do not know me judge my talent on the merit of my work? They do not know my thinking and they fail to ask me about my theories.* These executives based their selections on their own personal judgment. Roland strongly rejected this.

Philip Morris would be different, he hoped.

Ms. Marlowe, the young-sounding lady with whom he had spoken on the telephone, confirmed the appointment. She said that they were looking for fresh new talent for the packaging of future cigarette brands along with various other projects that management was considering. She seemed to be so inviting and he was so eager to work on a challenging assignment that he forgot to ask her whom he would see. He feared to ask her how the interview would be conducted. He wondered if he would show his work, or if they would view it without him. Most presentations were disastrous. His mind raced on ways to make this one different.

Suddenly, the elevator door opened. The taller of the two men walked out first, followed immediately by the woman who confidently strode up to the reception desk. Roland Levy paused. This was the meeting that he had worked so hard to achieve. Now, filled with anxiety, he barely moved as he left the elevator.

He met a public relations executive from Philip Morris some weeks before who invited him to be a guest at a meeting of the Industrial Designers Society of America. Talking to a member, Bill Predune, after the meeting, he exchanged business cards and learned that Ms. Marlowe was the person to contact for the firm's freelance package design assignments. "Don't mention my name," Bill had said, "but I know that they are looking for fresh talent."

A spark kindled in Roland's mind as he heard the fresh-talent phrase. He pondered its meaning. The account abruptly became very important. Maybe he really was the one Philip Morris was seeking. He could really be that one if they listened to his ideas and his theories and then studied his work with an open mind while he carefully explained the thinking that went into each project.

He suddenly found himself at the reception desk where he handed his card to a disinterested woman stuffing papers into various envelopes, answering telephone calls, and paying little attention to the visitors. The tall gentlemen had disappeared, probably through one of the doors leading to the offices. Maybe he would conduct the interview. Roland tried to remember his face, but it was a complete blank. Then he noticed the young woman already seated on one of the reception room couches, turning pages in a magazine. She seemed oblivious to both her surroundings and him. *Probably has been here before,* he thought.

It may have been ten minutes, Roland wasn't sure, when he heard the receptionist call, "Ms. Liforest, Mr. John Gillespie will see you now." Quickly, she gathered her things together, picked up her portfolio, walked through the door on the right of the reception desk, and was gone.

Why was she called before him and was she seeing his interviewer? The wait and the silence seemed unbearable. Was it twenty minutes? Could it be longer? He hadn't looked at his wristwatch when the door opened and a smiling Ms. Liforest walked quickly to the elevator with a brief wave and a smile to the receptionist.

"Mr. Levy, you're next. Mr. Gillespie will see you now. Just go through this door. He will be waiting in the first conference room on the left."

The receptionist smiled briefly for the first time. Slowly, he lifted his portfolio to the familiar place under his right arm, tossed his coat over his other arm, and walked through the door. His mind was racing with questions. Who was this Liforest person—an artist, an agent, or a packaging designer? He was to see the same interviewing executive as she. There was no time for explanations. Mr. Gillespie, a tall distinguished looking man in his forties, well dressed in a dark gray business suit with an initialed white shirt and foulard tie, smiled at him from the entrance to the conference room.

"It is nice to meet you, Mr. Levy. I'm looking forward to seeing your work." He quickly ushered Roland into the conference room

"Thank you, Mr. Gillespie. I'm glad to be here and I look forward to working with your company. Philip Morris is my favorite brand."

Switching his portfolio to his left arm, he extended his right hand for a brief handshake that Mr. Gillespie grasped firmly. Then the interviewer moved swiftly to a chair on the other side of the room so the conference table would be between them. "Let's get right to it," he said cheerfully.

Roland placed his portfolio on the table and awkwardly fumbled with the zipper while at the same time he tried to balance his coat on the arm of one of the chairs. "Show me the type of work that you do," said Mr. Gillespie as he sat down on his side of the large mahogany conference table. His eyes were glued on the portfolio and he smiled pleasantly with a confidence that seemed to be natural for a faceless executive. His tone, his smile, and his all too pleasant manner made Roland wish he had never arranged for this meeting. For the first time, he was actually seeing a face, an executive face, all accommodating and anxious to see his work.

Roland opened his black presentation case, the large leather portfolio that Sam Flax himself had taken from the back room of his Twenty-eighth Street art supply store and explained that even the account executive from Raymond Loewy's design office had admired it and bought one. Sam, a congenial man who owned Flax Art Supplies, was an old-timer in the business who had guided the careers of many successful designers. He urged them to invest in the proper equipment and often gave them leads to national accounts. When Sam made a suggestion, Roland always listened, and then struggled to make the purchase.

He knew that this portfolio was too expensive. He never told his wife that he had paid almost two hundred dollars for just a bag to carry things. This was different. It made a good first impression, like his dark pinstripe suit, his discreetly figured tie, carefully shined shoes, and the French cuffed shirt. The case containing his design work was a frame to emphasize the presentation.

"Mr. Gillespie," he began in a low hoarse voice, "I do not have samples of printed cigarette packages that I have designed. From the designs of candy, toy, and toiletries packages that I am going to show you, you will see how I have created strong brand marks and placed interesting lettering in strategic locations for instant communication."

One by one, he removed the packages from his case, carefully positioning them on his portfolio. With his finger, he pointed to the different graphic elements on each one to be sure that Mr. Gillespie's eyes were focused on the areas, letters, and colors of which he was speaking.

"Any trained and talented artist can cover the surface of these packages with design elements," he said, "but only the flow of visual communications makes them successful. All my designs have been created for impact effectiveness and quick purchase decisions."

The interviewing executive sat silently as Roland further explained his theories of no tan, color contrast, contours, and sans-serif lettering styles as motivators for consumer attention, interest, and ultimate desire for a product. He could see that Mr. Gillespie was troubled. Gillespie clasped his hands in front of him on the table and waited patiently until Roland seemed to be finished. Then he slowly began to speak.

"Mr. Levy, Philip Morris has been marketing cigarettes and other products for many years and has been very successful with its packaging. Many of our brands are best sellers in their markets. I do appreciate your taking the time to visit with us to explain your ideas and to present samples of your package designs. We really appreciate it. I will report this interview to John McGraw, our packaging brand leader.

Should he wish to see you, his secretary will call your office for an appointment. I thank you for your time. Please ask the receptionist to send in the next appointment."

Somewhat bewildered, in a daze, and extremely mad, Roland pushed the packages into his portfolio, grabbed his coat, and walked out into the reception room. Mr. Gillespie followed him to the door, nodded to the receptionist, and as if by code, she was already calling another young lady who walked passed him swinging her portfolio with her left hand and extending the right toward a smiling Mr. Gillespie. Everything was a blur as Roland walked into the elevator, reached the lobby floor, and quickly left the building.

He looked at his wristwatch. It was 10 A.M. Just across Madison Avenue, he spied a luncheonette, and fortunately, it was a one-way street with traffic moving uptown. At a fast pace, nearly running, with his overcoat under one arm and the precious portfolio in the other, he dodged cars and a bus to reach the other side. Once in the luncheonette, Roland settled down in a booth and ordered coffee with a buttered bagel. He tried to rethink the Philip Morris interview.

John Gillespie seemed to be a quiet, reflective man with an amiable personality. Why did he feel enraged when he left the interview? Certainly Mr. Gillespie was not displeased with his artwork. Maybe the problem was with his own attitude?

He knew that this was a problem. It wasn't his fault. He blamed it on the preppies who just wouldn't listen attentively to someone who was not one of their own.

Roland Levy always devoted many hours straining his creative efforts to produce designs that in his own mind fullfilled the objectives that he desired. Sometimes he created a cluster of shapes and colors that he felt would produce a feeling of excitement when viewed by an observant consumer. At other times he strained his creative talent to produce softness, rigidity, or even the feelings of playfulness and mirth.

"This is the function of an industrial designer," he told himself. "I must create a mood through my graphic and three-dimensional designs that will activate a consumer. The preppy boys just like to see pretty designs."

Alone at idle moments, he compared his beliefs concerning the function of a designer with the creative efforts of fine artists.

"They simply paint a scene to please their own emotions. You can see it in a somber watercolor landscape painting. The artist paints a meadow with flowers in the foreground, a peaceful lake in the center and then paints gray-purple mountains in a distance with a cobalt blue sky in the background. Hopefully, some art-loving person who shares that feeling may ultimately purchase the painting from a dealer to display it in her home . . . or it may never be sold.

"No, not for me," he continued. "As an industrial designer, I first interpret the needs of the consumer and through my training and talent I create the desired mood. That is my goal. When clients understand this they will contract for my services first and then ansiously await my solutions. This is the practice followed by the other professions.

"John Gillespie would have retained my services if he had simply taken the trouble to understand my objectives.

"Is my attitude wrong?" he pondered.

TWO

ROLAND LEVY always had mixed feelings. Why did he call on a large corporation like Philip Morris? He knew that they never retained small firms, especially a one-man shop with a part-time secretary and only one young artist assistant, a drop-out from art school, to help him with his work. Madeline was a gem, but the kind that only other artists could appreciate. She was very talented and capable with the skill to render precise lettering styles, but provocative on the telephone when the secretary was out and on some mornings, she arrived dressed in outfits that even embarrassed him. She loved to contrast orange knee length socks and Nike blue and white sneakers with black midi-pants and a red halter.

Certainly, he could not invite clients to his small office. It was cleverly arranged with Madeline's drawing table and her Mac computer in the middle room with enough space for him to work on a small drawing table on either side. But he was sloppy and careless with his tools and materials, so the room was never very neat. The front room looked more like an office with a small desk and computer for Maxine Nierman, a few framed photographs of design projects, and a small showcase for packages. The rear room was for conferences with a slide projector and screen, a glass conference table, and an assortment of second hand chairs. Most of the time, it served as his office and it was cluttered with art supplies as well as partially completed projects piled carelessly on a small couch. This was where he did his creative thinking.

The walls were unpainted. He had planned to coat them with brightly colored paint and interesting wall coverings, but everything else seemed to be more important. A good deal of his time was spent on writing sales letters that Maxine sent to firms whom he considered to be good prospects. Most of these were small businesses in downtown Manhattan, Brooklyn, and Queens. Experience had helped him to realize that letters sent to large firms never reached decision-making executives. The lower echelon people discreetly disposed of them.

It was impossible to make cold-calls on prospective clients. They made you sit so long in reception rooms and, if someone would take the time to see you, it was often an arrogant purchasing executive or one of his assistants who wanted to know your price before he even asked what services you supplied.

"Industrial design?" they would question upon reading his business card. "What's that? Oh, you do the artwork for packaging. Are you a printer, too?"

By this time, Roland Levy would be ready to scream, to pounce on them with anger, or to just run in the opposite direction. Out of courtesy, he always stood still, smiled slightly, waited for the questions to stop and their negative response to take over.

"We get all of our art work from our printers—that's why we give them the business. Just ask one of the printers. It's nice to meet you, come back another time, I'm very busy just now."

They were all alike, just doing their good-will jobs. He remembered every interview. He especially remembered the few people who asked him to make design suggestions. "For free!" they would say. "Just give us some color sketches and a few good ideas. If we like 'em, we'll give you a chance with our printer." The thoughts and the memories were depressing.

His mind wandered back to the Philip Morris interview. The preppy executives who work for large firms are different. Sure, they only like to associate with their own kind, but they are less abrupt and they do work with industrial designers. Perhaps he should have showed Mr. Gillespie some full color renderings of his suggested redesigns for popular food products. He definitely should have carried a small slide projector and, if he could find a screen or a clear wall in the conference room, he could have shown the slides that he had made to illustrate his design theories. But he had so many mixed feelings.

Suddenly, he noticed Ms. Liforest, the woman from the elevator at Philip Morris, at a booth at the far end of the luncheonette talking to a neatly dressed older woman. She was looking at a pad placed between them and appeared to be describing or designing something.

Did she get an assignment from Mr. Gillespie? he wondered. *Did she push her way in front of me and take the one design assignment that Philip Morris had available?* Without any hesitation, feeling sorry for himself, but angry that someone else had achieved the goal he was seeking, he stood up and walked directly to her table.

"Are you Ms. Liforest?"

"Yes. Didn't I see you just a short time ago at the Philip Morris office?"

"Yes. My name is Roland Levy. They invited me for a presentation, but I don't think that it went too well. I'm an industrial designer. What do you do?"

"Why don't you sit down, Mr. Levy. This is my friend and partner, Elaine Waltham. We're artists' representatives. You know—spots, renderings, and cartoons. We rep for a number of different artists."

"Is Philip Morris a client?"

"Well, John Gillespie has asked me to supply some cartoons for a sequence they're planning. It's my second assignment with them. We're discussing it now."

"I must get back to my office. Do you have a card? Maybe we can talk about it at a quick lunch some time?"

Roland took the card, picked up the check at his booth, paid the cashier, and left the luncheonette in a huff. He had to think this thing out more clearly in the privacy of his own office.

Walking at a quick pace along Madison Avenue, he tossed his coat over his shoulder as a cape and let his precious portfolio swing forward and back as he held it tightly in his right hand. He passed the elegant store fronts with their display windows discreetly displaying fashion wear, jewelry, and cosmetics. He crossed the busy side streets, half running and dodging the cruising taxicabs and the angry horn-blowing drivers who seemed to be in a hurry to go somewhere.

The buses on Madison Avenue all traveled uptown and he hated the crowded downtown buses on Lexington Avenue, just one long block toward the east. Roland loved New York but he hated the successful executives. He hated the long walk from their prestigious office buildings on Madison Avenue between Fortieth Street and Fifty-Seventh Street to his office in the lower rent district near Twenty-Ninth Street.

He stopped abruptly in front of an art gallery and framing store to look at a watercolor painting displayed in the window.

"Someday," he whispered to himself, "I'm going to paint like that."

THREE

"SO, HOW did you get the name Roland?" she asked with a pleasant smile. Susan Liforest liked to start a conversation on a personal level.

They were seated opposite each other at a small table toward the back of the Weathervane Inn on Madison Avenue. Susan was wearing a blue business suit with a white opened collar shirt and Roland wore his usual gray pinstriped suit with a striped silk tie. For the first time, he looked at her face without anger and jealousy. She was very pretty with big sparkling brown eyes, which were accented by thin black eyebrows and long eyelashes that seemed to emerge in a playful manner from her lightly sun tanned face. As she spoke, her lips smiled constantly and the rich red glow brought warmth to her face. She did have the annoying habit of touching her black shoulder length hair and moving it carelessly behind her ears. *Just a few years out of college,* he thought. *She still uses those uncertain, but playful movements and expressions of a charming college senior.* Her question took him completely off guard and he answered truthfully, with just a few seconds of hesitation.

"You're a little nosey. I just adopted it for business. My old friends and my parents call me Rube. My real name is Rueben Levy. It just didn't look classy enough on a business card, so I changed it to Roland. Don't you think it adds distinction?"

"Distinction, perhaps, but it certainly is not as glamorous as my name. Do you like Liforest?"

"It is a very interesting name. Where did your family come from? Somehow, I detect a bit of a French rhythm in your manner of speaking. Were you born in Paris?"

"No, Brooklyn. It was Levins when I went to college. But there are hundreds of Susan Levins. Now I'm Susan Liforest. Distinguished, right?" She laughed.

Her face lit up with a broad grin. They were quite compatible. As she talked, he had gradually moved his head and arms closer to her and was uncomfortably seated on the edge of his chair leaning across the table in a rather conscious effort to close the space between them.

"Where did you go to college?"

I started at Stern College on Lexington Avenue. It's a school for orthodox Jewish girls, but after one year, I had enough of the gals and my parents approved my going to Buffalo."

"Did you major in art?" This Susan Liforest was intriguing and he wanted to know much more about her.

"Well, it was that way in the beginning. You know that the State University at Buffalo has a fine museum and a great art faculty, but most of the art majors were so good. I felt that my talents just couldn't measure up. I like business, so I transferred to marketing and that became my major."

As she talked, flashing her sheepish grin, fingering her hair and flicking her eyelids to accent a particular sentence, his interest slowly turned to desire. He had to see her again.

"Do you live in the city?"

"No, I have a studio apartment on Queens Boulevard. I guess that you call it Forest Hills. It is only a block from the subway, so it is a hop, skip, and a jump into the city."

Roland looked at his watch, it was 2 P.M. and he still had hours of work that he had scheduled for the afternoon. Signaling the waiter, he requested the check and they both rose to put on their coats.

The waiter held Susan's coat. She turned to face him, slipped her two arms into the sleeves, and then asked Roland, "Will you button it up for me? The buttons are in the back."

As his fingers carefully pressed the buttons into each of the four holes, he wondered where and how she always found someone to help her put the coat on and even to take it off. What did she do at night? Was this just a ploy to have any man nearby attend to her needs? *Poor helpless little me, I need you to help me button my coat. She is irresistible,* he thought, *but I have to admit that with or without a man's assistance, she looks beautiful in that coat with its smoothly tailored front and flared-out back.* It was her need for a man's hand, or even a woman's, that puzzled him.

By this time, they were outside in the cold January wind and she was waving her hand in the direction of the Madison Avenue traffic to attract an uptown cab. As the first cabby stopped, she opened the door with her right hand, turned, blew him a casual kiss with the left, slung her shoulder strap bag on the seat, and as soon as she was settled in the cab, it literally flew into the traffic pattern on the right.

As Roland walked the one block south to his office building at 79 Madison Avenue, his mind raced with thoughts. He thought about Phillip Morris, felt anger toward the preppies, and felt desire and fantasy toward Susan Liforest, but his mind cleared instantly as he walked into the building and took the elevator to his twelfth floor office.

Maxine Nierman was waiting for him when he entered the office. She had a list of telephone calls, one she thought was most important. It was from an irate folding box salesman who had given him a lead to a toy manufacturer more than a week before. She wondered what had taken Roland so long to follow up on this.

He walked with her through the studio to his private office, waived to Madeline, and told her that he would be with her in just a few minutes. He hadn't really discussed the Philip Morris interview with anyone since he had other scheduled meetings on Wednesday and the follow-up with Susan Liforest was at lunch today. With so much out-of-the-office activity, this Thursday afternoon was going to be a busy one.

Maxine was a beautiful woman. She was tall and athletic looking with streaks of premature gray in her closely cropped hair. Although she was only nine or ten years older than Roland at twenty-nine years old, she had married quite young, but divorced her alcoholic husband after seven years of difficult living. Her second husband, a prominent attorney, about twelve years older than she, succumbed to a heart attack two years before. She had known Roland through a mutual relative and had always liked him, so when he needed a secretary, she eagerly asked him for the job.

"Was the lunch productive?" she questioned. "What kind of a gal is that young lady and can she get you into Philip Morris?"

"I'll need some time to think about it. She has some interesting contacts. We'll talk about it at the end of the week."

Maxine reviewed the telephone calls, the letters, offered numerous suggestions, and then, on a small pad held in her left hand, she wrote the information that he was giving her including four letters she was to compose, type, and mail with her initials instead of his signature. She turned to leave, but then suddenly gave him a peck on the cheek with wet lips and whispered, "Go get 'em, my favorite designer."

Alone in his office, Roland's thoughts quickly turned to Susan. *What should we do next?* She had enticed him thoroughly, creating a real conflict between seeing her as a social date or as a business contact to acquire new and more prestigious clients. If she had opened the Philip Morris account for one of her freelance cartoonists, she should be wonderful as a sales person for his creative industrial design talents. Suddenly, he heard the telephone ringing. Madeline appeared from nowhere carrying a group of color sketches that she was anxious to show him. Maxine was buzzing him to pick up the telephone.

"Is this Mr. Levy?" A pleasant sounding woman's voice asked. "Mr. Henry Isserman of the Ideal Toy Company would like to speak with him."

"Yes! I would be pleased to talk with Mr. Isserman."

"Hello, Levy, this is Henry Isserman. We've had two or three talks in my office and you have been writing to me since last Saint Isenstein Day, whenever that was. Maybe I have a project for a good industrial designer if you can get your ass down here on my time."

"Thank you, Mr. Isserman. Can I see you first thing tomorrow morning?"

"Hey, buddy boy, that's too fast. I'll be all tied up for the next few days and then I am due at the Housewares Show in Chicago for a week. Call me when I return and we'll set a date. If you are in Chicago, I'll see you there. Maybe we could have dinner one night."

"That's a good idea, Mr. Isserman. I have a number of clients who are exhibiting at McCormack Place. Maybe I'll see you there or my representative will contact you at your booth."

"Good! We're considering two other firms besides your outfit. The quicker we can talk, the sooner I'll make the decision. I'll be staying at the Hyatt."

Well, Roland pondered this invitation. *What now?* Surely he could not drop everything and fly to Chicago to meet Henry Isserman, but if he could send a salesperson, his firm would look very professional and a good salesperson could make additional contacts at the show. All the large toy and housewares firms would have exhibition booths at McCormack Place.

Roland had never been to Chicago. It was frightfully expensive. A few years ago he had attended a trade show at the New York Coliseum but it was a disaster. After four hours spent in visiting many of the display booths, he felt that he was merely wasting his time. The company representatives were all too busy with sales presentations to wholesalers and retailers and, although they were friendly, even telling him very funny jokes, they were totally disinterested in his company and his services.

He had heard that the Chicago Housewares Exposition was very different. Unlike the New York show, everyone who attended the Chicago Exposition was anxious to make contacts for both selling their merchandise and buying special professional services, lower-cost product components, and even creative advertising, public relations, and design services. Top business executives like Henry Isserman always spent several days at the Chicago show. They hosted big dinner parties, conducted national sales meetings for both company salesmen as well as independent sales representatives, and encouraged new business contacts. But Roland convinced himself that the show was too expensive for him to attend. Not only were the hotels expensive, there also was the air fares to Chicago and return, the expensive restaurants, the eager taxicab drivers, and even the long distance telephone calls back to his office.

If he could find some outgoing person to attend the show and represent his company, they could develop new contacts. This person would see a company's line of products, provide him with a list of suitable companies for his creative design work and supply the names of decision-making executives. Maxine could write sales letters to them and sooner or later he would acquire new industrial design clients.

His mind raced with ideas. How about sending Maxine? She knew his business and she always made a good impression with his clients. Then he thought about Paul, his old college friend who recently left a somewhat dead-end marketing position. But Paul would want a big cut and in his strong salesmanship manner, he might even want a partnership in the business. *Not a bad idea,* Roland thought. Maybe this was all a little too soon. Then he pondered a thought that had been floating through his mind since he met Susan Liforest. *She would be great.*

FOUR

WHEN HE telephoned Susan on Wednesday afternoon with an invitation for lunch on Thursday, she had responded immediately and said that she knew the Weathervane Inn. She had arrived promptly and seemed interested in maintaining a relationship. The lunch conversation had been free and casual with most of the talk about her. He really was not interested in talking about himself. Roland was seeking to start a relationship, but was not sure of its direction.

Roland was married to Bea, an elementary school librarian whom he had met while at Brooklyn College. Since their wedding two years before, they lived in a one-bedroom apartment in Brooklyn Heights, paid for mostly from her salary. They both knew that to expand his business, it was necessary to retain most of his earnings for later investment. He was operating as a corporation, Roland Levy Industrial Design, Inc., and although the firm paid all his expenses, he could only allocate a small salary for himself "I'll make it up in a few years," he explained to Bea. She was completely agreeable.

Susan Liforest was not the first woman who had sparked his interest. *Artists always have relationships,* he rationalized. But, at this moment, his thoughts were strictly about business. She was a natural salesperson.

So, at 9:30 P.M., while Bea was reading some book announcements and library material, he picked up the telephone in the bedroom and dialed Susan Liforest's home number.

"Susan, this is Roland Levy. I'm sorry to call you so late, but I just arrived home."

"It is nice to hear from you, Rueben. I'm usually up quite late."

"Hey! Quit with the Rueben stuff. Let's keep it Roland. I'm building a business."

"I'm sorry about that. You will have to tell me more about you. You were such a good listener at lunch. I guess that I talked too much. I really don't know anything about you. We'll have to do lunch again soon."

"Susan, how would you like to spend a few days at the Housewares Show at McCormack Place in Chicago?"

"What a lousy proposition," she laughed. "You could suggest New Orleans or even Las Vegas."

"No, I need someone to represent my firm at the show. I can't go. I'll pay all expenses—airfare, hotels, meals. Then I will pay you twenty-five percent of the fee for all projects resulting from your contacts at the show, and one firm, the Ideal Toy Company, is ready to sign up."

"It sounds very interesting. What is your average fee?"

"About three thousand dollars."

"Let's see, that's $750. I'll have to think about it."

"Can you meet me for lunch at 12:30 P.M. tomorrow? Same place."

"Okay, Rue—I mean Roland. We'll talk then."

Roland was not very good at deal making and he knew that to bring Susan Liforest into his business, he would have to provide her with a generous financial sharing as well as a social relationship, neither of which he was in a position to offer. It was clear to him from the Philip Morris encounter that he needed a charming sales representative, his own talents too often were not only limited, they seemed to hinder future sales growth. Design and merchandising principles were paramount in his professional life and the prospect of acquiring a new client was tied to that client's wholehearted approval of his beliefs. When they showed an understanding of his ideas and he felt that there was mutual respect, he was ready to start any design project. The use of design to achieve competitive distinction was a management strategy that Roland approved. His problem was with interpersonal relations with those executives whom he called "preppies."

Occasionally, when he investigated the backgrounds of executives in the larger food, pharmaceutical, and beverage firms, a Brooklyn College or City College graduate emerged. But they had graduate degrees from mores prestigious institutions. In his mind, the University of Pennsylvania, Bucknell, Cornell, Williams, and other colleges with ivy coated campuses were the social breeding grounds for most middle managers in these large product-marketing firms, and they preferred to do business with their own breed. When he met an executive who had prepped at a fancy secondary boarding-school, he was sure that they looked down upon him, his talents, and his ideas.

Henry Isserman was an entirely different breed. He had a sweet disposition and a vile mouth to disguise it. Short, rather plump, with a round face, large eyes, and a perpetual smile that befriended everyone, he listened to people quietly and then blasted forth with his opinions. Henry's collar was open and a striped silk tie drooped from his neck. While he chewed on an unlit cigar, Henry listened to Roland's ideas and then snapped, "It's about time that some artist thought a little more about communications on toy packages than just fancy lettering that's so pretty no one can read it. If you can do what you say, Buster, maybe we'll let you get into the pissin' contest for design jobs around here."

He was a little rough with his talk, but Roland was sure that he knew the toy business and had years of experience with bad packaging designs. His job as vice president of marketing was to oversee both the packaging and the advertising for the Ideal Toy Company. Two independent sales representative firms handled sales, one for the chain stores and the other group for the wholesalers and independents. Roland liked him and wondered whether he ever finished college. Rumors among the toy buyers who frequented the showrooms at 200 Fifth

Avenue were that Henry was expelled from three different colleges. One popular rumor was that he was caught screwing a history professor on top of one of the chemistry lab tables.

Roland thought, *Surely Susan could stimulate his interest and hopefully intrigue him enough to want to work with us. But would she want to be involved in the design work? Could she be content as part of the team, or would she want to be a leader? How would Bea react if she knew that I am spending business hours alongside a vibrant and attractive woman? What about Maxine and Madeline? Would they resent her intrusion on their office harmony?*

Roland could not wait to find out. He was convinced that he needed Susan to snag Henry Isserman and he dreamed that she could open doors with the big boys like Philip Morris. The rest he knew that he could handle when it came up.

FIVE

SUSAN LIFOREST stood in line at the check-in counter of the Chicago Hyatt Hotel, six tired looking men before her, all with large briefcases dropped beside them and clothing carriers suspended from straps over their shoulders. *I spotted some of these guys on the flight down,* she thought. *They must all be here for the Houseware Show.* During the three-hour flight from LaGuardia to O'Hare, she dozed off a good deal of the time, closing her eyes as the evening sky turned from dusk to darkness. The taxi ride from the airport was pleasant, but the bitter cold wind from Lake Michigan flaked the trees with snowdrops and chilled the January air, sending shivers through her entire body. She was not a lover of cold weather and if Roland had not offered this special deal, she would be warm and comfortable in her parents' apartment on this Monday evening at 9:30 P.M. She smiled as she remembered telling Roland that she had her own apartment. "Well, some day soon," she whispered.

"Do you have a reservation?" The clerk asked pleasantly, smiling at her after filling the room requests of the men in line before her.

"Yes. Mr. Roland Levy reserved a room for me for two nights."

"Here it is. It is a guaranteed reservation. Everything is in order. You have a nonsmoking single room on the sixth floor."

She picked up her briefcase and overnight bag, and walked to the elevators arranged around a circle in the lobby, each within full view as they whined up and down under the guidance of uniformed operators. She was wearing her winter coat with the buttons in the back and was well aware of the stares from several of the men, but her thoughts were of Roland and the selling task she would begin the next day.

Since Roland Levy had entered her life, many things were changing, and these changes were occurring far too quickly. At lunch on Friday, he had spent an hour explaining his theories about product and package design. Some of it made sense to her, but many of his ideas were too advanced for her thinking. Good artwork was most important to her. She enjoyed selling it, loved to look at it, and believed that a good package was a beautiful one. Hand lettering was very important to her and she believed that it must be painstakingly executed along with appropriate illustrations created by a very talented artist. Her several years in partnership with Elaine Waltham had strengthened these ideas. The client was the judge, she was convinced, and she found it easiest to sell something that he liked. "Give it to them just the way they like it and they will buy it," was her favorite saying. Now, what was she doing with a guy like Roland Levy who did everything his own way? Clients had to believe in his theories, understand his concepts, love his designs and artwork . . . or he wouldn't work with them.

He had discussed his feelings concerning Mr. Gillespie and why the Philip Morris interview soured. "Gillespie had his mind made up against me before I even came in," Roland explained with some bitterness in his voice. "He didn't even pay attention when I was talking. He was very different when you talked with him." She knew what he meant. She had felt that way when he began to explain his design theories to her. After the first few sentences, he stopped looking at you, turned his gaze to the ceiling, and seemed to be in a world all by himself. *That will turn anyone off,* she thought. *Poor Mr. Gillespie, a perfect corporate executive, was probably wishing for a double Martini.* No wonder the interview was a flop. If she and Roland could come to an agreement, she was sure that she could get John Gillespie's attention long enough to at least give Ruby a chance. And even if he presented a design that was too progressive looking for this conservative firm, and if John felt that it would give the firm a marketing advantage, he would convince John McGraw, the packaging brand leader, to at least market test it. *But all this is in the future,* she thought. *The problem now is Henry Isserman and the Ideal Toy Company.*

Carrying only a light overnight bag, her attaché case sparsely filled with careful selections from Roland's work, her luggage was not heavy and she did not have the patience to wait for bell-hop service. Once in her room, she removed her coat like a sweater, lifting it over her head and sliding her arms out, one at a time. Carefully, she hung up the coat without opening the buttons, removed the navy blue pantsuit that she wore for traveling, kicked off her shoes, and opened the water faucets in the bathroom tub. *After the tensions of this day, a soothing bath would be sheer delight,* she thought. She double locked the room door, leaving the bathroom door wide open, shed her hosiery and bra, dropping them on the floor, and stepped into the warm water with a sigh. Stretched out and loving the comforting feeling of warm water engulfing her tired body, she was content to stop thinking about business until the next day.

The sharp ring of the telephone abruptly disturbed her tranquil mood and she reached for the extension that hung from the wall at the left side of the tub.

"Susan, this is Roland. How was your flight?"

"I slept most of the way. I guess that I was a little tense. I'm in the bathtub now and it is divine." Nervously, she moved her right hand to her thigh and her fingers gently touched her crotch. She smiled. *That man does have an affect on me. Watch yourself, Susie girl.*

"You do sound tired. Is everything all right?"

"Oh, yes, but I still have to wash and dry my hair and get things ready for the morning."

"I just wanted to welcome you to Chicago and wish you well tomorrow. Have fun!"

"Thank you," she laughed as she touched her body again. "Thank you for calling. It is a bit lonely here. Goodnight."

"God," she whispered, "that man has a strange affect over me, but I can't let him know just yet. Remember, Girl, this is a business relationship and in his world, it is business first. If I let the jerk lay a hand on me before he opens his wallet, it just isn't going to work out."

As she emerged from the bath covered with two towels, she looked at her hair in the mirror and decided that with a little brushing and blowing with the dryer in the morning, it will look just fine, especially since she was planning to wear a hat. She slid into a nightgown, turned off the lights, and felt the warmth of the bed linen and the blankets as she tucked them around her.

Her thoughts turned to Mr. Isserman. Roland had said that he was very different from John Gillespie and he was confident that she could sell him their package design services as easily as selling him a piece of pie. *What kind of pie?* she wondered as she dozed off. *I wish Roland were here.*

SIX

THE HOUSEWARES Show was enormous. She realized this as she joined the dozens of men and women who ignored the large spread of continental breakfast tidbits in the hotel lobby and lined up alongside the four buses marked "McCormack Place Special" in order to be among the first to arrive at the show. The bus gathered speed as it traveled alongside Lake Michigan on the four-lane highway. She watched the traffic slowly churning in the other direction toward the busy uptown section of Chicago. The majestic blue hued buildings of the McCormack Place Exhibition Center emerged suddenly and were contrasted against the darkened waters of Lake Michigan on one side and with the gray sky high above, she felt like she was entering a fairyland. The bus whizzed past the parking lots and the view of the palace disappeared. They were parked in a large underground area and the driver was watching as, in an orderly fashion, the passengers left the bus and lined up before one of the small tables in the lobby to receive entry badges. She found the escalator going up to the exhibition floor, adjusted her identification badge, and clipped it to her lapel. She then looked about for the Ideal Toy Company exhibition booth. That was to be her first stop.

The seemingly endless array of exhibition booths, some looking like small country homes, a few two-story structures, all with colorful signage and large billboard-sized photography, were breathtaking to her. Smiling sales representatives, anxious, hurrying store buyers, and new business seekers like her filled the large hall. As she walked along the fairways with her coat neatly folded across her left arm, and the important attaché case clutched in her right hand, she was greeted with smiling "good mornings" from the men in each of the booths she passed. She spotted a doll company sign, but it bore a name that she was unfamiliar with. She then passed a mirror manufacturer, a toaster company, and a display of irons and ironing boards. She realized that with hundreds of exhibition booths, she would have to ask directions from someone if she wanted to locate the Ideal Toy Company booth before the day was over.

She stopped at the next booth along the way, the Westclox Time Company, a two-story structure filled with photos and displays of packaged clocks in various sizes and colors. A middle aged, well-dressed woman greeted her with the usual smile. "Can you help me?" Susan asked. "I'm looking for the Ideal Toy Company."

"Sure can," the woman replied. "I'll look them up in the directory." Picking up a large book from the nearby counter, she quickly checked the index and came up with L2516. "If you continue along the fairway until the next opening, you will be on the L line. Just follow that until you come to 2516. It may be a long walk."

"Thank you so much. You are very kind." As Susan left, the woman handed her a business card, which she quickly put into her suit jacket pocket. "I'll return to Westclox later," she mumbled aloud as she walked along. "I'd like to work with that woman. Maybe Roland can design a whole new clock packaging program."

She was excited now as she walked along the L fairway, looking anxiously at all the varied booths, waving at sales representatives who greeted her with their charming "Good morning," and alert to find booth number 2516. Many booths had their numbers covered with signs and photos, but then on the left she spotted a two-story unit that looked like a child's play house with huge block letters in red and blue reading "Ideal Toy Company."

The booth was about forty-feet long, about seven or eight feet deep, with bright lighting and large photographs of kids playing with toys. On tables, hanging from cords, and displayed on shelves were hundreds of toys and their packages.

"Can I help you, young lady?" said a happy voice from a tall man with a moustache in a red sports jacket with black pants, a white shirt, and multi-colored bow tie. "I'm Jack, the sales manager of the girls' toy line. Do you have a business card?"

"No. I rushed out too quickly to have any printed. I'm Susan Liforest representing the well-known firm of Roland Levy Industrial Design. I stopped by for just a few minutes to say hello to Mr. Henry Isserman."

"Hey, Henry, there's a lovely lady here to see you."

The man standing and talking with a group of four men at the far end of the booth turned around and shouted, "Send her down here, Jack. I go for broads. I mean, lovely ladies."

His face was covered with a huge grin as she approached and reached for his extended hand. He wore a dark blue business suit and a light yellow shirt, which was open at the collar so his tie hung straight down without a knot.

"So, what did you say your name was, and have you had your break-fast yet? We can have a quiet one in the office upstairs. I even think that there is a small kitchen."

Susan didn't plan on letting him off the hook so easily. She had dealt with brash guys like this before. *If this is his game, I am going to parlay it into an expensive dinner at the hotel,* she thought.

"Had it at 6 A.M. when I began my day," she lied, smiled, and blinked one eye coyly. "Do you play all night and then sleep late when you're away from home at a trade show? She knew immediately that this was a little brassy, but she was intent on stimulating his interest. After all, she was in Chicago to convince him that Roland Levy was the designer he needed, and the first step was to make him aware of her presence. The rest of the selling task would depend on her instincts.

Henry's grin quickly turned to laughter and he chuckled, "So, if you're not the breakfast type, let's at least get to know you. My name is Henry. Who are you?" His eyes stared directly into hers and for a second, she felt a shiver through her body. *I'll have to watch myself with this guy,* she thought.

"Henry, my associate, Roland Levy, asked me to look you up while I was at the show. We'd like to work on the packaging designs for your new toys. My name is Susan Liforest."

He held her hand for what seemed like an unusually long time and then as he dropped it, he asked, "Is this a project that you would work on?"

"Of course. Roland's design theories guide all our work, but I coordinate things between the studio and the clients. So, you'll be seeing a lot of me."

Henry Isserman turned to the men whom he had been talking to, excused himself, and asked Susan to follow him to a display area in the center of the booth. His smile was gone now.

"This is the new line of Ideal Games that I want to have packaged. I've worked with the best game designers and we know that we have a winner here. The games have all been patented, the molds and the dies are now completed, and we are ready to start production. What you see here are handmade prototypes. I need a designer who thinks with his head and not his ass and I already have four firms that I am considering for the job. Why should I give it to you and Levy?"

Susan stood silently, fearful for every word she might utter. Henry beckoned to one of the men he had been talking to, asked him to bring two coffees, and then stood waiting for Susan's answer. She tried to imagine what Roland would say, but her mind was a complete blank. Casually, as if in a daze, she fingered one of the items on the shelf.

"This is beautiful. It looks so challenging. I'll bet that every parent in America will want it for her kids. You have to be careful that the package does not get in the way."

Now Henry was silent. He waited for the coffee and when the man returned, he took the two cups, handed one to Susan, and from the lines that appeared on his forehead, it looked like he was deep in thought. "Very interesting," he said, looking at Susan. "Last week I had some guys in my office from two different industrial design firms and as soon as I showed them the items, they began to describe their packaging concepts. It made me so nauseous that I wanted to throw up. I threw them both out instead," he laughed.

"Well, Roland and I believe that the package is only there to sell a toy or a game. We won't do a thing until we understand the item, its play value, and how we think the kids and the parents feel about it." Susan really wasn't sure how she felt, but she was quite sure that this was the kind of answer that Roland would give.

Henry spoke slowly, "I told your boyfriend that this would be a pissin' contest, but you just won it with spit. If you can keep ass-wise thinking out of this and create a good packaging system for this line of games, you and what's-his-name can have a fuckin' big project. Let's discuss it at lunch or dinner." As she stood there, smiling, her big eyes looking appealingly at him, her fingers playing carelessly, perhaps nervously with her hair as it touched her shoulder, he found her unusually appealing, and she sensed it.

Susan knew that luck had been with her for a split second. She had managed to say the magic words even though she was not exactly sure what she had said, but she did know very clearly that this was the time to get out of there. *Let him want me,* she thought as she picked up her attaché case with one hand, took another sip of the coffee, and then, placing the cup on a shelf, she slung her coat over her arm and said softly, "I have a number of appointments this morning. I'll be back at the

Hyatt before 5 P.M. Call my room, 611, and I'll make some time to talk with you about taking on this project." Without offering her hand, she walked out of the booth quickly, looking only in the direction that she was walking.

"Fuckin' broad!" he said as she was out of hearing distance. "Room 611? Well, either I'll get in her pants tonight or I have found the package design firm that I've been looking for. Okay boys, back to work!"

■　■　■

Susan walked slowly with a big lump in her throat and heaviness on her chest. She wasn't sure what she had done, but it looked like she had a date for dinner and a leg on the Ideal Toy project. Now she had to find that nice woman at the Westclox booth. She needed a woman to talk to, a woman who knew her way around this show, before she could think about lining up some other prospects. She was sure that Roland would telephone again tonight and she hoped that she could give him a favorable report.

As she approached the Westclox booth, she waved to the woman who was now talking with several men. She waved back, excused herself from the small group that were probably company salesmen, and extended her hand.

"Did you find the firm that you were looking for? This show is so enormous that I'm afraid that if I leave this booth, I'll never find my way back."

"Say, can you get away for a few moments? I noticed a small cafeteria nearby. Would you like to join me?"

"Sure, that sounds good. My name is Ellen Burton," she said as they walked toward the tables. "I see from your badge that you are Susan Liforest from an industrial design firm. I'm a brand manager at Westclox for their boudoir line of electric alarm clocks. It's a new position for me, so I'm very excited. This is my first time in Chicago. I live in a suburb of Atlanta, about ten miles from our headquarters." Both she and Susan ordered toasted bagels with coffee from the service counter and as Susan reached for her purse, Ellen said, "This is my treat. The firm

gives me an allowance for all expenses at this show. And, we're interviewing a few design firms while I'm here. Do you do packaging?"

Susan smiled to herself and held back her answer while she bit into
her bagel and sipped the coffee. She studied the woman across the table
from her. She was medium height, with an athletic figure; about thirty-
five years old with jet black hair that fluffed, fully encircling her head.
Probably washes it herself with a black color to hide any hint of premature gray,
she thought. She looked like any of the pretty southern belles she had
seen in all the magazines, but her manners and composure were certainly
the result of years in competition with men in the corporate world.

"Yes," responded Susan after several more bites. "I'm here just for
today to see several of our clients. Maybe we can talk about it later."

"That's a good idea. I have a full calendar today with appointments,
staff meetings, and schedule time that I must stay at the booth to talk
with buyers. Where are you staying?"

"I'm at the Hyatt and yes, I'm the only one at our firm who had
the time to travel here."

"That's great! I was wondering how to get away from my group of
guys this evening. Are you free for dinner at the hotel? It will be my
treat."

"I'd love to, probably around 7 P.M. After walking the aisles of the
show, I'll need a warm bath before dinner." Suddenly, she thought about
Henry Isserman. This could be the magical formula. Henry would go
wild over this southern gal and she could keep both prospective clients
interested in her while she went off to bed alone so she could discuss
the day's activities with Roland.

Susan was not perturbed by foul talking men like Henry. During
her growing-up years she had heard every coarse word from the boys
at school and even from the girls as they displayed their bravado during
their girls-only gab sessions. But when men directed these words at her
or even used them in her presence, she was not sure how to respond.
Do I act sophisticated and respond with similar words as some gals do? she
whispered to herself. *No! Men like Henry Isserman treat women as sex*

objects. For me, it is best if I just ignore his comments. I need his respect and his business and I just can't let myself fall prey to his foul remarks.

She looked at Ellen Burton as she walked back to the Westclox booth. *She is lovely, so self-confident, and probably very successful in her world filled with men.* With her coat and attache case on her arms she followed the sign to the checkroom. With woman like Ellen to learn from, she felt that she could make some real contacts, hopefully even friends, at this huge trade show.

SEVEN

SUSAN LIFOREST picked up the Housewares Show brochure at the information desk and casually browsed over the list of exhibiting firms, placing a check in the margin whenever she found a familiar name or one that looked like a worthwhile prospect. There was O'Brien Paint, O'Cedar Mops, Parker Bros. Games, and then suddenly, in alphabetical order, she saw Philip Morris, in capital letters, at booth G1609. With a careful look at the floor plan on the last page of the brochure and she was eagerly off in the direction of the booth.

Philip Morris was located at the end of a long fairway, highly visible from several directions. The booth was considerably smaller than most of the others, only about ten-feet squared with a huge color photograph of the upper section of a Marlboro package along the back wall, a three-dimensional cigarette partially extending from the top. On the display was a sign, "Please Smoke Outside. No Smoking Indoors."

As Susan approached, six men and a woman were talking in the open area. One of the men looked up, smiled, and offered his hand. "I'm Jim Henderson," he said. "Where are you from and can I give you some packages of Marlboro?"

"No thank you, Jim. I'm Susan Liforest from an industrial design firm. Glad to meet you. I work on art projects with John Gillespie in New York. Is he here in Chicago?"

"Glad to meet you, Susan. I'm not sure when he is due to arrive. Let's ask Lester. Lester Brooks, say hello to Ms. . . . is it Liforest? Lester works with him in New York. I'm from the Memphis office. Is John Gillespie coming to the show?"

"Sure thing, Jim. He should be showing up early tomorrow. Do you know John well, Ms. Liforest?"

"We're working on a few things now, but we would like to do more of your packages."

"Well, Gillespie and John McGraw handle that. When I see him, I'll tell him that you're here."

"Thank you, Mr. Brooks, and thank you all for your hospitality. Good luck during the show."

Susan left quickly, pleased with the greeting she received. She really did not want to see John Gillespie, but she reasoned that it would make her firm seem more important if he knew that she had traveled to Chicago to attend this show, and although their relationship was rather formal, she thought that he was somewhat fatherly to her. Hopefully, the men will refer to her as a packaging designer and that would make it easier for the transition to Ruby's firm. *I'll see him in New York,* she said to herself. *It's too dangerous in this town. I have enough trouble already with Henry.*

For the remainder of the morning and the early afternoon, Susan walked about the show stopping at all the booths checked on her list, collecting business cards from executives whenever she felt that the firm had packaged products. She wished that there had been more time in New York to print her own business cards. Her plan now was to send a letter to each of these prospects, seek to establish a relationship, and then to entice them with suggestions to improve their packaging. She had an elaborate marketing plan in her mind—telephone calls, E-mail, messengers, even pigeons, and she was very anxious to discuss it with Roland Levy.

At 5 P.M., stretched out on her bed with just a light robe, Susan waited in her room for the call from Henry. He was reasonably punctual. The call came ten minutes later with charm and humor, but his need to be crude she felt was just a mask to cover either his emotions or his intelligence.

"Hi, Boobala! My little cutie! Are we going to make out tonight? I've reserved a place for dinner in the hotel dining room at 7 P.M..That's a good start. Right, Babe?"

"Sure, Henry, I thought that you wouldn't mind if I brought my pretty girl friend, Ellen Burton. She is a southern belle with Westclox and she would like to meet you."

"Ah, a ménage à trois or do you gals call it a tete-a-tete? Bring her along. Nights are very exciting at the Hyatt."

Susan was pleased with his response. She had figured him to be a big talker wise guy on the outside, but a little pussycat underneath it all.

Henry was seated at a round table at the corner of the dining room next to the window when she arrived. He was dressed in a dark business suit. The maitre d' ushered her to his table. He stood up politely and offered her the chair on his right. She could hardly recognize him in a navy pin-striped suit, white shirt, and softly patterned silk tie. With his clean-shaven face, he looked like any successful business executive, but when he opened his mouth, he sounded like the same old Henry.

"Where's what's her name? You know, the broad from Westclox?"

"Ellen should be here any minute. She probably had meetings all day at the Westclox booth. Oh, there she is now."

Ellen Burton was standing next to the maitre d' when she spotted Susan, waved, and walked toward the table. She wore a long off-white dress that fell to the middle of her calf, her well-formed legs carelessly reaching down to her black high-heel strapped pumps. The elegantly tailored dress with long sleeves and an open neck was printed with tiny floral designs that were subtly colored in light green, blue, and orchid hues. She smiled. Her jet-black hair reigned like a crown over her head and white sparkling pearls loosely encircled her neck. Ellen wore matching drop-down earrings that framed her soft, delicately tanned skin. She looked like the southern belle waiting at the esplanade for her admirers to escort her to the ball.

Henry jumped to his feet when she approached, took her extended hand, adjusted her chair, and said, "My God, Baby, you're beautiful! Hello, Ellen. I'm Henry. You know Susan. I hear that you are with Westclox. We gotta do a deal together with a clock and a doll or battery operated toy. We'll talk about it later. How about a good gin martini and some French wine during dinner?"

"Mmm. After the day that I just had introducing our new line of boudoir clocks to retail buyers, I could use a good one. Make mine dry with Bombay Gin, straight up with an olive."

"Just straight Perrier for me," said Susan. "I have work to do tonight to prepare a report for my boss."

Henry frowned, turned to Ellen, "Here's to a charming evening, my dear. Ideal Toy and Westclox have a great future, but let's put that on hold. Tonight, we'll talk about you and the great traditions of the south."

Throughout the meal, Henry's attention was focused on Ellen. She winked, she laughed, she touched his hand as he poured the wine, his hands found her lap, he rubbed her thigh, their gazes met frequently, and Susan was pleased with the way things were working out. When she finished the main course, she looked at her watch. It was after 8 P.M. She promised to see them both the next day, explained that she had a conference call with Roland and some clients, and left the table quickly. Henry waved as she sauntered away and Susan blew him a kiss from the restaurant door.

Henry wasted little time. By 8:30 P.M., he and Ellen left the restaurant for a bottle of great California wine that he said was in his room. They never touched the wine. Alone in the elevator, he moved behind her, gently kissed the back of her neck, and for the few seconds before the elevator door opened, he pressed his body against hers and cupped both breasts with his hands. She slowly rolled her neck, placed her left hand gently over his fingers, and then moved her right hand to his buttocks to push him closer to her.

In the hall, they held hands. He opened the door quickly, flipped the light switch at the entrance, opened his tie, and threw his suit jacket on the couch. She stood quietly near the door, her small purse dangling from tiny leather over-the-shoulder straps, both arms folded casually across her chest. "You have a large, beautiful room, Henry. All mine has is a bed, dresser, and television."

Henry was not interested in small talk. He moved toward her, opened his belt, dropped his pants and whispered, "Come on, Southern Doll, I'm one of the boys. Grab me and bite me."

She walked into the room, tossed her purse on the cocktail table, and sat down on the couch. "I've seen enough southern boys in my limited days, Henry. Stop acting like a crude little boy and let's make love or I'll leave." By this time, he had removed his under shorts and stood before her with an erect penis. She gently took it in both hands, cupped his testicles, and said, "If you don't immediately lie down in bed with your shoes off, I'll leave you with this big thing dangling."

He knew that she meant it. Henry removed the rest of his clothing, pulled back the covers, and waited for her to join him in the large bed. It seemed like forever to him.

She carefully removed her dress, slowly unhooked her pearls, and then spent a few minutes to remove her earrings before going into the bathroom. He heard the door close, then the toilet flush. She walked out of the bathroom entirely nude, turned off the light, and lay down on the bed next to Henry.

■　■　■

Ellen awoke, disturbed by his snoring, and slowly removed the covers on her side of the bed. The illuminated clock on the desk indicated 3:00 o'clock and, from the sound of his low but steady snoring, she was sure that Henry was fast asleep. The amount of alcohol that she had consumed at dinner clouded her thoughts slightly, but she had been in this predicament before. *I must get dressed and return to my room before he wakes up. The guys in my company may have telephoned my room last night and they may be on the phone again this morning.*

Swiftly she gathered her watch, jewelry and earrings, dressed quietly in the dark and then, carrying her shoes and her purse, she slowly opened the door and emerged into the dimly lighted hall. *It is better this way,* she murmured to herself. *He is a very likeable man. I am anxious to learn how he plans to do business with our firm.*

EIGHT

SUSAN LIFOREST skipped breakfast and with her attaché case and overnight bag in hand, she joined the crowd from the Hyatt on the early bus to the show. While talking to Roland the night before, she had decided to offer quick farewells to Ellen and Henry, hopefully to meet with John Gillespie for a few minutes, and then take the noon flight back to New York. Roland was anxious to reopen talks with Philip Morris. He was convinced that John avoided business relationships with poor guys and preferred to associate with his own group of preppies and ivy leaguers. With Susan as his contact, he had his mind set on convincing Gillespie that this poor guy had the fresh ideas and talent that could significantly improve his packaging. The more that she thought about it, the more that she knew she had to look for John Gillespie first. Departing from the bus in a hurry, coat under her arm with her two bags, she walked along the long fairway to the Philip Morris booth.

"Susan Liforest! I'm so glad to see you," said a smiling John Gillespie as she approached the booth. He placed her coat and bags on a small table, reached for both of her hands, and introduced her to the group of Philip Morris executives who were clustered together in the center of the booth. "You met Jim Henderson yesterday. Jim and I started Princeton together and we've been with PM for a good many years."

"Yes," said Henderson, extending his hand. "You're the packaging design lady. We sure could use your services."

"I didn't know that you did packaging design," John said. "We need some people in that area."

"It's a great new connection. We'll talk about it when I see you in New York. I have a flight to catch and a few stops still to make at the show."

"Better hurry." He kissed her on the cheek and she walked away quickly, grabbing her attaché case, overnight bag, and coat.

She had mixed feelings about meeting Henry or Ellen. Perhaps it would be easier to speak with them over the telephone. She smiled as she recollected the events of the previous day and night. It was clear that Henry had only one thing in mind and to her surprise, the proper looking Ellen Burton turned out to be an experienced corporate playmate. She was somewhat embarrassed to face either of them. She decided to talk to Ellen over the telephone, woman to woman. Susan thought this would be best rather than eye-to-eye. Sometimes the gals at school would talk about their sexual encounters, but Ellen was a real pro, the kind that could handle the boys at night and still work with them in the serious daytime business of designing, producing, and marketing merchandise. Susan let her imagination wander about the evening. She convinced herself that if they did sleep together, they would probably just ignore it this morning, but she just couldn't. If it worked out, and she hoped that it did, both Ellen and Henry would be very friendly to her. She slipped her coat over her head, left the exhibition hall, and hailed one of the waiting taxis for the trip to the airport.

Seated comfortably on the plane, she tried to imagine Henry Isserman as her lover, this crude talking, somewhat sloppy man, filled with charm and a determination to get what he wanted. At their first meeting in the Ideal Toy Company exhibition booth at the Housewares Show, he sent out signals by inviting her to breakfast and then dinner.

If it wasn't for the chance meeting with Ellen Burton, she would have been over her head with problems that called for answers and actions that she would be unable to handle.

John Gillespie is different, she thought. Gillespie was a soft spoken gentleman, prep school trained, ivy league college, affluent Christian home, assured that he would achieve success in corporate America and, even if he faltered somewhere along the route, family money and wealthy in-laws would always take care of him.

■ ■ ■

Roland Levy was waiting for her at LaGuardia Airport. He took her bags, carried them to the car, and didn't stop asking questions or talking as they rode along Northern Boulevard and over the Queensboro Bridge until they reached the parking lot on Second Avenue and Thirtieth Street. In the office, Roland was seated at his desk and Susan lounged lazily on the couch. He was overjoyed to learn that the entire trip had only cost an additional forty-six dollars in out of pocket expenses for taxis and tips. But she had a notebook with several pages filled with names to contact, plus successful interchanges with Ideal, Westclox, and Philip Morris. He had to quickly make a deal with this woman. She was really the key to his future business expansion.

Roland was anxious to learn more about the Housewares Show. He had heard stories from the guys about the evening parties, the drinking, and the bed swapping. He was embarrassed to ask Susan about the one evening that she spent at the hotel. She had called from her room at about 8:30 P.M. to recount the day's activities and the dinner with Henry and Ellen, but what did she do during the rest of the long Chicago night? He had an urge to telephone her at 11 P.M. to discuss some ideas for the next day, but he was afraid that she would be out of her room. What if a man answered the telephone? With a woman as an associate, he could wonder and even fantasize about her adventures, but they were really her secrets and her private life. All he should be involved with was her daytime business activities. But Roland was curious.

"Well, my little Ruby-call-me-Roland, let's make a deal," said Susan, wishing to stop all the questions and conversation about the show. *I have told him just enough,* she thought. *Let him imagine the rest.* "I think we can work well together. The show contacts will take several weeks to develop and with Westclox, Ideal, and Philip Morris, I'm going to be a busy gal."

"What are you looking for?" asked Roland with some hesitation.

Susan had mixed feelings in this area and had mulled it about in her mind frequently during the Chicago trip. She was aware of Roland's weak financial position; his business was just creeping along, but she was convinced that her efforts would bring in many substantial accounts. She paused for a second and then responded in an assured manner that surprised even herself, "Guarantee me twenty-five thousand dollars this year with a five thousand dollar bonus if I exceed one hundred fifty thousand dollars in new business."

Roland's mind raced with figures. He reached for a sheet of lined paper and listed existing salaries, rent, telephone, art and office supplies, insurance, auto expenses. He stopped, added it all up, and frowned as he added a wishful salary of thirty-five thousand dollars for himself. *It's a gamble,* he thought, but he was determined to start working with Susan immediately. "Okay, but we'll give it a six-month trial. Twelve thousand five hundred guaranteed and if it looks good, we go all the way."

She smiled. Roland had to act like a boss. It was more than she was earning with Elaine Waltham and it certainly offered more opportunities for growth. "You know that it's not the way I want it, but I'll take the chance. Set up some space for me around here, give me a telephone, and I'll start immediately. First, I must call Elaine Waltham. She's expecting the call. We discussed this change before my trip. She wants to continue alone as the rep for our artists. She'll do well without me. You know, I think you and I will make a great design business team."

NINE

THE IDEAL Toy Company was located in a group of old factory buildings in the Borough of Queens, a short distance from New York's
Borough of Manhattan across the Queensboro Bridge. The parking lot
was huge, divided into three sections, with signs for employee parking
only and special spaces for about one dozen named executives. Vehicles
occupied all the half dozen or so spaces carefully marked "Visitors with
Appointments Only." Roland found an unoccupied employee's space at
the far end of the lot and maneuvered his car into that space. It was 9
A.M., there was a light but steady rainfall, and Roland said to Susan, "If
that guy hasn't come to work yet, it's just too bad. I'm sure Henry won't
mind if we take the guy's space."

With Susan wielding an oversized umbrella overhead and Roland
carrying a large portfolio under each arm, they made their way across
the parking area to the front door. "Henry Isserman's office please," he
informed the guard at the front door. "He's expecting us. We're from
Roland Levy Industrial Design on Madison Avenue."

They were given clip-on badges, ushered to a visitor's elevator, and
emerged on the sixth floor in the executive area where Henry's secretary, a short gray-haired lady of about sixty, met them with a cheery,

"Hi! Henry's on the telephone; seems like he always is. Would you like some coffee? Just help yourself, it's over there," she said as she pointed to a coffee urn and several glass coffee pots.

With coffee cups in hand, each carrying a portfolio and Susan with the rolled-up umbrella, they followed the secretary into a small atrium before the doors to three executive offices. They sat down on the two lounge chairs pointed to by the secretary, placing their gear on the couch. In just a few moments, they heard a beaming voice coming from the nearest closed door, "Okay, Mabel. Show them in. I got a very busy day. I spent too much time in Chicago firming up that deal with Westclox. Now we gotta work on the packaging and the boss lady, a Ms. Burton or something, wants Susan here to work on it."

For a few seconds, Susan smiled from ear to ear. She was laughing to herself and trying to conceal it from Roland. *Ellen must have really worked this guy over,* she thought. When they entered the room, Henry was seated at a huge desk filled with papers, toys, and clocks. He rose, shook Roland's extended hand, patted Susan on the rear, and quickly brushed her face with what seemed like an embarrassed kiss on the cheek.

"This Westclox broad is coming up to New York in two weeks, maybe even sooner if I can help it, and we gotta have a slick presentation for her. She wants a family design of six packages. I get first crack at the layouts and then she and I will work together on approvals after she gets here." He moved back to his chair behind the desk, they both remained standing and he pointed to two large corrugated boxes placed on top of each of the guest chairs.

"Everything is included in these two boxes, except the contract, which is in front of you on my desk. We pay six thousand dollars for the whole design job. Production artwork is extra. It's as simple as that. Westclox wanted in that way 'cause they pay sixty percent, we only pay forty percent. You guys won the pissin' contest for this one and another one for Ideal Toy. Sign it now and come back next week. If I like it, you get the next one, too. Now get the fuck out of here. I'm busy."

Overwhelmed, overjoyed, and completely stunned, Roland picked up the two boxes, Susan took both portfolios and the umbrella, and they hurried out of the office, down the elevator, and stopped at the front door without saying a word. "Stay here with the packages, I'll get the car and drive up. It's just too wet out there." Taking the umbrella, he ran to the car, backed out of the parking space, and raced to the front of the building. It wasn't until they were both in the car that he let out a loud, "Holy cats! How did you do it, Susan? You're wonderful!" He reached across from his seat, kissed her on the cheek, and panted with excitement as he exclaimed, "I don't know what you did during those few hours in Chicago, but you sure tamed him. Now we have our first serious design assignment to work on."

Susan was thinking about the money—six thousand dollars on her first job and the promise of much more to come. She would earn her keep in only a few months. She wondered how much money Ellen made a year and if she was having an affair with Henry.

They rode back to the office in compete silence.

TEN

ELLEN BURTON always dreamed of becoming an actress like Greta
Garbo or Marlene Dietrich, a femme-fatale who captured the most
sought after man, the one who appeared to be most powerful. He need
not be handsome, just a leader of men who would stop during mortal
combat just to admire a woman, a man who appreciated the curve of a
woman's leg and the sensuousness of her figure. She would talk end-
lessly to her schoolmates about her ambitions, about the sirens she
admired, and the parts she planned to play during her theatrical career.

Her devoutly religious parents encouraged her performances in
church pageants and they always applauded her dancing although she
was sometimes a step ahead or a gesture behind the other girls whenever they performed in chorus. At St. Michael's Secondary School for
Girls, she usually took part in all the plays. Her voice was slightly hoarse
and she did not project well, but Ellen applied herself earnestly and felt
more alive, more connected to herself, and happiest when she was per-
forming on a stage.

Growing up in St. Louis was a happy time for Ellen, dampened only
by her father's frequent illnesses. John Burton was a maintenance engineer at Emerson Electric Manufacturing Company, a steady job that he

liked, but illness and minor accidents kept him home more often than his foreman liked. To conserve his energy, two or three nights a week he would get into bed shortly after dinner, leaving all the household chores to Ellen and her mother, Eunice, a volunteer at the parish who would rush off to attend evening meetings on Tuesdays and Thursdays. Ellen was generally left to herself to complete minor tasks, prepare her schoolwork, and then dream of the exciting moments when she was in the company of leading Hollywood actors.

Her best friend, Bess Morgan, an avid reader of Jackie Collins' novels, telephoned on Tuesday and Thursday evenings to relate the current saga or intimate love making that she read about. Exaggerating sometimes, excited always, the two girls would giggle and laugh and Ellen would try to recreate the lines in her own way.

"Ellen," said Bess one evening, "they were doing it standing up!" Ellen was silent. She listened quietly and when Bess hung up the telephone, she pictured herself in that pose with the captain of the football team at St. Louis High. He was a ruggedly handsome guy she had only seen at one game, but he was her hero during her last semester before she entered Washington University. Bess had no interest in college, she just wanted a clerical job where she could meet boys and find "Mr. Right."

Ellen settled into college life. Her father and mother finally agreed that she could live in the dormitory providing that she spent two weekends each month at home. At first, she loved the weekends at home and the chance to spend the time and a few double dates with Bess. But the boys, their jobs, and the local conversation bored her. She could not wait for Sunday evening when her mom drove her back to the college campus.

The Washington University Women's Dormitory Number Three was located on a side street just one block away from the quadrangle. She loved the quiet location and was pleased with her roommate, Fran, a college junior. Both were serious students. Ellen's father had insisted that she study mechanical engineering. "There are lots of opportunities for woman engineers," he used to say, "and they make a very good living." She still dreamed of an acting career and joined the freshman follies hoping for a chance to partake in one of their productions.

After two years of math, physics, strength of materials, and general drafting, she switched to business management; it seemed so much more interesting and practical. She was not anxious to sit before a drawing board or a computer to plan gearing and mechanisms. Business subjects seemed to be more related to people and she loved the challenge of marketing new products. She had taken enough courses in math and science—now it was to be merchandising, finance, and marketing. Fran had graduated, gone home to Berkeley, California, with several offers of engineering positions from technical firms there. Her new roommate, a freshman, was seeking to major in business management.

By the time Ellen graduated, she was sure that she had made the right decision. Job offers were plentiful from large Midwestern manufacturing firms for graduates with interests in advertising, sales, and marketing research. Bess had married one of the younger executives at the St. Louis Tool and Die Company and she was pregnant. Allen, her husband, was restless working in St. Louis and had sent resumes to many large companies in neighboring cities. One day, shortly after graduation and while Ellen was discussing a job offer from Emerson Electric with her father, Bess called and was very excited. "Ellen, we got the position," she shouted. "Allen is going to work in the product development department of a large clock manufacturing company in Atlanta. He's leaving next week and as soon as he can find a two-bedroom apartment, we're going to settle in our new home. You must come down and visit with us. We're both so glad to be leaving St. Louis."

Ellen spent the month of July living at home and considering where she would begin work in September. Although St. Louis was hot, there were cool concerts in Forest Park and Tea Dancing on Saturday afternoon at the Forest Hotel. The local boys were attentive, but she was bored living with her parents. The dream of an acting career was still her fantasy while the reality of a career in marketing was growing stronger each day.

At the end of July, she received an invitation from Bess to visit her new home in Atlanta. "You must stay for one week," Bess had said. "We have a spare room and the baby isn't due until November. You'll love it here; it is so peachy." It was Ellen's first trip away from Missouri. By the second day, she was imitating the slow drawl in the speech of the local residents; by the end of the week, Bess and Allen would giggle at her imitation of a southern belle receiving guests at a formal ball at Tara. Before she left for home, with Allen's help, she met with the human resources director at the Westclox Company, matching his speech word-for-word with her newly acquired southern accent. She left her resumé with him, although she felt that the interview went badly. She really had no work experience, but her college grades were over 3.4 and he seemed to dwell more on her engineering education rather than the courses she had taken in marketing.

A week after she had returned home to St. Louis, she received a letter from a Mr. Armond Duvalle, a vice-president of Westclox, inviting her for an all-expense paid two-day visit to Atlanta for a job interview. The Burtons were unhappy. John had wanted his daughter to work for Emerson Electric. He was sure that she would make a good sales engineer in their appliance division. But she was nearly twenty-two, ambitious, and anxious to live alone in another city. More than anything, she dreamed of becoming a southern belle with the accent, clothes, and mannerisms.

Ellen Burton started her career with Westclox as a trainee in the marketing department. She was the only woman. The twenty men included three vice-presidents, twelve sales representatives, three brand managers, and two market research executives. In her talks with Beth, she referred to them as, "Good old southern boys. You know, the kind that just have to put women down." But she was content to make their coffee, wash the cups, and even bring lunch to their desks when they were busy. She didn't resent too much their conversations with the jibes against women, and their complete satisfaction with a world run and occupied by men.

"We're training you for a sales position," Pete Walsh, the sales manager, would say, "and it is important that you know the company culture. You can't represent us until you become one of us," he would say with a smile. "And that will take a little while." Her job was to send welcome letters to new retail customers after a salesman had made the initial contact and then, after the first order, to speak to the buyer with her beautiful southern accent to determine if everything was appropriately delivered. Buyers from the Midwest and New England were delighted with her accent and the sales force boys were quite pleased, although they teased her about it.

Despite the frequent pleasures, a routine office job was dull for an ambitious woman. After two years, she wanted to meet some of the buyers, make more lasting personal contacts, and she even had her own ideas about the appearance of some of the clocks that they marketed to women.

Late one afternoon, with all the sales reps out in the field and Mr. Walsh working alone in his office, she thought it to be the appropriate time to speak to him about her promotion. Ellen knocked on his door and entered when he responded with a cheerful "Come in!"

Pete Walsh was a tall man with a slight pot-belly, tightly combed straight black hair that was graying at the temples, wire-framed glasses, and an ear-to-ear smile that seemed never to change under his rather bushy graying moustache. He was seated behind his big desk surrounded by photographs of his family and of various important looking people with whom he was shaking hands. As Ellen entered the office, he arose from his chair and went to the center of the office with his hand extended to meet her. She had waited a long time for this moment and without any preliminary conversation she blurted, " Mr. Walsh, I have been doing a good job in this office for quite some time. You promised me a promotion to the sales staff. Isn't it time?"

He stared at her for a moment. "As a matter of fact, young lady," he said, "this sure is the time to show you how to get ahead in this business. Close the door!"

Obediently, she turned, walked to the door, slowly closed it, and turned back to face Pete Walsh. She stopped suddenly, her mouth opened, and she couldn't believe her eyes. He had dropped his pants, held his erect penis in one hand, encircled her waist with the other, and whispered, "Honey, get down on it and make me feel good!"

He grabbed her hand, placed it on his penis, still holding her tightly around the waist. Ellen had experienced several relationships in college and one since she was living in Atlanta, but this was different. This was her boss and it could cost her job. She stood still—it may have been a few seconds—she was afraid to move her hand. She felt the penis throbbing. He whispered, "Oh, damn," and she realized that his orgasm had started. Roughly, he pushed her down, she fell to her knees, and his penis brushed against her cheek. As it softened, he said, "Honey, you'll make a good salesman, but you had better brush up on the duties of being a good southern belle."

She ran from his office, grabbed her things, and went home. She was too embarrassed to call Beth, too frightened to eat dinner, and was unable to sleep. The next morning, she arrived at the office on time, fearful that this would be her last day, and began to prepare the coffee. Mr. Walsh had not yet arrived, but several of the sales representatives were already sitting at their desks reviewing memos and telephone messages.

"Say, Miss Burton," called Harry Livingston, a salesman who regularly contacted department stores. "Pete Walsh called me at home last night. He said that you were to start with me this morning as an assistant. He wants me to break you into sales."

ELEVEN

Roland Levy was happiest when leaning over a large slanted drawing desk facing a clean roll of velvet-smooth tracing paper surrounded by sketch pads, color markers, pencils, triangles, some curve templates, and a few pieces of folding box board. He had explored computers and the various new programs to prepare artwork on the computer, but he felt cramped and uncomfortable watching an illuminated screen and drawing with that device called the mouse. The freedom offered by the expansive and usually cluttered drawing desk offered few restraints and his hands moved freely across the space, guided only by his inspirations, some sparking exciting directions, others just replaying time-worn themes.

This morning, a twelve-inch doll was posed in a sitting position at the left corner of his desk. The doll was propped up by a bookend, and from time-to-time, Roland would move the bookend to another position to change her pose, arms outstretched, arms folded, one behind the other, kneeling, crawling, and even climbing. Next to the doll was a Westclox alarm clock with a pale pink face color, cherry-red numbers, and white rotating arrows pointing to the numbers as they rotated around the circle. In front of him, on the expansive tracing sheet, he had drawn numerous sketches of this clock, some with eyes and smiling lips, others depicting cherubic faces, and even poses of dolls with hands gracefully pointing to the encircling numbers. Some of the numbers had doll-like features; others resembled rattles, teething rings, and a few baby elephants. All the sketches were in color. *Pink and blue are not the only colors for babies,* he thought. *I can use russet and green, citron and orange, and perhaps I should explore multi shades of pastel tints that vignette into almost-white tints.*

He always felt more secure with his graphic design work once he had determined the overall theme of a project and at least the shape of the outer container. But, until he had a conference with Henry, Ellen, and Susan, there was no clearly defined product including both the clock and the doll. *However, if I can pose the doll into an appealing position and then create a relationship between the clock and the doll, I will be able to determine the physical shape of their package,* he thought.

He had not met Ellen. He called her the "Westclox Lady," but he anticipated her desire to feature the clock equally with the doll. "The clock is so small and the doll is so large," he muttered. Suddenly inspired, he cut a freely formed cloud-like shape, which was slightly larger than the diameter of the clock, and fixed it behind the clock. Then he posed the doll in a reclining position within a rectangular shape leaving ample room above the doll to center the cloud-encased clock. His hands moved very fast as he sketched the full size doll and clock in color, leaving room for a cute message.

What should we call the product? he questioned himself. Answers flowed along with ideas for clothes, color, box shape, and lettering styles. *Mary.* "Mary Tell-Time," he thought. *Maybe just "Sleepy Time," or even "Baby's Busy Day." We'll dress the doll in pajamas,* he thought. But as ideas floated before him, he resolved to discuss them with Susan. After all, she was a girl and should know more about little girls and their dolls . . . but most important, she knew both Ellen and Henry and may be able to suggest ideas that would appeal to both of them.

Roland knew that whatever theme they selected, he could create an outstanding package.

Roland was secure with his design solutions. His creative mind worked at computer speed as he envisioned alternate concepts, disregarding some, enlarging upon others, combining, reducing, and maximizing elements that seemed to both logically and aesthetically bring him closer to a solution.

His mind tried to imagine a toy that would not only please Henry, but also make him so excited about its marketing potential that he would encourage both his firm and Ellen's to invest heavily in its promotion.

"Madeline!" he called to his assistant. "Take these three sketches and make more finished comps. They must be in full color and make sure that we have equal prominence for the logos of both Ideal Toy and Westclox."

As she entered the room, she looked at the clutter on his desk— half-drawn sketches, pencil notes, some adorable doll poses, and she smiled when she saw the doll. "Oh! She's awful cute. What are we going to call her?"

"I'm not sure yet. I put some names on my sketches and when you are done with the comps, we can see how it all looks. It's designed for a three-year-old girl, so we must keep it juvenile with a lot of contrast in the color. Try some pink and blue tints with a Prussian blue and a lot of white, then get into the oranges and browns and maybe we'll arrive at a color scheme that both mothers and three-year-olds will be attracted to. The client group is going to be our biggest problem. The woman is from a conservative southern company and Henry is the kind of guy who can go for a far out approach. But, before they put some real money into this product, it must look like the cutest novelty doll set on the market."

Madeline took the sketches, the doll, and the clock back to her desk to work on the project immediately. Roland sat quietly at his desk; his mind was racing in many directions. Madeline's comps were really only a first step. He'd hang them on the wall and then have a long meeting with Susan. Maybe Maxine could join them for a few moments. He wanted to listen to other opinions to be sure of his creative direction before the presentation to Henry.

As he thought about the project, he knew that Henry was the pivot, not Ellen, and he knew that he could not have a design meeting with the both of them. Yes, Henry would see his designs first, two finished models with the clock and doll interchangeable, and he imagined that he would place them on a toy shelf with other Ideal projects, think carefully and then, if he liked the concept, burst into a big smile. Then it would be up to Henry to convince Ellen Burton that they had a marketing winner.

Roland Levy remembered his childhood years living in his parents' tiny apartment. While his father and mother were asleep, Roland would sit with a sketchpad until the early hours of the morning, carefully drawing chairs, the window, even the radio. He wanted to be an artist like the men and women who painted pictures that hung in the Brooklyn Museum. Teachers praised his work and after school, he rushed home to make posters and signs for many of the clubs. He was in high school when he first read about Art for Art's Sake. He also learned that artists often went unpaid for their work. They painted first and then waited years to sell paintings and gain recognition. Therefore, many escaped from their talents to work as salesmen, teachers, and in many menial jobs. At Brooklyn College, working part-time as a salesperson at Macy's and a clerk at the post office, Roland tried to prepare for other work, but he always felt more comfortable with a pencil in his hand and a clean sheet of paper in front of him. He visited the large advertising agencies in New York seeking art assignments, but they wanted to see his portfolio, a resume of art school courses, and prior work. These agencies were all located in elegant office buildings with well-dressed men and young women at the reception desks.

Someone told him about the new field of industrial design, which was taught at Pratt Institute. He couldn't afford the tuition; it was difficult enough to stay at a free school like Brooklyn College with all the expenses for books and the contribution he had to make at home. However, he realized that the library was the answer. So, he spent most of after work and after school time in the library at Pratt as well as the main Brooklyn branch. He read the art and design periodicals, was inspired by the book by Harold Van Doren, and gradually his career direction emerged. It just seemed natural. He would become an industrial designer and create beautiful products and packaging that would be so attractive that consumers would rush to buy the products.

From the telephone directory, he copied the list of folding carton manufacturers located in Brooklyn and Queens and visited each of them asking the receptionists whether they had an art department and then if he could see the art director. Finding most of these facilities in industrial neighborhoods and in factory buildings, his jeans, sneakers, and sweater seemed quite appropriate and once he had made a contact, Roland offered to do free lettering, small paste-ups, and any artwork that a busy art director would assign to him. Through the last two years of college, along with his job selling ladies shoes at R. H. Macy and Company, he provided small artwork projects for two congenial art directors. They liked his careful lettering, but most of all, they liked his ability to complete and deliver all assignments on time. They permitted him to wander into the factory and he gradually learned how the folding cartons were made.

When he graduated from college, he printed business cards, solicited artwork from all the carton companies, and worked diligently in a corner of his bedroom. He hated working on the designs created by other artists. He longed for the chance to create packages for major brand marketers.

On alternate Sundays he would devote several hours to the advanced study of packaging by slowly walking along the busy aisles of the neighborhood A & P supermarket. He would stop in front of interesting displays to study how they were arranged and he would select outstanding folding boxes, place them in his cart, and carry them home for further study. He was particularly watchful for those with attractive colors along with those he considered to be well designed. But it was the intricacies of color printing and folding box construction more than graphic design that interested him.

Roland had spent many hours in box manufacturing plants watching both the printing and die-cutting processes. He stood in awe before the horrid, noisy, and foul-smelling machines as they turned out beautiful packages. He was excited to learn that only four different colored inks were used to produce mouth-watering photographs of food as well as the faces of the beautiful people that glamorized many packages. The four colors are cyan blue, magenta red, lemon yellow, and black. He searched the printed surfaces of boxes with a magnifying glass to study the many different colors that could be attained by printing "dots" of the four process colors. After each supermarket study tour he felt that he had acquired considerable knowledge, but his mother complained, "Ruby, why did you buy this product? You know that your father and I can't eat this food."

It took several weeks to understand how flat pieces of boxboard folded up into beautiful three-dimensional shapes. After removing the contents from the boxes, he would study the creases and the cuts in the board and then try to immitate them on sheets of paper.

This was a tedious self-study program, but Roland Levy was determined to become a professional industrial designer. He could create effective designs. Now he was ready, he thought, to work on any national brand. "But, how can I tell them that my office is in the corner of my bedroom?"

TWELVE

"HI, SWEETIE," Susan brightly announced to Roland as she strode into his office wearing a pale blue business suit with a pink scarf loosely tossed around her neck, falling carelessly over her shoulders. "I've found just the place for us to settle down. All we need now is a collection of new furniture."

"Good afternoon, Susan," chirped Maxine as she whisked past her desk. "Where have you been all morning? Dream up any new ideas?"

Roland just grunted. The thought of moving, with all its expenses, was the furthest thing from his mind. He knew that the place was too small for the expansion he has envisioned, but did she have to do it so quickly?

"Where is it located? On Madison Avenue? Near some of the big guys?" He asked half-heartedly, hoping perhaps that the location was wrong for his long-range plans.

"Well, practically. You go up to Fifty-fifth Street and then make a left turn onto Madison Avenue. There, on the north side, just two buildings from the corner is a five-story old mansion that has been serving as an apartment house for the past ten years. The owner is now converting it into offices. I met with her this morning and we worked out a great deal . . . with your approval, of course," she quickly added.

Hearing all this conversation through the open doors, both Maxine and Madeline burst into the room. "Oh, Fifty-fifth Street is a great address," interrupted Maxine. There are so many good places for lunch and it's near the Modern Museum and the stores on Fifty-seventh Street."

Roland just shuddered as he imagined all the costs, but Susan continued to talk. "The space available is the top floor, the fifth story. The elevator opens to a small reception area with three doors leading into the offices. It's perfect. There is room for a large studio with some windows; there is a great deal of closet space; there are three perfect offices; and," she added with glee, "there is even a small, well-equipped kitchen for lunches and for washing the paint brushes."

Madeline and Maxine were clearly excited. Roland's mind was racing. He had a meeting with the bank that afternoon and he couldn't do anything without the loan. To make things worse, he hadn't discussed the matter with Bea. He wasn't sure how she would feel about his going out on a limb with their savings and then borrowing so much money just because he felt that he had to expand. He couldn't remain just a little guy. Now was the time to join the top firms on Madison Avenue. Susan was his crutch to his dream of a big firm.

"Let's look at it this afternoon," he said to Susan, "but now, I want to go over some sketches on the Ideal and Westclox project. Do you have anything ready, Madeline?"

Madeline went into the studio, returned with three partially completed comps along with the doll and the clock, and proceeded to post them on the wall. "Work on some other job while we discuss these," he directed her and moving some papers from his small couch, he asked Susan to sit down with him to discuss the comps.

"You can stay also," he said to Maxine. "I need another woman's point of view."

He put the doll and the clock on his desk and the three of them looked carefully at the drawings on the wall. Maxine was the first to speak.

"You know that I have two sons, but if I had a daughter, I would buy her one of those. All three are the cutest doll sets that I have ever seen."

Susan was more critical. She rose from the couch, removed the scarf from her shoulders, and placed it in front of one of the comps. "The pink must be soft and actually feel as delicate as this scarf. The doll's hand must be touching the clock. Everything must be extremely soft . . . and girlish," she added.

"Suzie," said Roland, overjoyed. "That is just the type of comment that I was looking for. Those are the feelings that this item should communicate. Moms and dads, and even grandparents, should look at it and say 'How cute! We must buy it for our little girl.'"

Susan smiled. She always felt good whenever Roland agreed with her. She woud even feel better if Ellen Burton agreed with her. She was the person who really gave her the assignment and she was the person she had to please.

Roland thanked Susan and Maxine for their help, removed each of the three comprehensive renderings from their place on the wall, and placed them on his drawing table. Then, turning toward Susan, he said, "Before you leave, Suzie, can I keep your scarf on my desk for a few hours?"

THIRTEEN

THE REAR of the Ideal Toy Company building contained six loading docks for both the receiving of raw materials and the shipping of finished merchandise to wholesale warehouses and retail stores. Each of the outgoing docks was designated by a color painted in a large circle on the floor at the edge of the bay with a number painted in white in the center. Bay number one was red, number two was green, and number three was dark blue. The company had eight large container trailers, each with the company name boldly lettered on the rear and both sides. Three of them were always docked in the outgoing area with their rear doors open to the shipping department. Five others were on the side, out of the way of traffic, and one by one, they would be moved into the dock to replace a filled one. Independent tractor owners would drive in on schedule, hitch a filled trailer, and drive off with the rig to the contracted destinations. The larger chain stores would send their own trucks and they would usually dock at the incoming bin for the hour or two needed for loading.

One company clerk was stationed at each loading dock. He carried a clipboard with the day's shipping list scheduled for that bay. The checking of orders and their shipping destinations was a tedious task and each clerk was familiar with the line of toys as well as the names of most of the distributors. They knew the stock number codes for items as diverse as tea sets and drink and wet dolls, and their task was to avoid any mix-ups. Dealers wanted their orders filled properly and on time, and special sales and promotions often depended on meeting these schedules.

While production runs were in progress on the line of injection molding plastics machines, finished parts were placed in baskets and moved to the toy assembly department. More than twenty women connected the parts and placed them carefully into beautifully designed and printed packages. The finished packages traveled on a conveyor to the carton section where they were placed in dozen and two-dozen corrugated containers and then binned in the large warehouse section of the plant. Drivers of forklift trucks, following customer order lists, picked the filled cartons and carried them to the shipping department. The items ordered by each distributor were placed on four-foot pallets to a height of about five feet and strapped with plastic tape to secure them for transportation. Shipping clerks carefully clipped the order slips to the top of each load before forklift trucks moved them to the loading docks.

Lou Mangini was a loyal five-year employee of the Ideal Toy Company. Lou was in charge of shipping bay number one, the red bay. He was always shouting, red-faced with anger, and was unfriendly to the drivers. But Lou was careful, checked each order, and avoided any incorrect shipments. He was a local, about thirty-one years old with a continuing run of local girlfriends. He had worked for Henry Isserman as an assistant toy designer when he first joined the company, but he was transferred to shipping and for the past year, he had been an outgoing loading clerk.

Lou was a loner. He loved to work alone and he applied himself diligently to each project, ignoring time and only finishing a project when he felt satisfied with it. At first, Henry gave him complete freedom to be creative on his assigned projects and he seemed pleased with some of the preliminary sketches. But as the weeks went by, there was nothing among Lou's sketches that was close to a finished toy design.

Henry explained that although they worked all year, clearly detailed toy items needed to be presented to key store buyers by the end of November and working models finished by mid-January. If the trade responded favorably, additional models would be completed and introduced at Toy Fair in February. Production had to be completed by July for the items were planned for Christmas sales.

"Stop toying with ideas," Henry would yell at Lou in an angry voice. "Your job is to design toys; the kids will do all the playing. Stop playing with yourself and give me some fucking good sketches. I'll tell you if I think it will sell and then we'll make a rough model. Gimme ideas! I know what the kids and their moms will like."

Lou would shudder whenever Henry yelled at him. There were two women and one other man in the creative toy design department and they would smile whenever Henry showed his anger. They knew that it was always short lived. Ten minutes later, Henry was all smiles with suggestions and new ideas. But Lou hated to be singled out and showed his embarrassment with a red face and downcast eyes. He loved to imagine new toys and he felt that his ideas were good, but he could never please Henry.

Henry ruthlessly shot down a water-shooting game, which Lou believed to be a great item for an eight-year-old boy. "I just don't like water for toys inside the home," criticized Henry. "Eliminate the water and let the kid shoot a light at the target. And for Christ's sake, change the black pistol. It looks too real." Lou was devastated. He loved water toys, especially guns, and he believed that kids loved them, too.

He was only about five-foot-four-inches tall, but with his narrow hips and broad shoulders, he looked somewhat taller. He had a large nose, "A common trait in my family," he would say, and a small mouth that was partly covered with an uneven black moustache. He wore wire-framed glasses for close work and his usual dress was a gray turtle-neck sweater, blue jeans, and faded white tennis shoes.

"These are my work clothes," he would explain to anyone who was dressed more carefully. "When I go out, I dress the way my girlfriends like a guy to look—fancy sweater, argyle socks, and dark brown shoes. Guys like me only wear ties to church."

Lou lived with his mother, but their relations were strained and he was home irregularly. Margaret Mangini had her own friends, her beer, and her television. She just took the few dollars that he gave her every week and from time to time, she would ask, "Louie, when are you going to find a nice girl and settle down?"

The Ideal Toy Company traditionally produced twenty new items every year, generally repeated at least ten items from the past year, carried ten best sellers from years past, and then made about a dozen staple items that were common also in the lines of their competitors. Their purpose was just to fill out the line to about seventy-five to eighty items that were reproduced in the catalog with certain items extended in different colors, different sizes, and at differing price ranges. Henry's staff developed most items, but each year, searching for new ideas, he interviewed freelance toy designers and inventors. When a concept seemed to be an innovation, he retained the design firm to develop the whole project, including its packaging. He depended on his own judgment to produce a line of toys that would keep the firm in a major marketing position in the toy industry.

Harold and Irving Misson, two brothers who inherited the business from their father, ran the sales, advertising, and manufacturing. Harold ran the sales office at 200 Fifth Avenue in New York City while Irving was in charge of the large manufacturing and shipping facility in Queens. In January, the brothers would go to Hong Kong where they maintained a small office seeking new items that could be developed and manufactured there. In February, both brothers, along with Henry Isserman, the field sales force, and their sales representatives, would stay in the New York office and showroom to meet with buyers during the International Toy Fair. This was the most important time of the year. The opinions and advance purchase orders of the major toy buyers determined not only the fate of new items, but also the probable vol-

ume of sales for all items. Irving, Harold, and Henry would then esti-
mate how many of each toy item they should manufacture.

Toy Fair was a mysterious place where Lou Mangini dreamed that
someday he would visit. It was there that final decisions were made to
either manufacture or reject a toy. He wanted to know why his ideas
were not being presented to the important toy buyers. The sketch for
a space walker that floated among three planets and could be aimed at
any one was, he thought, his best idea. They all moved at different
velocities and when the child managed to propel the spaceman to one
of the planets, the planet automatically illuminated. He developed a
dog with an extended right paw. When the child shook the paw, its
eyelids opened, his head flipped up, and he wagged his tail. But Henry
criticized each one.

"Lou," Henry said one Friday morning, "you have to learn more
about the toy business. You have been here for a year and none of your
ideas have gone into production. You have to learn more about our successful toys. But most of all, you must learn how to work as part of a
team. I'm transferring you to the shipping department starting Monday.
You'll be part of the team there. If you want to stay with the company,
you'll join the gang, learn the line, and you will find out about our best
sellers. So pick up your things and get your ass out of here by the end
of the day."

He hated Henry because of the way he handled the transfer. He was
embarrassed in front of the others in the department. *I'm as good as they
are,* he thought. *I still have some great ideas. I'll show him. He'll want me
back . . . but I won't give him anything. I'll show my ideas to Mr. Irving. He's
a good guy.*

Lou was not liked in the shipping department. He did his work and
memorized the stock numbers, but he was not friendly with any of the
other men in the department. They kept him there for three years and
when Peter Agnello, the man in charge of shipping bay number one
suffered a heart attack, his boss suggested him for the job. "Lou is very
loyal," he explained to Mr. Irving. "He's smart too, but he is a loner. He

works best when you give him some responsibility. Try him out. He knows shipping and he's a weasel with our stock numbers. I think that he can replace Peter."

Henry did not hear about it for several weeks until he went to the shipping department to inquire why an order for an important customer was late. He was irritated and everyone in his way received a tongue-lashing. When he reached bay number one, he was surprised to be greeted by Lou Mangini.

"Good morning, Henry. Are you slumming?"

"So, you fucked up again, Lou," responded Henry in an irritated voice. "I don't know who was stupid enough to put you here, but you have been missing a number of orders. Let me see the shipping lists for the last few days."

"Yes, Sir. They are right here on my clipboard. Each day has another sheet. What company are you looking for?"

Henry grabbed the clipboard, flipped pages back, and settled on one sheet. "I don't see the name of Piggly-Wiggly stores on this sheet. You must have erased it."

Flustered and angry, Lou yelled back, "Go see the guys that fill the pallets for all the stores. If they send me a pallet, I ship it correctly. Any problem is theirs, not mine." He couldn't look at Henry; he hated him even more now as he watched him walk to the shipping department. "Bastard," he whispered under his breath.

A couple of days later, a whole pallet was placed at Lou's dock with a packing slip for Piggly-Wiggly. He kicked it first, checked his shipping list, and then ordered it on to the trailer.

Lou Mangini liked to visit toy stores on his days off. Dressed in jeans, alone or with a girlfriend, he'd walk into a store, study some of the interesting items, and then ask a salesperson which one they recommended for an eight-year-old boy . . . or a girl. He was always testing his own opinions. He had an idea for a new doll concept, but he was not ready to show it to Henry. When he worked in the department, he started to outline this new doll, but Henry stopped him. "Keep with boys' stuff, Boychick. That's where we need new items. When you grow a pair of big tits, I'll let you create girls toys."

He had an idea for a girl's doll with a voice mechanism connected to a clock that would tell the activity time of the day with a child's voice. He was too angry to show the preliminary sketches to Henry. For two weeks, he worked at home during the evenings to prepare a group of sketches for both the doll and the package.

"I've been working here for nearly five years," he said quietly. "Where am I going? I'm shipping toys instead of designing them." During a lunch break shortly after Thanksgiving, Lou walked into Mr. Irving's office, past his secretary, and spread his portfolio of sketches across his desk.

FOURTEEN

ROLAND AND Susan clipped on their visitor badges, greeted the guard cheerfully as they entered the Ideal Toy Company building, and walked to the passenger elevator. "Mr. Isserman said to send you right up when you arrived. His office is on the sixth floor."

"Thank you," said Roland Levy with a smile. "We expect to be visiting with you quite often." Both he and Susan were each carrying a large portfolio and he also held a large corrugated carton, carrying it by a handle attached to the string encircling the box."

When they arrived on the floor, they heard angry voices shouting threats. Mabel Lieberman, Henry's secretary, was sitting on a couch with her hands over both ears. She motioned for them to sit down, but she didn't rise to greet them.

"You can't come in here, Irving, with this little whore and tell me that I have to feature some crap brained idea of his in next year's line." It was Henry's loud voice filled with anger. "Who does this cunt lapper think he is to go over my head and take some stupid new item directly to your attention? This is my department and he once worked for me. I fired him then and I'd do it again now."

"Henry, he was afraid to show it to you for exactly that reason. He tells me that you would not consider anything that he designed as worthwhile. So, he did the right thing. He came to see me."

"Irving, I won't waste my time looking at his drawings. I don't want to see him in this office or anywhere, and whatever he wants to show me, he probably stole."

"I hate you! I'll kill you!" a third voice threatened loudly.

Suddenly, the door opened and a short, broad-shouldered man with a black moustache charged out of the office and ran to the staircase. A few minutes later, Henry emerged from the office talking to a well-dressed tall man in his fifties. Henry smiled when he saw Susan and Roland and stopped to introduce them.

"Mr. Irving Misson, I'd like you to meet the principals of our new design firm. Ms Susan Liforest and Mr. Roland Levy. I have a high regard for their talents to create saleable toys."

"Henry has spoken a lot about you. I am pleased to meet you both and I shall look forward to your contributions. I'll leave you with Henry now. I have several appointments." Turning to Henry, he said, "I left the drawings on your desk."

As if on cue, Mabel rose from her chair and followed Henry into his office. They closed the door. A few minutes later, she emerged.

"Mr. Isserman has had a sudden interruption and a change in his schedule. He can't see you today. However, he asked me to request that you leave your portfolios and the box you are carrying. He may or may not look at it, but he will call your office tomorrow to schedule a new appointment."

Roland looked hurt and bewildered.

FIFTEEN

Late on Friday afternoon, 10 February, Susan Liforest returned to the office from meetings with several executives at the 225 Fifth Avenue Gift Building. As she whisked past the reception desk, hurrying for a quiet moment in her own office, Maxine Nierman called to her.

"Susan, I've had two urgent telephone calls for you from Ms. Burton who wishes for you to call her at the Beekman Tower Hotel just as soon as you get in. She says that it is very important."

"Ms. Burton? Heavens! She must be in town. She wrote that she would be in touch whenever she came in. Please call her, tell her I'm very busy, but if she is free, I'd love to have dinner with her tonight."

Damn, she thought. *I hope she's busy. I have an understanding with John Gillespie to have dinner with him tonight. His wife has gone to Chicago to see her mother for the weekend and just now, I feel completely drained.*

Hearing her voice, Roland came charging out of his office. "Suzy," he said in an excited voice. "Henry wants us to present the comps for the three new Crazy Cat games at 3 P.M. tomorrow afternoon. The meeting is at the New York showroom with the Misson brothers and the whole sales force. Ask Madeline to show you the comps. The stuff is beautiful. We need you at the meeting.

"Such short notice. I have a busy weekend, but I'll try to be there. I just heard that Ellen Burton is in town. She's probably here for the meeting."

She followed Roland as he returned to his office and sat down on the couch, still wearing her coat and scarf. "In this business, everything seems to happen at once," she said in a low, troubled voice. "I've been calling on Mr. Gillespie of Philip Morris for the longest time and I've listened to all of his excuses. Finally, he says that he has a promotional brand of cigarettes that needs a new package and he promises to introduce me to the director of all their food-marketing projects. I think that we are finally getting somewhere with that company. I was hoping for a bulls-eye this weekend."

"Has he let you in on any of their new product plans?"

"Better than that," she replied. "I've seen some of the comps that were prepared by their old design firm. They were beautiful, but he explained that they were rejected because they did not reflect the marketing direction. He has a lot of confidence in your analysis, Ruby, so I think we really have a good shot at some big fees here."

Roland smiled. *She likes to get personal with her Ruby stuff. Damn. She had better not do that at a client meeting. Those preppy bastards snubbed me when I explained my design theories,* he thought. *Now, they have laid an egg with their own kind and they want me to save them.*

He looked up at Susan as she rose from the couch and prepared to leave. Grinning sheepishly and trying to conceal his angry feelings, he said, "Great work, Suzy. Keep close tabs on him. Feed me his goals and we'll develop the best damn selling packages that he ever imagined."

"Oh," she said as she approached the door. "Ellen Burton wants me to call her back. I'll speak to her from my office."

Roland leaned back on his chair. *She's quite a gal,* he thought. *I knew that she could break into that preppy gang.* He looked down at his dull shoes and his pants with all the wrinkles around his thighs. She dresses like a doll and must impress that crowd as excellent. She is quite an asset to this firm.

Susan walked across the reception room toward her office, waved, forced a smile to Madeline and Joe, the new artist in the studio, entered the room swiftly, and closed the door behind her. She sat up straight on the cushioned chair behind her small glass tabletop desk, still wearing her coat, and dropped her purse and her scarf on the floor beside her. It had been a busy day, all filled with promises, and now it looked like the weekend would be no better.

They had expanded, moved to new quarters, refurbished the premises, even hired a very talented new artist, but sales were not coming in fast enough to catch up with her own expenses. Except for a few double dates with old girlfriends, her social life was a bust. Ruby was a doll, but he was so obsessed with climbing the ladder of success that he never looked at her like a woman. "Just make more and more contacts," he said, "and the business will ultimately expand." All week, the middle-aged business executives charmed her with politeness while they slyly leered, held her hands, and made suggestive remarks. But she was learning to play the game with equal charm.

She looked around at her office, the smallest in the suite, with one large window facing some modern uptown office towers, a small closet, and a continuous band around three walls of the room of desk-high white cabinets with white Formica tops. In starkness, it resembled a physician's office. Opposite her desk was a small white leather chair, but under the desk, clearly visible through its glass top, was an orange colored wool rug.

The emphasis in the room was the enlarged full-color photographs of packages and small products that were mounted under glass and cleverly arranged at eye level on the walls. It presented a clear mood to any visitor that this was a design firm and that she was an important executive.

"Maxine," she said into the intercom on her desk. "Did you get a response from Ms. Burton?"

"Yes. She said that she would wait in her room until you were settled and then she asked that you please call her. I love her southern accent. Shall I get her on the phone for you?"

"Please."

"Hello Ellen," she exclaimed with some excitement as she heard her voice. "How are you? It is great to hear from you."

"I'm just on my way out, Susan. I have some meetings and then dinner at the Fifth Avenue Club with Henry and Mr. Irving Misson. I would like you to be there. Meet me at the Club at 7 P.M. You enter from the lobby at 200 Fifth Avenue. Just ask for Mr. Misson's table."

"Gee, Ellen, I have sort of a problem."

"Tell me about it later. See you tonight. Bye."

Susan held the telephone in her hand for several minutes after Ellen had said good-bye. She put her head down on the desk, shielded by her folded arms. Suddenly, she rose from her chair, stood at the window, and gazed at the endless chain of buildings and sky.

"Fuck it! These are my three most important clients. Damn. I just can't screw this up." Quickly, she dialed information for the Plaza Hotel and then asked the hotel operator to give Mr. Gillespie a message that she would be a bit late for dinner. Save a drink for me."

Then she grabbed her scarf and bag and walked into Roland's office, concealing her dilemma with a big smile.

"Burton's in town, I guess for tomorrow's meeting. She wants to meet me tonight at 7 P.M. Girl talk, I guess. It's best that you don't come. I'll call you about tomorrow's meeting. Bye."

Before Roland Levy could respond, she walked sprightly to the door, waved good-bye to the girls, and rang for the elevator in the corridor.

I'll think it all over in a hot tub, she thought.

SIXTEEN

SUSAN STOOD at the window of her eighteenth-floor studio apartment on East Twenty-eighth Street, gazing at the seemingly endless high-rise buildings that cluttered the New York space along the shore of the East River. Her gaze stopped at the elegant and stately United Nations Buildings, the Beekman Tower Hotel, and she smiled as she followed the gondolas that swayed above the river to and from Roosevelt Island. She loved New York and she particularly loved her upscale high-rise building with both a doorman and a concierge attendant.

During her childhood, she shared a room with her sister, Phyllis. Phyllis was five years older and was the pretty one in the family—so her parents used to say when they thought that she was not listening. "Little Suzy likes to draw," her parents said to each other. "She'll marry and be a great help to her husband." But they never said how she would help him.

Isaac Levins, her father, was a mildly religious man who insisted that both of his daughters receive a Jewish education and live at home until they were married. Phyllis left at nineteen to marry Jerry Brandt, a first year law student. It was a small wedding and neither parent was too happy. The young couple moved into the big Brandt house at Sheepshead Bay and Phyllis continued her education at Stern College. Jerry received his degree from Brooklyn Law School and, as expected, joined his father's Court Street firm. *Another accident chaser and Hadassah mama,* Susan thought. She wanted much more.

As a teenager, Susan had the room to herself and when she entered Stern College, her mother agreed to throw out the two twin beds and dresser and let her redecorate the room. The apartment was on the first floor in a four-story walk up tenement building in Bensonhurst, Brooklyn, and the girls' room was the first one on the left as you entered. There was a long hall with her parents' bedroom, living room, and kitchen at the far end. So, Susan made her room into a den with a couch that opened into a bed, two chairs with a coffee table between them, and a television set in the corner. She did her schoolwork on the couch with papers all over the coffee table.

Now, in her own New York apartment, she felt free. There would no longer be a light in her parents' bedroom when she returned home late from a date, and she would no longer hear footsteps in the hall behind her closed door when she talked with a friend or had a visitor in her room. Although she had her own telephone and close friends frequently came to visit her at home after she graduated from college, she hated her Bensonhurst address. When she started to work in New York, she had personal cards printed listing her address in a prestigious high-rise building on Queens Boulevard. However, she had her Brooklyn telephone number printed below this address and following it in parenthesis was "unlisted." A girlfriend from college lived in the building and she would call her when the doorman received mail addressed to Susan Liforest.

Susan Levins loved deception.

Slowly, she removed her clothes and slid into a hot tub filled to the top, head on a plastic pillow, suds bellowing on top of the water, and feet twisted together stretched out as far as she could push.

Playing the date game was a challenge in college because there were more male students than female, and they were always hungry for dates, especially during the cold winter semester when everyone preferred to stay on campus. She would accept a guy's offer for dinner, then break away with the excuse to study, only to meet another guy later in the evening to dance in the canteen. If the first one spotted her later, she would wave to him, explain that she finished her work early, and then introduce the two men. *College guys are so timid,* she thought. She could even have a third date in her room under the pretense of studying after the first two had gone to their dorms. It was an easy game in college, but when she returned home to her room in the family's Bensonhurst apartment, her dates were a bit older and were much more demanding. She knew she was a little wiser now. Susan remembered the weekend when her parents went to Atlantic City with Phyllis' in-laws. She had been dating Rudy Quigley. He knew that her folks would be away because she mentioned it to him when they arranged a Saturday evening date. But, on Friday night, she had agreed to meet a blind date, a young lawyer friend of her brother-in-law, Jerry Brandt, at her sister's new Manhattan apartment. They all went out to dinner at Ruby Fu's Restaurant.

The new guy, Dave Kaplan, lived in an apartment on Montague Street in Brooklyn Heights and he offered to drive her to her parents' apartment in Bensonhurst. Since it was only 10 P.M., she invited him up to her room, explaining that her parents would probably return before 12 P.M. In her cozy and dimly illuminate room, listening to symphonic music, Dave cuddled with her on the couch and she enjoyed his affection, returning his kisses as they both loosened their clothing. Suddenly, there was loud knocking on the door.

"Suzy, I saw the light on from the street. Are you awake? It's me, Rudy. Open the door. I know that you're the only one home and I hear your favorite Mozart recording."

The both stood up suddenly. She froze. With the buttons of both her blouse and his shirt opened, Dave said, "He's making too much noise. One of us should go to the door and shut him up. I'll go. I'll just put the chain on and tell him to go away. I'll tell him that I'm your cousin, Dave." Before she had a chance to respond, he had opened the door slightly and Rudy could see his opened shirt and ruffled hair.

"Who the hell are you?" screamed Rudy. "Where's that little whore?" He skipped down the stairs and bolted out of the front door.

Susan sat up in the tub. Although this happened a few years before, the scene was fixed so deeply in her mind that she feared any conflict that could possibly become unfavorable to her. In both her personal and business relationships, she took great pains to avoid misunderstandings. She tried to be precise in her appointments and to let everyone know that at that moment, they were her exclusive interest. When first out of college and working for Elaine Waltham as a business representative, Susan concentrated on one particular artist at a time whom she believed would be of most value to a specific company. Elaine loved her ability to secure steady work for some of the artists and she earned her commissions by working very hard to develop new business contacts with art directors and then to sustain their loyalty by delivering good work within their budgets and time schedules.

After a year of employment, receiving a small drawing amount and commissions rising as her sales increased, Elaine made her a partner. Instead of a commission on each sale, she received forty percent of the business profits minus taxes. But when Roland Levy's offer came along, it was hard to resist. She couldn't work with two partners, it was either one or the other, and she saw more of a personal future to be associated with a business owned by a man than being partners with a woman. She wanted to be with a firm that created the artwork, not one that just represented the artists. And besides, Ruby was a cute guy.

"Enough of this schoolgirl dreaming, Gal," she said aloud. "You're working with the big boys now. Get your ass into your best suit and show them all that you can play the game as well as any of them."

Slowly, still wrapped in a bathrobe over her wet towel, she sat on her vanity chair, studied her image in the mirror, and slowly brushed her shoulder length hair. She carefully applied minimal make-up to her face—some blush, a touch of mascara, and a careful coating of red on her lips. As she started to get dressed, she turned from the mirror and surveyed the room. It was all hers—one studio room that was tastefully decorated with modern designer furniture. A round granite-topped table adorned the entrance with four red cushioned wire back chairs with plastic legs, easy to lift and move about the room. Twin sofas in deep brown leather faced each other perpendicularly to the wide expanse of windows, one opening to a bed. The room also contained a large white marble cocktail table and a bookcase unit that concealed a television set.

She sat at the far corner of the room in front of her vanity table, which also served as her writing desk. But Susan was more comfortable writing from a reclined position on the couch with her legs draped over the big marble cocktail table. The open bathroom door revealed a full-length mirror and a shelf above the sink cluttered with bottles. She scanned the closet for her good black pantsuit, looked at the clock on the desk, and hurried to finish her dressing. With a last check of her makeup, she walked into the galley kitchen, sipped a partial glass of water from the refrigerator, and turned to look at the room once more before turning off the lights, grabbing her coat, and opening the door.

She hated to leave. She loved the room, her privacy, and the magnificent view from the windows. Opposite the elevator was a long mirror. As she waited for the elevator, she put on her coat and checked her appearance in the mirror.

It was 6:15 P.M. She asked the doorman to hail a taxi. She felt ready for Ellen Burton and the Ideal Toy boys.

SEVENTEEN

MARRIED MORE to his business than to his wife, Roland Levy spent few nights at home each week. Working at his drawing board until well past 12 A.M., he often dozed off on the office couch when he was too tired to make the subway journey home. Maxine Nierman had found him asleep on his couch several times and discreetly remarked, "Roland, you must have arrived at the office so early that you probably skipped breakfast. Can I order you something?" On these occasions, he would smile and reply, "Yes, I arrived very early and I guess that I just forgot about breakfast. Please order something."

One morning, Bea Levy called and Maxine, aware from the worried sound of her voice, said that Roland was still sleeping on the couch in his office and that he must have worked well past 12 A.M. On the nights that he came home, he would try to explain his intensity, his compulsion, his need to spend hours on each design, but Bea did not understand. "All my friends have husbands who come home for dinner every night. You arrive so late, on the nights that you do come home, that you just go right to sleep because you're so tired. We don't even go to the movies anymore."

Susan Liforest was different. She loved the designs that he created and she understood that he devoted long hours to create them. They discussed the designs, they discussed her sales approach, and they both shared the excitement when a new client retained them to develop a project. She solicited firms by telephone and mail, and diligently made sales calls on important marketing executives—many times, Susan brazenly walked in on them without an appointment. Roland joined her for closings and for occasional client lunches. But as they grew closer in their business relations, she yearned to be closer to him . . . and for shared pleasures unrelated to business. He never saw a movie, rarely watched television, never attended a concert, and the only music he listened to was whatever sound came from the radio near his desk.

She was sure that he needed more moments of relaxation and she was sure that he would enjoy her company in a social environment. But how could she make a date with a compulsively busy and married boss? Concerts, movies, and the theater were all far from his current interests.

Passing by the display windows of the Art Students' League on West Fifty-seventh Street one morning, Susan noticed a small sign announcing an exhibition of recent watercolor paintings by members of the league's faculty in association with some noted artist members of the American Watercolor Society. She knew that Roland loved watercolors. The opening reception for invited guests only was scheduled from 5 P.M. to 7 P.M. the following evening. This seemed like a good opportunity to share some leisure time with him. She went into the building and asked the young woman at the reception desk how she could obtain an invitation for the president of an industrial design company who was also a watercolor artist. She presented her business card and the receptionist placed his name on the guest list and gave her a printed invitation on which she wrote in the name, Roland Levy and guest. Now all that remained was to make a date.

Roland was not interested at first. "Maybe next year. You know that I have too many projects just now and my best concentrating time is at night. The staff leaves this office at 5 P.M. and that is my time to concentrate on design. No! Between 5 P.M. and 7 P.M. is too important. Why don't you attend the show and tell me all about it?"

"But, Roland, this is a showing of the work of some of the finest watercolor artists," continued Susan in what seemd like a losing situation. "It is your chance to meet them in a social setting and talk about real art, not packaging or product design." It took only a moment or two for him to look up from his desk and ask with a boyish grin, "Should I wear a suit and a tie?"

"Wow!" said Susan to herself as she left his office. "He is more difficult to sell than than our biggest client."

The following day, Susan left the office early and returned at 5:30 P.M. just as Maxine was leaving. "Susan, going on a big date with one of the clients? You look lovely."

"Yes," she lied. "Big night. He is going to pick me up at the office."

"Take a tip from an older gal. Pick the rich ones. They may be lousy lovers, but their money buys lots of pleasures."

"I'll remember that, Maxine. Thanks. See you in the morning."

Roland was absorbed at his desk with a series of color sketches when she opened the door to his office. She stood there in her long black shift with slits on each side, black hosiery, and high heel pumps, her hair freshly set with bangs gently kissing her eyebrows and falling to within an inch of her shoulders on each side.

"Suzy, you look so glamorous," he said abruptly standing up from his desk. "Big date?"

"No, dear," she winked as she spoke. "Just an opening reception at the Art Students' League. Did my date forget all about it?"

"Oh! I guess that it just slipped my mind. But I have a clean shirt and a sports jacket in the closet. When are we due?"

"Right now! We should leave here just as soon as you get dressed. It is just a short walk. If we get there at 6 P.M., we'll have plenty of time to see the paintings and meet the artists."

They walked slowly along Sixth Avenue, turning at Fifty-seventh Street, she holding his arm close to her body to steady herself and he, alerted to the sensual scent she was wearing, matching her walk step by step. They climbed the stone steps together and entered the gallery of the Art Students' League. A young lady collected their ticket, ushered them to the bar, and handed them a program listing the paintings, the artists, and the suggested prices. They each selected a glass of wine and then walked together to the exhibition area.

"Look, Suzy! Here is a painting by Don Kingman. Notice how freely the washes appear and how the composition keeps your eye moving within the painting. Beside it is a John Marin. He loves big color areas and avoids small details. And Herb Olsen. He paints children so beautifully with delicate colors."

Roland was happy and excited. He had often seen photographs of these watercolors, but the originals were so much larger and more colorful. As he walked around the gallery, stopping at each painting, Susan held his arm tightly.

Standing for a few moments in front of a painting by Cathy Johnson, a pretty woman with gray hair asked, "Do you like the colors?"

"Yes," replied Roland. "They are so soft and they reflect the mood of a moonlit evening. I love the way the washes of lemon yellow seem to be peeking through the cobalt blue and gray of the sky. I wish that I could paint like that. It is beautiful."

"Oh, thank you. I did that one at Block Island last summer. I teach watercolor painting at the league. I'm Cathy Johnson. Why don't you register for one of my courses? Do you paint in oils?"

Roland was silent and too excited to talk. Susan extended her hand and said, "Cathy, this is Roland Levy, the noted industrial designer. I'm Susan Liforest, his assistant. He is one of the busiest designers in New York."

"I'm very glad to meet you both. Why don't you join me at the bar for a drink? What kind of design work do you do?"

Roland and Susan discarded their wineglasses and ordered martinis; Cathy asked for plain ginger ale on ice. "Our firm designs small products and their packages along with the trade marks and identification programs needed to sell complete product lines," replied Roland.

"So you must do color sketches and renderings. Do you use watercolors?"

"Occasionally. Most of our renderings are with markers. Then we make accurate paperboard models using colored papers and tempera paint. We must try to imitate realism."

Cathy Johnson extended her hand and said, "Call me here at the league if you wish to join one of my classes. They are calling me to meet some other important people. Good luck to you." She left the bar and walked to a small group of men and women who were standing in front of one of her paintings.

Roland was happy and excited to be in the company of so many fine artists. Susan put her glass down on a small table and asked, "Don't you think that we should have some dinner? The Russian Tea Room is just across the street and that is where most of the artists will be going."

"So, why not? Suzy, you look so pretty and you have been struggling to keep up with me all evening. I'm so glad that we came. Let's join them."

The Russian Tea Room is a long, narrow restaurant with small tables set closely together and Russian art objects interspersed at every open area. As they sat down, Cathy Johnson waved to them at a crowded table near the back of the room. There were some artists seated at other tables, most in groups of four. Susan was happy to be alone with Roland. They ordered Borsht, Shashlic, and some red Russian wine. They talked about the paintings, the artists, and the Art Students' League.

There were cabs waiting outside when they left the restaurant. Roland nodded to a driver and as soon as they both were seated inside, the driver took off. The cabby asked, "Where to?"

Roland turned to Susan. "Shall we go to your new apartment? Give the driver the address."

"Of course. It's Twenty-eighth Street and Second Avenue."

Roland was very quiet in the taxi. When they arrived at her apartment building, he got out with her and signaled the driver to wait. He walked with her to the front entrance door, turned to quickly kiss her on the cheek and received her full lips for a longer time than he expected. "I must get back to my design work. I have so many new ideas; I'm bursting. Thank you, Suzy. It was a great idea and I loved every minute." He turned around abruptly and returned to the cab.

She watched him as the taxi drove off. "Well, it was our first date. I have to work on him. He has great potential." She waved to the doorman and rang for the elevator.

EIGHTEEN

THE FIFTH Avenue Building stretches between Twenty-third and Twenty-fourth Streets on the west side of Fifth Avenue and continues along those streets almost halfway to Sixth Avenue, towering above all its neighbors and imparting an old world elegance not shared with any of the adjacent commercial structures. Diagonally across Twenty-third Street, rising unobstructed from the apex of the triangle that is formed by the crossing of Broadway with Fifth Avenue, is the world-famous Flat Iron Building. Pioneering architect Louis Sullivan, who it is said inspired the later creative work of Frank Lloyd Wright, designed this building before World War I. This construction innovation received its name from its early use of steel framing and its unusual triangular shape. Originally, the owners designated it as the Fuller Building. Between both buildings, facing them from the other side of the wide thorough-fare, is Madison Square Park with its walks, benches, and statues that tell its Civil War history.

The Fifth Avenue Building also has a long history. It was erected as a hotel when Twenty-third Street was uptown and horse drawn car-riages with uniformed drivers waited patiently at its front door to take ladies shopping at Wannamakers, Lord and Taylor, and the other fine stores that dotted the neighborhood. Well dressed ladies and gentlemen leisurely strolled in Madison Square Park and dined in the elegant restaurants along Twenty-third Street and Fifth and Madison Avenues. Gradually, as New York splendor moved further uptown and commercial ventures multiplied along Twenty-third Street and Broadway, the hotel became home to business enterprises. It went into considerable neglect during the depression years, reemerging after World War II with the growth of new business ventures. First came the custom tailors, catering to the same elegant people who had enjoyed the comfort of the Fifth Avenue Hotel. Then, firms in the men's fashion industry rented showrooms in the building and gradually it lost its splendor and joined the group of buildings along Broadway and Fifth Avenue that competed for the leasing of office space.

The toy industry breathed new life into the building. As important office buildings became market buildings, so did the 200 Fifth Avenue Building. Gradually, toy, doll, and game sales offices moved into the building, encouraged by Helmsley-Spear, the building owners and rental agents who limited tenants to only that industry. The Toy Manufacturers' Association established it as the setting for the International Toy Fair, their central marketing showplace where individual firms could present their product lines in the privacy of their own showrooms. The entire industry could now attract wholesale and retail store buyers from all over the world to come to this one central market location.

The marketing of children's toys, dolls, and games to consumers is a multi-step process starting with designers and engineers who first create innovative products to be manufactured. Then it is the function of manufacturers' representatives, independent wholesale distributors, and company sales organizations to show the products and solicit sales from retail store buyers. Ultimately, the manufacturers advertise as also do the retail stores that display and sell these products to consumers. Market weeks are organized by trade associations in many industries in order to show in one location the entire gamut of new products that will ultimately be available for sale. A central location to view product lines saves considerable time and money for busy marketing executives and retail store buyers who otherwise would be forced to travel to many different locations.

The major buying season in the toy industry lasts only six months each year: April, May, June, July, August, and September. In such a short market span, manufacturers must have their product lines determined with prices and quantities set by the end of February.

To accomplish this, new products in the toy industry are first produced in limited quantities so manufacturers can test their sales potential by soliciting the opinions of the company sales force and the national representatives, and then testing the eagerness of large retail chains to make early buying decisions. From these preliminaries, quantities and prices for most items are determined at Toy Fair. But every year, each company seeks one hot item that is strong enough to carry the whole line.

When products are produced overseas, the buying season must start even earlier because of shipping schedules and longer manufacturing delays. Toy Fair is always a busy time for both buyers and sellers. Major manufacturing and marketing decisions must be made between Washington's Birthday and 28 February. However, consumers in retail stores do not purchase the vast majority of toys, dolls, and games until Halloween and Thanksgiving. The largest sales occur during the two weeks before Christmas. The actual orders for this merchandise by retail stores are not generally received before April and May with deliveries starting in June.

In early January each year, the housewares industry sponsors one of the largest trade shows at McCormack Place in Chicago. The Ideal Toy Company, along with many other large toy firms, exhibit their products at this show since buyers from multi-product stores like Wal-Mart search the exhibitors for new and interesting items. Nevertheless, the major international market for toys is at the 200 Fifth Avenue Building and, because of overcrowding, the market extends to the neighboring showroom building across Twenty-fourth Street at 1107 Broadway. A bridge extending from the ninth floor of the Fifth Avenue

Building connects both toy buildings. Firms without showrooms in either of these buildings exhibit their new lines at the showrooms of their manufacturers' representatives and at the Javits Center. The Toy Manufacturers Association leases this convention hall during the last weekend of Toy Fair to provide selling space for smaller U.S. firms and Asian and European firms.

The Ideal Toy Company occupies a large showroom and office space on the tenth floor of 200 Fifth Avenue Building. It is the permanent office suite for Harold Misson and his two sales executives along with the advertising manager and several secretaries. They maintain the showroom and are hosts to visiting buyers throughout the year. Mr. Harold only travels to the Queens factory for special meetings and product conferences with Irving or Henry. During Toy Fair and for several weeks before and after, Irving Misson coordinates sales with manufacturing from an office next to his brother's. Henry occupies a desk in the showroom where he can demonstrate the new items to buyers. Irving and Henry have the task of preparing the exhibition of the new items. Harold develops the sales catalog, the consumer and retail advertising, and all three men work on the pricing and the quantity of each item to manufacture. Both Irving and Harold travel to European and Asian countries to arrange for foreign manufacturing and scheduled delivery dates.

During the first week of Toy Fair, most of the executives stay at hotels in the neighborhood since they entertain the important buyers throughout the day and the evening. This year, Henry refused a room at the Prince George Hotel on Twenty-eighth Street, insisting that he needed to escape from the local industry excitement in order to sleep at night. Instead, he registered at the Beekman Tower Hotel.

Susan Liforest's cab stopped in front of the large canopy that extends from the edge of the sidewalk to the huge archway at the entrance to 200 Fifth Avenue. As she paid the taxi driver, he said, "This is it, ma'am. It's quiet now, but in a few days, this place will cause a traffic jam. Have a nice evening!"

The street was dimly illuminated, but the lobby of the building was blazing with bright light as she entered. There were a few well-dressed men talking, all with their coats on, probably confirming the next morning's appointments before they left for the evening. The lobby was painted gold with huge chandeliers suspended from an enormously high ceiling. Banks of elevators lined both sides of the lobby. Two of the elevators had their doors open and uniformed operators stood in front of each one.

"Can you direct me to the Fifth Avenue Club?" Susan asked the first uniformed operator.

"Just walk to the end of the lobby and go through those double doors," he replied as he pointed the way for Susan.

The long lobby led to a smaller rotunda and the side entrances to the building from Twenty-third Street and Twenty-fourth Street. In the center was a wood framed glass double door with very small lettering on the glass, "The Fifth Avenue Club." A uniformed attendant was standing inside the door.

"I'm Ms. Liforest. I'm here to meet Mr. Irving Misson of the Ideal Toy Company."

"Yes, ma'am. Just have a seat in the lounge. I'll tell Mr. Irving that you are here. Welcome to the club."

"Susan. It's so nice to see you," exclaimed Ellen Burton emerging from a door at the end of the hall and walking toward Susan. "You look great, as usual."

Wearing a long dress with an open back and a small orchid on her shoulder, Ellen reached out to kiss Susan on the cheek, take her hand, and lead her into the dining room. There were only a few tables occupied in the large room, all with groups of six or seven well-dressed men who seemed to be talking more than they were dining.

"Susan, you know Henry. This is Irving Misson, but everyone calls him Mr. Irving. He's one of the good guys who run Ideal Toy. Henry calls him Izzy when no one is around." Ellen winked. "Guys, this is my good friend, Susan Liforest, of Roland Levy Industrial Design."

Henry grinned and didn't bother to stand-up, but Mr. Irving signaled the waiter to take her coat, rose from his seat, and offered her the chair next to his. He was a tall, distinguished looking middle-aged man and was slightly bald with a gray moustache. He wore wire-framed glasses over bright blue eyes and his small, smiling mouth seemed a little strange on a somewhat long face.

"Miss Liforest, Henry is so pleased with all the splendid work created by your firm. We are looking forward to a very successful Toy Fair. What would you like to drink?"

"Just some red wine, please. I have quite a busy evening ahead."

"Oh! I'm sorry to hear that, but I am glad that you were able to join us, even for just a short time. I was anxious to meet you before tomorrow's meeting. As you probably know, the first sales meeting before Toy Fair officially opens is the most important. This is when our national sales reps get to see the line and hear about our pricing structure. Your firm has done some beautiful work for us in a very short time. Ms. Burton also shares our enthusiasm with the line of Tell Time Baby Dolls. It should be our hit item for the season."

"Our marketing people are very happy, Susan," Ellen added. "Mr. Carrol, the president of Westclox, plans to visit during Toy Fair."

Henry was very quiet. He just grinned now and then and concentrated on his dinner.

"Will there be a big crowd at tomorrow's meeting, Henry?" asked Susan.

Putting his fork and knife down, he looked up at her and said, "There better be. Forty guys work with our reps all over the country. I invited them all. There are about ten of us from the home office. So, we'll have enough folding chairs and I ordered about thirty-five box lunches and lots of soda and snacks. Some guys like to go out for a bite with friends from other firms. This is buddy time in the toy industry."

He looked at Irving Misson and said, "I hope that there are no uninvited visitors." Then he added, "Nor any objections to our lines."

There was a sudden silence. Then Susan asked, "Are you expecting any?"

Mr. Irving moved his chair back slightly. "Well," he seemed to fluster. "We, that is Henry and me, got into a little misunderstanding concerning one of our lines. We paid a little money and I think that we settled it. Didn't we, Henry?"

"I'm not so sure, Izzy," replied Henry. "I just don't trust that son-of-a-bitch. He has it in for me."

There was silence at the table. Susan began to stir as if it was time to depart. Ellen asked Susan, "Can I call you later?"

"I'm going to the ladies room before I leave, Ellen. Would you care to join me?"

As Susan and Ellen walked away from the table, Ellen asked, "What's up, Babe? Your boss sneaking away from his wife for a little rendezvous with you?"

Susan checked her make-up, applied some fresh lipstick, and said, "Worse than that. He's too fucked up with his design work to even think about me. I have a late dinner date with an older guy whom I've known casually for a few years. I'm supposed to meet him at the Palm Room of the Plaza where he is staying for the weekend. His wife is away. He could be a great client if I handle him right."

"Honey, I'll let you in on a secret. There is no right or wrong way. Keep your goal clearly in mind. You know what the guy wants. It's one of the perks guys seem to think comes with their job. Remember that you're just as smart as he is. It will go any way that you want it to go. My creed is very simple. Know the guy first, then give a little to get a lot."

"Thanks, Ellen. I knew that you would understand. I'll see you at the meeting tomorrow. Ask the waiter to get my coat. I'll say good-night to Henry and Irving and excuse myself. Say, who is that fellow they were talking about?

"Let's leave that for next time."

NINETEEN

Roland Levy met Susan Liforest in the crowded lobby of the Fifth Avenue Building at 2:45 p.m. on Saturday. When he approached her, she was somewhat surprised.

"Why Mr. Levy, sir. You look as distinguished as any guy in this building." He returned her comment with a smile and a wink.

He was dressed in a pin-striped dark gray suit, a deep maroon and gray striped tie, and a light gray shirt with sleeves that extended long enough to show a white French cuff linked with a simple silver cuff link. She had never seen him so properly dressed. He can be so handsome, she thought.

"Hey, Preppy!" she continued to kid him "You look more affluent than the prep school boys. I always knew that you could play the part well."

Joe, the new artist, was standing beside him carrying a large corrugated box and struggling with a portfolio. Roland carried a smaller box. Neither wore coats, although it was a cold Saturday afternoon.

"We came by cab from the office. Joe is going right back since he has some work to finish on packages for Block Drug. Say, you look spiffy."

Susan smiled. She was wearing the same black pantsuit that she wore the previous day. *No one will notice,* she thought.

Roland blushed. "I tried to call you last night, but I guess that you turned your phone off. You looked so tired when you left the office."

She didn't answer and they entered the crowded elevator. "Tenth floor, please," he told the operator.

The expansive Ideal Toy offices had a large retail store display window on each side of the glass double door entrance. A green and white striped canopy extended over them into the corridor by at least three feet; the Ideal Toy Company lettering was along the edge. The glass surfaces were covered from the inside with white wrapping paper adhered to the windows with Scotch tape. Roland imagined that these windows would spotlight his designs during Toy Fair and he envisioned all kinds of props and positions to display the merchandise.

As Roland opened the door, a guard greeted them with a clipboard containing names. Please give me your name so I can check it on this list. This is a private meeting limited to only Ideal Toy marketing people."

Joe placed his package and the portfolio on a table and left immediately. As soon as the guard located Roland and Susan's name, he called Henry who picked up the packages and ushered them into the large showroom, which was crowded from wall to wall with men and women, all talking at the same time and all leisurely dressed in casual weekend clothes.

"Hey, you all," said Henry. "I want you to meet our design people. Here's Roland Levy and Susan Liforest. You've seen their work in the great stuff we have on display up front. They brought in more of our items for us to look at."

He led them to two empty chairs in the first row. "We saved these for you. Say, are you guys going or coming from a wedding?"

He returned to his seat at the center of a long table, facing the group with Mr. Irving and Mr. Harold on either side of him. One of the men opened the corrugated boxes and placed the new designs on the table and the illustrations from the portfolio on an easel.

The front and both sides of the windowless room were covered with toys, dolls, and games, along with their various store displays. In front of the room, in a large and well-illuminated display area, were about a dozen dolls. They were posed in various positions holding a cute Westclox clock in one hand and were dressed for parties, picnics, gardening, and other play activities. In bold lettering above this display was a sign reading:

THE NEW INNOVATIVE DOLL LINE
CREATED BY ROLAND LEVY INDUSTRIAL DESIGN
AN IDEAL TOY/WESTCLOX COLLABORATION

Susan smiled and proudly tapped Roland on the knee. He was too excited to feel anything. Then she spotted Ellen sitting on the side in the row behind her. Ellen whispered, "See me when we break. You look as good as the designs."

The new designs included three games with brightly colored plastic pieces packed in a rigid box, a contruction toy with multi-colored pieces that combined to form several small houses, and a tractor with a trailer containing several small toys.

"Hey, Roland!" Henry called out. "Come on up here and tell us about the new stuff that you just brought in. You have to sell it to us first. Then we'll all go out and sell a million of them."

Roland rose from his seat, walked to the front, picked up one of the packages from the desk, and started to explain the sales advantages of the concept, the lettering, and the colors when loud shouting interrupted them.

"I'm Lou Mangini and this is my friend Maryann. We're here to see my designs. I created a new line of dolls and at least half a dozen other toys. I'm going in and you can't stop me."

The door opened suddenly and Lou and Maryann walked into the room waving and smiling to Mr. Irving Misson. They were both elegantly dressed in black suits, he with a red tie and she with a yellow, red, and gray silk scarf around her shoulders. As they walked to the front of the room, Lou saw the large sign above the dolls.

"That's a damn lie. I did it. I did it!" he shouted. "And I created some other stuff in this room. Come on, Maryann, let's get the hell out of here." As he reached the door, he turned, glared at Henry, and said, "I'll get you, you bastard!"

Maryann pulled him by the arm, trying to get him to leave peacefully. His tie was loose; his face was flushed. "I'll get them yet," he yelled as he left the showroom.

There was not another sound in the room. Henry looked at Irving and they both stood up.

TWENTY

BEATRICE LEVY sat behind the big art reference desk in the Brooklyn
Central Library at Grand Army Plaza. She was gazing out of one of the
two huge windows that funneled in the morning light. Although the
February sky was clear, there was no bright sunlight to cheer up the
normally dismal room. She liked this more than the brightly lit school
library.

Art scholars prefer it this way, too, she thought. With so few people
engaged in art research, she imagined the souls of the great artists to be
asleep inside the bindings of the photo reference books. Occasionally,
docents and curators from the neighboring Brooklyn Museum of Art
would seek her advice to locate history books depicting the lives and
discussing the paintings of artists whose work they planned to exhibit.
During January's college recess, several scholars from Columbia and
Brooklyn College spent a few hours each day gathering information for
their research studies. Now, they were back at school with little time for
outside library studies.

Her mind wandered to Ruby. "He works so hard and we are still so
deeply in debt, more than we have ever been. My salary pays all the

household bills," she mumbled, moving her lips slowly. "But he works so hard, sleeps in the office several nights a week, and when he comes home, he is always hungry. He doesn't even take showers or change his clothes when he's away from home, and he is always too tired to talk with me."

Feeling sorry for herself was neither a pleasant nor a frequent state of mind for Bea. She always greeted people with a smile along with some happy words and when asked about her husband, she replied, "He now has some of the largest toy, clock, and food companies as his clients." But her patience was slipping and she was quite annoyed with Ruby.

He's such a good artist and is very intelligent, too. Why can't he take a regular job? We can't have children while he's having a good time playing big shot designer. I work to support him, and I keep postponing my Masters of Library Science at Pratt Institute, she thought.

"Bea," whispered her friend Shirley from the General Circulation Department. "Are you dreaming of warm nights on the Isle of Capri or a quiet dinner on the patio in Bermuda? Snap out of it. It's February in Brooklyn and it's cold. Are you free for a Big Mac at McDonald's tonight? Fred is bowling with the boys from the office."

"I really could use a little company tonight. This is Toy Fair time and Ruby is working late again. I'll meet you downstairs at 5 P.M." Bea was an alert looking woman with a pretty face, a broad smile, and a continual weight problem that dieting never seemed to help. She wore her light brown curly hair in a boyish manner that made her appear a little taller than her five-foot-two-inch height. She dressed in simple, casual clothes, buying almost nothing new, using her entire income to maintain her household and wondering whether Ruby would ever make a decent living. Each day her anger toward him increased.

Shirley and Bea left the library and walked across Eastern Parkway, then Franklin Avenue, and the short Plaza Street block until they reached the subway station on Flatbush Avenue. They huddled together as they walked. The air was clear and cold, but the snow had been removed a few days earlier and, at 5 P.M., the massive monumental arch at the Plaza seemed to add a mood of protection and warmth. Next to the black wrought iron railings that surrounded the subway stairs was the entrance to the new McDonald's.

After ordering and receiving their burgers, fries, and coffee, they sat down in a booth at the side of the room, furthest away from the food counter. Bea smiled at Shirley and thought, *We have known each other for a long time and as far as I can remember, she always seems to be there when I need her.*

"Tell me, Kiddo," said Shirley. "Do you think that he is playing around with someone else? We've been friends since high school and I remember Ruby when you first started to date him. What's eating you up?"

"I'm really worried, Shirley. I'm getting deeper into debt every day. I can't keep it up. Since Dad is gone, Mother now lives alone and she has asked me to give up the apartment and live with her for a while. I'm frightened and I don't know what to do."

"You know that I am quick to give my opinions and my advice, Bea, but leave me out of this one. Fred and I have had our arguments, but I have never thought of leaving him. Killing him, yes. But leaving him . . . that's a very serious move."

"I can't even get him to talk about money or our debts. I'm beginning to think that it is a sickness with him and he won't give up until it kills him . . . or me. We haven't gone out to dinner or seen a movie together in over a year. I think that Mother is right. If I move out for a few days, he may miss me and come crawling back."

"But, what if he doesn't? If he has a floozy on the side, your moving out will just play into their hands."

"I guess that I just don't care anymore, Shirley. I've cried myself to sleep many nights. I'm still young enough to make a new life for myself if I have to."

They drank their coffees slowly. There seemed to be nothing more to say. As they put on their coats to leave, Shirley asked, "When do you think that you will move out?"

"Mother suggested Sunday."

"I'll speak to Fred tonight. Get your things together. I'm sure that he will want to help. We'll pick you up in our car sometime in the afternoon and move you to your mother's. I don't like the idea, but this is what friends are for."

The both entered the subway station together. The two women hugged each other and as soon as they separated, Bea broke into tears."

TWENTY-ONE

Toy Fair was a busy time. It was market week for the world-wide toy industry and the excitement continued both day and night. Retailers met with the manufacturers, sales representatives met with their customers, advertising and marketing executives sought new selling themes, and old friends and competitors joined each other for a drink or a meal. Design firms were busy, too, zealously seeking new contacts and trying to gain publicity for the designs that they had created.

Although the wrapping paper "blinds" were removed from the showroom windows, all the new toy items were closely guarded. Most new items were not patented and there was always the fear that a competitor may learn of an innovative new toy. If start-up costs were low, or if it naturally fit into their line, these competitors would offer it to the larger retailers, like Toys "R" Us or Wal-Mart, with a promised delivery date far into the future. If you could deliver by August, a major buyer may give you a temporary order to assist you with a bank loan, but you had to promise a big discount.

Anyone passing by the Fifth Avenue Building knew instantly that there was an activity inside involving toys. The Disney firm had a giant Mickey Mouse balloon floating near the front entrance and a ten-foot teddy bear sat alongside the door. A large display window to the left of the entrance featured specially selected toys along with a message from the Toy Manufacturers Association. Display windows within the entrance area highlighted the toys of several well-known manufacturers. All day long, young men and women wrapped in winter coats and scarves distributed circulars to those entering the building inviting them to special showrooms where new items were on display and where deals were available for buyers who placed early orders. But, by 7 P.M., the hoopla had dispersed and although there were still people in the lobby and on the street, they were mostly on their way out to dinner or to private parties.

Lou Mangini parked his automobile on West Twenty-fourth Street near the corner of Sixth Avenue at 8:30 P.M. on 27 February. The street was dimly illuminated from two towering streetlights and all of the local retailers along Twenty-fourth Street had already closed their window display lighting. Even Ralph's Pizza and Fast Food had closed for the evening. There were a few other cars on the street, probably belonging to residents in the six-story loft condominium building in the middle of the block. Lou and Maryann emerged from the car, locked it, and walked swiftly along the dark street toward Fifth Avenue, arm in arm, she swinging a small purse and he carrying a plastic bag rolled up under his arm. The Twenty-fourth Street freight entrance to the building was closed tightly and one truck was parked near the driveway ready for a morning delivery.

The few people talking in front of the Fifth Avenue Building muttered greetings and the couple smiled in return as they entered the building. The lobby was fully illuminated and one guard stood talking to a man and woman who seemed to be leaving.

"Busy night," said the guard as they entered the elevator. "Even when we are not very crowded, you should still wear your badges."

"Oh. Thanks for reminding me. I must have left it in my other jacket. I'll wear it when I leave the building."

"Well, if it's after 9 P.M., I'll be on my way home. That's my quitting time. Be sure to sign your name in the book on the stand near the front door if you leave after 9 P.M. We check it each morning to see which offices stay open late. See you in the morning. By the way, the elevator is on automatic. All the operators just left five minutes ago."

"I'm familiar with it. I've signed the book before. See you tomorrow."

Maryann smiled. "Lou, you play the part very well. Hopefully you'll be one of them next year."

Sooner than that, I hope, he thought, but he was still steaming with anger against Henry. "Mr. Irving tricked me, gave me a few measly bucks for my ideas, and now they are going to make millions."

"Things will work out well, Lou, but first you must control your anger. It only gets you into trouble."

They stepped out of the elevator on the tenth floor and as soon as Maryann emerged, he quickly reached inside, pressed the button for the third floor, and moved away just before the doors closed. The lights were on all over the floor and the show windows of the Ideal Toy Company were still brightly illuminated. He stood looking at the windows for several minutes, studying the wide assortment of toys. Then he rang the doorbell. When he was sure that no one was inside, he opened his small bag and took out a string of door keys. Pete, one of his boyhood friends who had a few tangles with the police, gave him the keys when he faithfully promised to return them at the end of the evening. After only trying five keys, the lock turned and the door opened.

"Follow me, Maryann. Don't make any noise and lock the door after you. We don't want any unannounced company."

He found the wall switches and the room was brightly illuminated in seconds. He stood there gazing around the room for a minute or two and then quickly turned them off. *A guard or someone working late in another showroom may see the lights and investigate,* he thought. From the small bag under his arm, he removed a powerful flashlight and then walked slowly around the room shining it at all the various toys and games.

"There must be over one hundred toy items here, Maryann, and many of them were developed from my ideas. Henry said that I was no good . . . and then he stole my ideas." He opened the small bag that he was carrying and took out a folded black garbage bag.

"Open this bag all the way and hold it open. Follow me around the room. I want to fill it with the toys that I created."

They walked slowly around the room collecting bounty from numerous displays. He opened the boxes, folded or crushed them, and stuffed them, along with the toys, into the plastic bag. It took no more than ten minutes for them to fill the bag. When he came to the Tell Time Baby Dolls, he started to curse loudly.

"Lou, you're making too much noise. Just take one doll and let's leave. I'm frightened."

He grabbed one of the dolls, pushed it into the bag, and then, taking the filled garbage bag from Maryann's grasp, he closed it with the extended tie strings.

"Wait outside the showroom for a minute, Honey. Keep the door unlocked. I'll hold the bag. There is something else that I want to look at."

Maryann left the showroom, closed the door, and waited patiently in the corridor for about two minutes, when suddenly she heard him shout, "If I can't kill you, Henry, I'll beat you just as I'm doing to your precious line."

Terrified, she ran into the showroom and turned on the lights. He was swinging a toy golf club in all directions, breaking displays and destroying toys.

"Stop!" She shouted as she tried to grab Lou's arm. "Please, we're in enough trouble already. Let's go home. If you continue with this craziness, I'll just leave you here and take the subway home."

Quietly, he picked up the bag of toys, followed her out of the showroom, and carefully locked the door. Then he led her to the stairway. Although the bag filled with toys was heavy, they walked down one flight of stairs and walked across the ninth floor connecting bridge to the 1107 Broadway building.

"You take the elevator, Maryann, and I'll walk down the stairs. Give me some time to walk down with this load. When you get to the lobby, tell the guard that the restroom you regularly use on the fourth floor is locked. Ask him to open the door to the ladies room in the rear of the lobby. When you're both away from the front door, I'll walk out the front door with the toys. It's a dark street and the bag is black, so everything will be all right. I'll put it in the trunk and wait for you."

Although the bag of toys was quite heavy, Lou carried it like a trophy with a smile and a feeling of pride. He imagined that they were his toys from his concepts and he would now study and improve them. The lobby at 1107 Broadway was small and the stairway was near the front door. Checking first to see that it was empty, Lou walked swiftly to the revolving door, pushed the bag ahead of him, and was on the street in seconds.

Broadway and Fifth Avenue cross in front of the toy buildings and the buses, automobiles, and taxi cabs are routed in several directions by both street signs and traffic lights. In the evening, downtown traffic continues to rumble by while the uptown traffic slows considerably. The address of 1107 Broadway is the last Broadway address before the street numbers continue on the other side of Madison Square Park. The toy building takes up half of the block along Broadway between Twenty-fourth and Twenty-fifth Streets, sharing it with an office building.

Lou walked casually out of the building as though he was carrying a bag of office garbage to deposit into a street receptacle. He turned the corner and continued on Twenty-fourth Street until he reached his car. He placed the bag in the trunk and waited in the driver's seat for about five minutes until Maryann joined him.

It was about 10:30 P.M. when they arrived in front of Maryann's father's wood frame house in Middle Village, Queens. He placed his right arm around her shoulders and moved closer to kiss her.

"Please, not tonight," she whispered. "I've had all that I can take. You did a terrible thing tonight and I'm ashamed of myself for helping you. Lou, you must change your ways. Papa only knows you as a guy with a steady job. If he knew what we did tonight, he would never let me see you again."

"Maryann, I want to make something of myself and in order to do it, I have to take a few chances. I have many ideas, but I never had a chance. Let's think things over. I'll call you in a few days. Thanks for believing in me. I needed you tonight. You give me strength."

He reached over to kiss her goodnight, but she opened the door and ran up the few front steps to her door. She removed her key from her purse, opened the door, and then waved goodnight. He closed the car door and sat there for several minutes thinking. Then he drove home.

■　■　■

The following morning, Henry and Ellen were having breakfast at the luncheonette in the building when Mr. Harold passed by their table.

"Henry, we had a little trouble in the showroom last night. My brother arrived early and he discovered it. We decided to do nothing about it now and I want you to ignore it, if you can. I've ordered some men from the factory to come up here this morning and we'll get it all fixed up. I've got a Toy Fair to worry about, not some delinquent stupid kid."

They all left the restaurant immediately and Henry was shocked with the mess in the showroom. "That little bastard. Only Lou would do this."

"Henry," said Irving, "remember what we said. Forget it. We'll get it repaired. Let's concentrate on selling some merchandise. This is Toy Fair and we have some very hot items."

TWENTY-TWO

HENRY SAT comfortably in his first class seat aboard a Boeing 747 heading for Atlanta, Georgia. Toy Fair had ended a few days before and Irving Misson suggested that he visit the Westclox plant to select the appropriate clock and to coordinate their clock production with the production of the dolls at the Ideal factory in Queens. "It is important that you meet all the key executives," he said. "We may need to talk to them on the telephone later if we have to make changes in design or even in quantities." He always worried about production.

During the flight, the two young flight attendants served him several glasses of beer and a roast beef sandwich, returning frequently to listen and to laugh at his weird stories and jokes. He claimed that he was a British secret service agent sent to investigate a murder in Peach Tree Plaza. The murderer's identity was unknown, but he usually left a doll at the crime scene. This time he left a clock. He was on his way to Westclox to study all the different clock styles. "When I identify the style and decode the message, the British Secret Service will be able to name the murderer." It all sounded so reasonable to the flight attendants, but Henry didn't look British. On his lap, he had a small portfolio of drawings, all depicting clocks and dolls. He pointed to one and said, "If this is it, I will have the name of the murderer," he boasted.

In between his beer drinking and his flirtation with the flight attendants, he was seriously studying a number of typewritten pages clipped to a small portfolio, which he kept under the clock drawings. These pages included sketches and schematics of various toys, some in full color, others in bold lines. The sketches all seemed to be of innovative toys. Henry made notes on a small black covered pad, which he kept in his inner suit pocket.

When the plane landed, he waved good-bye to the girls and pulling a black travel case on rollers, he walked to the baggage retrieval area of the airport where he spotted Ellen Burton waiting patiently for him. Still holding the pull strap with one hand, he grabbed Ellen with the other and holding her tightly, kissed her for several seconds.

"Ugh! I can taste the beer," she said with a smile. "But it is good to see you."

"I couldn't wait to get my arms around you," he whispered into her ear. "You know that I just flew down to Atlanta to see you. I thought only of you during that miserable plane ride. And now I just want to be alone with you."

"Henry, let's save all that for later. I'll drive you to the hotel so you can settle in. Then, we'll go to the plant. Peter Walsh and Harry Livingston are waiting to meet you. And maybe if he is still in his office, Mr. Carrol, our president, may want to say hello to you. Ugh! I still can taste the beer. Here's some gum. Chew it before you meet them."

"Honey, I just want to meet you with my pants off and the lights out."

Ellen was dressed in a blue blazer with a light gray skirt, black hosiery, wide high heels, and a soft tan blouse with ruffles around the collar. Her hair and eyes were carefully made up and her lips were a dark red color. She looked the part of a competent woman executive. *The same old Henry,* she thought as she opened the front door of her car and they both sat down. It was a light tan Lincoln Continental with leather upholstery and beautiful interior panels made of wood. *She must be doing it with one of the bosses to get a car like this,* he thought.

Anticipating a typical dirty remark from him, Ellen said, "Westclox gives the top marketing executives a forty-thousand-dollar allowance every three years to buy a new luxury automobile. I bought this one about three months ago." He muttered something about having an old Pontiac, but she was too busy driving through traffic to pay any attention. When they reached the hotel, she parked at the entrance while Henry registered, placed his bag in the assigned room, and returned to the car, all within fifteen minutes.

He looked more relaxed as they drove to the plant and he admired some of the local buildings, the Atlanta skyline, and the beautiful trees. The Westclox plant was about fifteen minutes from the city line. They drove up to the employees' parking lot where, near the entrance to the building, there was a sticker and parking place marked "Burton, VP."

"I'm impressed," said Henry. "I didn't know that southern guys gave that title to southern broads. What did you do to get it?"

"I worked very hard and was better than the boys at their own game," she responded quickly. "Oh, there is Armond Duvalle. He has been looking forward to meeting you."

"Hi, Ellen. This must be the famous Henry. I'm very glad to meet you. Pete and Harry are in the conference room. You are right on schedule. Let's go in."

The meeting was very formal, although they referred to each other by their first names. The men kept their jackets on and the only tie that was out of place was on Henry's ruffled shirt. He had opened the knot and it was loosely hanging from his open collar. Henry explained how the marketing of toys differed appreciably from housewares and he stressed the importance of being ready for volume production two months after Toy Fair.

"Our clock doll concept is a creative innovation," he explained, "which we very effectively presented to the biggest chain store buying executives at Toy Fair. They agreed with us that it could become a high volume seller. Now we must send them samples for final review by their buying committees. They are committed for a first order in minimum quantity. It is important that we help them to feel that every mother, grandmother, and little girl will not only love it, but that they will also buy it for themselves, their relatives, and friends. If the chains re-buy after their initial order, which I think that they will, we will have a multi-mil-lion dollar seller for several years, and we must feed them a healthy advertising allowance to keep our production running smoothly."

Henry then informed them that he would select the clocks in the morning and then remain at Westclox until the industrial engineers could give him a production schedule that he could coordinate with Ideal.

Pete Walsh thanked him for coming down to meet them. "Stay as long as you think is necessary. Mr. Carrol wants you to be our guest during your stay here. Our firm will pick up all the costs at the Hyatt Hotel for both the room and your meals. It's southern hospitality," he replied. "Since this is Ellen's project, she will be available to help you with any of the information that you need from Westclox. It is after 5 P.M. and most of us have evening appointments. We'll probably see you tomorrow and hopefully in New York during next year's Toy Fair." They all shook hands and the three men left.

"In your usual way, Henry, you've charmed the charming Southern boys," remarked Ellen. "They think that you are all business all the time, and they wouldn't believe me if I told them anything different. So, big boy, we have tonight for ourselves, but tomorrow I have a busy day at the plant."

"Okay, Dear. We'll dine at the hotel," he said, "and then spend a night on the town. Then we'll head back to the hotel room for some good champagne and a little warmth. Tomorrow, I'll finish my business and take off later in the day."

The evening progressed slowly. First, they had drinks at the hotel bar, then dinner at a steak house downtown, and a few dances at the Kit-Cat Club. Then Henry became restless. Holding her closely on the dance floor he asked, "Shall we spend the night in the bedroom of the gracious home of a beautiful southern belle, or do we do it in the back seat of your car?"

"No, my big northern brute," she whispered into his ear. "It's more exciting for a southern belle in a man's hotel room. I'll join you for a couple of hours, but then I must go home. I have to change my clothes, pick up some important papers, and arrive at my office in the morning ready for a busy day. Call me there at 9 A.M. after everyone has arrived. I will ask you if you had a good evening and we will send a company car to pick you up."

"Honey," he responded, "you've played this game before. As long as we have a few hours to rub tummies together, I'll make you happy."

What a nasty remark! He is sweet deep down and so charming with men, she thought. *Why does he have to be so crude with women?* She took his arm and they walked out of the club where an attendant was waiting with her car. "Peach Tree Hyatt," he said to her and then settled back in his seat for the short ride.

The lobby of the hotel was quiet when they arrived and parked the car. Looking like a couple on their honeymoon, they held hands until they reached the elevator. Wasting no time, upon Henry's insistence, they went right to bed.

At 12:30 A.M., Ellen awoke. She was ready to dress and leave for home. She saw Henry sitting behind the desk working on some papers under a dim lamp. He was entirely nude.

"No bathrobe? Do you think that you look more beautiful in your birthday suit?" asked Ellen.

"Both—a short time ago, you loved my nude body."

As soon as she finished dressing, she walked closer to the desk to see what he was doing, but he quickly covered up some of the pages. "It looks like you are studying pictures of toys. Is that your new line?"

"Ellen, some guys are making a fortune from new toy innovations. I'm trying to cash in on it, too."

"Well, I have enough problems. It's time for me to go. Call me at 9 A.M." She kissed him on the top of his head and was out of the door before he could reach out for her. "Keep away from bad deals, Honey," she whispered as she closed the room door and walked to the elevator.

Henry stood up after she left, walked to the door, locked it, and turned on the lights. Holding some of the papers in his hand, he said in a low voice, "Someone is going to make a fist full of money if he plays his cards right. I have met most of the top guys in the major toy firms and boy, would they love to get their hands on this list. But how can I show it to them? Irving and Harold will skin my ass."

He picked up the extra blanket from the bed, wrapped it around his nude body, and sat down on the chair facing the desk. He studied the list of toys again and made check marks on a sheet of paper containing the names of over a dozen toy manufacturers. "I have to find a guy who is hungry enough and maybe even dumb enough to take on the big guys who thought this up. You have to take a chance when there is big money at stake."

Throwing the blanket back on the bed, he turned out the lights and tried to sleep, but he was too wound up with his thoughts. Tossing, turning, and not able to sleep, he emerged from the bed about an hour later.

I have to see Lou as soon as possible, he said to himself. *He may be a small time crook, but he has some good connections. With my knowledge, I can steer him in the right direction, give him a few bucks, and ultimately I can get a big piece of the action.* He smiled as he drifted off to sleep.

TWENTY-THREE

As THE first rays of the morning sun slipped through the venetian blinds and teasingly sent striped highlights over the desk and drawing table, Roland Levy slowly opened his eyes and pushed the blanket up over his shoulders. He had slept soundly on the couch, quite used to the reduced heat in the building at night, but always feeling cold in the morning when the stream heat started to warm the room. He slept better in a cold room, he told himself, but he found it difficult to first fall asleep, sometimes lying awake for almost an hour creating new design solutions in his mind and dreaming of the acclaim he would ultimately receive from those faceless executives. This was one of those mornings when he just wished that he could lie in bed a little longer, but he had some changes to make to one of the new Westclox package designs.

The office and studio gang rarely arrived before 8:30 A.M. and they never came into his office. To ensure that he had his privacy, he always locked the door before going to sleep and that could be anytime after midnight. This morning, he had an important conference with Susan Liforest at 9 A.M. sharp. Darn her. She was always early, well dressed, and fully organized for that time of the morning. And she was always probing and asking him how he felt and what he did the night before.

He so much wanted to tell her, but he was afraid that she would not understand. He was also afraid that she would offer suggestions, just like his mother, which he neither cared to hear nor would he ever even consider.

When they expanded the offices four months before, they had leased the full floor and extended the art studio and the new photography studio in order to accommodate a larger staff. Susan had suggested that they build a private executive bathroom exclusively for his office. "Clients," she said, "should not have to go into the studio to pee." Another little perk he gave into was the small pink powder room exclusively for her use in her office.

It was 6 A.M. He arose quickly, clad only in under shorts, did some stretching in front of the window, washed, and shaved. He then carefully folded the big white quilt that served him so well all night and placed it in a large white corrugated box on the top shelf of his closet. This was his secret. Carefully, he chose one of two suits that neatly hung on hangers in the closet and one of the three starched shirts hanging beside them. It was now 6:45 A.M. and he was fully dressed. He called the deli across the street to have a buttered bagel and a cup of coffee sent to his office, unlocked his office door, and walked down the hall to the art studio. He had worked in the studio for several hours after everyone had gone home the previous night, but he was still not satisfied with that Westclox design.

There were now six designers working in the studio and to oversee every project, he had to devote longer hours than when he had just one assistant. His somber mood suddenly changed as they came in and he greeted everyone with a smile, a good-morning, and a complement for the design work they had completed. When the new design studio director, Peter Smith, arrived, he sat beside Roland at the desk and they both looked at the Westclox package design perspectives in color on the computer monitor and then, on a sketchpad, Roland drew the changes that he thought would improve the design.

"Stick with it, Pete," he said. "This one is really going to be a winner. We're meeting with the Westclox executives sometime next week, so we have enough time to make it perfect."

Turning to the rest of the staff, he said, "I got in early this morning and I have been studying all of our jobs. Everyone seems to be progressing extremely well. I've left sketches on your desks with various suggestions, which I hope will be helpful. If you wish to discuss anything, just call me. Try to stick to your deadlines, but remember, if you can create something better, just design it and forget the deadline. Our job is to create the best designs . . . whether or not we meet deadlines. I'll be back to look over things in the afternoon."

As he left the studio to return to his office, Maxine Nierman arrived and soon after her, Sarah Smith, the new bookkeeper. Everyone seemed so happy in the modern, brightly illuminated office with white ceramic tile floors and light warm pastel colors alternating on each wall. This was another one of Susan Liforest's ideas, which Roland was very happy to approve. It gave the office a distinctive appearance, which he thought reflected the high level of taste that was necessary in a design office.

It was just a few minutes past 9 A.M. when Susan Liforest entered carrying a large corrugated box, which she supported precariously with both arms, letting her purse dangle from a strap around her shoulder. Nodding good-morning and smiling to everyone, she walked into her office, placed the box on her desk, removed her purse, dropped it along with her coat on her chair, and reached across the desk to check her telephone messages on the answering machine. Satisfied that things were under control, she quickly walked into her powder room, checked her face in the mirror, and fluffed her hair. She lifted the box to a comfortable position, supported by her chest and both arms, and walked into Roland's office, pushing open the partly closed door with the package.

"Come in, Baby," said Roland. "From the size of that package, it looks like you have brought us a big breakfast."

"Better than that. Ask Maxine to call the deli to send up some real breakfast. This will be a long meeting. We have a whole new line of

Kraft food packages to discuss. Ruby, starting with what is in this box, we're going to become one of the biggest firms on Madison Avenue."

She placed it on the desk, opened the top, and one by one, she carefully removed about a dozen packages. Susan arranged the packages neatly in a circle around the box. Some were plastic tubs with snap-on covers, others were folding paperboard boxes and a few were plastic wraps, both clear and opaque white. Then she proudly leaned over the desk as if to protect all her new possessions.

"I'm so excited, she said. "These are all new items for cheese and soy products. The marketing manager wants one coordinated line with a new logotype, new colors, and a brand image that is to stand out on the shelf as a gourmet line . . . but with a promotional price. Here is a copy of the report from consumer testing. It was conducted from three focus groups along with an evaluation and projected target market statistics compiled by the marketing manager. They have given us four weeks to come up with a first conference presentation. But, do you want to hear the best part?"

"Yeah. Don't keep me in suspense. So far it looks great, Susan."

"Well, they asked if we could keep the job within a budget of seventy-five thousand dollars and complete the twelve packages within four months."

Roland walked around the desk and kissed her on the cheek. "Let's call in Maxine right away and dictate a retainer agreement. We can start just as soon as they sign."

"Okay. We're in pretty solid with Kraft and Philip Morris since you did that great design for their new cigarettes. But Roland, these guys in big companies do a lot of socializing. This is how they meet with everyone, exchange ideas, and most importantly, it's where they give out business. I've been playing this alone and it's getting to be a bit uncomfortable. I know that you can't have cocktails or a late dinner out every night, but could you make and appearance and bring Bea every now and then?"

Roland sat back in his chair. He had kept his secret for six months; now he would have to tell her. Susan looked beautiful. Although he worked closely with her in the office every day and frequently spoke to her on the telephone at night when she was at home, he had refrained from talking about his personal life. She was always curious. He never talked about his wife. Never called her. She met her once briefly, soon after she joined the firm. She was just leaving when Roland asked her to stay for a few moments to meet Bea. It was a pleasant meeting, no more than a few minutes and Bea had wished her good luck in her new position. She had said that Ruby was looking forward to her helping him create a successful business.

"Can I come with Bea?" Roland repeated. He turned and looked out of the window instead of looking directly at her. He was silent for at least a minute. "Well," he finally said, "she is now living with her mother."

"Oh! Ruby, I'm so sorry. What happened?"

"I really don't know." He paused and suddenly felt a heavy load leave his mind. He would tell her everything. "I guess that she just got tired of me running my own business. She wanted me to take a job, have regular working hours, and a regular salary." He paused again. "One night she was there, fast asleep when I came home late. I left early in the morning when she was still asleep. When I came home that night, she was gone. Her clothing was gone, too. She left only a short note."

"So now you live alone in the apartment?"

He felt a little embarrassed. "No, we lost the lease."

"So where do you live?" she asked with some hesitation and walked slowly to the couch and sat down with her legs curled under her.

He smiled to himself thinking how stupid this must sound to her. "Well, I stay at the Y a few nights a week, but most of the time, I guess I just work."

Maxine walked in with her dictation pad and the conversation stopped suddenly. As he started to dictate a contract and a work order, Susan rose to her feet, smiled at Maxine, and then she excused herself in order to make some important calls from her office. When Roland finished dictating, Maxine left, very excited about the prospect of so much new business. He rose from his chair, walked to the window, and just stared at the windows and the faceless people working in the office building across the street.

TWENTY-FOUR

"SUSAN, THIS is John. Good morning!"

"Hi! It's 9 A.M. Saturday morning; this is my time to sleep," answered a rather tired Susan Liforest, holding the telephone receiver to her ear with her head on the pillow.

"What time did you leave? I must have been fast asleep."

"I guess it was about 2 A.M. The hotel concierge called a limo and I guess that I was home by 2:30 A.M. How are you?"

"Not so good."

"Was it something we ate for dinner?"

"No! My wife knocked on the door at 8:30 A.M. this morning. Fortunately, I was alone and in the shower when the porter showed her in. She came down from Westport to wish me a happy birthday before the Philip Morris conference started today. They know her at the Plaza since she lunches here often. Boy, was I glad that she didn't catch you in the room."

Susan was wide awake now and getting angrier as he talked. "So, happy birthday, you louse. You're a lucky man that your wife loves you. What was not so good?"

"She found your white handkerchief on my bed and got very angry. But there were no other signs and I explained that I probably picked it up from my desk after a meeting in the office and just forgot to leave it with the secretary. So, everything seems to be okay now. She went down for a cup of coffee while I'm getting dressed."

"John, we must break it off. Let's keep our relationship for business. We can still be good friends." Then she added, "I thought that you were leaving your wife."

"Susan, you must understand that I need Lorraine. Her family has been in the tobacco and oil businesses for over fifty years. My job, my home, my friends, and my style of living all depend on her. But I really need you, too."

"So long, John. I'll see you on Tuesday for the meeting in your office." As Susan hung up the telephone, she sank back under the covers throwing the pillow over her head to let out a shriek, "Damn! Damn!" Her thoughts were racing in all directions and she began to sob. *I just can't believe those guys, even the nicest ones . . . and I can't resist them either*, she thought. *Take hold of yourself, Susan. You're playing in the big leagues now and these corporate gentlemen are not always the way they appear to an innocent Jewish girl from Brooklyn. Hmmm, I guess I'm not so innocent anymore.*

It was the little tip from Ellen that saved her from an embarrassing confrontation and maybe the end of all her business with the Philip Morris executives. That dear Ellen. She went through it all on her way up as a woman executive in an "old boy" southern business hierarchy. Ellen had said, "If you're going to spend the night with the guy, never, never, take him to your own apartment or even your own hotel room. Men just never leave when you want them to. And it can get very sloppy. The secret is to go to his room and when he falls asleep, put on your clothes and leave as fast as you can. Believe me," she had emphasized, "it gives you the advantage."

It sure does, Susan thought.

Susan was too disturbed to sleep or even to just lie under the covers. She put on her robe and walked barefoot to her small kitchen. She put the filter, coffee, and water into the coffee maker and sat at the small table watching the dark liquid drop from the filter into the glass coffeepot. She had to erase John Gillespie from her mind, no matter how gallant and sincere he appeared to be. He was a louse. As she sat there, her thoughts gradually turned toward Roland Levy. A year before, she had dreams about Roland and he seemed to be somewhat responsive in a timid way, but as the business expanded, his involvement moved more deeply into a pattern of devotion entirely to his work. Although he was quick to agree with her ideas and to support her selling efforts, he rarely looked directly at her and during a meeting, he would talk to himself just as easily as he would talk to her. She loved her job and even felt somewhat secure with the boss, but she wanted more.

She searched for possible relationships with clients and prospective clients, first seeking more business and then fantasizing about with whom she would want to spend more time. Most of them were older men anchored to their jobs with framed pictures on their desks of smiling wives, happy kids, and some even had grandchildren. A few, especially in the larger corporations, looked at her somewhat as a cute play toy and these were the guys she had to sell, not flirt with. She had already gone too far with John Gillespie.

Roland Levy was there every day, waiting for her, smiling, and was ready to discuss her plans as well as her problems, even calling her at home at night. But she knew that he was married and she feared that an angry wife could ruin all her business plans.

But, Bea had left the nest. Poor Roland no longer had a wife, a home, or even a real bed to sleep on. Was that the way he really wanted to live or was this the time for her to become more helpful, maybe even more personal?

She dressed slowly, returned the coffee cup to the kitchen, closed the bed, dressed, and left the apartment. As she emerged from the elevator, the doorman greeted her with a friendly smile and wished her a nice day. It was a bright June morning with a temperature of about seventy degrees. She started to walk toward Fifth Avenue without a planned destination, just a morning walk on a nice day. When she reached Madison Avenue, she saw the trees at Madison Square Park and walked into the park to sit on a bench. The park was somewhat crowded with kids on bicycles, mothers with strollers and carriages, and weary elderly folk reclining on the benches, some throwing bread crumbs to the birds. Then, across the wide intersection of Broadway and Fifth Avenue, the Fifth Avenue Building cast a shadow that seemed to be pointing directly at her. Magically, as if guided by a super hand, she slowly walked toward the building.

Looking into the relatively deep display windows at the front of the building, she studied the dozen or more toys along with their packages that were neatly arranged along with the names of the companies that had developed them. There were two items from Ideal Toy Company, one was the water shooting machine gun that Roland had developed and the other was a very cute tea set that she did not remember seeing before.

A man standing nearby was also looking at the toys. He had black hair and a thin moustache and was wearing a dark suit, white shirt and tie, somewhat out of place for a casual Saturday stroll. He smiled at her. "Do you like toys?" he asked Susan.

"I guess that I never grew up. I still love to look at them."

"My name is Lou and I'm a toy designer. Can I buy you a cup of coffee in the luncheonette? It's only open for breakfast today."

Lonely, angry with all the men she knew, with time to waste, Susan looked at him and thought, *Maybe I'll pick up a few leads. I won't tell him who I am.* She turned toward him and said, "Well, I have about a half hour before an appointment with my hair dresser. I'll join you for a cup."

He talked about various toy ideas, did not mention any firms, but said that he had an appointment in the building at 10:15 A.M. When she was ready to leave, he gave her his business card. It read, "Lou Mangini,

Inventor and Toy Designer, 129 136th Street, Middle Village, Queens, NY." The name meant nothing to her. She put it in her purse, thanked him for the coffee, and left the building. *I'll give the card to Roland,* she thought. *He may be interested.* But then Susan wondered, *Where have I seen him before? Oh, well. I see so many people every day. He just looks like someone that I've bumped into.*

Lou stood looking at the display windows until Susan disappeared from sight. He quickly entered the building, walked into an empty elevator, and pressed the button for the tenth floor. The Ideal Toy showroom doors were locked. He pressed the button at the side of the door and waited for two or three minutes. Just as he turned away and started to walk toward the elevator, the door opened and Henry emerged. He closed the doors behind him, locked them with a key, and beckoned to Lou to follow him to the staircase.

"We're going down two flights of stairs to the eighth floor where I have a small office. As I said on the telephone, I have a proposition that can give you a fist full of money if you are smart."

"I just came to listen. Maryann says that I should keep away from you, but I could use some money," said Lou. "What kind of deal do you have in mind?"

Henry approached a door at the end of the hall near the freight elevator, opened it with a key, and Lou followed him into the room. It was a small storeroom without a window, furnished with a small desk, three chairs, and a file cabinet. "Sit down and listen to what I have to say. I know a lot of guys, but I picked you. I have a check in my hand for $500.00 made out to cash. It's yours and there will be plenty more. Are you interested?"

Lou took the check, folded it, and placed it in his pocket. "What's the deal?"

"I want you to do a little investigating. How you do it is up to you. I want you to go into showrooms and get catalogs, photographs, and specifications of the new innovative toys that toy companies are developing. This should be simple for a clever guy like you. Ask some of your cronies if they know anybody who would like to put a squeeze play on some big toy companies. This is a multi-million dollar deal and you can make over a hundred thousand dollars in just a few days."

"Ha! Smart guy," said Lou. "I know a guy who is already working a squeeze on toy firms. I'll think about it . . . but I'm keeping your check anyway, you bastard."

TWENTY-FIVE

ROLAND LEVY sat at the head of his new conference table. His tie was loosened and pushed to the side, his shirt collar was open, and both cuffs of his white shirt were rolled back. Roland was holding a thick mechanical pencil in his hand and starring at a pad of drawing paper that he had placed in front of him. Seated, one on each side of the table, were Susan Liforest and Frank Smith. At the other end of the table, neatly dressed in a dark business suit with a blue shirt and striped tie, was Lou Mangini. He appeared quite confident and seemed to be in control of the conversation.

"All the big toy companies are lost without inventors who create the new toys each season," he repeated himself. "They can't face the reps and retail buyers at Toy Fair with last year's line. And the timing is right since they start looking at new ideas at the end of the summer. This is when I come in."

"Yes," said Susan, "but when do we come in?"

"You are the third design firm that I spoke to on the telephone and the only one to ask me to come in for an interview. I need a place to work and I suggest a trial period of two months. I can't get to the big toy companies to show them my ideas. They won't see me, but they will see you because you are already their designers. My girlfriend's father insists that I get a steady job or he won't let me see Maryann. My idea is that you pay me a weekly salary and show my work as designed by your firm. If you receive royalty payments, I get a percentage in addition to my salary."

"But how do we know that you can design top creative toys?" asked Peter Smith. "We're pretty good ourselves."

"I'm a specialist. This is all I do." He then opened the suitcase he had brought with him and one by one removed sketches and paperboard models of various girls' and boys' toys, which he described and then placed on the table. Peter studied some of them more closely, picking up both the models and the sketches. "Not bad. The ideas seem fine, but the designs need a lot of work."

Roland stood up after a quick look at each of the items and said, "Mr. Mangini, I like the idea, but it will take me a few days to think it over. I will also need to discuss it with my associates and with one or two of the toy firms that we work with. Thank you for sharing your ideas. Miss Liforest, give him your card. Today is Friday. Call her on Tuesday afternoon and she will tell you our decision. It's nice to meet you." He left the room quickly with his sketchpad under his arm and returned to his office.

Lou packed his things into the suitcase, shook hands with Peter and Susan, and left. Susan turned to Peter and said, "I think that I met him a few months ago. He had an appointment with a toy firm at 200 Fifth Avenue. I gave his card to Roland. I'm sure that he did not recognize me. He seems like a nice guy. What do you think?"

"I like the idea, Susan. If we can suggest new toy lines, we can develop much more business with each of our regular clients. I wonder what Roland thinks of the idea. He didn't say anything during the meeting. You know, we do have plenty of room for him in the studio."

Susan left the conference room and returned to her office, satisfied that the decision would be left entirely to Roland. He was the one who had spoken to Lou on the telephone and he invited him to present himself to them in the conference room. She wondered why he was not working for one of the toy firms and if he had ever worked for one of them. Henry Isserman had toy designers on his staff. *Oh, well,* she thought. *It's Roland's problem.*

■   ■   ■

Everyone in the office was delighted with the conference room. As soon as it was completed, it became almost indispensable with client meetings for both Roland and Susan. Peter Smith used it to meet with suppliers whom he did not want to view the work in progress in the studio. In recent months, business had expanded considerably with complete lines of new products from Kraft Foods, Westclox, Merck Pharmaceutical, Ideal Toy, and some of the more recent new clients. Delivery service people were frequently going into both of their offices and many projects that were confidential were often carelessly exposed. The building owner had offered them more space and Roland knew that to handle all this new business, expansion was necessary. He therefore leased the fourth and fifth floors, plus a reception room and office on the third floor, planning this for pick-ups and deliveries and for a new clerical and financial office.

Susan was furious when she first saw the expansion plans that Roland had drawn up. She loved the idea of the conference room. Her office could now be more personal with less clutter from all the comps and samples that she used to encourage sales. This would all go into the conference room. However, the proposed changes in Roland's office surprised and angered her.

"Ruby, what are you doing? This should be an office, not a hotel. You have planned a whole wall for a Murphy bed and two closets, and I see that you have extended your bathroom to include a shower and sauna. Don't you ever want to leave this place?"

"Susan, the cost of this expansion represents everything I own. Bea is suing for a divorce and she wants as much as her lawyers told her she could get. Fortunately, this business is a corporation and it is highly in debt, but because of your efforts, we do have the contracts to pay things

off and to ultimately make money. So, until this is over, I'm not drawing a salary, I have no home, no car, and I plan to live in the office. This
building once was a residence."

"So tell me, what do you think about this toy inventor?" she asked,
abruptly changing the conversation to a subject she could handle with
less emotion. "You know that this is the guy whom I met at the Toy
Building. I gave you his card."

"I must still have it in my desk. The guy called and what he offered
seemed interesting. We have a number of clients who are interested in
new ideas. Certainly, there is Henry. Then there is Banner and Fantasy
Toys and maybe even a half dozen others. I'd like to try him out. Call
him on Tuesday and let him come in. We'll work out a deal. His face
looks familiar. I may have seen him at one of the toy firms. If he is good,
we will benefit."

Susan loved his ability to make quick decisions and to provide log-
ical answers to problems. Three years before when he invited her to join
his one-man design firm, she had hesitated at first, but then felt attracted to him by his directness, his determination, and his quick decision
that she would fit into his plan to build a large industrial design organization. Whenever she had some doubts or failed to close a design contract, he was there with support and confidence that it would be better
next time. She loved these manly traits and even when she faced the
reality of his marriage, she felt that she was part of him during the
longest hours of the day. Now she had mixed feeling about his new
freedom and the changes in his personal life.

Her mind often wandered before falling asleep at night, picturing
Roland with her in romantic settings at a beach in Southern France or
drinking champagne on a bear rug in front of a roaring fireplace in a
small chalet in the Swiss Alps. He would look deeply into her eyes, hold
her tightly, and say all the things that she wanted to hear.

The intercom on her desk signaled a telephone call. Maxine said,
"It's a man, but he says it is personal and won't give his name. Do you
want to take it?"

"Sure, why not?"

"Hello, Ms. Liforest. It's Lou Mangini. We met in your office this morning. Would you like to join me for a cup of coffee across the street? I have something that I would like to discuss with you."

"Can't it wait until next Tuesday? Mr. Levy will make his decision then."

"Well, it's about Ideal Toy."

Susan had other things on her mind and to have coffee with this new toy inventor just did not interest her.

Maybe if I sat with him in a restaurant he would remember our first meeting, she thought. *I guess that Henry Isserman did not hire him. I don't want to hear the details. Since Ruby has decided to let him work in the studio, sooner or later he will tell us everything.*

"I will speak with you on Tuesday," she said and hung up the phone.

TWENTY-SIX

LOU MANGINI worked diligently at his drawing board, ignoring the computers, making full size pencil illustrations of each of the toys he proposed. A few of the sketches were made with considerable details showing the toy as it would appear during different stages of play, but most of them just conveyed an idea. Each evening Roland would study the concepts after everyone had gone home and in the morning, he would offer both suggestions and encouragement to Lou.

"Lou, this circus toy seems like a good idea, but you must focus on a child below ten years old. Six to eight is about the best range. That is the age group other than pre-school whose parents buy most toys."

"I'll keep that in mind. Roland, I've created at least a dozen good concepts during the month that I have been here."

"Keep it up, Lou. In another week or so, I would like to get your sketches together in a portfolio and start making presentations to the toy companies."

Lou discussed his ideas with the other designers in the studio during coffee breaks and he frequently went to lunch with any group that would invite him to join them. He even asked Susan Liforest if he could call her at home, but she had said, "Lou, let's just wait until the end of your two- month trial."

During the day, as he worked at his drawing desk, he presented an appearance of full confidence. At night, in his room upstairs at his mother's home in Queens, he was very restless. Toy ideas were not easy to create. He often went to the Toy Building on Fifth Avenue to study the items in the window and he would read about new toys in *Playthings Magazine*. Then he thought that if he actually entered the toy building at night and looked into the showroom windows, he might find something that would inspire him.

"Hello, Pete, this is Lou. I've got to talk to you."

"Sure, Lou. Come around the corner. I'll meet you in front of my house. We'll take a walk. I like to walk at night."

As they walked, Lou explained his idea. "I'm getting stale on toy ideas, but I just need to see some of the concepts that the toy companies are now considering, especially Ideal Toy. I'd like to get into their offices at night, but I have to do it secretly so I don't get in trouble with my job."

"Easy as eating a piece of cake. You can borrow my keys."

"But, I'll need something else. If someone spots me, I want to look like a burglar to scare them so I can sneak away. Can you lend me a ski mask and a gun?"

"Buddy, you're like a brother to me, but even to my brother I'll have to charge fifty bucks to borrow the piece. No bullets."

"That's great. Here's two twenties and a ten. You're a great friend."

Pete took a key ring from the chain of keys dangling from his jeans and gave it to Lou. Then he reached under his sweater and removed a holster from his belt. "Don't show this piece unless you get caught and need it to scare someone as you run away," he warned.

Lou put the holster around his belt, felt the ugly contour of the gun, and the two friends parted.

The next evening at about 11 P.M., Lou arrived at the freight entrance to the 200 Fifth Avenue Building. He was wearing a black turtleneck sweater, black pants, and an old pair of black sneakers. There was no one in sight, so he took his time to open the padlock carefully, release the chain, and open the lock on the twin steel doors. He entered the building easily. All he had to do now was slowly walk up the ten floors to the Ideal Toy Showroom.

Carefully, he unlocked the showroom door, turned on his flashlight, and entered Harold Misson's office. Fumbling through his desk drawers, he found a folder marked "New Toy Concepts." From the cabinet behind the desk, he located a lined legal pad and sitting down on Mr. Misson's chair, he copied all the information that he could find. Hearing the security guard's footsteps in the hall, Lou quickly closed the desk drawer, tore out the pages from the pad, dropped it nervously on the floor, and walked to the outer door. Lou waited for the officer to key-in his station and then to leave the floor. In the dark, Lou left the showroom and silently walked down the ten flights of stairs, secured the freight doors, and walked slowly to the subway station in front of the building.

■　■　■

During his review of work done the next evening, Roland became excited when he saw some of the new sketches on Lou's desk. "Now, he has some good practical toy ideas. I just can't wait until I show these to Henry. I'll surprise him and drop in to his office in Queens tomorrow morning. Good ideas shouldn't wait."

On the morning following Lou's secret visit to Ideal's office, Mr. Harold Misson entered his office and he felt that something was wrong. He was a compulsively neat man who carefully cleared his desk each evening so that he would be ready to start work promptly or even to conduct a meeting in his office in the morning. He was somewhat perplexed when he saw the partly opened drawer in his desk and the legal pad on the floor. He called his brother at the factory.

"Irving, I don't think that anything is missing, but I think that someone was in my office last night. The only thing I worry about is the new toy concepts."

"Harold, let's not take any chances. Alert security that we had a break-in and arrange to have an armed guard on duty when you leave the office. This is very serious. Some competitor can steal our new toy concepts and beat us to the market with our own toys. I'm really worried."

The agency sent an armed guard, a man in his sixties who had been an officer in the New York Police Department and now worked part time for a security firm to add to his city pension. He met with Harold at 5 P.M. the next afternoon and they decided that he should just sit in the private office until he heard an intruder.

"Then," said Harold, "hold the guy until you get the NYPD. We are going to demand full charges. If he shows up, we're depending on you to collar that son-of-a-bitch. I don't care who he is. Do I make myself clear?"

When Harold Misson left, he locked the doors in the usual manner, turned out all the lights, and told the building security guard that he had a private cop guarding his office all night. The private guard spent some time studying the suite, noting where the doors were and where the light switches were located. Then he took out his loaded service revolver, checked it carefully, and placed it on the desk within easy reach. Then he sat down on the couch in the office and proceeded to scan through one of the toy magazines. He dozed off as soon as the sun set and the office became dark. But, with years of training, he was a light sleeper.

At about 9:30 P.M., he awoke suddenly hearing a key turn in the door and then what sounded like footsteps in the showroom. Quickly, he reached for his gun and the large flashlight that he had placed next to it on the desk. Standing up with one foot in front of the other facing the office door, he held the flashlight in his left hand, the revolver in his right, and aimed both of them at the office door.

Silently, the door to the office opened. He could feel the slight breeze that came from the showroom. Instantly, he pressed the button on the flashlight, shining the bright light directly on the face of the intruder. Lou stepped back, totally surprised. This was something that he had never expected. He froze for several seconds. His mind worked rapidly. He reached for his gun.

"Give me all the money you got," demanded Lou in a loud voice. "I've got a gun and this is a robbery."

Frightened on seeing the gun, the guard cried, "Put your hands up, drop the gun, or I'll shoot."

Lou turned and ran into the showroom, turning over tables as he passed them. The door was locked and he searched his key ring for the right key. Suddenly, the guard turned on all the showroom lights. Lou circled the room, running with his gun extended in shooting position.

"Stand back while I open the door or I'll shoot," he threatened.

He raised his arm and pointed the gun at the private cop. Frightened with a gun pointing at his face, the cop fired two shots. The first one caught Lou in his shoulder. He threw a chair at the display window and charged against the broken glass with his body. After the second shot, there was a loud shriek and Lou fell face down to the floor.

The guard dialed 911. In what seemed like minutes, the shaking guard was sitting on a chair in the showroom, all the lights were on, and the room was filled with cops and the emergency medical attendants were leaning over Lou who was lying face down on the floor.

"Call Mr. Harold Misson," the private cop said to the officer in charge. "I had to shoot the intruder. He was going to shoot me."

TWENTY-SEVEN

ROLAND LEVY hired a limo and driver at 8:30 A.M. to drive him to the Ideal Toy factory in Queens. Neatly arranged in a portfolio were copies of the latest toy sketches, which he found on Lou Mangini's desk. He had made color copies from the originals and returned those to Lou's desk. He was anxious to get Henry's opinion.

Since he had arranged to meet the limo driver on the corner of Fifty-fifth Street and Madison Avenue, he was out of the office before any of the staff arrived. While driving over the Queensboro Fifty-ninth Street Bridge, he opened the portfolio just to look at some of the sketches once more. He was pleased with the concepts and felt certain that Henry would like them, too. But Henry was hard to predict. If everything went well, he would put Lou Mangini on the staff with a regular salary.

The limo driver approached the front door of the Ideal factory and asked, "How long do you think that you will be? I'll wait about fifteen minutes and if you are still busy, I'll take another call. When you want to go back, just call the office for another limo."

"Thanks. I may not even get to see my man since I didn't make an appointment. But what I'm bringing to him may get him to keep me there for a while."

He greeted the guard, pinned on a badge, and took the elevator to Henry's floor. As he walked to the reception room, he heard loud voices and above it all was Henry yelling, "It is a shame that they didn't kill that thieving bastard. Izzy, you have to throw the book at that guy. He must be working for a competing toy company. What kind of a firm would hire a little crook like him?"

Roland stood at the secretary's desk and asked if he could have a moment with Henry.

She didn't even ask Henry. "Mr. Levy, he's in a furious mood this morning. I don't really know what's up, but I think that someone got shot. Why don't you call me later and we'll work something out."

Fortunately, the limo was still waiting and Roland put the portfolio in the back seat and then moved in beside it. He sat silently, somewhat perplexed. They agonized through the morning bridge traffic into Manhattan and he was back in the office by 10 A.M.

As he approached his private office, Susan was waiting at the door. "Ruby, am I glad to see you. We've been invited to lunch by the preppies at Kraft Food. There will be about four of them and they want us to meet them at 1 P.M. in the garden room of the Four Seasons. Two of the guys are from Andover and Williams, but don't worry, Baby, you look great in your new suit."

"It's been a tough morning, Sue. I rode all the way out to see Henry, but he had some kind of a problem and it was a wasted trip. Could you do the lunch without me?"

"Absolutely not. These guys want to talk with you. They see enough of me. And they want it on their turf. You couldn't get into the Four Seasons without them. They have accepted you as one of them. Stop playing rich kid, poor kid. You've made it."

"Shall I change my tie?"

"You look fine. I'll pop into your office at 12:30 P.M. and we'll cab over. We can't be late because those guys live by the clock. And, be prepared to drink a dry martini," she added with a wink.

■ ■ ■

The usual east side New York traffic slowed the cab somewhat, but Roland and Susan reached the entrance to the restaurant at precisely 12:50 P.M. They were greeted at the door by a guard in uniform who checked their names on the reservations list and then directed them to the garden room where the main waiter ushered them to Gordon Vaness' table. The four men already seated there stood up as they approached and Gordon said, "So, this is the elusive Roland Levy. I'm so glad to meet you. Sit down and have a drink. How are you, Susan?"

"Just fine, Gordon. Roland, this is Paul Rowan, Walter Cunningham, and Doug White. They are all product managers in the food division of Philip Morris. It's the biggest and the best in the world, isn't that true guys?" They all smiled and extended their hands.

"Delighted to meet you," said Roland. I've spoken with you several times on the telephone, Gordon. Paul, Walter, and Doug are very familiar names from our correspondence and your frequent conversations with Peter Smith, my studio manager. We are all very pleased with the opportunity to work with you."

"Then let us all join in a round of martinis," suggested Paul Rowan. "I'm thirsty." Turning to Roland he said, "We're counting on you to help us grow even bigger."

"Let's drink to that with a couple of martinis," answered Roland firmly. He felt comfortable with these men. They loved the work that he had created for them and as long as he could continue to produce the same level of design work, he knew that he would continue to be very important to them. The luncheon conversation was very general with remarks about sports, vacations, and humorous anecdotes about some of the Philip Morris executives.

As the coffee was served, Gordon Vaness said, "Roland, we are planning a major advertising campaign and we would like you to meet the account executive at the agency. His name is Lester Greenberg. You know that we work with BBDO. Lester is vice president.

"Have Lester call me and we will invite him down to the studio to acquaint him with our staff and our work."

"That is just what we want. You have done such a fine job with our various Kraft brands that we want you to work with the agency to develop a new look for our Miller beer. You give us a great product appearance and he'll advertise it," Gordon Vaness said, showing his confidence in Roland Levy Industrial Design.

"Yes," he continued. "If it goes well, we'll all get a big kiss from our board of directors and you can make a fist full of money." Then he laughed, "If it flops, we all get a big kick in the ass from the CEO. But don't even think about that. I'm glad we had this luncheon, Roland. I feel pretty confident now that I have met you."

As Roland and Susan got into the taxi for the ride back to the office, she grabbed his hand, kissed him quickly on the mouth, and in an excited voice said, "Ruby, baby, you were wonderful. You're in now. They loved you. Now we have to give this agency guy the same treatment. They just gave us their prime beer product."

Roland was silent. The surprising kiss kindled his emotions. She was a beautiful and emotional woman whose belief in him had transformed his one-man business. He sat silently as the cab moved slowly through the traffic. When the cab stopped in front of their building, he paid the driver, turned, put his arms around Susan, and kissed her on her lips with a partly opened mouth. "Thank you, Susan. You're wonderful."

They left the cab quickly, barely looked at each other as they entered the elevator, and when they reached the reception office, Maxine had telephone messages for both of them. Roland's message was from the Marge McDermott Model Agency explaining that the girl who was to pose for the photo on the front of a Banner Toy package would not arrive until 6 P.M. Her mother had a late hairdresser's appointment. Quickly, he arranged for one photographer to work overtime in the photo studio, called Marge back to confirm the shooting time, and began to arrange the props for the evening shoot. The entire staff left at 5:30 P.M., including Susan, who didn't even say goodnight.

By 6:00 P.M., the backgrounds and the props were all in position. The photographer was set to take the preliminary Polaroids and then shoot the four-by-five view camera for the overall scene. Roland would use the hand-held Nikon for the action shots. Elizabeth was adorable, experienced with studio lighting, and she knew how to hold her smile and her position when told to do so by the photographer. With her mother working along with them to keep her clothing looking neat and fresh, the shoot took only about an hour and a half. The little girl was so tired when they finished that she found a comfortable spot on the studio couch and fell asleep. The photographer remained in the photo studio to clean up and prepare the negatives for a pick-up by the lab. Roland went to his office, his mind racing on that last kiss that he gave to Susan and his feeling that he wanted more.

He was hot, sweaty, and tired from the studio lights. Roland also felt tension from moving about the room in a squatting position to obtain the right angle for the camera. He opened the Murphy bed, removed all his clothing, placed it on a chair, picked up some papers on his desk to read, and walked into the sauna to relax and focus his mind back to the office work that he loved.

Suddenly the door opened and Mrs. Mona Rivers, Elizabeth's mother, walked barefoot into the sauna with a large towel wrapped completely around her.

"Elizabeth is sleeping. Your photographer said that you would be in your office. I didn't realize what a lovely place this is." Roland was too shocked to answer.

"Oh, it is too hot in here and it will ruin my hair. Get me a shower cap. Let's cool off in the shower." She took his hand, pushed open the door of the sauna, and led him out.

"There is a cap on the wall next to the shower," he replied hesitantly.

As she put the shower cap carefully on her head to cover all the hair, she reached for his hand again, the towel fell from her body to the floor, and they both entered the shower nude.

Mona Rivers was a beautiful woman, probably in her mid thirties, with a girlish figure that she seemed proud to display. Roland, although married for several years before Bea left, was still somewhat shy with woman. He had surprised himself with the outward expression of affection for Susan that he felt when they were leaving the taxicab. But this woman was hard to resist as she snuggled into his arms under the shower and pressed her body close to his. He was aroused, excited, and pleased with this beautiful and willing woman in his arms.

"Let's get out of here," he whispered into her ear while opening the shower door and leading her out of the bathroom. He rubbed her back and a bit of himself gently with a towel and they both moved to the bed in almost the same motion. As he lay down partly on top of her, she pulled his face toward hers and said, "Roland, before we begin anything, I want you to promise that you will recommend Elizabeth to Marge McDermott for a television commercial. Marge said that she would give her a spot if you agreed."

At this moment, Roland would have recommended her for a prime-time commercial part anywhere. "Sure, she's gorgeous and cooperative. I'll speak to Marge." Not another word was said. Mona mounted him and neither noticed that the door opened slowly and Susan Liforest looked in.

TWENTY-EIGHT

SUSAN LIFOREST sat on the couch in her office with her feet tucked under her. She was staring at the mysterious shadow cast by the one light in the room, a small lamp next to the couch. She held a wrinkled handkerchief in her hand. She had been crying. About an hour before, she heard quick footsteps moving from Roland's office down the hall toward the photo studio. There was no conversation. Just a woman running home from a man's room. *Who is she?* she asked herself. *How long has this been going on? Why didn't I suspect something? He hasn't slept with Bea in a very long time. And why does this bother me so much?*

Her despair was suddenly interrupted as the door to her office opened and Roland Levy stood there with a surprised look on his face. Wearing slippers, dressed in pajamas and a bathrobe, he smiled when he saw her. "Susan, I came in to turn the light off. I didn't know that you were here. When did you come in?"

"Oh! I came in about fifteen or twenty minutes ago. I had to pick up some things for a meeting tomorrow morning," Susan lied. "I'm getting ready to leave." Abruptly, she arose from the couch and hurriedly left the room leaving the door open and the lamp on. She reached the elevator very quickly and before he could say another word, she was gone. He stood at the door wondering about this unusually strange behavior. Walking into the room to turn off the lamp, he noticed her handkerchief on the couch and, in a matter of fact manner, he picked it up like a crumbled sheet of paper and tossed it on her desk. *She must have forgotten this,* he thought. *It feels like a good handkerchief. She may look for it when she comes in tomorrow.*

As she stood alone in the elevator, Susan felt nauseous. She hadn't eaten anything since lunch. She hailed a cab as it sped by the building, sat nervously during the short trip to Twenty-eighth Street, and did not smile until she received a friendly greeting from the night doorman in her apartment house. Her thoughts continued to wander. *Did Roland have a girlfriend? Was that Bea in bed with him? Is she taking him back?* She was angry with herself that she had shown affection for him in the taxi-cab. Why had she waited so long to show him how happy she was and how much she cared about him? She wanted him to see her as a woman, not just a pushy selling machine.

It was 9 P.M. and she had to talk to somebody. Her first thought was to call John Gillespie. He would make up some excuse to his wife, drive in from Westport, give her just the comfort that she wanted, but the dog would want to spend the night with her. No, she was ending that. Then she thought about that toy inventor who wanted to take her to dinner. He probably wanted to talk to her about some work that he did for Ideal Toy. "This is a good time," she said, "for me to get to know Lou Mangini. He seems like a nice guy. He lives in Queens. I'll get his telephone number from information."

"Hello, is Lou Mangini at home? This is Susan Liforest." A woman with a deep Italian accent answered the telephone. "No, Lou is not here now. Often he comes in very late and sometimes he sleeps at his friend's house."

"Thank you. I'll speak with him tomorrow. Just tell him that Susan Liforest called."

Depressed, lonely, and hungry, she found some food in the refrigerator, turned on the television, and sat up until after midnight.

Roland spent the evening working in the studio, went to bed at midnight, and wondered if Susan was feeling well. He had meant to phone her, but once he became involved with the studio work, he completely forgot. He couldn't forget Mona Rivers. He would call Marge McDermott in the morning and give Elizabeth a good recommendation for the television commercial spot. But he would ask her never to send the kid to him for a studio shot. Marge wouldn't even ask why. She knew all about striving mothers seeking stardom for their daughters, frowned upon it, and if he had told her about Mrs. Rivers, Marge would have blacklisted her child.

The morning was busy with telephone calls and visitors. Roland had waited patiently for a telephone call from Mabel Lieberman, Henry Isserman's devoted secretary, but she hadn't called. Anxious to show him Lou's toy inventions, he called her to make an appointment. She turned the phone over to Henry immediately. "Roland, or whatever you real name is, buddy boy, if you have toy ideas to show me, I want to see them. Come see me at 5 P.M. today."

Peter Smith walked into Roland's office at 12 P.M. to tell him that Lou Mangini had been absent for two days. Since he hadn't received a telephone call from him, he just assumed that he had quit. "He might have used up all his ideas and just walked out. Maybe he got a better job with a toy company," he said.

"Clear off everything at his desk, Peter, and bring it all into my office. He had a few good ideas. I have a meeting tonight with Ideal Toy. According to our agreement with Lou, all of his work in this office belongs to our firm. Hopefully, one of his ideas will be worth the money that we have already paid him," Roland said.

"Incidentally, have you seen Susan today?" Peter asked.

"No. Madeline was asking for her. I'll call her later," answered Roland.

He left the office at about 4:00 P.M. and the limo reached the Ideal Toy factory forty-five minutes later. He told the driver, "This will be a long meeting. I'll telephone the dispatcher when I'm finished and ready to return to New York."

Henry was happy to see Roland. He asked how his little chippie was and said, "I am indebted to her. She introduced me to that chick from Westclox and we will do over a million dollars with that line. Now, let me see what you've got in your portfolio. Another couple of million dollars and I'm off to Paris, the Riviera, or just to a beautiful whorehouse in South Carolina."

Roland opened the portfolio and Henry flipped through the sketches. His face turned white. "Mabel," he yelled. "Get Mr. Irving in here immediately. As for you, you son of a bitch, I never want to see you again. Get the fuck out of here, you crook!"

TWENTY-NINE

"SUSAN, THANK God you're home," exclaimed an exhausted and angry Roland Levy from an open and unprotected pay telephone somewhere on Manhattan Avenue in Maspeth, Queens. "I'm a little out of breath. I've been running aimlessly in this dreary factory neighborhood searching for a telephone. I just had a terrible scene with Henry and I have to talk with you."

"Can't it wait until tomorrow? I'll see you in your office in the morning."

"No. It's pretty bad. Can I come to your apartment? I'll call my limo service from here and I can get there quickly."

Susan remembered Ellen's rule—no male clients or business associates in your apartment at night. "I'm just going out to dinner and I'm very tired. Besides, I have things that I plan to do tonight."

"Let's meet for dinner. There is that little French restaurant on Twenty-eighth Street between Madison and Lexington. I should be there at 7 P.M. Take a table and wait. My limo may be delayed. I must talk with you."

Susan Liforest was very unsure of her feelings. As she hung up the telephone, she thought that it would be nice to have a quiet dinner with

Roland in a romantic French restaurant. But, he sounded like a wounded pussycat and she didn't care to nurse his wounds with a vision of that other woman lying in his bed. Susan didn't know if she would continue working with him without the possibility of a future relationship.

She had spent the afternoon at home on the phone following up on her plan to hire one or two account executives to handle the daily contact with the big international firms that were now retaining Roland Levy Industrial Design to create new brand images and complete lines of family related packages. Roland had suggested that she search for a middle-aged artist who was seeking sales and client contact work. They had discussed it several times until she finally convinced him that all the big clients wanted was a representative from the design office to sit in on some of their planning meetings and to keep in frequent contact with them as the design work progressed. She preferred a dignified looking man in his late thirties who was educated in marketing, preferably from an Ivy League college, or at least have an Ivy League image. During the afternoon, she had spoken to six men whom she felt somewhat filled this description and she had scheduled interviews with them in the office for the next day.

She quickly showered and dressed for dinner, carefully selecting a flattering blouse and carefully brushing her hair so it fell naturally to her shoulders. She arranged a silk scarf around her hair to keep it in place and left the apartment for the short walk to the bistro.

Roland was sitting in a booth in the back row with what looked like a martini in one hand while the other was holding up his chin with a clenched fist. His collar was opened, tie loosened, and his hair disheveled. This is how he always looked when he had a problem, but his face usually broke into a big grin after just a few minutes of discussion with her.

"Baby!" he said softly as he rose slowly when she approached. *His suit is a mess*, she thought. "Thanks for coming. Sit down and join me for a drink."

"A dry gin martini," she requested from the young waitress who approached the table.

"I can't understand it, Suzy. Henry just threw me out of his office and he was so mad that I think he will black list us from the entire toy industry. All I did was show him my portfolio of Lou Mangini's toy inventions." He spoke hurriedly and with short breaths.

"Lou wanted to tell me something about Ideal, but I never gave him the chance."

"Forget about him, Sue. We have to get to Westclox before he gets us kicked out of there, too. Can you call Ellen Burton? Maybe even at her home tonight?"

"Ellen is in Taiwan with a group of product brand managers from Westclox. They are checking on the production run for several of the new lines, which we designed. She is not expected to return until the beginning of next week."

"Well, it is nice to have dinner with you. It has been a long time." His face brightened up with a big grin. She felt more comfortable now, but she could not remove the image of that nude woman in his bed and the thought that it might have been his wife.

"Have you seen Bea lately?" she asked coyly.

"No. She talks to my lawyer. She wants an uncontested divorce. My lawyer thinks that she may be planning to get married. We've been separated for more than a year. I guess that she wants children." The grin had disappeared as he talked and the forlorn look returned to his face.

"Well, don't you?" she asked.

"Of course I do, but Suzy, for the past three and a half years, with your help, I have been parenting a business with long hours and many problems. There's still time for a family." Then he added, "Don't you think so?"

She just nodded as dinner was served and having had little to eat at home all day, she was quite hungry. As he ate his dinner, he seemed to be more pensive with little to discuss other than the opinion that the onion soup was too salty and the lamb too greasy. *Nothing can please him tonight,* she thought. The level of noise had increased, the other tables were all filled with diners, and there were some couples waiting at the door.

"It is uncomfortable to talk here," Roland said, looking at the closeness of the tables and catching occasional words from neighboring conversations. "Let's find a small luncheonette where we can have coffee and talk. There must be one around the corner on Lexington Avenue."

The waitress brought the check, the hostess thanked them gracefully, and they left the restaurant holding hands. *He's just holding on to me for safety,* she thought, but she continued to hold on to him firmly. Lexington Avenue was dimly illuminated with one overhead street lamp and all the stores were closed. They continued walking slowly toward Third Avenue, which seemed to shine more brightly from the entrance lights on several high-rise apartment buildings.

"Suzy, don't you live in one of these buildings? If it isn't too late, I could help you make some coffee. I really need to talk."

Well, Ellen didn't say that you couldn't break the rule if you wanted too, she thought. "It is late and we are both tired, but I have some coffee cake and we can put on some decaf. My apartment is just around the corner."

Seated on a couch holding the coffee cups, they began to talk about the future of Roland Levy Industrial Design without Ideal and the many small toy firms that had been the nucleus of the business. Susan discussed her plans to hire two account executives and the interview scheduled for the next day "You know, Ruby, the business has really grown away from low end jobs from small toy companies that question every fee that we charge. We now work with giant firms that pay high fees for the quality work that we produce. Kraft has just opened the door for us to work with their advertising agency, one of the largest in the world. Things are really very bright. Forget Henry Isserman. You were just trying to help him and something exploded. Why don't you call Lester Greenberg the vice president of BBDO and invite him down for lunch tomorrow? We can have something catered with waiter service and eat in the conference room."

Roland was no longer listening. He had fallen back on the couch and was fast asleep, still holding a piece of coffee cake in his right hand. It was now 10:00 P.M. She rose, lowered the lamp, opened the closet to search for a blanket, and covered Roland as he lay fully stretched out on the couch.

He's such a cute guy, she thought. *I'll just let him sleep. The problem with Henry must be more serious than I imagined.* She undressed in the bathroom, slipped into her two-piece manly pajamas, quietly opened her sleeper couch, and without making another sound, stepped into the bed and snuggled under the covers. *He is so close and yet so far away,* she thought.

She was awakened from her sleep at about 2 A.M. in the morning by the sound of a voice. Roland was talking on the telephone. When he saw her sitting up in bed, he put the telephone down, walked over to her, and sat down on the end of the bed. "Thank you, Suzy. I feel a little better and I'm going back to the office. The limo will be here in a little bit to pick me up. I'm so grateful to you."

Slowly and nervously, he placed his arms around her hips and pressed his lips against hers, softly but firmly. Seconds passed. She held the kiss and instinctively threw her arms around his neck. She pulled her face away for a second and then, propelled by a long desire, reached for his lips again and gently pulled him down closer to her. She was partly under the covers, but they held each other close for what seemed like an endless time. The lobby phone interrupted with a message from the doorman that the limo had arrived.

"Come in early for breakfast," he whispered in her ear. He left abruptly and after he was gone, she laughed at his appearance, which was completely disheveled. *What would the night doorman think? Who cares? I love the guy.*

THIRTY

ROLAND LEVY had little sleep that night with images of children's toys all aligned in battle formation with Henry leading a charge against him. At 6 A.M., he arose from bed, took a shower, and dressed slowly. He was anxious to review the work in the studio and was sitting at Peter Smith's desk making some sketches when Susan Liforest arrived.

"I wasn't sure if you would be up so early, but I brought some bagels and hot coffee just in case. We have orange juice in the fridge."

"Thanks, Baby, I'm hungry. Let's go into the conference room. We have to plan our day before the phones start interrupting." As they settled into the armchairs and Susan arranged the breakfast food on the conference table, he said, "Thank you for being so patient with me last night. With Henry gone, I felt that my whole world was slipping." He paused and then added, "All except you. You're right. I'll try to get that agency big-wig here today. You interview some of the guys for the account executive job and I'll get Maxine to give us a list of all the large international firms that we are doing work for." Suddenly he began to laugh. "Maybe we are now too big and too expensive to work with Henry and the other toy manufacturers."

Susan smiled and took a sip of her coffee. *He's "out snobbing" the snobs,* she thought. "Honey," she said softly. We have a great organization and all those guys are in business to make money, not bear grudges. When they need us, they will come crawling back. But, in the meantime, let's just keep working with our other clients."

Since the door to the conference room was open, Peter Smith interrupted. He was carrying a group of color prints, which he tacked evenly on one of the cork display panels and focused the spotlight on them. "Roland, I just printed these from my computer. Here's the new look we have been trying to achieve for the Miller line. What do you think?"

"They look pretty good, but try increasing the M of Miller no more than one eighth in height and condensing the whole word so it is in the visual center of the circumference of the label. It will help us to emphasize the new lettering of the brand name. Try to also emphasize the reds and yellows and subdue the greens and dark browns. Remember, we're developing an image for the young beer drinkers and we want to separate this label from any association with older brands." Then he looked at Susan. "Maybe we should leave these color prints on the wall for the BBDO guy?"

"Gosh, not without a cover," said Susan. "We must be very concerned with secrecy, especially around the guy who is running their advertising program."

"Right," said Peter. "I'll get someone from the studio to come in and tack cover sheets over them, which you can remove at your discretion."

When Roland and Susan were alone, he said, "I'll work in the studio this morning to try to pep up some of our projects. Ask Maxine to invite Lester Greenberg of BBDO for lunch here, today if possible, and when you get a live wire or two among the guys that you are interviewing for account executives, invite me in just to offer another opinion. Since you will work closely with them, you really should make the final selection." He rose from his chair, walked to the door, smiled, blew her a kiss, and whispered softly, "You're the greatest."

She sat for quite a while and then called the porter to clean the table and vacuum the conference room. If Lester Greenberg accepted the invitation for lunch, they would be ready for him.

About 11 A.M., Maxine Nierman buzzed Susan on her intercom. "Susan, there are two gentlemen here who showed me their police badges. Where is Roland? He doesn't answer his page."

"He was working in the studio. He may be in his office. I'll go in and see if he is there." The door was closed. She knocked once and then opened it slowly. Roland was seated in his desk chair with his head on the desk cuddled in his arms. The poor guy was so exhausted that he must have fallen asleep again. As she walked in, he raised his head and smiled. "I've been falling asleep frequently," he said smiling at her. "What's up?"

"Ruby, Maxine says that two men from the police department want to see you. She is trying to reach you on your intercom."

"Hi, Maxine. Ask them how much of a donation they expect us to give and then just write them a check. I'll sign it."

"No, Roland. They insist on seeing you. They are walking toward your office now."

The two plain clothed detectives walked into the office and, looking at Roland, one of them asked, "Are you Roland Levy, sir? Roland nodded. "May we sit down? We have some questions to ask you. This lady can leave."

"No. I'd like her to stay. What are your questions? I'll be glad to help, but I have a busy afternoon."

"Does a man named Louis Mangini work here? If he does, what is his job?"

"He did work here for about a month, but he left suddenly. He was a toy designer. Has he gotten into an accident? Where is he?"

"Don't you know where he is?" asked the other detective. "He says that you know all about it."

Roland looked at Susan. "No, he just stopped coming to work. Where is he?"

"In the hospital nursing a gun shot wound with a twenty-four hour guard, waiting to be arraigned in court. So far, he is charged with a break-in, armed robbery, defacing a business premises, and theft of valuable documents."

"So what has that got to do with us?"

"He gave us a sworn statement that he works for you and his job was to infiltrate toy companies and steal their new toy ideas so that you could develop them first. He told us about the clock doll and a number of other toys. The Ideal Toy Company has filed charges against you and asked us to bring you in for questioning."

Both Roland and Susan froze in their chairs. There was silence for several moments. "This is all absolutely ridiculous. What do you want me to do?"

"My only suggestion is to call your lawyer. We have instructions to take you to the station for questioning. This is a serious charge against you. Someone has been shot and valuable papers have been stolen."

Nervously, Roland buzzed Maxine and asked her to get Sol Lefkowitz on the phone. "He's handling my divorce, but his firm has a full legal practice."

"Tell him to meet you at the 102 Precinct on First Avenue. We'll have to take you with us."

Both officers stood up, asked Roland to come forward, and while he was walking toward them, one officer handcuffed his wrists behind his back. Moving to opposite sides, they each supported him by one arm and before a shocked Susan and a bewildered staff, they led him out of the building and to the police vehicle parked in front of the door. "Can I come with you?" asked Susan.

"Meet us at the station with the lawyer."

THIRTY-ONE

THE 102 Precinct occupied an overcrowded three story building on East Seventy-first Street with police cruisers angle-parked in front as well as at various spots along the crowded one-way street. Law enforcement personnel in blue uniforms loitered in small groups on the sidewalk. The police officers moved away from the double-door entrance as if prompted by a signal when a police cruiser double-parked in front and two plain clothed officers emerged, leading the handcuffed Roland Levy into the station. No one paid much attention until a few moments later. All heads turned as Susan Liforest, wearing a short skirt, arrived in a taxicab, paid the driver, and hurriedly walked into the building, a cell phone in her right hand talking to someone at Sol Lefkowitz's law office. He was explaining to her that they had sent an attorney to the municipal court to apply for bail as Rueben Levy was a first offender, but that they really could not accomplish anything until he was finger-printed, photographed, and officially charged with a crime. Since the law office was on Madison Avenue and Sixty-first Street, they promised to send a young lawyer to the 102 Precinct to be sure that Mr. Levy received his legal rights and to receive a copy of the charges for the lawyers to study. They instructed her to sit in the reception room and not speak to anyone until she had spoken with the lawyer. But as soon as she sat down, two officers approached her and asked how they could be helpful. She just smiled, thanked them, and explained that she was waiting for her lawyer.

In another room in the station, Roland Levy was experiencing a deep depression. He was angry at himself for being in this predicament, angry at Lou Mangini for putting him there, annoyed and particularly angry with the police officers, and he was feeling totally humiliated by Henry, who apparently had spread all this venom about him. "Why does he want to punish me in this way?" he sighed as they were photographing his head from different angles. "This is all one hideous mistake," he cried to the photographer who appeared totally disinterested.

A young looking lawyer with a visitor's badge on his jacket lapel entered the room and introduced himself to Roland. "Mr. Sol Lefkowitz asked me to meet with you and to see how helpful I can be here. I'm Jimmy Fields, an attorney in the criminal division of our firm. We have another lawyer talking to the judge right now to see what we can do to get you bailed out." As they talked, a uniformed police officer approached, pushed Roland's hands behind his back, placed handcuffs around his wrists, and led him to a holding cell already occupied by six or seven men. He opened the steel door, removed the cuffs, and gently pushed him inside, closing the door immediately. The other occupants moved away and Roland stood somewhat dazed looking out through the bars. Jimmy stood outside attempting to relax him.

Suddenly, Susan approached the cellblock accompanied by a uniformed officer. When she saw Jimmy Fields' badge she cried, "They said that you could get him out. What is he doing behind prison bars? He didn't do anything." She put her face as close as she could in the space between the bars and he tried to kiss her. They stayed there for several seconds. The police officer turned his head and told Jimmy that they could only stay for five minutes.

Jimmy asked Roland, "Do you have a house, a car, or some tangible assets that can be used for bail? If not, we will have to locate a bail

bondsman to put up the bail money. In the meantime, you will probably have to spend the night here with these guys," he said as he nodded his head at the men in the cell. "They are probably too drunk to
even notice you. In the morning, they will take you to court and we'll
work on getting you out."

Turning to Susan, Jimmy said, "Return to the office and get as
many signed affidavits from persons who know the circumstances of
this charge. We'll need them in court. And," he took an envelope from
his inner jacket pocket, removed a printed sheet of paper, and said, "Mr.
Lefkowitz asked me to have you sign this retainer agreement. Our firm
will do all we can to fight this thing for you."

Susan listened to the lawyer's conversation as if he was talking about
someone else, not her poor Ruby who never did a dishonest thing in
his life. She signed the agreement form as an officer of the corporation,
kissed Ruby through the bars again, said good-bye to Jimmy, and
returned to the office as quickly as she could.

Maxine was the first one to greet her as she entered the reception
area directly off the elevator. She had been waiting patiently all morning and had a worried look on her face that seemed to ask, "What is
going to happen to us without Roland? It's all a mistake, isn't it?" she
finally asked. "Roland has never done anything wrong in his life. What
did those detectives want with him?"

Susan explained the situation created by Lou Mangini, which
erupted with the hostility of the toy company executives who feared
that their secret designs had been stolen and may be sold to the competition. "They call this industrial espionage, and it's a serious crime. No
one has spoken to Lou, so we do not know what he was up to. Roland
knew nothing at all about this, but the police are questioning him. That
is all I know."

When Peter Smith came into the reception salon, she was too
drained to continue any further with explanations and asked him to
please refrain from talking about it in the studio until 3 P.M. when she
would explain the situation to the whole staff. She quieted his anxiety

by telling him that it was one big police department mistake and that Roland would be back at work the next day.

Maxine reminded her that there was one prospective account executive already waiting to see her and that two others were scheduled for later in the afternoon. She also informed her that Lester Greenberg's secretary had called and said that he wanted to meet them for lunch the next day, but preferred a first introduction at the Friars Club instead of in their offices. Susan asked her to please confirm the time with Mr. Greenberg and that she and Roland would meet him there. Hurriedly, she pushed the elevator button to go up to her office and said, "Maxine, please usher the man waiting to see me into the conference room in about five minutes. I must wash my face before I do anything else. I'm completely worn out."

Susan opened the door to her office and stood silently at the entrance surveying the room, feeling its warmth and the closeness it made her feel to Roland, whose office was adjacent to hers. Unlike anyone else, he had listened to her needs, accepted her little foibles, and had given her the opportunity to fulfill her aspirations. The office had become her private domain where she renewed her energies. She healed herself from the abuses she encountered in the harsh environment of representing a design firm as a woman in a world dominated by aggressive men who constantly challenged her ability to make decisions. Here in this quiet ambience, she nursed her ego. Today, she felt helpless with the vision of Roland handcuffed and confined to a prison cell with drunkards and criminals.

It was only five minutes, but Susan felt that it was much longer. Somehow, she had removed the clouds of depression, her lively walk returned, and there was even a spring in her step as she emerged from her office going directly to the conference room. Roland was depending on her and she had to control her emotions. The future of the business was very important to both of them.

"Good afternoon, Mr. Brunswick. My name is Susan Liforest. Mr. Levy wanted to meet you, but he was unfortunately detained. I am the vice president of marketing and should we come to a mutual under-standing, you will be working with me along with Mr. Levy and Mr. Smith, our design director. Do you have any problems with that?"

"Not at all. As you will see in my curriculum vitae, I have worked for major advertising firms for fifteen years and very often the leader-ship is by creative women."

Bruce Brunswick was a slim man, nearly six-feet tall with a tanned complexion, black hair flecked with spots of gray, and a relatively long face that seemed to widen when he smiled. He smiled often during his conversation, a friendly upturn of his lips, which seemed to be contagious.

"Your background is quite impressive," said Susan, returning his smile as she glanced over a two-page sheet that he handed to her. "Our business is continually expanding and our clients have asked us to assign account executives for various design work in order to coordinate their objectives with our creative efforts. You will not be soliciting new accounts, just working as liaison between them and us. Is this what you would like to do, Bruce? If you don't mind my calling you by your first name. We try to be informal here."

"That is exactly the position I am seeking. I did client liaison for Y&R and J. Walter. But advertising client relationships dip as agencies are changed and the campaign creative process gets shorter. It is my hope that an industrial design firm has a continuing client relationship through various products, their packages, and their retail displays."

"Well," said Susan, "this is what we try to achieve and to accom-plish this the role of an account executive is most important. I note from your resume that you attended the Friends Academy both in New York and in Riverdale. Then you attended Bucknell University with a major in marketing and advertising. If our firm provides the challenge and the opportunity that you are seeking, let us set another date and meet together with Roland Levy. Please call our office tomorrow. It has been my pleasure to meet with you. I'm sorry you had to wait, but next time we will try to be more prompt."

As he left the conference room, she called Maxine on the intercom. "Has either of the other two men arrived? This last gentlemen appears to have just the background that we are looking for."

"Mr. Conwell is here now and the other gentlemen said that he will arrive at 4 P.M."

"Thanks, Maxine. Send Mr. Conwell up to the conference room."

Henry Conwell was a heavyset man of medium height with a high balding area on the top of his head and graying hair falling along the sides. The same graying hair was repeated in his bushy moustache, which appeared to be neatly trimmed. He wore wire-framed glasses that seemed to disappear over his big eyes. He smiled as he walked into the room and extended his hand to Susan Liforest.

"It's nice to meet you, Ms. Liforest. We spoke on the telephone. I've been in advertising for about fifteen years, but I have never been in an industrial design office. When I was at BBDO, I saw your company name on some of the packages we were promoting. Beautiful art work."

"Yes, Mr. Conwell. Mr. Levy is a top designer and we do have a very creative art staff. Have you ever worked with an art studio before? Our artists get a little temperamental and dislike making any changes to their work. But we're selling it to our clients and it is the account representative's task to aid the client in selecting the best designs. Often, we use focus groups and mechanical testing to supplement our decisions. Is this something that you would like to do?"

"That has been my forte in the advertising business, but advertising campaigns change too frequently. After all these years, I think that I will be better suited to a design studio."

Susan listened attentively as he talked about his prior work, his education in art history at Cornell University, and his earlier art work at the Chaite Academy, a prep school. *This will be a difficult choice,* she thought. *Since these first two men really have similar backgrounds and, if Roland and Peter Smith feel comfortable with them, they would each be an asset to the firm. Ironically, they are both the kinds of guys that Roland calls "prep-*

pies." But this is actually what we need to expand our work with the big international firms. Breeding is so very important.*

When Henry Conwell left, Susan went into the studio to explain the unfortunate situation that followed the work of Lou Mangini. She said that Roland did not know about Lou's previous connection with Ideal and that Lou was just a criminal. "Industrial espionage is a crime. It is stealing somebody else's ideas. Evidently, that is what Lou was doing and that is how he got his ideas. It's a terrible thing. But what is worse, we did not know anything about it."

She asked everyone working on toy accounts to discontinue their design work immediately. She told them that Peter would confer with each of them to start work on some of the newer appliance and food projects. As she left the studio, she told Peter Smith that she was preparing some affidavits, which she would give him later about Lou Mangini. She hoped that many of the designers would sign their names to it.

When she had a writing problem, Susan Liforest went directly to Maxine who always seemed to know the right words to use on any important document. "I'll just turn this over to her and whatever is done, I will take to the lawyers tomorrow. Really, none of us knew anything about Lou. Once he tried to tell me something about Ideal Toy, but I stopped him," she mumbled.

It was approaching 4 P.M. and Sol Holtsman, the third candidate for the account executive position, was due for his interview. She had two calls to clients that she wanted to make before the meeting and she had to call Westclox to find out when Ellen Burton was scheduled to return. "Oh, Ellen," she whispered. "I really need you now. Things have gone far over my head and I'm scared." She mumbled a few four-letter words under her breath and quickly walked to her office to make the calls.

THIRTY-TWO

ROLAND LEVY spent most of the night in deep thought. He covered his head in the gray prison blanket when the intense smell, the moans and the snores of his fellow cellmates, and the sometimes flickering of the overhead fluorescent light created restlessness that was difficult for him to endure. When he did doze off for what seemed like only seconds, his dreams of making love with Susan Liforest were clouded with an image of monsters lurking in the shadows. These monsters were dark unidentified shadows that had suddenly crept into his life just as he saw his goals come closer to reality.

Things were going so well. He had done nothing wrong to deserve Henry's fury. The horrendous humiliation of being led from his office in handcuffs like a common criminal angered Roland. The fear of losing all his contacts with the toy industry, the small firms that were his first clients, was a major blow to him. They had all treated him so well. He could work so easily with the one owner or two battling partners who with limited capital, operated small factories and warehouses and had parts made by equally small businesses in Taiwan, Hong Kong, and other Asian countries. They didn't care how he dressed. They never criticized his worn shirts, wrinkled pants, and dusty shoes. All they wanted were good ideas and good designs.

The toy industry suited him well. Each year, they introduced new items that needed special design work and attractive packaging. The business owners and their executive assistants, like Henry, could not draw, could not create toys, and could not design packages. They hired creative people to do this. Most of them worked very cooperatively with designers. Henry was difficult. He challenged creative designers, bullied and pushed them until they produced something different and outstanding, which he could proudly make part of his product line. Roland thought that he understood his needs and they had a mutually friendly relationship. But it was all over now.

He did not understand Lou Mangini's role in all this. The detectives had told him that Lou was imprisoned in the hospital because he had been shot during a hold-up and that he, Roland Levy, was being held in prison because he hired him to steal ideas. Roland was never given the chance to defend himself. Henry lost his temper and forever banished him from working with toy manufacturers. Henry was his friend, he thought; now he was his jailer.

His thoughts wandered to the executives who worked for some of the big international firms that he wished would become his clients, and indeed some of them had. These were the firms with faceless men whom he wanted so much to please and whom he feared so much, the men who appeared meticulously groomed with striped silk ties and gold cuff links, always with leather attaché cases dangling from one arm. He imagined them as young men in prep schools, athletes in Ivy League colleges, and now members of fine country clubs living in the big white colonial houses in Connecticut. These preppies made him feel self conscious and embarrassed that his clothes were not as well tailored as theirs. Roland was embarrassed and worried that they would immediately discover that he was not one of them, not educated as they were, not dressed as they were, and he feared that they would not listen to his ideas, reject his small firm, and criticize his designs.

They accepted Susan Liforest. They always spoke highly of her. She dressed appropriately, was comfortable in their environment, and they listened to her and accepted her opinions concerning designs. She feared Henry Isserman and cleverly avoided any confrontation. She reached him through the charm of Ellen Burton. How he envied her polished ways. He was too straight, too forward, always emphasizing his own ideas rather than coordinating them with clients.

He was attracted to Susan at their first meeting by her assurance in the Philip Morris offices and when she joined his firm, he admired her natural ways with all the executives whom she approached for business. She assumed that she would be successful, if not at first, then eventually. He feared the mysterious power of preppy executives and anticipated their rejection of his ideas.

"You challenge them, Ruby," she had said several times after working together with him for several months. "Whether you want to or not, you actually court their rejection. Just be friendly. Share your ideas with them. They are intelligent men. They want to learn more and if what you say appears to benefit them, they will want you on their team."

She is wonderful, he thought. *And I love her.*

"Mr. Levy," called a prison guard. "Get dressed. Here is some breakfast. In ten minutes, the detectives will be here to take you to court."

The court session moved very quickly. Along with two other men from his cell, Roland was handcuffed, led into a prison van, driven to the court house, and held in a locked room for about twenty minutes until a uniformed guard called his name. His handcuffs were removed and he walked into a large courtroom surrounded by two officers and was led to a chair at a table facing the judge. He sat down next to a lawyer whose face was unfamiliar and whose name he could not remember two minutes after he had introduced himself. The lawyer spoke to him in a soft, pleasant voice.

"Good morning, Mr. Levy. We have a promise for a bail bond and now it is just up to the judge to hear the charge, set the date of a further hearing, and then set the bail. You'll be a free man in a short time."

Roland just wanted to see Susan and then get back to the office. He felt sick, he looked sick, and his clothing was a mess. He heard the judge and lawyer talking, he stood up when directed, and when the lawyer said, "Not guilty" and the judge asked him if that is how he pleads, he repeated, "Not guilty." The lawyer led him from the court-room and down the steps at the front of the building. A driver held the door open to the rear seat of a dark colored limo and he hurried inside, brushing against Susan who was sitting inside with her arms outstretched to him.

"Ruby, dear. Thank God you're out of that horrible place," she said. "We'll be back in the office in just a few minutes. You'll feel better there." He just smiled, too tired and too depressed to say anything until they entered the elevator in his building.

"Since I could not sleep in that foul smelling place, I was able to do a lot of thinking, Suzy. We've become an important industrial design firm and we are growing every day. We have to drop those little time consuming toy firms and concentrate on the major consumer business-es that really need us."

"That's my goal, too," said Susan. "But just now, you had better shower and dress. We have lunch scheduled at 1 P.M. with Lester Greenberg at the Friars Club."

Still very tired, but with a determination to quickly remove any scars that stemmed from the ordeal he had just been through, he shed all his clothing and sat in his sauna at high heat wrapped in a towel for about ten minutes. Then, as cold water from the shower enveloped his body, cleared his head, and sent tingling waves down to the tip of his toes, he felt ready to go back to work.

Susan had made up her mind that she wanted Bruce Brunswick as her account executive and was anxious to discuss this with Roland as soon as he was dressed. There was at least an hour before they were scheduled to leave for the Friars Club, and she sat in her office review-ing his vitae with Maxine. "It is so important to have a person with the right personality to interact with our new clients. Their opinion of our firm comes from our presentations to them and from the people who make these presentations. Roland makes sure that our designs are great, but we must do everything possible to help our clients feel the same way."

"Susan," said Maxine with a look in her eyes and a tone in her voice that seemed to express admiration, "where did you learn all this? You are such a natural. Roland was so lucky to find you. We have all come a long way."

When Maxine left, Susan took all her papers into the conference room, called Peter Smith to join her for a brief meeting, and then called Roland. He entered the room about ten minutes later, fully dressed with a jacket and tie, flashing a big grin on his face.

"Now, where were we before we had this little interruption?"

"Peter and I were evaluating Bruce Brunswick's vitae. He was the first man that I interviewed yesterday. Roland, you must meet him as soon as possible. I think that he is perfect to start on the Kraft food account," she said.

"See if he can come in tomorrow. I could see him in the afternoon. Now, I would like to prepare for the luncheon meeting with Lester Greenberg. He is a very important contact. What do you know about him?" Roland asked.

"Well, we can't ask for a curriculum vitae on every guy before we meet him for lunch," said Susan teasingly. "From what I can gather, Greenberg is an important man at the advertising agency and has been around major firms for a long time. Everyone seems to like him."

THIRTY-THREE

THE FRIARS Club occupied a four-story building on West Forty-sixth Street surrounded by shops and offices. It had been a club exclusively for actors and it gained considerable fame for the ribbings, which comic actors engaged in with each other and the annual testimonials to leading show people. Still claiming mostly a theatrical membership, the club accepted members from leading business firms who wished to use its luncheon and dinner facilities for business functions.

Susan and Roland arrived by limo, hurried up the front steps, and entered the reception area. "We're here to meet Lester Greenberg," Roland said to the middle-aged man in a tuxedo who stood at the entrance to the front dining room.

"Mr. Levy?" he asked. "Mr. Greenberg said that he may be a little late, but that I should usher you to his table and suggest that you order a drink and some of our hors d'oeuvres. Please follow me."

The dining room was filled with people at each table, talking almost continually as they ate with middle-aged waiters watching over each table and bus boys removing dishes just as soon as they appeared to be empty. As soon as their drinks arrived, a tall, distinguished man in his late fifties, tanned, with a small gray moustache, graying hair with a slight bald spot on top, and a smile that showed gleaming white teeth, arrived at their table.

"Don't bother to stand up. I'll shake your hand sitting down," said Lester Greenberg. "I've been looking forward to meeting you both. Years ago I worked for Raymond Loewy, the famous industrial designer. I did public relations from his Chicago office. I loved it. Tell me about your industrial design firm, Mr. Levy."

There was something about Greenberg that Roland liked immediately. "Well, we're a small firm, but we do the same work—product design, packaging design, corporate identification, and a little bit of hand holding to help our clients understand the marketing value of better design. We were hoping that you would come to our office to see our set up and some of our past designs."

"We'll schedule that on another day. I wanted to meet the people first. Now I have. Mr. Levy, may I call you Roland? And you, Ms. Liforest, may I call you Susan? My name is Lester, but everyone calls me Les. I see that you have already had some drinks. I'll just order one and then we'll concentrate on lunch."

The talk was very general as they ate with Lester Greenberg, rising frequently to shake hands with and share a comment with several different men who passed by the table. "You seem to know many people here," commented Susan.

"Well, I'm at the club for at least one lunch or dinner every week and on Thursday I have lunch here with the Executives' Association of Greater New York. This is a group that you should think about joining, Roland. It's the best-kept secret in New York and it brings in more business than any other group. If you're interested, I'll tell you about it at another time. Let's make a date to have lunch at your office."

"We have made a good start on the Miller designs and we would like to go over them with you before we go back to Philip Morris. Today is Tuesday. Can you do it on Thursday?"

Les took out a small leather-bound book from his pocket and scanned an appointment list. "Gee, I'll have to call you when I return to my office. If my secretary can move some things around, I can be free on Thursday. The PM boys want to work fast. I'm delighted that you have made a good start. That was Raymond Loewy's old trick. Surprise the client by making a group of sketches in advance of the meeting. It used to work for him."

Susan called the limo service while they were still eating lunch and the driver was standing in front of his car when they emerged from the building. "Can we drop you off?" asked Susan. "No," Les responded. "I have to stop on Madison and Forty-sixth before I return. That is just around the corner. Thank you for the offer, though. See you on Thursday."

As he left, they entered the limo. Roland was so tired. He rested his head on Susan's shoulder until they reached their office building. Then, they each adjourned immediately to their separate offices.

Roland sat behind his desk and began to make notes on a large pad. What did he want from Lester Greenberg? What did L. G. want from him? The most important benefit would be his enthusiastic approval of the Miller designs. This required staging with considerable help from both the art studio and the photo studio. His mind weighed several presentations. He needed to talk to Peter Smith right away.

"Peter," Roland said on the interoffice telephone, "I need you and a photographer to help me set up a slide and mock-up presentation of the new Miller designs for the day after tomorrow. Please ask one of the photographers to come into my office with you so we can discuss it."

Roland started to make sketches. First, he drew a series of beer bottles including the existing Miller bottle. Then he quickly sketched the same grouping with the new bottle in the foreground. He roughed it into a six-pack and then he roughed a group of six-packs on a retail shelf. By that time, Peter and Carl came in with a portfolio filled with the new Miller artwork.

"My idea, guys," said Roland while pointing to the sketches on his desk, "is to make up a series of two and a quarter projection slides to show how inferior the old bottle looks in comparison with all the other popular beer brands. Show another shot of the same group of beer brands highlighting our design. Finally, show a glamorous shot of the bottle alone using a complementary background, flowers, a sports scene, or a supermarket. Whatever works. Make it sing. Then, after this last slide is screened in the darkened room, we turn the lights on and give him two finished package dummies. Can you do it in a day and a half? And what do you think of the idea?"

Peter was the first to respond and he had a big smile on his face. "It's a piece of cake, Roland. Our design is so good we can really make a terrific presentation. How do you feel, Carl?"

"Just give me the art and the comps. We'll take some great shots."

"That's great, guys. This presentation is very important. Take my sketches and if you need anything else, just call me."

When they left his office, Roland started to think about the Executives' Association. He had heard some favorable comments concerning that group, but really knew nothing about the members or how the organization functioned. Maybe this was a chance to get in with the preppies. It would be great to have lunch at the Friars Club once a week. If everything worked out well with Les, maybe he would invite him to attend a meeting.

Still tired from his prison ordeal, but invigorated with new enthusiasm stemming from the Les Greenberg meeting, he walked into Susan's office. She was on the telephone, but motioned for him to sit down. As soon as she put the telephone down, he started to talk.

"Susan, the studio is working on a great presentation for Les. We're going to screen some slides and wind up with some pretty good comps. I feel that he will be impressed. Order some food so we can avoid going out to a restaurant. And, what have you heard about the Executives' Association?"

"Really nothing. Les mentioned it at lunch, but I think that the marketing vice president of Philip Morris also mentioned it some weeks ago. Other than that, I know nothing."

"Thanks, Suzy. We'll ask Les to tell us about it."

THIRTY-FOUR

LESTER GREENBERG was late and both Roland and Susan were anxious. The appointment was for 12:30 P.M., but by 1 P.M., he had not arrived. The caterer had started the lunch menu and was annoyed when Susan insisted that he delay his service until their guest arrived. Lester's office had called at 12:45 P.M. and again twelve minutes later. His secretary explained that an important client was trying to reach him. When he arrived at 1:15 P.M. with the excuse that he was tied up at a prior meeting, Susan gave him his telephone messages. He just flashed his contagious smile, looked completely relaxed, shook his head, and said that clients were always trying to reach him.

"We all lead a busy life," he said looking at Roland. "If I took every phone call from clients when they wanted to talk to me, I would never get any work done. When I return to the office, after I review the day's work, I take an hour and return everybody's phone calls. I'm more relaxed then, they are more relaxed, and we all stay sane and happy. This is a crazy business, isn't it, Roland?"

"Suzy, do me a favor," he said as he sat down next to Roland, placing his leather briefcase on an empty chair along with his coat. "Please have one of your young ladies call my secretary and thank her for tracking me down. Tell her not to call anymore. I'll take care of everything when I return to my office later this afternoon."

The three of them were seated at the end of the large table in the conference room; this was a luncheon setting with silverware, napkins, and stemware at each place. "Susan has arranged this luncheon with a very talented French chef who gets very temperamental when his favorite dish is served cold," Roland said, "and since it is after 1 P.M., we should start now and we'll present the Miller project while we're having coffee."

Not waiting for his approval, Susan left the room and returned with a uniformed waiter who glided into the room with a chrome metal and heavy glass cart carefully arranged with drinks, ice cubes, extra glasses, plates, and a covered terrain containing hors d'oeuvres.

"Martinis, of course," offered Roland.

The waiter served the drinks along with a plate of lobster tidbits, each with a plastic toothpick protruding from its center. He left quickly when he finished his service and returned with a Caesar salad in a large bowl along with various anchovies, sauces, croutons, and dressings, which he mixed on his cart and then served on individual plates. As they were finishing the salad, he returned with three covered dishes containing Chilean Sea Bass, a vegetable and a potato, and after removing the salad dishes, he opened the covers and placed a dish carefully before each of the diners.

Roland was not very comfortable with this elegant service in the office. "It is necessary," Susan insisted, and she was annoyed when Roland firmly rejected serving a fine French wine. "You must treat these guys with simple elegance," she had said. "If you want to do business with them, you have to behave like one of them." He knew that his future business was now dependent upon them, but he had a difficult time separating from the warmth of his mother's family style service on the kitchen table. *How did Susan acquire such sophistication?* he questioned.

The luncheon conversation was very general. Les talked about some of the client account executives that he said knew nothing about modern advertising. They were just hacks waiting for sales to go down so they could condemn the advertising agency. "Those guys hate creative people," he said. "We have to keep them away from the art directors and copy writers. Right now, they have a bug for designers. They don't know any designers, but they talk like they do."

"We don't know any either, do we Susan?" Roland asked with a big grin.

"Speaking of designers," said Susan, "can you tell us about the Executives' Association and how a great design firm like ours can benefit from it?"

Les appeared eager to change the subject. "Great idea! It is a wonderful organization. My firm has been a member for over twenty years. I've been the delegate for the past two years. Several design organizations would like to join, but we haven't found the right one. We're still looking." He winked at Susan. "A firm must be well respected and must have an outstanding person as their delegate, either the big boss or an important vice president."

"Can you tell us a little more about the organization itself?" asked Roland. The waiter was just beginning to remove the dishes and serve coffee. Roland was anxious to get on with the Miller presentation, but he was curious about this unusual organization.

"They say that the idea started with Ben Franklin," said Les as he sipped his coffee. "It was discontinued after his death, but emerged again about a hundred years ago and there are now Executives' Associations in more that ninety cities throughout the U.S. and several are active in Europe and Canada. Our organization has been in New York for over sixty years. The idea is very simple. We accept one member for every business category. We have one banker, one stock broker, one medical group practice, one plumbing contractor, one legal firm, one accounting firm, and oh, yes, one advertising agency. That's me. Want to hear more?"

Susan looked at Roland. "We sure do. What's the purpose? Is it like Rotary?"

"Well, Rotary, Lions, Optimists, even the Chamber of Commerce are all business social groups in which members meet for lunch and may or may not do business with each other. But the Executives' Association is different. We do not perform any public service or charity. We're organized only to give and receive business from each other and to provide leads and introductions to other members to help them increase their business. We do not have speakers at our weekly luncheons. While we eat, we explain our various businesses and then offer leads to each other. This is fully organized. We have an office in mid-town, two full time executives who organize every meeting, produce a weekly newsletter, a semi-annual directory, and keep a record of all new business that members receive or give. It's a great organization."

"How many members do you have?" asked Roland.

"Close to ninety, just now, but only about sixty come to each weekly luncheon. Whether you attend or not, dues are payable in advance. If you don't attend for several weeks, you could lose your membership. Since we only have one firm in each category, there are usually firms waiting to join. But a business firm may be proposed by a member whenever there is an open category and then the firm is thoroughly investigated by the executive director and the membership committee." He smiled, "I'm on the membership investigation committee."

"Well," said Roland, as they all seemed to be finished with their coffee. "We're interested, but maybe we can talk about it later. I'm going to call our art director, Peter Smith, to start the presentation." Turning to the waiter, he said, "You can clear the table now, but leave the coffee cups and bring in a pot of hot coffee."

"I'll call Peter on the intercom," said Susan.

Peter entered the room accompanied by two young art assistants. Roland introduced them to Les Greenberg and just as planned, the slide presentation began. Peter opened a sliding door in the rear wall behind where they were seated to reveal the projector, already loaded with slides, and at the opposite end of the room, one of the assistants parted two doors to reveal a large screen. The lights were turned down and the presentation started.

Roland, standing next to the screen with a pointer, explained each slide as Peter timed the slides to his conversation. In the darkened room, Susan's eyes were on Les Greenberg. He was quiet during the presentation and started to speak when the lights were turned on, but Peter interrupted him.

"Mr. Greenberg, this is our current recommendation." He handed Les a bottle of Miller with a beautiful label wrapped around its circumference.

Les was quiet for several minutes, turning the bottle around in his hands and looking closely at the lettering, graphics, and color.

"Guys," he said, "you really have something here. I liked the whole presentation. We will have to run some focus groups, discuss it with the client, and coordinate it with our advertising exposure. Maybe I can get more design work for you from some of our other packaged goods companies."

"We'd love to work more closely with your agency," said Susan.

"Take me around your studio. Let's see some of your other work. If things work out, I'll arrange a meeting with some of the top guys at our shop. Who knows? Maybe they will point you in the direction of some of our clients. But remember, an advertising agency makes money by placing advertising in the media. We don't make it with design. But good design keeps ads running for longer periods. That is our overall goal."

The studio tour went very quickly. There were a few delays when Les stopped to talk with the two designers who were creating the graphics for the line of Kraft Lite Cheeses and to look at some of the comprehensive food packaging designs that were on display on one of the shelves. He ignored the work of designers who were creating new forms for products and displays, but stopped at everyone's cubical to say hello and shake hands. He followed Roland into the photographic studio and was delighted to see all the props and lighting equipment.

"You know, we don 't bother with photography. We send it all out to the best photograph studios and assign an art director to coordinate the shoot," explained Les.

"Well," Roland responded, "we take our own shots, retouch them, color print, and place them just where we want them on our packaging design comprehensives. When the job goes into production, the client sometimes selects a well-known photographer who takes his own shots, but he follows our layout."

The tour ended in Roland's office where Les reclined on the couch with one foot resting on the marble cocktail table. "This was very worthwhile. The Philip Morris guys were right when they asked me to look at your setup. Hopefully this will ultimately be profitable for all of us."

"I hope so," said Susan. "We have just hired a new account executive who is anxious to work closely with the Kraft executives. We would like you to meet him whenever it is convenient. He's a Cornell man."

"Really? Me too. I'm also active with the alumni association. By the way, I am also active with the Fieldston alumni group. A number of the guys at the agency went there. We all grew up in New York City and didn't want to leave until college. Did you attend Ethical Culture too, Roland?"

Susan interrupted, "Roland is an artist's artist. He just went to art school." Roland smiled at her very pointed response. *Suzy is a smart gal,* he thought.

"Are you free for lunch next Thursday, Roland? I would like you to be my guest at the next Executives' Association luncheon. Can you meet me at the Friars Club at 12:15 P.M.? Just tell the hostess that you're waiting for me. We'll sit together so I can introduce you around. Lunch starts at exactly 12:30 P.M." Not waiting for an answer, he stood up, spied his coat and briefcase, along with the bottle of Miller beer that Maxine, on Susan's instructions, had carried into the office earlier and placed on a side chair. Les tossed the coat over his left forearm, pushing the briefcase firmly under his arm. He held the beer bottle carefully in his left hand as he offered his right hand to Susan and Roland. As the elevator door opened and Les entered, he turned and said, "See you next week at the Execs," and then he flashed his approving smile just before the door closed.

"Ruby," exclaimed Susan as the elevator descended. "You made it. You are now one of them!"

"Thanks to you, Baby. It really was a great show."

THIRTY-FIVE

Sunday morning started with a telephone call from Ellen Burton. Susan Liforest lay in her bed half sleeping, half thinking, sliding her head further under the heavy blanket, inch by inch, as the sun's rays slipped slowly through the tiny spaces in the venetian blinds, gradually flooding the room with a warm radiance that blended with her romantic dreams.

The shrill rings of the telephone abruptly interrupted her mood.

Sunday mornings were always difficult and very lonely. She had enjoyed a quiet dinner the night before with Jerry Malone, a charming young sales executive with Kraft foods who loved to tell humorous stories about the foibles of food shoppers in supermarkets. He had called her several times until she finally agreed to have dinner with him explaining that, "My boyfriend is out of town on a business trip and I must be home by 10 P.M. to receive his call." She needed the company, but was too involved with Roland Levy to think of starting another relationship.

Poor Roland. His divorce was pending, attorneys were reviewing his assets, he had neither an automobile nor an apartment, he lived rent-free in the office, and he was now facing a criminal charge from Ideal Toy Company, once his most important client. As the firm's reputation grew and more designers joined the art staff, he increased the time devoted to creative work, personally reviewing every studio project, but was still always available to encourage and assist her marketing efforts.

When the phone rang for the first moment, it seemed like a wishful dream—maybe dear Ruby was calling to greet her on Sunday morning and assure her that his thoughts were entirely about her, but the second moment erased that thought. Maybe it was Jerry Malone, the nice guy who just wanted to thank her for her delightful dinner companionship. By this time, she was wide-awake and was sure that it was her mother. Susan hadn't spoken to her in several weeks and was thinking of calling and visiting her today; it would be just like her mother to call first.

"It's nice to hear from you," she said in her sweetest tone as she reached across the bed to pick up the telephone from the cocktail table.

"Don't try to sweet talk me, Ms. Liforest," Ellen Burton hissed. "I'm calling you at home as a friend because my boss has broken off all ties with your crooked firm. I still can't get myself to believe it, but when Henry and Irving both spoke to my boss and explained how you stole creative ideas, even our Westclox doll line, and then sent this poor guy to spy on Ideal Toy, I actually cried. You and your boss did a terrible thing. Henry says he wont stop until he gets this Levy guy for good."

"Oh, Ellen. I tried to call you right away, but you were overseas. It is all one big mistake. Roland didn't do anything."

"I'll be in New York sometime this week whenever I catch up with all the paperwork on my desk. I won't call you, but if you feel the need to speak with me in person, you can try to catch me at the Beekman Tower Hotel. I can't promise that I'll see you. Henry is sick over this tragedy. He says that he was sucked in by the nice-guy attitude of Mr. Levy. Good-bye."

The warmth left the room. Only the icy tone of Ellen Burton settled on all the furniture.

Roland Levy was up at 6 A.M. eager to start his day. He enjoyed Sunday. It was his time to be alone, to pursue his art, to dream, to think about the future, to be really creative. Rain, snow, warm or cold, he loved to spend the entire day in the studio without interruptions from people, telephones, clients, and all the responsibilities that involved so much of his time as the chief executive of a large company. How did it get so large? He wanted everything under his control and as his reputation grew and the work expanded, control was gradually slipping away.

Still clad in pajamas, slippers, and a robe, he walked from his office into the studio on the way to breakfast of a bagel and coffee that he had prepared in the small kitchen the night before. The top floor of the five-story building contained the graphic design studio, the kitchen, and the offices of Roland and Susan. The elevator door opened into the studio, which occupied most of the space. Each artist had a right-angled cubicle with a drawing table, computer-equipped desk with adequate shelving, and storage space. Peter Smith, the art director, occupied the cubicle next to Roland's office. Each time he left his office, Roland stopped to talk to Peter, but this morning, he just sat down on Peter's chair and surveyed the various projects. There were ten designers assigned to this studio and Peter carefully reviewed all their work. Roland picked up two large renderings of Kraft packages, placed a sheet of tracing paper over each, taped it securely in place, and picking up a black pencil, carried them with him into the kitchen.

Sitting on bar stool, waiting for the coffee to heat, he studied each rendering. With bold, black strokes, he made several revisions on each. Propping them up on the counter and leaning against the wall, he studied them as he ate his bagel. I see where I have work to do today," he said. "It just does not look the way I would like it to."

He walked back to the studio carrying the two renderings and returned them to Peter's desk. Then, he went from cubicle to cubicle, sitting on each of the chairs and studying the work on the computer and drawing tables, writing notes, making small sketches, and evaluating all the design work. His entire morning was spent in this fashion often talking, singing, and enjoying a most pleasant time.

At 12 P.M., he felt somewhat satisfied, exhilarated with the numerous challenges to his design ability, pleased to be alone with his thoughts, and happy to once again feel the joys of being an artist. He returned to his office to shower and dress in a pair of wrinkled jeans with a faded blue sweat shirt and his well-worn sneakers, and then once again returned to the kitchen and removed a wrapped turkey sandwich from the refrigerator along with a can of Pepsi. Thusly armed, thinking of it as exercise, he walked down the stairs to the floor below.

The fourth floor contained the industrial design studio, the photography studio, and a small shop for constructing packaging and product models along with an occasional small set for a photo shoot. There were seven designer's stalls in the studio, the same units as in the graphics studio, and there was still room for a few more. The photo studio was a windowless area with electrical outlets and cords extending from both the walls and the ceiling. All of the equipment was locked in several closets along one wall and the opposite wall was scarred with hooks and bar extensions to hold large rolls of colored background paper.

Roland moved around the studio checking the work of each designer and making some of his own sketches. By 3 P.M., he had reviewed all the projects in the studios on both floors. He particularly loved the third floor, the newest construction. He walked down one flight of stairs to look into the conference room, and then into the new large office to be shared by the account executives. There were two smaller rooms for private meetings with suppliers and clients. He had designed an overall concept for the building when they first moved into the top floor space, but he never expected to realize his aspirations so soon. An elderly lady, whom he had never met, owned the building. She was anxious to have only one tenant instead of the six that occupied it at that time. The real estate agent told Susan that the owner inherited it from her parents and that she was born in the building. Each time that Roland wished to expand, she provided the additional space by offering the other tenants desirable space in one of her other buildings. The first floor of the building still had a small office for a three-person accounting firm and the partners were out on audits for most of the day.

The entrance to the building contained a comfortable reception area that was furnished with a couch and several chairs. On a small table was a telephone to speak to the receptionist on the second floor. The door to the street was always locked with an intercommunications system to the receptionist. On some days, a guard sat at a small table and opened the door for special clients. A glass door at the far end of the reception area led to the elevator alcove. Above the elevator was the sign, "Roland Levy Industrial Design, Inc.," with a small directory that instructed all visitors to stop at the second floor. Adjacent to the elevator and facing the rear was a double door with the lettering, "Joseph J. Sorrentino, CPA."

Roland finished his tour with the second floor, the business area, containing the office for the two secretaries, the bookkeeper's office, a large room for receiving and preparing deliveries, and the client reception area and "showcase." On the walls were framed renderings of products and packages and two lighted glass showcases filled with various packages designed by the firm. He sat down on one of the leather chairs to look over the scene. He had worked hard to build this business and now Ideal was seeking to destroy it.

Suddenly, the telephone rang with a clamor that broke the silence and changed his mood. *Who could be calling on Sunday?* he wondered.

"Ruby, it's me," said Susan Liforest. "I just spoke to Ellen. She called ripping mad. I have been crying all morning since I spoke with her. She has taken this Lou Mangini thing very badly and is calling us thieves. She will be in New York sometime next week. I hope that we can get to talk with her."

"Are you free for dinner tonight?" he asked. "Let's talk about it. How about the little French restaurant that we like on Twenty-ninth Street? Is 6:30 P.M. okay?"

THIRTY-SIX

ELLEN BURTON sat across the table from Roland and Susan at the penthouse restaurant of the Beekman Tower Hotel. It was early evening on Thursday. She had arrived in New York on Tuesday and spent all of her business hours with buyers and merchandise managers from F.A.O. Schwartz, Toys-R-Us, and J.C. Penny. Tuesday evening, she was so exhausted that she fell asleep in her room at 7:30 P.M., forgetting dinner entirely. On Wednesday, she walked through New York stores noting the placement of Westclox items and checking the inventories on the clock doll line. She met Henry Isserman for a Chinese dinner at the Dragonseed Restaurant in the evening and they walked back to her hotel, saying good night in the lobby. Tonight was to be different. She had her hair set and her nails manicured. Ellen had relaxed in a warm bath and now she was looking forward to meeting Henry and planned to spend the evening with him at the hotel and then drive with him to LaGuardia International Airport in the morning for her flight back home to Atlanta.

Ellen looked lovely. All the tiredness and strains of business seemed to have left her eyes and she was relaxed, but annoyed that she had to meet with both Susan and Roland. Susan had left messages for her every day and when she finally reached her that morning, Ellen agreed to see her alone for a few minutes in the penthouse lounge. She was dressed in a dark blue pantsuit with a light blue blouse and a pink scarf that draped softly about her collar with both fringed ends falling gracefully together below her bosom. Her jet black hair had tiny gray highlights as it curled over her ears with simple bangs that seemed to kiss her eyelashes each time she moved her head.

She had one hand on her left ear fingering the dangling silver earring while with the other hand she pointed directly at Roland. Although there were filled wine glasses on the table, nobody had taken more than a sip.

"If I didn't have warm feelings for Susan, I'd never be here. We were going to talk, woman to woman, for just a few minutes. Now that you're here, I'm going to direct my questions at you. It is 7:15 P.M. now and Henry is picking me up at 8 P.M. He will be furious if he hears that I have been talking with you. So you must be out of this hotel in thirty minutes. If you want to say something to me, you better do it now. I'll just listen."

Roland first looked at Susan and then turned his head to look directly into Ellen's eyes. "Lou was hired by me to design new toys. I never checked his background. He worked in the graphic studio and our art director thought that his idea sketches looked good. After a few months, he suddenly disappeared. Since he did not show up, we all thought that he had just walked away from the job. Thinking that some of his ideas may be good for Ideal Toy, I brought them all in to Henry. That is when he suddenly exploded."

"That's the truth, Ellen," interrupted Susan. "We had no idea what Lou did after he left the office."

"What about the doll line? Henry says that Lou showed him the idea sketches for the doll and the clocks before he saw your sketches. Did he develop that first?" Ellen sounded very angry.

"Absolutely not," said Roland. "We designed that line. I have no idea how Lou got into it. This whole thing makes me furious. This guy turns out to be a crook and I go to jail. We have a growing business with some of the most respectable clients. These unfounded accusations can put us out of business."

Ellen looked at them both for a few seconds and then said, "I don't know whom to believe. Keep away from Henry. I'll try to set up a meeting between you and the Misson brothers. Let them sort it out. I only want to cry and that will kill my make-up. Don't call me. I'll see if I can get them to come to your office. Now leave the hotel instant-ly . . . and don't let Henry see you." She stood up quickly, ignoring her wine glass, signed the check with her room number, checked her lip-stick with a mirror from her shoulder bag, and walked quickly toward the elevator.

Roland was both confused and angry. He could not understand why Henry Isserman was so furious. He turned everyone against him and refused to even see or talk with him. Obedient to Ellen's warning, he reached for Susan's arm and they both hurried to catch another ele-vator. In just a few minutes, they were out of the building. Hastily they walked up to Fifty-seventh Street where they hailed a cab to return to the office. Neither was hungry. Both were confused. They just wanted to talk.

"Susan," said Roland as they sat on the couch in his office, "we have a good chance to stop this thing if we can get Harold Misson up here to see our offices. He seems to be an experienced businessman. Hopefully he will see how absurd this whole thing is. If he agrees to drop the charges, this whole episode will end quickly. I'm just scared sick in fear of the press. If I have to go to court, these stupid charges will be all over the newspaper."

Susan snuggled next to him and he placed an arm around her shoulder. "It feels so comfortable," she whispered. "Let's forget all about this tonight, but I must go home soon. Friday is a busy day."

"Maybe we can get your boss to give you the day off," he said with a wink and a smile as he moved closer and pressed his lips to her will-ing mouth. "But if you insist on working tomorrow, let's enjoy ourselves here tonight. We'll call the limo service to take you home before midnight. Do you know that I love you?"

As Susan rode home in the limo, exhausted, deliriously happy, and excited that her love for Ruby was returned with equal emotion, her thoughts turned to the meeting with Ellen. She had been so happy to see her, but she was disturbed by Ellen's insistence that they avoid any confrontation with Henry. She thought that Ellen was afraid of Henry's anger. It was not even suggested that they meet and discuss the situation with him. No. Henry must be in a rage. Instead, she suggested that they meet with Irving and Harold Misson.

Henry was always cheerful and fun to be with and he seemed to appreciate Roland's work. All their meetings and design presentations were so very pleasant that both she and Roland considered him to be a friend and the Ideal Toy Company to be a special client, one that even the studio designers felt would appreciate their creative efforts. The romantic involvement between Henry and Ellen seemed to be spontaneous from their first meeting in Chicago to their private interludes each time she came to New York. Ellen was single, probably had been married before, but Susan realized that she knew very little about her past. She knew that she lived alone, had climbed the ladder in her large company, and was now one of their key executives receiving a high salary with an expense account and company stock options.

She knew nothing about Henry. He never talked about his family. Irving Misson once referred to his admiration for Henry's wife, but she did not seem to have any presence in the business, no family pictures on his desk, no participation in company affairs. Susan thought this was strange. He acted like the debonair bachelor, free to pursue romantic affairs.

Yet Ellen was afraid of this jovial and likable man. Was she afraid that he would cause a public scene with Roland? Lose his temper and physically confront him? Or, was she fearful that he would be angry with her, just look with disdain at Roland, and then turn his rage on her for the rest of the evening, ruining her planned romantic evening?

She began to think that there was something more to this incident, more than Ellen, Roland, and she had been told. Henry was so furious that it was even spilling over to his relationship with Ellen. Did Irving Misson know about his affair with Ellen, or was this relationship hidden from everyone except she and Roland?

"Miss," said a hoarse voice from the front of the limo, breaking her thoughts. "We're here! Let me escort you into the lobby. I don't see the doorman."

"Oh, that's kind of you. At this hour, he is probably sitting on one of the couches. Thank you. I'll be fine."

The doorman rose as she entered, smiled pleasantly, and escorted her to the elevator. When she entered the apartment, she kicked off her shoes, unbuttoned her blouse, and walked toward the bathroom. The silence and her thoughts were interrupted by the telephone.

"Goodnight, my love," was Roland's pleasant greeting. "I'll see you tomorrow."

"I love you," she whispered, and they both hung up their phones. "I guess that I worry too much," she said as she fell into bed and was asleep in minutes, still partly dressed.

THIRTY-SEVEN

LESTER GREENBERG of Batton, Barton, Durston, and Osborn, charged into the building, his silk necktie was hanging from his open collar, his suit jacket was somewhat disheveled and his voice was hoarse.

"Where's Maxine?" he questioned the receptionist as he emerged from the elevator. "I've got to see her right away and then I want Roland and Susan to met me in the conference room. I have been on the phone all morning and we have a bombshell."

"Good morning, Mr. Greenberg," said Maxine as she walked into the reception area from her adjacent office. "What can I help you with?" The receptionist looked up at Maxine and then moved away from her desk expecting some hostile remarks from this seemingly very disturbed executive.

"All hell broke loose at our agency this morning when we read the news article in *Advertising Age* about your stealing secrets from competing toy companies. This is industrial sabotage and our gang wants no part of it. In fact, they won't let you into our offices. I have to see Roland and Susan immediately. Get me some coffee and I'll wait for them in the conference room."

Maxine was stunned, fearful for Roland, and too nervous to respond. She ushered him into the conference room, asked one of the girls to bring him some coffee, and then took the elevator up to Roland's office. It would be better to tell Roland face to face. She could explain it better than over the intercom. Lester was so angry and maybe he would calm himself somewhat as he sat alone drinking coffee.

Roland responded quickly when he saw the troubled look on Maxine's face as she conveyed Lester's message. "Thank you for coming up. I'll get Susan. Tell Lester that we'll be down to see him in just a few minutes. Set a coffee service for Susan and myself. Friendly talk flows better when you're all drinking coffee." He was worried and frightened about this unexpected visit, but bravely felt that he could handle it effectively.

When Susan and Roland entered the conference room, they were all smiles. "Good morning, Lester," said Susan, walking over to him and extending her hand.

"It's not a good morning," snapped Lester. "Not only have the guys at my agency closed the doors to your firm, but the president of the Executives' Association saw the *Advertising Age* story and blasted me for ever bringing you to our luncheon, and he threw out your application for membership. I'm here on my own. Talk. Tell me what this is all about. I want to hear it straight from you." His anger seemed to grow as he spoke.

Roland sat quietly for a few moments as one of the office girls entered the room with a pot of coffee and began filling the cups. As she left, he stood up, pushed his chair in, and walked next to Lester. Facing him from a standing position he looked down as his upturned face and said, "Lester, we have a problem. None of this is true. A man who worked here has somehow gotten himself into trouble and he is using me as a scapegoat. We're designers. We develop ideas—we certainly don't steal them." His face was flushed as he talked and when he finished, he sat down, resting his elbows on the table and supporting his head with his hands.

"We're trying to get the owners of the Ideal Toy Company to sit down with us and listen to the whole story," said Susan, looking intermittently at Roland, then Lester. "Because of this vile charge by a former employee, Roland has spent a night in jail and now he is waiting to present his case before the grand jury. The whole thing has been a nightmare."

Lester's tone quieted somewhat. "What can we do right now? Everything has been stopped between us, our agency business, Philip Morris, everything, until I tell them that this thing has been cleared up. It better be good because we all run highly ethical businesses and we can't afford to be associated with any crooked schemes."

Roland began to tell the story, starting from the original telephone call and interview with Lou Mangini, his work in the studio, and his subsequent hospitalization from a gun wound.

"How can he get away with this kind of accusation?" questioned Lester. "It's his word against yours."

"Not quite," said Roland. "We have statements from Peter Smith, my studio director, and all the staff members concerning his work at the drawing board. He was the only one working on toy designs. And we never really inspected his work until he left."

"What is this deal with the owners of Ideal Toy?"

"Well," said Susan, "we are trying to get Irving and Harold Misson, the brothers who own Ideal Toy, to sit down with us and listen to the story. If they drop the charges, our attorney says that will end this horror."

"Maybe I can help. I'd like to try anyway," said Lester. "The president of our agency knows Harold Misson. They are members of the same country club in Westchester. I'm not promising anything, but maybe they can start the ball rolling."

"And, one more thing," continued Lester. "We have retained Dan Rothe of Rothe Public Relations, one of the most respected names in the PR business. Dan personally knows all the editors of our trade papers. He is not a magician, but he will work on your behalf to minimize any strong hostile articles about you and your firm."

"Thank you, Les," said Susan. "As I see it, the most devastating problem will be our reputation with the top people in the toy and housewares businesses. After this affair is all over we will need extensive public relations to enhance our image. Is this something that Dan Rothe does?"

"Susan and you too Roland, my friend," said Les. "I am surprised that you do not have a PR firm on retainer. I'm going to ask Dan to make a luncheon date with you. Many of the journalists on the staff of newspapers and magazines respond to the news releases sent to them by the PR firms retained by the brand marketing firms. They often do not include the name of the design firm in their stories."

"So," said Roland, "if we have our own public relations firm on retainer, our firm would be written up in some of the important publications."

"Your work is so good," said Les, "that a good PR firm could be most helpful to you. It has been a great help to our agency."

Roland was quiet. *More expenses,* he thought.

As if she were reading his mind, Susan said, "Roland, it is a great investment . . . not an expense."

THIRTY-EIGHT

HAROLD MISSON always felt comfortable when he was dining at the Fifth Avenue Club. Maybe it was the lavishly furnished room, or the very attentive waiters and their captain. Maybe it was the feeling that he was among so many friends, all in the same business, sitting at near-by tables. Everyone said hello, inquired about business, and often said something nasty about the building, one of the showrooms, or one of their competitors in the toy business. They chuckled with each other and seemed to be playing a game that they all enjoyed.

This was Wednesday evening, all the sales representatives were on the road somewhere, and the club was reasonably deserted. There were only three other tables occupied by diners and at each one he was sure that a chain store toy buyer was discussing his order after an afternoon of studying the line in the showroom. But the diners whom Harold had invited to join him for dinner were not toy buyers. In fact, most of them were really not in the toy business. The six of them were there to listen to Roland's story.

John Hecht, chairman of BBDO, had persuaded Harold to hold a meeting with his brother in order to find the truth about the break-in and the stealing of ideas. He did it just to please Lester Greenberg. "We have no real interest in this," he had told Harold, "but one of my key executives is tied up with this design firm on several projects. Trade espionage is very serious for all of us in business and if this guy is a crook, Lester should know about it."

Irving Misson was very negative about the meeting. "I can't tell Isserman that I'm doing this. He is furious and won't be happy until Levy is sent to jail," he told Harold. "But, as a favor to you, I'll join you at the club. Hopefully, we'll all enjoy a good dinner."

Irving met with his brother and John Hecht in the Ideal Toy Company showroom a half hour before the 6 P.M. scheduled dinner and the three of them enjoyed reminiscing about their relationship of a few years before when BBDO had been the agency for the Toy Manufacturers' Association and both Harold and Irving had been on the board. There were always charges among the member toy manufacturers that some firm had copied their hot item and was offering it as a loss leader. But they usually settled the disputes amicably. These reminisces were good for a few laughs and they were all smiling as they stood shoulder to shoulder in the elevator as it descended to the lobby. They entered the Fifth Avenue Club with Harold Misson leading the way.

They were seated and had ordered a round of drinks before the Levy party arrived. Harold spent a few minutes walking around to each of the other tables in order to greet the buyers whom he knew and to shake hands with other toy company owners. Then they waited patiently for nearly fifteen minutes for the others to arrive. Harold had requested six table settings, but he was not sure if Roland Levy would be alone or with his associates.

Roland Levy was not alone and he did not look very happy as he arrived surrounded by Susan Liforest, Ellen Burton, and Lester Greenberg. "So now we are seven," said Harold Misson as he extended his hand to each one and offered a chair to each of the ladies.

Lester Greenberg introduced himself as he quickly moved a chair from a nearby empty table and sat down in the space next to Irving Misson. "I know that John Hecht did not expect me and I want to apologize to him and to you all for joining this group without an invitation. The four of us have just finished a meeting in my office at the agency and this story as Roland and Susan unfolded it was a shocker to both Ellen and myself. I felt that I just had to join you here tonight and help them to convince you that they were duped, tricked, and falsely charged."

"I don't believe it," said Irving raising his voice in an excited manner. "Henry has spent hours going over this whole situation with me, showing me all the drawings and blaming himself for being duped by these two double crossing conmen . . . and woman."

"Please," Harold interrupted. "Let's have a quiet dinner first and then we'll listen to their excuses. Stealing toy ideas before they are patented is despicable in the toy business and the grand jury will hear the case next week. We're here to listen and not interrupt. I'm hosting this dinner as a favor to my old friend, John Hecht. So, let's eat now and talk later."

Roland Levy was nervous during dinner, sat quietly avoiding conversation, and occasionally looked at Susan who smiled faintly in return, but did not engage in any of the table talk. Ellen, sitting next to Susan, kept up a lively conversation with John and Harold, first about their new marketing program and ultimately about golf and the country club to which most of the executives at Westclox belonged. The club in Westchester that both the Missons and Hecht belonged was very casual, according to Harold, and was a great source for business contacts. "Not so in Atlanta," explained Ellen Burton. "We're very formal, dress codes are required even on the golf course, and dresses and jackets are a must in the dining room. For us, it is a place where we get to talk with one another in a neutral setting and your golf score rates higher than your position up the ladder or even your sales record."

"Well," laughed John as he gently patted Harold on the back. "At five dollars a hole, I usually take these guys for enough money to pick up the tab for drinks and cigars. We have a shotgun tee-off tournament every year, but most of us are not serious golfers. But, let's get serious now. I asked you all to come here for a purpose."

As he spoke, the waiter and bus boy began to clear the dishes from the table and Harold ordered coffee for everyone plus a bottle of brandy. "This always helps a discussion."

"So, tell us, Mr. Levy. Why has the district attorney called a grand jury to review charges against you?" asked John in a stern voice. "Irving and Henry are going into court against you because they are convinced of your guilt. What do you want to tell us here that they have not heard before?"

Roland cleared his throat and started to talk when Les Greenberg interrupted. "John, we've all heard his story several times. It seems that Susan and Ellen have had several meetings together and before we gathered for this dinner, I listened to them and to Roland for about an hour. This has become a very delicate situation and you may not want to expose it in a public courtroom."

"Why not?" questioned Irving in a loud voice. "We don't care who knows about his thievery. Henry says he is a crook. My brother, Harold, and I come from a family that has always been in the toy business. Grandfather started it in Germany and we worked with Dad as kids growing up in the toy business in New York. Everybody knows us and we know them. It's a small industry of medium-sized companies with only one or two giants. Henry has been with us for five years. I hired him as my assistant and he has grown with the job. Today, he is in charge of all new toy ideas. He actually creates our line of toys every year and so far, we have been ahead of all our direct competitors. We're out first with the new ideas . . . and it is all due to Henry Isserman."

"This is a bit embarrassing," said Lester, "but from what Susan and Ellen have told me, it seems that Henry is more involved in the conspiracy than Roland. Let me ask you a question, Harold. Have your new items for last year and this year been in any way similar to your competitors?"

"Don't interrupt him, Irving," said John Hecht. "I don't know what he is driving at. Let Harold answer the question."

"It happens from time to time. Maybe toy guys think alike. A few of my friends called me at Toy Fair to congratulate us for our new line. Each had one or two innovative items, which they were surprised to find in our line also. We laughed about it—friendly competition. One guy got really angry, but I turned him over to Henry. Never heard anything further. Our Tell Time Baby Dolls are leading our girl's line and no one else has anything like it. Irving runs the factory and he makes the decisions on new items. Every week he sends a folder up to my office with a description of the new items that he is working on. To tell you the truth, I don't even look at it. I put the folder in the bottom drawer of Henry's desk here in the showroom office."

Susan waited until he was finished and said very slowly, "We believe that many of the ideas in that folder are toys being developed by your competitors. They get the ideas first; somehow, Henry finds out about it and then develops their idea as his own and puts it into his line before they do."

Everyone was silent for a few moments and Ellen Burton started to speak in a slower than usual Southern way. "I'm very fond of Henry Isserman. We worked closely together and incorporated the ideas of Roland Levy into a best selling clock doll line. But I believe that Henry had a secret deal with Lou Mangini and others to copy the best ideas of competing firms. When Roland went to see him with sketches that Lou had made for these toys, Henry was shocked. He thought that Roland had discovered his secret. He became excited, angry, and maybe even frightened. But he saw a way out. Blame Roland for stealing his new ideas. He probably frightened Lou with a long jail sentence and got him to blame Roland for his break-in at Ideal Toy. It all makes such sense. I cry every time I think about it. I can't believe it and yet it makes so much sense."

Susan broke into the conversation and began to talk quickly, "Henry's anger was just too much against Roland. He wouldn't talk with him. He just wrote him off as a crook after working with him so closely for a long time. And then he shut him out of the industry by passing the word to all his competitors. It seemed so strange. The lawyer defending Roland asked if we thought that it was a set up. Roland asked him to engage a private investigator to look into it. That's where the matter stands just now. Roland is furious."

"Roland, you've been silent. I guess that you are very angry," said John Hecht, "Why did you come here tonight and what are you planning to do? You are the patsy, if what they are saying is true, and you have the most to lose."

Once again, Roland started to speak and he was interrupted. "Let's stop right now," said Irving Misson. "This has gone too far. I must call my lawyer tonight. Some fears that I had are coming into focus. Until we learn the truth, we must stop the grand jury. Harold, you and I will talk alone for a while upstairs." Turning to the others around the table, he said, "Please do not act or say anything about this until I call you tomorrow. There are many things that you do not know that we must look into. Let's say goodnight now. You can stay here and finish your coffee. Harold, please come with me to your office. I need to talk with you."

THIRTY-NINE

HAROLD MISSON'S office was at the far end of the toy showroom behind the clerical office where his secretary kept the files, the duplicating machine, fax, and other office equipment. There was just her desk, her chair, and one chair for a guest. His office was small and sparingly furnished, which was somewhat unusual for the chief executive of a large firm, but the men who were born into the toy business generally prefer to sit behind the huge old oak desks that were used by their fathers. It gives them a feeling of continuity and even superiority over the newcomers who entered the business in the late fifties and sixties. Harold's desk chair was relatively new, but its black leather arms and wingback gave it an old fashioned look. "The firm was started in Europe," he was proud to explain to toy buyers who sat on plain oak chairs in front of his desk as they scanned the adjacent wall entirely covered with framed black and white photographs of his father and his uncle working inside the pre-war German factory, a picture of them in front of their first American office on Essex Street, and a large photo of them at the ground breaking ceremony for the Queens factory. "The Borough President shoveled the first hole," he told everyone.

The only other furniture in the room was a large wooden bookcase and a small wooden desk with a glass top, which was used by Henry for three weeks in February during Toy Fair and two weeks in June during the Summer Fair. The desk was next to Harold's and Irving often used it whenever he was in the office. Tonight he sat behind the desk facing Harold who stood at the large double window looking out at the lights on Twenty-third Street. Neither one had anything to say since they returned from the Fifth Avenue Club. They could be together for a full hour, as they often were during Toy Fair, each deeply involved in his own thoughts and both respecting the privacy of each other.

Both brothers were satisfied with their roles in the business and where it was common in the toy business to have frequently fighting partners, Harold and Irving ran the business successfully with mutual respect for each other's duties. Both had a son in college and Harold also had a single daughter who had just started a career as a kindergarten teacher. He often thought about a son-in-law in the business, but never discussed it with his brother.

Harold lived in New York City and during Toy Fair, his wife often joined the sales team in the office working closely with his secretary to assist new toy buyers and to join her husband in the evening when he invited the important retail executives to dine with them downtown at the Gotham Restaurant or uptown at the Essex House. They were his favorite places, generally too far up or downtown to be frequented often by other toy manufacturers.

When Milton Misson turned over the business to his two sons, his own brother had died and the business had lost its challenge for him. Harold was his oldest son, a graduate of the University of Pennsylvania, and had been employed for the past year in the marketing department of Proctor and Gamble in Ohio. He missed the glamour and excitement of New York and when his father offered him a chance to work in the family business, he eagerly accepted. Irving had studied engineering at Cornell and was always fascinated by plastic molding technology. Once Harold had made the switch and was working for Ideal

Toy, Milton called both sons together and explained his plan to have his sons operate the business. Within two years, each son implanted himself in a distinct phase of the business—Harold in management and sales, Irving in product development and manufacturing. Harold moved to an uptown apartment house on the West Side of Manhattan. Irving purchased a house in Queens so he could be near the factory and the manufacturing processes that he loved. Milton retired with a big party and until his death, spent spring and summer in the family home in Belle Harbor and as the cold weather approached, he moved to Palm Beach, Florida. He was pleased with the continuity of the business and very proud of his two sons.

"Since Toy Fair, Harold," said Irving interrupting the long silence, "I've had an uneasy feeling about Henry. The line had several items too closely similar to items developed by Banner Toy, Eagle Toy, and even Hasbro. I thought that it was just coincidence, but I began to think that we know very little about Henry."

"How long has he been with the firm? More than four years."

"Well, I think it was nearly five years ago in February when I put a large display ad in *Playthings Magazine* seeking an executive to run our creative department. Henry was working for Aladdin Toys in Nutley, New Jersey. He came to see me at the plant and we just hit if off instantly. He liked our line, made some good suggestions, was very humorous, and I took a chance and hired him instantly. He started work in April and he has been with us since then."

"Why did he need two months to change jobs? It seems like a long time."

"I never asked him," said Irving. "I was busy and soon after he started, I gradually turned over the department to him. To tell you the truth, I really know very little about him. I was just anxious to get a new toy line together each year and Henry always came through. During the past several years, I've sent him to the Housewares Show, the London Toy Fair, and even the Hong Kong Market. He only stayed a few days at each place, but he always came back with good ideas. And you know how well he gets along with the toy buyers during the week or more that he spends at the New York showroom during Toy Fair."

"But, Irv, we have a problem now and Henry seems to be right in the middle of it. I don't think that we can solve it by just talking to him. I have an idea, but I don't think you will like it." Harold moved away from the window and sat down on the chair behind his desk. "Do you want to hear it?"

"Well, we have to do something. This poor guy Levy will be going to jail and everyone at dinner tonight thought that he was innocent. What do you have in mind?"

"I met a private investigator a few weeks ago at the country club. He is a lousy golfer, but he was telling us about the spying going on in the computer industry. I'd like to talk to him about this. His name is Murray. I have his card somewhere." Harold opened the top drawer of his desk and found the card among a neat pile of various unrelated business cards.

Irving reached over for the card, glanced at it inquisitively, and Harold said, "He has an office in the Fisk Building. A private investigator. Let's talk to him. Maybe he can help us straighten out this situation."

Irving replied, "It's a good idea. I hope that he can uncover some real facts." He smiled at his brother.

FORTY

MURRAY APPLETON was a man of medium height with bushy pepper and salt hair, glasses, and the kind of face that would trigger a friendly smile from a total stranger were he sitting next to him on the subway. Although he had a somewhat expanded chest with broad shoulders, his waist looked to be about a size thirty-two and at first meeting, learning that he was a detective, anyone who expected him to look like James Bond would be very disappointed. He wore tight fitting, crumpled blue jeans with a gray turtle neck sweatshirt and dirty white sneakers, which he rested on the lowest drawer in his desk as he sat on his chair facing his visitors. He was sitting there talking on the telephone and drinking from a bottle of water as both Harold and Irving Misson were ushered into his office by the short blonde receptionist.

"Hi, Harold. Be with you in a moment," he said as he turned quickly away from the telephone. "Thanks, John," he continued addressing the voice at the other end of the line. "We'll sum it all up tomorrow and I'll be in to see you with the final report within a day or two. Relax, if you can. When you see the photographs, you will feel much better. So long!"

He rose, quickly meeting the two brothers in the center of the room and shaking their hands individually with a firm grasp. "Pardon my dress. I just came back from a three-mile run in Central Park. My daily body conditioner. It's about the only exercise I get these days. You must be Irving. I'm glad to meet you. Why don't you sit here on the couch." He motioned to the brown leather couch at the side of the room and he sat opposite them on a matching leather chair.

"Tell me your problem. On the telephone, you spoke about industrial espionage."

"Well," started Irving, "we would like to learn everything we can about an employee. Is this something that you can do? It must be done secretly because we do not want him to know that he is being investigated."

"You see," continued Harold, "if everything turns out well, we still need him to do his job. He has been a trusted executive and we hope that he will continue to serve our company in this role in the future."

Murray relaxed on his chair and as he leaned back, his blue jeans slid up, fully revealing a small brown holster strapped to this right ankle with an ugly looking revolver partially concealed within. "Oh! Excuse me. I always take this piece with me when I go to the park. You never know!"

"Well, that scares us," said Harold. "This is a simple investigation. We don't want anyone to get hurt. We already had one man injured because of gun play."

"Tell me what troubles you about this man and what it is that you want to find out. Then all I need to know is his name and address. The rest of it is my job. I have been doing private investigations for twenty years, mostly on referral from attorneys. During the last few years, there has been a bash of industrial espionage cases from some of the largest firms in New York. We're pretty good at that." He smiled at them as he said it.

"We think that his man has been stealing ideas from our competitors, improving them, and putting the items into our line before the other company has started production. He has accused a man we know of stealing from him. All we want to learn is the truth about what has been going on."

Murray rose from his chair, walked to the desk, and buzzing the intercom, he asked, "Rose, can you come into my office for a few moments?" He moved back to his chair, then stood up again when Rose came in, and ushered her to the empty chair opposite the couch on the other side of the cocktail table.

"Rose is one of my discreet investigators. She's licensed and has been with me for six years. We have two others, experienced and licensed men who are currently in the field working on a confidential matter. I would like Rose to hear your story, but first I will tell you how our fees work and about how long each investigation usually takes. We'll get a better idea after the first two days of investigation. As you know, we are very experienced in discreet investigations."

"I do most of the cranial investigation," said Rose. "I was a librarian before I joined Murray and you will be surprised with all the information that is available. As a trained investigator, I also do field work where my appearance opens doors that may be closed to the men."

Irving sized her up quickly. She was about thirty, had a good figure, a bright smile, a pretty face, and was very disarming. "Rose, when Henry Isserman sees you, he will make himself very appealing."

"Don't worry a bit," said Murray. "Rose can handle him. I direct the team and each of us has another job to do to quickly get the information we seek. Our fee is one hundred dollars a man-hour, plus expenses, billed and paid for each week. Operators work no more than four hours a day on each assignment. Every two or three days, I will give you a report if there is anything interesting. Sometimes it only takes a week to give you the answers you seek. Sometimes it takes longer. We never know until we get involved in the case. Are you ready to tell me all about it?"

Irving began by telling Murray and Rose the whole story about Henry Isserman, Lou Mangini, and Roland Levy. Harold broke in from time to time to tell him how they would like to avoid the grand jury hearing for Levy. "I just do not want to see the firm's name brought into court and ultimately into the newspapers. We make toys and we must look like a firm that parents can trust."

Murray Appleton taped their information, gave them both a business card, and ushered them to the door of his office. "We'll start your investigation on the day after tomorrow and I'll call you a few days later. I'll tell your secretary that I'm, Murray, your golf buddy and we'll talk in golf terms. You never know who will be listening. With your permission, I would like to speak with Roland Levy and maybe indirectly to Lou Mangini. Glad to meet you, Irving. Good-bye."

As they rode down the elevator, Harold remarked, "Hemsley took over this building when the Fisk Tire Company left. Did you see the lobby when we came in? He sure modernized it. Let's stop in at that Chinese Restaurant off the lobby. I'm a little shaken after this meeting. I really need to relax with a drink."

Harold opened the door to the restaurant and they both walked in. "Hal," said Irving abruptly. "Stop and stand still for a moment. Isn't that our Henry sitting in the first booth with those two men? Let's get out of here before he sees us. He is supposed to be in the factory. I wonder what he is doing way up town on Fifty-seventh Street."

"You work with him, Irv. I suggest that you call your office and ask to speak with him. Here, use my cell phone. That man may only be a look-alike. Don't use the phone now. Wait until we're outside."

They hurriedly walked out of the building, through the turn-style doors on to Fifty-seventh Street, and then crossed the street to enter the lobby of the old General Motors Building. There were no cars on display since GM sold the building, but the lobby was traditional in appearance with its clutter of marble and its bank of elevators. There were exit doors onto Broadway, which they scurried through and then crossed Broadway walking east on Fifty-eighth Street. Here, Irving stopped and leaning against a building, called the factory.

"Irma, this is Irv Misson. May I speak with Henry?"

"I'm sorry, Mr. Irving. Mr. Isserman is not here. He left this morning and said that he would return at about 2:30 P.M. He has received a few calls. Shall I tell him that you called?"

"No. Forget about it. It's nothing important. I just wanted to tell him when I expect to return. I'm on my way back to the office. If any one has called for me, just put the list on my desk. Thank you." He closed the phone.

"It was him in the restaurant, sure as hell." said Irving. "I've worked with Henry long enough to know what he looks like, even from the back. I'm going to call Murray and maybe he can tail the guys. They are probably still eating and talking."

Murray Appleton received Irving's call politely, listened to a rather vague description of the men, promised to look into it, and Irving then gave the phone back to Harold. "That guy is so matter-of-fact about things. I hope that he knows what he's doing. I've had enough for one day. I'm going to take the Sixth Avenue subway and then a cab to the factory from the first station in Queens. I'll call you at home tonight if anything comes up. So long."

Harold continued to walk along Fifty-eighth Street until he reached the Essex House. He was all shaken up from the meeting with Murray and slowly walked into the hotel, found his way to the bar, on the lobby floor, asked for a dry martini, and sat down on a stool facing the big windows with a view of the park. He sat there for what seemed like an endless period with his mind wandering about thoughts of James Bond and *The Thin Man* when he felt a tap on his shoulder.

"Aren't you from Ideal Toy Company?" asked a pretty looking woman with long black hair that seemed to cover one eye and tease the corner of her mouth each time she spoke.

Awakened from his daydreaming, he turned as she sat down on the leather barstool next to his. "Yes, I'm Harold Misson. Have we met before?"

Looking at his glass, she ordered a dry martini that the bartender served rather quickly. "I'm one of the buyers for Kid-N-Kaboodle. We met at Toy Fair when I gave you a trial order for a few of your items. My name is Sydelle Marcus."

Harold's mood changed instantly. He smiled, extended his hand, and said, "Oh, yes. Now I remember you. How did you like Toy Fair this year? Are you on another buying trip? How long will you be in town?"

She smiled. "Harold, you must be a great salesman. You ask so many questions that it will take me a long time to answer them."

"Well, let's finish our drinks and go for a walk in the park. It is such a beautiful day and Central Park is blooming at this time of year." He took both checks, left a ten-dollar bill and five singles on the bar. They stood up, emptied their glasses, and walked out.

FORTY-ONE

Roland Levy loved New York. With both his home and office on Fifty-fifth Street and Madison Avenue, he felt part of the excitement, part of this huge business metropolis, a place where most of the world's major corporations maintained their United States headquarters, most of them located just blocks away. The New York that he both loved and sometimes feared were the corporate board rooms along with their adjacent private offices of preppy business executives. These offices were all lavishly furnished with beautiful reception areas that were the domain of their lovely young women with cultured voices who welcomed you with studied courtesy and considerable respect. From his windows, he gazed at their huge buildings and smiled often when he dreamed that he was part of this enormous scene.

He barely remembered the earlier years when he feared these faceless men and shuddered as he was cordially ushered into their offices. He was so sure then that they did not understand him, did not understand his work, and that they ridiculed his choice of shirts and suits. Now he had five suits in his closet with Paul Stuart labels, six cotton shirts from The Custom Shop, and at least a half dozen silk ties. Then there was the gold cuff links given to him on his birthday by Susan. He was different now and he not only looked the part of a successful business executive, he felt like one.

New York was not all perfect. He couldn't stand the subway, hated the buses, and vowed that he would no longer walk down busy Madison, Fifth, or Park Avenues carrying his tell-tale portfolio. "I would look like a hungry freelancer soliciting hourly work from art directors," he mumbled. The limousine service was his answer and he traveled in their black Lincoln Towncars to all client meetings watching other New Yorkers as they waited for changing traffic lights to cross busy intersections and then walked with the slow flow of pedestrian traffic along the sidewalks. New York was a beautiful place, but he preferred being a perpetual spectator.

As he sat behind his desk studying a model of a new hair dryer design, part of a line of women's hair and facial products being developed for Revlon, he was interrupted by a call on his intercom.

"Mr. Levy, there is a Mr. Murray Appleton here to see you. He does not have an appointment, but he says that it is important. He has been asked to meet with you by Mr. Harold Misson. Shall I send him up to your office or will you meet with him in the conference room?"

"Yes. Ask him to come up here. Please ask Susan to meet with him first and then usher him upstairs to my office. I'd like her to join us for the meeting. Mr. Misson telephoned this morning to inform me that Mr. Appleton had something important that he wanted to see me about. I have no idea what it is. I guess that we'll find out soon enough. Thank you."

Murray Appleton entered Roland's office in step with Susan, both of them smiling as if responding to a humorous story. Murray was dressed in the business attire of an executive.

"What's the joke?" asked Roland as he extended his hand to Murray and welcomed him into his office.

"Oh," said Susan. "I asked Mr. Appleton, Murray, what he did and he said that he was a stand-in for James Bond except that he married his client." She smiled as she said it.

"Mr. Levy, may I call you Roland? Harold Misson has retained me to investigate the situation of industrial espionage that seems to be the charge against you made by Henry Isserman and acted upon by the police. So far, we have only engaged in preliminary work and the charge against you doesn't seem to be well documented. Tell me, did you steal ideas from other firms and try to sell them to Ideal Toy?" He winked as he spoke.

"Absolutely not. Lou Mangini, our short-time employee, worked on toy ideas under a special deal. I have no idea where he got his ideas. I thought that he developed them himself."

"Well, Roland, at this early time in my investigation, I believe that you are in the clear. Somebody made you the patsy and I'm trying to get enough evidence to have Ideal Toy Company call off the charges and the grand jury."

"You're a blessing from heaven. How can I help?"

"I've been led to believe that somehow Henry is behind all this. You know that the Misson brothers know very little about him even though he has been a faithful executive for several years. Just a few days ago, we spotted him in a restaurant on Fifty-seventh Street talking to two unknown individuals. My investigator listened to their conversation with a surveillance apparatus from a neighboring booth. He taped their conversation. They were asking for extra funds in order to copy the blue prints of a new toy series just being developed by Mattel."

"Well," said Susan, "there's your evidence. We never stole ideas. You have them red-handed, as you detectives say."

"Not quite. They haven't done anything yet. We must find him with someone else's blueprints in his hands. Then, we must learn what he's going to do with them. At that point, we'll get the other firm to go after him for stealing. It's a little complicated. I'm here now to ask you some questions.

"My first question," he continued, "is this. What do you know about Henry? His job, his attitude—how he has behaved with you before this incident?"

"Well," said Roland, "he is the vice president of marketing and advertising for Ideal Toy Company. That is a very big job. He is in charge of new toy ideas and packaging. In fact, he was the one who gave this firm one of its first big jobs. I thought that he was my friend."

"I always had some restraints and some fears concerning Henry," replied Susan regarding Murray's question. "Frankly, I was afraid of him. Fortunately, when I first met him in Chicago, I was able to introduce him to Ellen Burton. She could handle him." She smiled as she said this. "Ellen has had some misgivings herself lately. She wouldn't tell me what they were, but I think that she was afraid of his anger. I think that he acted very nervous and that was one of the things that bothered her."

"Ellen told us of her suspicions before our dinner meeting with the Missons," said Roland. "It was something that Henry told her that convinced her that he was falsely accusing me. She was sure of it, but she still wanted to protect him. They do have a successful business relationship. I guess that is why they hired you."

"Do either of you know anything about Henry? His wife, his family, his home? His background?" asked Murray.

"Not a thing," responded Roland. "I've asked questions, but I can only speculate. No one whom I spoke to had any real knowledge of Henry's background. I don't think that he was intimate with any one at Ideal Toy. Friendly, yes. Even well liked by most of the people. It seems to me that the toy business is his whole life. He knows everyone."

"One of my investigators, her name is Rose," said Murray, "ran a full check on him starting with the New York Motor Bureau. We have his license number, his car, and his home address. He is separated from his wife and has a small apartment in Queens, but the address listed at Ideal Toy is that of his wife who has a home in South Orange, New Jersey. He keeps his personal life very secret."

"Ellen Burton has spent a lot of time with him. Have you spoken to her yet?" Susan asked.

"Rose had a long interview with her yesterday and that is why I'm here," Murray replied. "She was very helpful and suggested that I speak to both of you. I'm trying to work fast. I have two investigators in the field listening to Henry's telephone calls and following him during all his activities outside of Ideal Toy. Have you seen this?" He removed a copy of *Advertising Age* from his briefcase and read the headline, "Noted Industrial Designer, Roland Levy, Charged With Stealing New Toy Inventions. Grand Jury Indictment Expected."

"Unfortunately," said Roland. "The grand jury is expected to devour me sometime at the end of next week. Somebody must do something or I'll be in jail for something that I didn't do. I guess that you need new evidence."

"That's my job. If I can produce enough evidence, they will drop the case." He stood up, shook hands with Roland and Susan, and winked as he left.

FORTY-TWO

THE TOY industry is one of the most vibrant businesses centered in the United States with grown men and women seeking to satisfy the ephemeral needs of the smallest consumers. Traditionally, it is sexist with dolls and tea sets created for little girls and wheel toys, guns, and action play toys created for little boys. However, these little consumers change their interests as they grow and few of the previous year's toys will satisfy their needs today. Toy industry executives fiercely compete with each other to introduce new items, which give them a marketing edge over competitors.

The vast majority of toy sales to consumers are made after Thanksgiving as gifts to children for Christmas. But immediately after New Year's Day, toy sales suddenly drop slowly, picking up momentum through the year until once again, they magnify at Christmas. The world's toy industry leaders meet in New York at both the Toy Building and the Javits Center for several weeks each year during February in a massive demonstration of show-and-tell. The toy manufacturers secretly reveal their new items to the retail store buyers and a yes or no nod from important buyers determines the life or death of a new toy.

Innovation and creativity make the toy business challenging and executives seek to surround themselves with staff members who have the skill to develop new ideas, substantially improve old ideas, and understand the timeliness of their ideas to motivate both children and their parents. Sometimes the timeliness is more important than even the creativity of the toy itself.

Murray Appleton pondered this belief. It was strange that certain innovative ideas suddenly emerged at each Toy Fair. Six different companies had the same item, all somewhat different, but one company had developed the item first and that firm received the bulk of initial orders. In many cases, Ideal Toy was ahead of its competitors. Why?

He asked himself this question over and over again. There was another question that puzzled him. Why was Henry so angry with Roland when he showed him the sketches that Lou had made for new toys? It evidently was Lou Mangini who had stolen these ideas from sketches that he found in Henry's desk at the Ideal Toy showroom. Did Henry make those sketches? If he did, or even if he didn't, why did he hide them in the bottom drawer of a desk that he only used during Toy Fair?

Murray Appleton did not believe in secretaries. "They just sit around and chew gum," he would tell everyone. "I'm the gum-shoe here and I don't chew," he would wink. Anyone who was in the office answered the telephone and when they were all out, there was the telephone answering machine and the facsimile machine. During the morning hours, Murray, Rose, Jack, and Bill were usually in the office going over time sheets or discussing their combined efforts on some of their cases. This morning, the four of them were sitting together on the couch and chairs surrounding the table in Murray's office.

"I've gone through all the records at the Motor Vehicle Bureau, the United States Postal Service, and I've questioned a number of people who knew Henry Isserman, even his former wife," said Rose. "He has had a number of jobs in the toy business during his forty-two years, lived in a number of different places, but he has never been in any trouble."

"I have been tailing one of the men whom Rose first spotted at the Chinese Restaurant," said Bill. "His name is Joe Casey and he is on parole for a bit he did for shoplifting. No other record. He is twenty-five years old and I don't trust him. He's got some kind of a racket."

"Well, Tony Nelson, the other guy, is the strong man. I tailed him to the gym," said Jack. "He looks and acts mean."

"Rose," said Murray. "I think it is time that you carefully review the police records for both of those guys. They seem to be working some kind of a scheme. Maybe Henry is part of it. Maybe he was a dupe. We have to check his bank account. But, sure as hell, Roland Levy had nothing to do with these guys. I'm going to tell Harold Misson to drop the charges against him. Then we must find out why Henry made him the patsy."

"So, we have two guys, Joe Casey and Tony Nelson, who have some kind of a money making scheme involving the toy industry," said Jack. "Let's go fishing. We should take mug shots of each of them, call on the top guys in toy companies, show them the pictures, and see if we get a bite. Either Henry is one of the instigators of the scheme, or he is buying their illicit services. If he's buying, some other guys in the business are also buying."

Rose stood up from her seat on the couch and moved to the window. "I've got a feeling about this," she said slowly. "I don't feel that either of these two guys is smart enough to master mind a scheme so big that Henry would place a man's career in jeopardy in order to protect himself. He threw Levy to the wolves because he feared someone or something. I think that Casey and Nelson are just messengers and this is a ring organized by someone big in the toy industry and he has guys like Isserman shaking in their boots."

The telephone rang. Murray went to answer it and the meeting ended.

FORTY-THREE

THE EXPLOSION sounded like a dull thud, but it could be heard by the people who lived in the apartments above the stores on Flushing Avenue and some of them, awakened at 2:15 A.M. by the noise, leaned out of their opened windows to look for the cause. There was silence for some minutes after this first thud, but it was soon followed by a louder one that brought sleepy faces to the opened windows on this warm, sticky night. Then a gunshot sound echoed through the darkened and isolated street, a car engine started with a loud whine. Screeching tires skidded on the road and loud voices shouted from the car as it raced along the street. From the opposite direction, the sirens of a speeding fire truck awoke everyone else who had been asleep and several persons, hurriedly dressed, began to gather on the sidewalk in front of their buildings. Their eyes focused in horror on the building across the street.

The Ideal Toy factory building was on fire. The blaze illuminated two windows on the top floor and the explosions had burst the glass, forcing the flame, the smoke, and a foul odor to escape into the hot summer night. The sleepy neighbors covered their mouths with handkerchiefs.

Two fire trucks raced to the scene and parked in front of the building. Ladders were extended, hoses were unrolled, and firefighters in protective gear climbed on to the ladders and as others moved into positions directing water hoses on the building, the firemen carrying hoses and pick axes entered the building from the two exploded windows.

Then, two police cruisers, with sirens blazing, arrived closely followed by an ambulance. Attendants quickly removed a stretcher from the rear door, entered the building, and soon emerged with a covered shape in the stretcher. As the ambulance left the scene, the police officers encircled the fire trucks, the cruisers, and the front of the building with yellow tape marked "Crime Scene. Stay Back Ten Feet." The fire diminished quickly, but the fire trucks and the police cruisers remained as the police and firefighters thoroughly inspected the building.

Irving Misson was awakened from a deep sleep by a telephone call from the police department. "There has been a fire at the Ideal Toy Company factory," said a somewhat bored voice from the Queen's police department, "and your name and number are listed as the person to call for all emergencies."

"Oh! My God! Was anyone hurt?"

"I'm not sure. I believe that there was a shooting. Please come as soon as you can. The building is still smoking."

Shocked, still not quite awake, and disturbed by the news of a shooting, Irving asked, "Was somebody shot? Was the fire on the factory floor, the storerooms, or in the offices? We have orders that must be filled."

"I think it was just a couple of offices. I don't know if they shot the perpetrator. Please come down as soon as you can." He hung up.

Irving dressed slowly, awakened his wife, and explained that there was just a small fire at the plant and suggested that she remain in bed. He was frightened, not quite sure of his next move. Should he call Harold at 3 A.M. or should he call Murray? Maybe it would be best to call his lawyer. As he backed his car out of the garage, he reasoned that it was best to see the factory first and determine the damage before calling anyone. The factory was his responsibility and Harold wouldn't expect to be called until Irving knew all the facts. It was normally a half-hour trip from Forest Hills, but with no traffic, he arrived in fifteen minutes.

"You can't park here," said the tall policeman as Irving Misson stopped his car in front of one of the fire engines and darted out toward the entrance to the building. "Get back into the car and move it."

"I'm Mr. Misson. This is my building. Who's in charge?"

"Just park it across the street, then meet me at the front door. I'll take you to the lieutenant."

"Thank you." Irving moved his car, locked it, and walked across the street to the entrance to the building.

"You're the owner? I'm Lieutenant Brown," said the officer at the front door. "We have just started the investigation. It looks like arson with a couple of homemade bombs that went off on the top floor and started the fire. The security guard was shot. On the way to the hospital, he said something about two men."

"When can I go in?" asked Irving impatiently. "I must see the condition of the office. Did you get any water on the dolls or the packaged goods? This is our delivery season."

The lieutenant led him through the first floor of the factory where there were many puddles of water, but no damage to any of the merchandise. They slowly walked up to the sixth floor executive offices and Irving couldn't control himself. "Who could have done this terrible thing? There are papers all over the floor, cabinets broken into, and everything is wet and has a horrid odor."

As they walked downstairs, Irving turned to the lieutenant and asked, "Was it the security guard whom you said was shot? How badly was he hurt?"

"We have no information. He was taken to the hospital. Do you know him?"

"No, we use a security service. The day men are regulars, but the guys that cover the evening and early morning hours change frequently. All the information about the service is in my desk, probably soaked with water. Can you tell me which hospital he was taken to? There is nothing that I can do here. I'm going home to make some calls."

The lieutenant promised to obtain the information and Irving Misson walked slowly to his car, started the engine, and looked sadly at the police cars and fire trucks parked in front of the factory. Irving drove home very slowly. His wife was waiting for him as he opened the front door.

"It's a mess and our security guard was shot, but I think that we can open the factory in the morning. Henry's office was all burned out and mine is soaked with water. I must call Harold. He'll be angry if I wait until morning. Why don't you go back to bed? I'll join you in a few minutes. I could use another hour or two of sleep."

Harold listened to his brother very quietly, annoyed that he was awakened, but pleased that Irving called him as soon as he did. He promised to meet him at the factory at 9 A.M. His mind raced with thoughts about Henry. *What was so important in Henry's office that forced someone to burn it? Was it that guy Lou who broke into the showroom? No— he is still in police custody—maybe still in the hospital. Henry must be in some kind of trouble. Is this a warning?* "Stop being a detective," he mumbled. "You have already hired one. Call Murray Appleton. That's his job."

Murray was a light sleeper and answered his telephone on the first ring. He listened silently, didn't ask any questions, and said that he would like to meet both Harold and Irving at the factory at 12 P.M. He promised that he would be there with one of his investigators.

Irving couldn't sleep. He lay in bed thinking about the fire. *Why would the perpetrator be so desperate as to shoot a security guard? What will we do next? This is the toy business. We make things for kids. What do gangsters want with toys?* The more he thought about the fire, his fantasies wandered, and by the time he arose from bed at 7 A.M., he was frightened. He dressed, drove to a diner for breakfast, and was at the plant by 8:30 A.M.

Two police officers were at the front door talking to the security guard and some of the workers who had just arrived. Irving greeted them all, told them that it was safe to go back to work, and that he was investigating the fire in Henry's office. Harold arrived promptly at 9 A.M. and the two brothers sat down to talk in a small sales office on the second floor. The injured security guard was still in a coma, but was expected to live. They waited for Henry, but by 11:50 A.M. when Murray and Bill came in for their meeting, Henry had neither arrived nor telephoned.

Murray and Bill inspected the damage to Henry's office, Bill made some notes, and they both returned to the second floor office. "These are dangerous characters and this was just a warning to Henry," said Murray. "He's scared now and over his head in some deal. He probably will talk, if we can find him. Give me two more days. But don't do or say anything to anyone except that this was merely an accidental fire." The detectives left quickly.

FORTY-FOUR

ROLAND LEVY sat wrapped in a towel on the wood slat bench in the sauna under a dimly lit overhead light at 7 A.M. The timer was set for thirty minutes. Many questions were still unanswered and his mind wandered, individually considering each of them. He could not understand the apparent tie between Lou Mangini and Henry, and was puzzled by Henry's horrible accusation that he was responsible for Lou's crimes. Now he was told that Lou was in jail and Henry had completely disappeared, left his job, and vacated his apartment a week before with his Buick Park Avenue still parked directly in front of his building. The lawyer told him that his case was dropped, that the Misson brothers had dropped their accusation of him, and there would be no further criminal or legal charges. But he wondered if his client's would understand that the criminal charges were completely false. Both *Advertising Age* and *Playthings* must run stories to explain the mix-up.

The bell rang softly and the gas flames around the coals within the gas sauna heater gradually diminished. He rose from his seat, still wrapped in the towel, placed each foot into a white rubber sandal, opened the sauna door, dropped the towel to the floor, and entered the adjourning shower stall. It was 7:30 A.M. He reminded himself that he was to meet Susan Liforest and Ellen Burton at the Beekman Tower Hotel for breakfast at 9 A.M. The first spray of cold water tingled through his whole body and he gradually turned the warm water knob until he felt warm and cozy once more.

He dressed quickly, donning a white shirt with blue pin stripes, white collar, and French cuffs, and a broadly striped tie with alternating blue, white, and sand colors. *Suzy likes this combination with my oxford gray suit,* he thought, remembering the early days when she urged him to discard his jeans and wrinkled cotton pants in favor of a business suit. "Since you want to live and work in the corporate world," she said, "you must dress in a fashion that will make others believe that you belong there."

Peter Smith arrived at 8:15 and they made a round through the studio. At 8:45 A.M., he met the limo driver in front of the building and they drove to the hotel.

When Roland entered the restaurant, Susan and Ellen were seated at a table with a carafe of coffee and two half empty cups in front of them. He smiled at them both, shook their extended hands, and sat down opposite them at the table. They had arrived a little earlier since Ellen had already checked out of the hotel and had a scheduled flight back to Atlanta at 1 P.M. He asked Susan how she was feeling and she responded, "A bit tired, but ready for an exciting day. How are you? I already told Ellen that you left my apartment at 12:30 A.M. We don't have any secrets." She blushed slightly and then smiled.

"Oh! Come on guys. We've got a lot to talk about," interrupted Ellen. "I spent a good part of yesterday talking with Harold and Irving, and then I spent some time with Murray Appleton and his staff. I am so worried about Henry. Murray and I even went up to his apartment. He left so hurriedly there were papers and discarded clothing all over. I was crying through most of last night. He must be in trouble or he would have called me."

"What really happened?" asked Roland. "All I know is that Henry's office was bombed, a security guard shot, and a lot of papers burned and water soaked. Then someone realized that I was a patsy and dropped the charges against me after they nearly put our whole firm out of business."

"Let's order some breakfast," said Susan. "We'll talk as we eat."

They gave their orders to the waitress and as soon as she left, Ellen continued talking. "Murray explained that his investigators tracked the two men who were seated with Henry in the Chinese restaurant and he gave their home addresses to the police. He believes that they were probably the men who planted the bomb and shot the security guard. The police arrested them yesterday on suspicion, but they can't hold them too long. So far, the men are scared and refuse to talk, but they are just tough guys. The security guard is still in the hospital, but his condition is improving and they expect to bring him to headquarters to identify the men."

"Do they have any idea who was behind the scheme or even what they were after?" asked Roland.

"So far, Murray has a few ideas," said Ellen, "but he is still working on the case. He thinks that there is some higher up group or even one top figure that organized this crooked scheme. Murray believes that they hit about thirty toy companies for many thousands of dollars each, and that this is just the beginning. Henry probably went along with them at first. You know that he is a very curious fellow. Eventually, he either asked too many questions or he tried to stop working with them. Your sketches may have frightened him. Murray thinks that he believed you were in with them. He got you out of the way to save his own skin."

"I still do not understand what it was all about. What were they trying to do?" asked Susan. "What were executives like Henry paying for?"

"Well," said Ellen. "Harold explained it this way. He called it knock-offs. One company gets a hot toy idea and as soon as it begins to take off and they begin to make money on the item, the other companies copy it and sell it for less. The first company loses a lot of its anticipated sales if the knock-offs get on the market early."

"So how does the scheme work?" asked Roland.

"Do you know how many companies are making Tell Time Baby Dolls?" asked Ellen. "So far, there are six excluding Ideal Toy. I can't complain since we are supplying the clocks for all of them, but Henry was furious because they all went into production at about the same time. They weren't knock-offs. Somebody sold the same idea to all the competing companies . . . and they must have paid a lot of money for it. Irving is checking on payments that Henry authorized to designers and inventors. It must be over two hundred thousand dollars. Some of it must have been involved in this scheme.

"Bill, one of Murray's investigators, gave Harold his opinion on how the fraud may have operated," continued Ellen. She was beginning to talk quite loudly with considerable anger in her voice. "First, they sneak into toy firms looking for new items. He says that it is easy to get into most toy factories and showrooms because they are not usually guarded. If the guys know where to look, they can find the new items. Then they send someone to a toy company, show the marketing executive the new idea, along with some evidence that a leading competitor is going to introduce it into their line next year. Anxious to beat the competitor, the company executive may buy the plans for ten thousand dollars, maybe more or less. But instead of being exclusive, every company is sold the same set of plans."

"With an operation as big as that," said Roland, "they must have an office somewhere, a bank account, and even some unsuspecting workers."

"Murray told Harold that the scheme may have been started by some small toy design firm," Ellen said, her face now quite red and her expression showing her angry feelings. "He thought that it may have been taken over by one of the large crime families who saw an easy mark in the billion-dollar toy industry. They have the organization and manpower to contact the hundreds of toy companies all over the country. They may use college students, anxious to earn some extra money, to first show the idea for a new item, but they follow up with mobsters like the two guys that blew up Henry's office."

"Henry may have caught on to the scheme," suggested Susan, "and held on to some of the items without paying their price. Maybe that is why he met them at the restaurant in Murray's building. So they scared him and destroyed everything with a bomb."

"When you play games with the mob, you always lose," sighed Ellen. "Now he is either running away from them or they have injured him. Murray told Harold that they probably just frightened him to run away. He is too small a peg in their business to take a chance with a murder. He thinks that they are even going to let the two mobsters go to jail for attempted robbery. They have many more thugs to fill their shoes. They'll just wash their hands and continue the business somewhere else."

As the morning progressed, Ellen kept glancing at her watch. "It is time for me to go now," she said at 11:30 A.M. "I'll keep in touch and if you have any good news about Henry, please call me." She kissed them both and the hotel attendant whistled for a taxi, helped her with her suitcase, and she waved as the cab headed toward the Triboro Bridge to LaGuardia Airport.

FORTY-FIVE

"I'M FRED Winrich," said a good-looking, well-dressed, middle-aged man. "I'm the CEO of Winrich & Sons, Inc. We're plumbing contractors. We engineer, install, and service complete plumbing, heating, and air conditioning systems in major New York buildings. We have been doing this since 1903. I'm looking for leads to architects, builders, real estate developers, and owners or board members of large buildings or condominiums. This week, I wish to thank Conrad Fina for a personal introduction to Roy Batiste, the senior vice president of Hemsley-Spear."

It was Roland Levy's first meeting as a member of the Executives' Association of Greater New York. He listened attentively to Fred Winrich and then to Les Greenberg as he spoke about his advertising agency, BBDO. Then, he listened to the five other men and one woman who sat at his table as they introduced themselves and their businesses. They were all top executives from leading New York corporations specialized in different industries, and everyone was seeking contacts to expand their business. As a new member, Roland's turn was last. Looking at the faces of executives whom he once feared, he smiled to himself. Then in a soft voice, he proudly explained that his firm designed products, packages, and corporate identification programs for some of the largest companies. He said that he was interested in meeting the chief executive officers of major product marketing firms.

Jimmy Zamparetti of Best Employment, Inc., sitting next to him at the table, turned toward him and asked nonchalantly, "Do you want to meet the president of Mattel Toys?"

"I sure do," answered Roland in an excited tone. "We have been trying to make a presentation before one of their executives for several months."

Jimmy smiled. He was a heavy set, good looking man, dressed in a well fitted, double breasted dark blue suit with a dark red silk tie and a light gray shirt. His white French cuffs peaked out beyond the sleeves to expose gold sculptured cuff links. "I built my employment business from a one room office to a full floor on Wall Street in only twenty years," he said. 'I did it partly through leads from the Executives' Association and contacts on the golf course. I spent last week in Palm Springs. My wife and I joined a foursome with Henry Marts and his wife at the Marriott Hotel Golf Course. We later joined them for dinner at Wally's Turtle Restaurant. I didn't find out until dinner was over that he was the president of Mattel Toys. We're now interviewing executives in New York to fill two spots in his California firm. Since you're interested, why don't I arrange a dinner so you can meet him. Are you free some night next week?"

Les Greenberg, sitting on the other side of Roland, patted him on the back and explained, "See! Roland, baby. This is the way the Association works. You get one and then you give one. Aren't you glad that you joined?"

Roland was quiet for a few seconds than he looked at Jimmy and said, "Any night next week will be fine. I'd like to have Ms. Liforest, my vice president, join us for dinner."

"That's great," said Jimmy. "I'll call Henry and we'll all have dinner at Wally's. I should have two top candidates ready for him to interview in California next week, but we'll be meeting in the afternoon. Make reservations to fly to Palm Springs early Wednesday morning and check in at the Marriott. Tomorrow is Friday. I'll call you in the evening after I speak with Henry. You know that they are three hours later. When they start work at 9 A.M., it is 12 P.M. here."

Roland was a little uneasy. What had he done? It may cost five thousand dollars to spend a couple of days with Susan in California trying to land the Mattel account. His thoughts wandered. Suddenly, his fear of executives returned. He felt that he was caught in a trap. Les interrupted his thoughts.

"Mattel invests a fist full of money on product development and packaging. They must have an advertising budget in excess of forty million dollars on Barbie alone. My agency, BBDO, would love to have a piece of that account. Product development and packaging should be worth at least five million. And you have a chance to pitch your firm's creative ability to the top man in the company! It's surely worth the expense of a few days on the west coast."

Roland felt a little better. He thanked Jimmy and said that he would look forward to his telephone call. The executives at the table all turned their attention to the podium where Dan Rothe, of Rothe Public Relations, the president of the Executives' Association, started the roll call. There were sixty members present and during the remaining forty-five minutes, each one stood up, introduced himself and his company, and thanked all the members who had given him leads.

"Leads are the main purpose of this organization," explained Les Greenberg, "and more than seventy percent of them turn into profitable orders. Each week, our executive director, Karen Duncan, compiles a newsletter to all members listing the amount of business received. It's a whopper. Only about sixty of the ninety members usually attend each weekly luncheon meeting. Those not attending miss out on possible leads. With too many absences, firms are asked to leave. That gives us an opening to induct a new firm . . . and we get more leads." He chuckled.

As he left the meeting, Roland tried to remember the names of the people who introduced their firms at his table. He wanted to give Suzy their names and maybe she could recommend some of their firms to his clients. Maybe even solicit them for business. He remembered Sheldon Brilliat of Manufacturers Corrugated Company, and of course, Jimmy Zamparetti of Best Employment, Inc. Then, he had met Conrad Fina, president of the large insurance firm of Fina and Son. Jennifer-Lu Landau of Auto Leasing Center impressed him with her sharp wit and her salesmanship.

He wanted to meet the presidents of Right Time Moving and Storage, Mutual Parking, Skyline Displays, P-J Electric, and Chase Manhattan Bank as they introduced themselves during the roll call. *I'll have another opportunity next week,* he thought.

He shook hands with several people who introduced themselves to him as he left the dining room and walked down the hall. When he reached the front door, he spotted his limo driver parked at the entrance. Susan was sitting in the back seat writing in a notebook.

"What a pleasant surprise." He smiled, kissed her on the cheek, and sat down next to her. "We have a lot to talk about, but I need a rest first. That was a tiring ordeal."

"Don't get too comfortable," she said. "We're on the way to Revco. They are in the Lincoln Building at Grand Central. I've asked Bruce Brunswick, our new sales contact, to meet us there at 2:30 P.M. We're meeting with the president. Bruce has been working on this for several weeks and he set up this meeting today. I have made a number of notes about the company on this pad. Why don't you read it as we drive to their building?"

The limo driver proceeded along Park Avenue driving uptown, hindered by the slow moving traffic. He stopped for several red lights and moved frequently from the inner lane next to the flowering road divider and back to the center lane as cars slowed to make left turns. He was in no hurry. Roland needed the time to relax and to read Susan's notes concerning Revco. The driver finally stopped at the corner of Park Avenue and Forty-second Street.

"Your best bet is to get out now and walk across the street. If I make the turn onto Forty-second Street, we'll be in traffic congestion and the police officer may not let me stop the limo to let you out. The Lincoln Building is just a few steps from the corner with a subway entrance on one side and a large turn-style entrance."

"Thank you, Ferdinand," said Roland. "I'll call the dispatcher about a half hour before we leave."

"That's fine. If I'm available, I'll pick you up. If not, I'll tell the assigned driver to park at the Forty-first Street entrance to the building. It is less crowded there. You will find one of us there when you set the time."

They walked into the lobby and spotted Bruce Brunswick with a large portfolio under one arm and an attaché case dangling from the other. He was leaning patiently against one of the marble walls.

"Right on time," he said. "Revco occupies four floors in this building for their executive offices. But Mr. Duane Inmont, the C.E.O., wants us to meet him in a small conference room that he has reserved at the Lincoln Club on the fortieth floor."

"Glad to see you, Bruce," said Roland shaking his hand. "Susan tells me that you have already made a presentation of our work before some of Revco's executives. Evidently you have sparked some interest. It will be a challenge to meet with the boss and show him how good design can help his business. I'll let you and Susan take over at first since you are more familiar with the company and its products and then I hope to wind it up with the start of at least one project."

The express elevator took them to the twenty-first floor and then made local stops until it reached the fortieth. Several men entered on the upper floors and they all exited at the Lincoln Club. They followed the men as they left the elevator, turned right along the carpeted floors, and walked along a short hall that opened suddenly into a large comfortable looking lounge. There, a tall man with a blazer, white shirt, and blue striped tie greeted the men. The man welcomed them and signaled to a maitre-d', who ushered them into a large, but rather empty dining room on the right. Then, the tall man turned to Roland Levy who was walking in front of Susan and Bruce.

"This is a private club, you know. Do you have an appointment with one of our members?" His tone was quite unfriendly.

"Mr. Duane Inmont has invited us to meet with him here," answered Roland.

Instantly, his attitude changed. "Oh, yes. Mr. Inmont has reserved Conference Room C. It is the first door on the left at the end of this long club lounge area. Just knock on the door. He is expecting you."

As they walked along the lounge to the conference room, several of the men relaxing on soft leather chairs looked up and smiled. Roland nodded and returned a friendly smile. *This must be the mid-afternoon business break,* he thought. *This is where those prep-school snobby men gather. They really think that I'm one of them.* He looked down at his clean white French cuffs. "I look as good as they do," he mumbled under his breath.

Bruce knocked on the door marked "Conference C." Duane Inmont, a short and pudgy man with partially rolled up sleeves and a loosened tie, opened the door immediately. He had an impatient attitude with an obvious agility. "Glad to see you, Bruce," he said, extending his hand. "Call me Duane. So this must be Ms. Liforest and Mr. Levy, the design wizard I have been hearing about. May I call you Susan and Roland? We're all damn informal up here. Shake hands with the guys around the table. That's Darren Wagner, our product development chief, Hank Diffly, our marketing director, and Lewis Stanford, who heads manufacturing. You can call them all by their first names."

He sat down and motioned for them to take seats around a large oval table on which there was a corrugated box in the center. Bruce opened both his portfolio and his briefcase, standing to address the group.

"That's not necessary. These guys have seen what you have done for others. Put it all away," said Duane Inmont. "What I want to know in the next few minutes is what you can do for us. Darren has a working model of a new vacuum cleaner. Take it out of the box and let's all look at it."

Duane Inmost clearly was the boss. He was a man in his mid-fifties with a sun-tanned balding head encircled with graying hair, rim-less glasses, and a ruddy complexion from years of summer weekend sailing on his lake in Connecticut. The other executives were pale by contrast, in their mid-forties, and alert to all his authority. Darren Wagner, tall and handsome with blond hair and a bushy mustache, removed the corrugated cover and revealed a dull gray vacuum cleaner with a prominent Revco logo.

"Our competitors are selling this type of vacuum cleaner for seventy-nine dollars," he said standing and pointing to it. "It is a great chain store item. We can't get ours down below ninety-nine dollars. The stores would like to handle ours because it works better, we offer deeper discounts, and they make more money per sale. But . . ."

"But," interrupted Duane, "it looks like shit. I want a whole new image created for this Revco Wonder Electric Cleaner. I want a more feminine look that will appeal to women, a more friendly company logo, more attractive colors, and a self-selling display package that will show off this wonderful machine. Can you do it?"

Roland stood up, moved the model closer to him, and looked at it carefully for a few seconds. "We won't touch the mechanism. We'll design a new plastic housing edged in chrome. We'll coordinate the textures and develop exciting colors. Then, we'll create a new logotype and an entirely new package. By the end of the day tomorrow, you will have a complete proposal in your hands with all fees and a time schedule. This is the way we work. Both Susan and Bruce will be in touch with you."

"That's it," said Duane. "Darren already has paperwork for you to sign as a receipt. Take the damn thing with you and I'll speak with you tomorrow. I like the way you work." He stood up, followed by the other three men. They put on their jackets, straitened their ties, and accompanied Susan, Bruce, and Roland to the elevator.

FORTY-SIX

FROM THE patches of landscape visible between the clouds as they floated ethereally below the airplane, Palm Springs looked like a barren desert dotted frequently with irregular patches of green and surrounded by high mountains on all sides. Roland and Susan were puzzled by this strange landscape. The flight to Los Angeles from New York was uneventful, but they were looking forward to the short flight over the San Jacinto Mountains into Palm Springs. They expected to see a fairytale city cluttered with movie sets and the vacation homes of movie stars. Palm Springs was a disappointment. From their window seat in the two-engine airplane, all they saw was the dismal dunes. Los Angeles had sparkled. It was a magical world from the air with big buildings, wide city streets, and homes with tailored lawns. But Palm Springs looked like a barren desert waiting to be changed into a movie set.

As the small airplane sputtered and slowly descended to prepare for landing at the small Palm Springs International Airport, Susan suddenly called out, "Roland. It's beautiful. Those green patches are golf courses. I can see the palm trees and so many lovely homes."

In a few minutes, they were on the ground, descending the metal stairway from the plane, and walking into the Palm Springs International Airport. The baggage area was at the far end of the airport. As they walked under a long canopy, they could feel the pleasantly cool dry desert air floating in from the open sides. This was a refreshing change from the stale air conditioning during their long morning flight. Baggage retrieval was easy and Roland's automobile reservation from Avis was waiting in the rental car area.

Guided by an Avis map of Palm Springs, they drove along Tahquitz Canyon Way to Palm Canyon Drive. Turning left toward the Marriott in Palm Desert, they suddenly found themselves in the center of Palm Spring's historic downtown district. It was 4 P.M.

"This looks like such an exciting place," said Susan. "We'll just have to spend some time here after we complete our business."

"We've never taken the time for a vacation. You must have a lousy boss," Roland replied, winking at her.

They drove along Palm Canyon Drive and Route 111 for about twenty minutes, passing Frank Sinatra Road, until they reached Country Club Road. Then, following the map, they turned left and shortly found the road into the Marriott Hotel. Roland registered as Mr. and Mrs. Levy as Susan waited next to the bell captain with the luggage.

When they were settled in their room, he said, "I registered as Roland Levy and friend."

"And friend," she said snuggling up into his arms. "Is that all I am to you?"

"Well, I was a little embarrassed before the girl at the desk. She asked if I was here alone or with my wife. What was I to say? I said that she was that pretty woman over there with the luggage. She smiled and I signed as Mr. and Mrs. Levy." He blushed.

"Ruby dear," she said quickly kissing him on the lips. "What will we say to Jimmy and Mr. Marts?"

Just then the telephone rang.

"Roland, it's Jimmy. We're all set. Henry has a limo and driver. We'll meet you in the lobby at 7 P.M. I made all the reservations at Wally's. We'll have a private table in an alcove with Maurice as our table captain. Henry hired the two executives whom I presented to him this afternoon, so we're in his favor. He is looking forward to meeting you. Is your associate with you?"

"Yes. We're all set. And, you know that I am very grateful to you."

"You would do the same for me. I enjoy helping other guys build their business. It's my pleasure," said Jimmy.

"I need a bath and about an hour to sleep before getting dressed to meet them," said Susan as she removed her blouse and started the warm water in the tub.

"When you're finished, I just need a shower. I'm going to take the next hour to go over our presentation. It is going to be quite difficult to pitch a million dollar account during a social dinner. Important guys like Henry Marts still scare me. I hope that I brought the right clothes."

As he talked, she shut the bathroom door, stepped into the tub, and reclined in the soothing hot water. She thought, *He's at the top of his profession and he's still crying "poor me." I guess that I love him, but he makes me so fucking angry sometimes.*

Promptly at 7 P.M., Jimmy introduced Roland and Susan to his wife, Maria, and then to a smiling Marilyn and Henry Marts. "This is going to be a fun night," said Jimmy. "Henry makes wonderful toys, Roland makes them look better, and I play with them. I even have a Barbie, don't I, Maria? I keep it in my office next to my golf putter as a conversation piece. Everybody loves it."

"I bet that you don't have the new one," said Henry Marts. "We've created a beautiful Barbie on roller blades that you can put on and take off. Wind her up and she skates across the room. When Ruth Handler first created the doll, she did nothing but look pretty. We've made a modern woman out of her."

The limo driver greeted them at the door and in just a few minutes, they were at the entrance to Wally's Turtle Restaurant on Route 111 in Rancho Mirage. The hostess welcomed them at the reception alcove and ushered them to a table in the corner of the semi-private Foyer Room.

"Sit next to me, Susan. Roland, sit next to Maria. This way we can get to know each other," said Henry. "I enjoy good dining, but I enjoy business even more. So, we can talk about what you can do for Mattel all through this great dinner. Jimmy has been very helpful to me and he recommends you very highly. I only joined Mattel two years ago after a long stint at both Fisher-Price and Hasbro. I welcome new ideas."

The waiter handed them each a menu and then made several recommendations. "This is Wally's. You can have anything you desire. The chef will make it any way you like it and you can have as much or as little as you want. Can I assist you in your wine selection?"

"Jimmy, you pick the wine," said Henry. "Let's order and then I want to get to know Susan and Roland. I need a top creative firm to work on our new line, but I'm a tough guy to please."

Roland was happy that Susan was seated next to Henry. *He's one of those critical executives who still scare me,* he thought. *We've come all the way out here at our own expense. I must hide my fears and behave as an equally competent businessperson. Susan will charm him and I'll try to be the creative guy. God! I have a big shop with some great talent. We can handle anything. This guy looks like a prep. He's probably the third generation Marts. I hate him.*

"Henry, we are in our own building with full studio facilities, a dedicated staff, and we've created top selling lines for Ideal, Cardinal, Tyco, Empire, Irwin, and several other large toy firms," said Roland, gradually feeling his importance as a designer. "We no longer accept toy accounts on a project basis. We have too many top brand major product marketers. However, I love the toy industry and we are looking for one major manufacturer on semi-annual retainer. Maybe you are the company for us, maybe not. We'll have to see." His voice weakened as he finished the sentence.

Susan's eyes lit up. *He made it,* she thought. *Now he has Henry on the defensive.* She turned to Henry and said, "We recently turned Tyco down. We didn't have enough time to get a line of action toys ready for the February Toy Fair. But as Roland explained, on an annual retainer with one major firm, we can assign a full-time design team."

She always says the right thing, thought Roland. *I feel better with her support.*

Henry was quiet for a few moments and he slowly chewed his food. Jimmy started to break the silence with a joke when Henry looked up, dropped his knife and fork, and said, "I would like you both to come to our offices tomorrow morning to meet the staff and see our plans for the new lines. You'll fly with us in the company airplane and we'll get you back here by the end of the day. It's only about an hour-long flight. You won't need to check out of the hotel. Since that's all set, let's enjoy this fine dinner."

Roland just nodded. There was nothing to say. Henry made quick decisions. The conversation during the rest of the dinner was friendly; Jimmy told two jokes and by 9 P.M., Henry said, "I asked the limo driver to be here at 9 P.M. Let's go back to the hotel."

As they entered the Marriott, Henry invited everyone to take one of the little motorboats on the small lake that seemed to be part of the lobby. Steered by Venetian looking sailors, these little boats docked in the lobby where guests could board and travel to different restaurants and bars within the hotel. Jimmy and Maria gleefully joined Henry and Marilyn, but Susan said that both she and Roland were tired from the full day's trip and preferred to go to their rooms. They would see him in the morning.

"Wow!" exclaimed Susan as they reached their room and she sat down on one of the cushioned chairs near the window. "You certainly made a hit with that guy. He not only wants us, but he is also going to sell our services to his executives. We have nothing further to do until we see him again in the morning. Do you have any ideas?"

"Baby, I'm filled with ideas," Roland said as he snuggled next to her and pressed his lips gently against hers. "Why don't we just rip off our clothes and jump into bed. Maybe we will get an idea or two."

FORTY-SEVEN

THE AIRPLANE was more comfortable than either Roland or Susan had imagined. The cabin was very different from commercial airlines. All the seating was in a large U shape. The opening led to the double door where the two pilots controlled the flight. There was probably enough room for ten people to sit comfortably in the small space. Soon after take-off, the pilot announced that seat belts could by removed and Henry Marts walked over to where Roland and Susan were seated.

"This is a beautiful airplane, isn't it?" he asked. "It was one of the first big investments I made when I took over the company. These two jet engines can take me all over the United States. I travel now when I want to, not when the airlines decide to take me. And I can open new manufacturing plants in hard to access places where land and labor are cheap."

The flight lasted no more than forty-five minutes. Henry spent the time talking about himself and his plans for Mattel. The plane landed smoothly, a limo was waiting at the end of the landing strip, and in less than five minutes, they were in the office complex where they were ushered into the conference room.

"It was nice to meet you," said Marilyn Marts. "My driver is ready to take me home now. I only live a few miles from the plant. Henry is very happy that we all had a chance to meet for a social evening. Now he is anxious for you to start some really creative work for the company. I look forward to seeing you again soon." She extended her hand, both Roland and Susan took it, and she said good-bye.

When they were alone in the conference room waiting for Henry to return, Susan said, "Everyone thinks that we are already part of Mattel. Something is wrong here. We have not talked about fees, time, or patents. We don't even know the type of items that they want us to work on."

Before Roland could answer, Henry Marts entered the conference room followed by six executive, four men and two women. The men were wearing jackets and ties. except for the womn. The women wore pantsuits with a delicately flowered turtleneck. They chose seats on the opposite side of the conference table to Susan and Roland. Henry sat at the head of the table.

"Ladies and gentlemen," said Henry. "Before I introduce you to Roland Levy and his associate, Susan Liforest, I want you to know that I have asked them to travel across the country to meet with me and this morning, I brought them here in the company plane. They have an outstanding record in the design of marketable toys and I have decided to retain them as exclusive consultants to Mattel Toys. Susan and Roland, I want you to say hello to my group managers. Pearl Hagans is in charge of dolls, baby carriages, and tea sets; Clyde Jones handles all of our wheeled goods; Percy Goodman oversees all of our games; Bob Williams runs preschool toys; Judy Marcus is the leader of the kids' general toys division; and Larry Kaufman is the genius with our group of electronic toys."

Both Roland and Susan stood up and reached across the table to shake hands with all the executives. Roland was puzzled. *Has he decided to hire us without seeing our work?* Roland wondered. His doubts turned to confusion as Henry called for assistance and groups of Mattel toys were placed on the table.

"Roland," said Henry. "I have had my research department look into your firm, your clients, and your successful product designs from the moment that I agreed to join Jimmy Zamparetti and you for dinner. We spoke to the presidents of a half dozen toy manufacturers and they all gave you a rave review. Especially Harold Misson of Ideal Toy. He said that he caused you a little grief at one time, but that he apologized and he advised me not to let you get out of my sight. What do you think of that?"

"I guess that I'm embarrassed," answered Roland. "We work hard and we have a very fine creative staff. Susan and I came here because Jimmy said that we should meet you. I'm very glad that we did."

Susan joined in with, "I must confess that I have always loved Barbie. I really wanted to work with the company that created her."

"Well," said Henry, "we can't take the credit for Barbie. Ruth Handler created that image and we have been fighting to keep it alive with both little and big girls all over the world. I have a separate division for Barbie. Now that you have met the key players on my team and have seen a few of the new items, where would you like to go from here?"

Roland was pensive for a few moments. Then he said, "We have a few stops to make before we return to New York. I'll call my attorney to set up a retainer agreement, which he can fax to you in a few days. When we reach an agreement, send all your catalogs by overnight express and check the items that you wish us to consider first. We will organize our team and come back to you with a schedule."

Henry Marts stood up. The six Mattel executives all stood up; they shook hands once more, and left the conference room. Henry walked over to Susan and Roland. "I would like you to stay for lunch. I will have one of our guides show you through the operation here and after lunch, my pilots will take you back to the Marriott. You'll even have time to get in a few holes of golf."

It was a tiring day for both Susan and Roland. When they returned to the hotel, both of them went quickly to the telephones to speak to the office. Susan had a lengthy conversation with Bruce Brunswick and Roland discussed several design concepts with Peter Smith. He explained to Peter that he would give him the fax number of the hotel in Palm Springs where they expected to be the next day. He needed Peter to fax some of the product sketches to him there. They had room service send a light dinner up to their room and Roland called the Ingleside Inn in Palm Springs where he had a stand-by reservation starting the next day. The Inn had a cancellation and Roland and Susan's room would be ready by 2 P.M.

The Ingleside Inn is one of Palm Springs' treasures, a continental villa with elegantly restored rooms filled with antiques. It was the favorite of Garbo, Greer Garson, Marlon Brando, and even Salvador Dali. Located just steps from downtown Palm Springs, nestled close to the San Jacinto Mountains, the Inn was a lover's paradise.

As the Marriott bell captain placed their baggage in the trunk of their car, he remarked, "No golf clubs?"

"No," answered Roland, "we just didn't have time."

"Honeymoon," winked the bellman.

"Sort of," said Roland. He smiled as he slipped into the driver's seat of the vehicle and looked across at Susan.

"You seem to be having a good time," she said. "Was it at my expense?"

"No, my sweet. I was just thinking of the Inn."

They drove north along Highway 111 until it turned into Palm Canyon Drive, made a left turn at Tahquitz Canyon Way, and turned into West Ramon Road. There, they parked in the circular driveway behind an antique Cadillac roadster, and when Susan walked under the entrance canopy and saw the flowered tiny lobby, she grabbed Roland's arm and whispered, "I love it. It is so beautiful."

"Wait until you see the room," replied Roland. "They tell me that there is nothing like it anywhere."

"Ruby, it's breathtaking. I feel that we are in Paris with Dali, Picasso, and Gertrude Stein." She hugged him, kissed him on his ear, and said, "Let's walk in the garden near the pool. Then we can go to our room."

As they walked, holding hands, she suddenly felt cold. What was she doing with this man in this beautiful place? Did he want to propose? Did she want to marry? This was her boss. He owned the business. She was earning a high salary, had a lovely apartment, and had the freedom to do as she desired. This man was a workaholic, dedicated only to his design work, and just wanted a bit of womanly warmth and sex for pleasure. She stiffened.

"Roland, let's look at some of the art shops. They say that Palm Springs has become the home for many contemporary artists."

He jumped at the idea and they left the gardens of the Ingleside Inn and walked toward the center of town on Palm Canyon Drive. They stopped frequently before the huge illuminated windows of the art galleries, smiled at the colorful abstract paintings, and mimicked the facial expressions on the portraits of Indian Medicine Men. As they walked toward Tahquitz Canyon Way, they passed the old Plaza Theater where Jack Benny enacted so many of his early radio broadcasts. Photos of Biff Markowitz and his long-legged beauties looked down at them from billboards advertising the Senior Follies.

They passed numerous sidewalk cafes filled with laughing vacationers who looked up from their drinks to extend friendly greetings. The crowd at Peabody's Coffee Bar partially blocked the sidewalk and across the street the tiny tables at Einstein's Bagels and Starbucks Coffee were clogged with trays, cups, and happy couples enjoying each other's company.

Susan and Roland held hands and walked slowly past the huge mall structure dotted with even more restaurants, and at the far end they stopped to listen to the music of the Latin band playing at the sidewalk cafe of the Hyatt Hotel. When they reached Alegro Road, Roland pointed to a sign.

"Look Susie," he said. "This sign points to the mountain and the Las Palmas section of the city. Let's walk along Alegro Road. Some celebrities live there."

When they reached Belardo Road Susan said, "Rubie, there is an elaborate candelabra lighting fixture in front of this home. I wonder who lives here?" She stopped a distinguished looking gray haired man who was walking along Alegro Road "Can you tell me who lives here?" she asked.

"Well," the man smiled. "Liberace, the famous pianist, used to live here. He always had a candelabra on his piano. He died a few years ago. It's a Spanish Hacienda style home, very large with seven bedrooms and eight baths. Each one has gold plated faucets."

"Thank you," said Susan. "I'm so glad that you passed by. Can you tell me something about that huge building close to the mountain? It is beautiful with graceful curves and overhanging roofs."

"That's Frank Sinatra's synagogue," said the gray headed man. My name is Norman Brown and I was there when he raised three million dollars and then gave it to the Synagogue. Mr. Sinatra was a generous man who lived in Palm Springs for forty years. He hosted three expensive gala dinners attended by his friends and fans and then gave all the money to Temple Isaiah."

"What a lovely story," said Susan.

Mr. Brown continued, "There is a remembrance plaque with an eternal light on the wall in the Sanctuary for both Frank Sinatra and his mother. Why don't you walk up to the building. The brilliant new Rabbi, Jordan Ofseyer, would be pleased to welcome you. So will his friend, Father Andrew Green of the nearby St. Paul's Episcopal Church."

"Thank you," said Roland taking Susan's arm. "We have a long walk back to our hotel. We'll save that for another time."

FORTY-EIGHT

THE LETTER did not contain a return address. It was typewritten on plain white paper and the plain envelope was addressed to Roland Levy at Roland Levy Industrial Design, Inc. Maxine Nierman had opened the envelope as she did with all Roland's mail. This letter was one paragraph long, double-spaced, and the only identification was a rather cryptic signature. As she prepared to toss the correspondence in the trash, she suddenly deciphered the signature. It was "Henry."

She grabbed the telephone.

"Roland, we have a letter from Henry," she said in a very excited tone. "I think that it as an apology. Do you want me to send it up to the office now?"

"Please, send it up right away. If Susan is in, ask her to come into my office when the letter is delivered."

It had been six months since Henry disappeared and Roland often wondered what had happened to him. That horrible night in jail and the court appearance were still vivid in his mind and probably always would be. He could never forgive Henry for so strongly accusing him. Fortunately, Ellen Burton and Les Greenberg helped the Misson brothers to search for the truth. Maybe this letter would help them understand. He had really believed that Henry was his friend.

Maxine was too concerned to send the letter up with a messenger. She carried it to Roland's office herself and came in along with Susan. Both of them were excited. They had read the letter, but they waited without any comments until Roland had finished reading it. Then Susan asked, "What does it mean?"

Roland read the paragraph three times before he started to speak. "This is all in long hand. Henry writes that he is sorry if he caused any aggravation. He apologizes to me and writes that he now has a new life no longer with any connection to the toy industry. That's all he says. Why now? Why does he write a letter to me now? He has been away so long. Why not forget the whole episode?"

Susan was deep in thought. "Maybe Henry didn't write it. Maybe it is someone who thinks we know where Henry is and this may be his way to find out."

"Sure," said Maxine. "Now that we have the letter, we will call him on the telephone, if we know where he is."

"What you say is all very reasonable. I'm going to call Irving Misson. He knew Henry better that anyone else. Maybe he can shed some light on this. I'll hold the letter and as soon as I have any information at all, I'll share it with you."

The women left and Roland dialed Irving Misson's number at the Ideal Toy factory. "Irving, this is Roland Levy. I just received a strange letter, which we think was sent to me by Henry. I am going to send it to you by overnight mail. In my opinion, I think that he is in deep trouble and is signaling to us to help him. Maybe you should involve Murray Appleton."

Irving had very little to say until he had read the letter. They he called Roland, thanked him, and said that he was going to take his advice and send it to Murray. "It could be a ploy, a hideous joke, or a cry for help. We'll let Murray figure it out."

Murray Appleton worked very quickly. He studied the envelope, the postage stamp, the handwriting, and two days later, he called Irving with these facts. "It is Henry's handwriting, so we must conclude that he is alive. I'm not sure if he wrote it on his own or under pressure from someone else. The letter was mailed from Chicago. If you would like to go further with this, I can send one of my investigators to Chicago and I may have an answer for you in one week."

"I would like to find him and talk with him," said Irving. "Let's go for a week. Call me when you have some real information."

Bill, Murray Appleton's investigator, flew out to Chicago and settled in a rooming house near the Loop. He said that he was a salesman and needed the room just for one week. He had a good description of Henry and he searched for him in bars, cheap hotels, and in retail stores. He reasoned that a stranger needing money could always find employment in a stock room. After three days, he thought that he saw him unloading women's clothing from a truck into a discount fashion store. He telephoned Murray for further instructions.

Murray reasoned that he was hiding from some dangerous characters. If Bill, whom Henry did not know, stopped him, Henry could respond with violence. It would be natural for him to assume that his whereabouts had been discovered and that Bill was sent to harm him. Perhaps if he saw Irving or Harold Misson, he would be relieved, would explain his disappearance, and would accept their help. Murray felt that he had to advise them of Bill's successful investigation and to urge one or both of them to go with him to Chicago.

Harold's response was negative. "I'm furious. Isserman got himself into this by associating with some scheming criminal bastards and I'm not going to take time off to save him from them in Chicago. He hurt the company very much and he betrayed our trust. If Irving wants to go, he's crazy."

Irving was more responsive. "I worked closely with Henry and I'd like to give him the benefit of doubt. I don't know what happened, but if he is in serious trouble, I feel that I should help him. I can leave for Chicago in the morning."

Murray Appleton made all the arrangements and both he an Irving were on the morning flight. They met Bill for lunch and the plan was to have Irving wait outside of the store at the end of the workday and then walk up and talk to Henry. Both Murray and Bill would be nearby in case they were needed. Murray had reserved two adjoining rooms at the Hyatt hotel and that is where they planned to have Henry explain everything to them.

Irving stood on the street corner looking at a newspaper and leaning against the brick wall near the back door of the apparel building. He was nervous. He frequently looked up from his paper to see the reassuring faces of Bill and Murray who were standing at the other side of the door. He didn't have the patience for detective work. Suddenly, he spied Henry. He was sure that it was he. He wore faded blue jeans, a gray tee shirt, partly covered with a black motorcycle jacket, and dirty white sneakers. His face looked dirty, very tired, and he seemed to be deeply in thought.

"Henry?" questioned Irving in a soft voice as he approached him, walking very slowly.

Henry stopped suddenly at the sound of his name. He looked deeply into Irving's eyes, blinked as if awakened from a dream, and grabbed Irving, encircling him with both of his arms as if he never intended to let him go. Murray and Bill walked up to where they were standing.

"Irving! I'm so glad to see you," he exclaimed in a voice little above a whisper. "This has been a frightening experience. I'm all worn out." Irving felt tears because Henry's face was close to his. Henry broke away as he sensed the presence of the two other men.

"Who are they? What are you trying to do?"

Murray responded quietly, looking directly at Henry and smiling. "Ideal Toy hired me to find you. We would like to help you. You'll be safe if you come with us."

Bill walked to the intersection to look for a taxi and returned quickly with an old cab that had seen better days, but it was large enough to seat all four men. He sat in front with the driver and Henry was comfortable in the rear seat flanked by Murray and Irving.

"The Hyatt Hotel," said Murray, and the driver took off like he was starting the Indy 500. Upon reaching the hotel, Irving paid the driver and then he followed the others as they walked to the elevators.

Once in the room with the door locked, Murray called room service and requested drinks and assorted sandwiches. He had to talk to Henry first before he could make any plans, even for dinner. But Henry just sat on the sofa and looked at everyone suspiciously.

Irving was the first to break the silence. "Your office at the factory was bombed and the building set on fire. Did you know that?"

Henry nodded. "That afternoon I left for Chicago, running to save my life."

"Who was running after you?" asked Irving. "Will you please start from the beginning and tell us what this is all about."

Henry started to speak. His voice was very low and he stopped frequently to clear his throat. "It all started with the Tell Time Baby Doll. We gave the project to Levy, spent some money, and we got a beautiful doll and a great selling package. Then one day, you brought in a doll design and a package designed by Lou Mangini. It was practically the same thing. I tossed it aside and we produced Roland Levy's design and made a bunch of money."

"Then," he continued, "I began to see the same concept being produced by several other firms. They were not cheap knock-offs. Each company thought that they were first with the idea. Someone had sold each of the firms the same idea. I had a meeting with Lou and gave him some money, but he told me nothing. Then we caught him stealing our toy concepts. Although it was hard to believe, one day Roland Levy came to see me with a pack of sketches. And what were they? They were copies of our new secret items. This was no coincidence. The only way that he could have gotten to these ideas was theft. And that little weasel Lou said that Levy paid him to do it."

"But what caused you to disappear?" asked Irving. "You left your car, your apartment, everything. Who were you afraid of?"

"Well, I started to question Lou in the hospital. He assumed that I was involved somehow and asked me if I would be interested in seeing a friend of his who had some excellent new toy ideas. I said yes. A few days later, two guys came to the factory to see me. They asked me to give them a purchase order payable for one thousand dollars for five new toy designs. Curious, I wrote a purchase order and they arranged for a meeting in a restaurant at 250 Broadway. Their names are Tony Nelson and Joe Casey. One of them went to the cashier at the factory with the purchase order and received a check to the Main Line Development Company. A few days later, we met at the restaurant and they gave me the drawings for five items. They said that they had twenty more. I just could not believe it. The items were really good."

"So what did you do?" questioned Murray. "Did you make the items?"

"No! Being suspicious of Lou Mangini, I began calling up people I knew in other companies. Before long, I discovered that these same two guys had sold the ideas to five other companies. So, I called them and we had another meeting at the Fifty-seventh Street Chinese restaurant. We had five more after that, during which they gave me more items and collected about fifteen thousand dollars. Finally, I told them that I hid all their plans in my office, that I knew all about their scam, and that I was going to the police."

"What happened then?" asked Murray.

"Well, Tony came to see me at the office. He leveled with me and said that nothing would happen if I shut up and kept quiet. He said that there were some big guys with lots of money behind this. They had crews of young thugs who broke into toy companies and spies in other firms who sold them the ideas. There are many guys like Joe and Tony who push it. Before he left, he twisted my arm and kicked my stomach so hard that I was in pain for a week. At the end of the week, a little frightened, I was determined to go to the police. I was too embarrassed to tell you about it, Irving. Then, the shit hit the fan."

"Whom did you think you were dealing with?" asked Irving.

"I didn't know. I thought that it was some small time thugs like Lou Mangini. But one night, a guy rang my bell at home, forced his way into my apartment, and made a punching bag out of my face. He told me that some of the biggest guys in the toy industry were behind him and that they decided that if they found me in New York by the end of the next day, they would kill me. He then put my right arm on his knee and broke my wrist. I went to the emergency room at the hospital, a doctor put it into splints, and I slept soundly that night. I haven't slept well since that night. Early in the morning, I received a telephone call. The guy said, 'If we see you alive tonight, you'll soon be dead.' That was six months ago."

Everyone was silent. Then Irving asked, "Is the scam still operating?"

"I haven't heard a thing in six months. Maybe they have made their millions and have left the toy industry. I'd love to come back, but I'm afraid to go home. My name here is Charlie Smith. If you would help me find a job with a toy company in Chicago, I'd be very happy." He looked more relaxed now and Irving began to see signs of the old Henry Isserman.

"I have a few friends. I'll have Murray get you a new wardrobe and tell you whom to call for a job," said Irving looking down at his dirty clothing. "I'll send you your retirement fund and our law firm will help you to change your name." He shook Henry's hand, and said, "Goodbye, Charlie." Have a good life. You disgraced our company. Harold and I never want to see you again."

As soon as Irving Misson left the room, Murray Appleton beckoned to Bill to pull up his chair and move closer to Henry. The three men were silent for several minutes. Henry looked at each of them and asked, "I'm very thirsty. Do you mind if I have something to drink?"

"I'll get if for you," said Bill, getting up and walking to the cart containing drinks and sandwiches. "Are we going to eat this stuff, Murray, or are we going to have a real dinner downstairs in the hotel?"

"What do you say, Henry? Want to have a good dinner with us?"

Henry smiled for the first time and looked a little more relaxed. "If that is an invitation and you will pick up the tab, I'll join you."

"Irving made a deal with you and he always keeps his word, so what you say to us only answers our curiosity. But Bill and I know that you are a damn liar. You were trying to buck the mob with a deal of your own. You were in this crooked scheme so deeply that you pocketed one hundred thousand dollars. When the boys found out, you gave them fifty thousand, promised them the rest, and then fled to Chicago with the money. It is all used up now. When you first came to Chicago, you lived at the Blackstone, bought new clothes, and got a job selling men's clothing at Wallacks. But you were too visible when you realized that there were guys looking for you. So you moved to a rooming house, took the name of Charlie Smith, and got this job loading dresses. Now you are broke and you're looking for a handout."

Henry sat quietly. Eventually, with a glass of Pepsi in his hand, he looked at the two men and asked, "Are you cops?"

"Private investigators," said Bill. "And smart enough to figure out this whole deal."

"What are you going to do? All I have is about one hundred dollars plus this twenty that Irving gave me. When Irving sends me my retirement money, I can make a new start in the toy business."

"Let's go down to dinner," said Murray. "It's all on Irving's tab. Bill and I have reserved rooms at this hotel for tonight. In the morning, we'll help you get new clothes and make the call to the Stromberg Doll Company here in town. The owner is one of Harold's old Ethical Culture kids. They will do anything for each other. So, you'll get a job there as Charlie Smith and get back into the toy business . . . in Chicago. But there is one thing that you must promise me."

"And what is that?" asked Henry nervously.

"When you are on you feet again, you will send me a full confession of your involvement in this mess. I'll try to square it all up with Harold Misson so you can be a respectable part of the toy industry again . . . as Charlie Smith."

"Can you do me a favor?" Henry whispered. "Let Ellen Burton know that I made a big mistake. Tell her I'm well and making a new start. I'll call her in a few months. She's a terrific woman. Maybe we can start over again."

FORTY-NINE

THE MORNING meeting at Roland Levy Industrial Design, Inc. was always at 8 A.M. on Tuesday and attendance was always limited to those who had received invitations on Monday. Each meeting was timed to last for two hours. Frequently during the last half-hour, one or more executives from a client company would be invited. Roland explained that because of the confidential nature of their work, clients were not admitted into the studios. But during these meetings, all the designers involved in specific projects could meet with the clients and discuss their creative ideas.

Susan was always present as the vice president of marketing. She prepared a design evaluation report for each client's project and directed the work of the two account executives. Her special assignment was the responsibility for the group of designers who were working on the Mattel retainer. Bruce Brunswick, the account contact executive who concentrated on work for food and housewares companies, attended the meeting when one of the clients in his area were being discussed. Henry Conwell handled the pharmaceutical, appliance, and general product design contacts with clients. He too was frequently invited to attend.

Peter Smith, the design director, attended every meeting and sat close to Roland. Together, they started every design project. Roland provided his creative insights and they both smoothed out a design direction that Peter developed into renderings and models through the group of artists on his staff. The system worked very well.

There were twelve members of the firm present for the meeting on Tuesday, 7 August. As usual, Maxine had arranged several trays of bagels with butter, cream cheese, and fruit preserves, and there was both regular and decaffeinated coffee. When they finished the first hour and a half of discussion concerning design work and the overall philosophy of the firm, Maxine knocked on the door and Lester Greenberg entered. Because of the many common clients, whom they both served, he had met most of the members of the staff before. He sat down in the visitor's chair next to Roland after filling a cup with decaffeinated coffee.

"As you all know, Les is a vice president of BBDO Advertising Company, Inc.," said Roland. "I have the privilege to announce that yesterday that name left the agency forever. It is now the United States Division of Grande Lyons Freres, the largest advertising agency in France. How do you feel about it, Lester?"

"*Oo-la-la! Três bien!* We're all as happy as a lark. They are a great group and by joining them, we will have offices all over Europe and even Asia. We're a world agency now, not just New York, Dallas, and Chicago."

"Hopefully this will bring new clients to our firm as well," said Roland. "We may open a West Coast office to serve client firms in Pacific Rim countries, China, and Japan. Would you like to see us grow?"

There was applause and a bellowing of yes. The meeting ended at 10 A.M. and Les, Susan, and Peter Smith retired to Roland's office.

"Roland, have you ever considered selling your business?" Peter asked.

Susan laughed. "This business is Roland. Nothing in life is more important to him. Nothing!" She did not look at Roland, but when she had finished saying it, he looked directly at her.

"It has all been a dream. I started small and with the help of everyone in this office, it has grown into reality. I don't think that I can stop. It is my whole life. The clients, the media, and the consumers closely monitor both industrial design and advertising. All the companies travel a straight path along Madison Avenue. We took big chances and made an end run. That is what this business really is, an end run on Madison Avenue." Roland spoke softly and paused frequently.

They were interrupted by a knock on the door. Maxine opened it slightly to look in. "Susan," she said, "Mr. Berger, the New York representative for Mattel, is here for your appointment. Shall I send him to your office or to the conference room?"

"Thanks. He's a bit early. Ask Eric and John to bring the models into the conference room and wait there for me. Give Jake Berger a cup of coffee and tell him that I will be along shortly." Then she turned to Roland. "Do you want to come to this meeting? I would like to get some input from the sales reps, too. It really is not too important, but it keeps everyone happy."

"No, Susan. You have a good grasp of the design direction that we have taken. Peter and I have gone over everything. The designs should speak for themselves. Ask Bruce to join you. I'll join you for the next meeting. I'd like to discuss this French agency take over with Les and Peter."

Susan left in a hurry, leaving the door slightly ajar. Roland got up to close it. Peter asked Les, "Will the new owners change any of the key personnel?"

"From what I understand from the original negotiations, we will continue operating as we have in the past. They will send a corporate executive here to coordinate the new international set up."

"What about John Hecht?" asked Roland.

"Gone. Well, not just yet, but soon—probably in a few months. He is pocketing a lot of money. I don't know what he plans to do. Probably retire and play some golf," he chuckled.

"And what will happen to you?"

"You are looking at the new executive vice president," he perked up proudly. "I'm moving upstairs to a new office, a new secretary, and a lot more bucks, I hope."

Roland was silent for a few moments. Then he asked, "Was John Hecht happy to retire?"

"We don't know. But the deal was too good to turn down."

Peter rose and walked toward the door. "I like it here just as it is. Send us some more clients and I'd like it even more." He left the room, closed the door, and walked into the studio.

Les stood up, placed both hands on his hips and standing in front of Roland, said, "You know, if you sell this shop to a big foreign corporation, you too can make some big bucks and still stay on if you wish."

Roland smiled. "Suzy would never forgive me." The meeting ended.

FIFTY

ROLAND LEVY rang the bell for apartment 2B. There were twelve buttons on the console at the side of the locked double doors on Carrol
Street in Brooklyn. He walked up the three steps and stood on the stone
landing until he heard the buzzer and as he pushed the door on the
right, it opened quite easily. He had taken the subway from the Fifty-
ninth Street station in Manhattan, getting off the train at the Sterling
Street station. He walked the few blocks to number 1106. It was a brick
faced building, six stories high with steel fire escapes extending from
some windows on every floor and air conditioners protruding from
other windows.

It was Sunday and he was going to have lunch with his mother.

The elevator in the small and barren lobby was old and very slow,
just as Roland remembered it. His mother's apartment was just two
flights up. *A little exercise is good,* he reasoned as he walked up the stairs
breathing quite heavily.

"Ruby!" said his mother as she waited for him in front of the open
door. "It is so good to see you. Come in. I've prepared a nice lunch."

Roland hugged and kissed her and followed her into the living
room of the small apartment. Since his father was in a nursing home suf-

fering from Alzheimer's disease and showing no recognition for anyone in the family, she had moved into this studio apartment. "I like it small," she explained to Roland. "There is much less to clean and I have everything that I need very close to me. The neighbors are nice and friendly. I read a lot, watch television, and go shopping. It keeps me very busy."

She had been living in this apartment for two years and during that time, he had only managed to visit her on two occasions. One was her birthday and the other was on the high Jewish holiday of Yom Kippur. He looked around the room. Most of the furniture from the old apartment was cluttered along the walls. Against one wall there was a narrow bed without a headboard on which she had placed three large pillows to serve as a backrest. She sat comfortable on this while she beckoned him to sit on the large upholstered chair. "It is very comfortable," she said. "I do most of my reading in this chair. For television, I like to lie back on the bed. It is more relaxing to watch it that way. And, I love to sleep in a narrow bed. It is very cozy." She smiled.

"Ma," he sighed. "You know that I've asked you many times to let me buy you an apartment in one of the newer buildings."

"Yes, Ruby. You do enough already. Once a week you send that cleaning service. They clean the apartment in one hour. They wash my sheets and pillowcases, make the bed, and do any of the other wash that I give them. That's all I need. Doesn't the apartment smell nice?"

"Mom, I speak to you on the telephone at least once a week, but all we talk about is how you are feeling. This is a quiet Sunday and I'm not busy, so I thought that we could talk about other things."

"Ruby! You're thinking of getting married again. Is it to that nice Jewish girl in your office?"

"No, Ma. I'm not ready for that again. Let's have lunch. We'll talk in the kitchen."

The kitchen was a long narrow room with an alcove just wide enough for a small round table and three chairs. The table was set for two and she began to take some food from the refrigerator and warm up two dishes in the microwave oven.

"You know that I don't fuss any more. I'm warming up the split pea soup and I have some chicken and sweet potatoes that I baked this morning. We can talk as we eat."

"Ma, do you know what I do? You know what I mean, what I do in the office?"

"I tell everybody that you are a big industrial designer. You hire people to draw pictures for packages and other things. I'm so proud of you."

"Do you remember when I used to draw things?"

"Of course I remember. Did you see the drawing that you made of your father? It's framed on the wall. In the closet there are sketchbooks. You used to draw people in the subway. You are a good artist, Ruby."

As they continued to eat their lunch in the small kitchen, she asked him, "Are you happy doing what you are doing? You seem to be making a good living. Your father was so proud when he told everyone that his son was an artist. 'He draws like Rembrandt,' he used to say."

"These days, I hardly draw. I make a sketch or two from time to time, but I have many artists who work for me. They draw although today they all use computers. It is so much faster and the drawings look better. We can even make copies in all different colors. It has become more like science than artwork."

"But you like to draw."

"Well, I really like to paint in watercolors. Remember the painting that I made of the lake at Prospect Park? We gave it to Aunt Bess who lives right near the park."

"Yes! It is hanging framed in her living room. She loves it and tells everyone that it was painted by a famous artist, her nephew, Ruby."

Roland was silent for a short time as they removed the soiled dishes from the table. "Let's talk in the living room, Ma. I must get back to the office. I have some work to do and I'm having dinner with a friend."

Mrs. Levy walked into the living room, sat on the bed, and said, "Son, your father was not a rich man, but he always said that he was happy because he loved his work. His brother-in-law, Bess' husband, Joe, died of a heart attack at age fifty-two. He made money and left his wife in comfort, but he hated what he did. He sold aluminum siding. You know, Joe was a great musician. He played several instruments."

Roland looked at his watch and then stood up. "Thank you, Mom, you were very helpful. I'll call you and I'll come back for another lunch soon."

"Maybe you'll bring a girl with you."

He smiled as they waited for the elevator. He left the building quickly and walked to Eastern Parkway. *No,* he thought. *No more subway rides.* He hailed a taxi and rode back to his office.

FIFTY-ONE

ROLAND WAS seated at his desk alone in the office one evening soon after the Sunday lunch with his mother. Looking up at one wall, lighted with tiny spotlights from a track in the ceiling, he studied some large color photographs of his work, all beautifully matted, framed, and hung close to one another. Among the group were photographs of a stunning bottle and label for a Swedish Vodka, a chrome and plastic scooter for a child of ten, a high-speed liquid food blender, a few perfume bottles, and some large plastic toys. It was a display of a mature and talented industrial designer, although it only showed a handful of his work.

His thoughts went back to the days when he graduated from college and had set up his first office. He was anxious to become a professional member of the American Society of Industrial Designers. He had gone to his first meeting as a guest and someone gave him a lead to Philip Morris. Then, pleased with the contact, he applied for membership and was invited to meet with the chairman of the membership committee. He was nervous. Would they accept his credentials? He diligently prepared a portfolio with samples of his best work. Two package designs and one trademark had been designed for client companies. The other examples in his portfolio were illustrations of a toaster, an electric iron, and a telephone, all for non-existing firms.

Holding his portfolio with its precious samples, he took the subway to Fourteenth Street and then walked to Fifth Avenue and Thirteenth Street. The meeting was scheduled for 5:30 P.M. at the Salmagundi Club. It was a gracious old brownstone building nestled between two large luxury apartment houses with a turn-of-the-century stone banister that seemed to protect the long flight of stairs at the entrance. From a picture window on the ground floor to the right of the stairs, a lighted dining room was partially visible, obscured only by a tree and bushes blossoming in front of it on the small lawn. The window on the left side provided a partial view of an office that was visible through partly opened vertical blinds.

He had been notified that it was a regular dinner meeting with the usual get-acquainted cocktail hour first. His personal interview was scheduled after the members finished dinner. The leather portfolio containing all of his samples was to be shown to Belle Kogan, the committee chairman.

As he walked up the long stone steps, a tall man followed closely behind. "Hi, let me open the door," the tall man said as he moved in front of Roland and opened the right side of the large black double doors. "They often get stuck," he said as they both entered the small lobby. "My name is Egmont Arens. I haven't seen you here before. Are you a new member?"

"My name is Roland Levy and I have an industrial design studio." Egmont shook his hand and they both removed their coats and gave them to the checkroom attendant. Egmont then pointed to a showcase built into the wall close to the entrance doors. "That is the actual oil painting pallet used by John Singer Sargent. He was a member here at the turn of the century. He died in 1925. All the famous American artists were members of this club."

There was a large parlor room opposite the checkroom and since the door was open, Roland walked inside. The room was dimly lighted, furnished as a lounge with elegant couches, chairs, and tables that reflected the mood of this nineteenth century building.

"That's the members' lounge," said Egmont. "Our meeting is downstairs."

"What is in the other room?" asked Roland pointing to the closed door at the end of the lobby.

"That's the main art gallery. There is probably a show being exhibited now. It is closed at night since there is no one here to guard the paintings. Let's go downstairs. There is another gallery there. I'll buy you a drink and introduce you to the fellows."

They walked down the wooden stairs with dimly illuminated oil paintings lining the wall. From the lowest step, Roland saw the wood paneled dining room directly ahead with tables all set for dinner.

"We turn to the left. There is the gang all bunched up in the bar. Follow me. I promised you a drink."

Egmont seemed very well known. He shook hands with everyone, addressing them by name and promised to see them later. He introduced Roland to Bob Gruen. "He is the president of the New York Chapter." Then he spotted John Vassos. "This is the great John Vassos, Roland. He designed the first computer for IBM."

As they approached the small and crowded bar, he ordered two martinis and then he walked with Roland down a small flight of stairs into the gallery. "We have a small exhibition here of some of the members' work. That is one of mine," he proudly said as they walked closer to it. "It is a new x-ray machine for dentists. Next to it is a washing machine designed by Lurell Guild and over there is a photo of the new dishes designed by Belle Kogan." Each time that Roland looked at a design, he promised himself that someday he would design a better one.

When the cocktail hour ended, a bell sounded, and the members moved into the dining room. Seating was informal and Egmont urged Roland to accompany him at a large table where he seemed to know all the members.

"You know," he said to Roland, "most of the members here are graduates of the Pratt Institute's industrial design program. Alex Kostelow, sitting at the end of the table, is the professor who directs the program. He keeps in touch with all of his students. At another table you will find his wife, Rowena Reed. She is the professor in charge of the first year program. A few of the members graduated from Carnegie Tech and also from The Chicago Institute of Design. Every year more colleges introduce courses in industrial design."

When the dinner was over, the members gradually said goodnight and walked upstairs for their coats. Egmont wished Roland good luck and left the dining room. At a table near the window, two men and one woman were seated. Roland walked over to them. "Are you Belle Kogan?"

"Yes," replied a pleasant looking woman of about forty. "We have left an empty chair for you. Sit down, open your portfolio, and show us you work."

Roland remembered this ordeal very clearly. They asked him where he went to school, where he learned to draw, where he studied design. He ignored many of the questions and told them about his office, showed them his stationery and business cards, and then he explained all the thinking that went into his designs. They weren't impressed. "Come back next year," Belle Kogan said. "If your work improves, we'll consider you for membership."

"I'll never make it," he whispered. "The designers don't want me, the clients don't want me." Now, fifteen years later, his office and client roster was larger than most of theirs. But he still had the same fears.

FIFTY-TWO

"SUSAN, THE last two jobs were late and I was very embarrassed," said Bruce Brunswick sitting on the couch in Susan Liforest's office. It was Saturday morning and she had called this informal meeting to keep in close contact with her account managers. "Darren Wagner is a patient guy, but he had Hank Duffy, the marketing vice president, waiting for two days to show our rendering of the vacuum cleaner to his field representatives," he continued. "He was pissed, but fortunately everyone loved the designs. We were only one day late with the initial sketches for the new logo. Is there some way that we can keep our planned schedule? Revco is a great account and I don't want some other firm stepping in just because we take a little more time than we promised."

Susan chuckled. "Roland is the culprit. He seems to take a little more time to review each job. Have you seen his desk lately? It's a cluttered mess. I just have to goose him up a little."

"Well, I have found a solution," interrupted Henry Conwell. "I just tell the guys at Kraft that we have a genius at the head of our firm. He gets new creative ideas in the middle of the night. Then, in the morning, he inspires the art directors and what comes out is pure genius.

They love it. But, seriously, we have to keep to our schedules. It is good business practice and we're working with some of the biggest business-es in the country."

"Thanks for your time, guys. I really appreciate the great work that you are doing. I'll talk to Roland. Incidentally, isn't it cold in here?"

"It sure is," answered Henry. "That's why I'm still wearing my coat. Don't they deliver heat on Saturday?"

"This is an old building, which we have modernized," said Susan. "We have forced warm air running through the ductwork and electric heating panels additionally in the offices. I have my own portable elec-tric heater, which on cold days, I usually place near the window. I'll turn it on now."

The two men left her office, took the elevator to the street floor, and departed, making sure that the front door was securely locked. Susan moved to her desk and spent about a half hour going over her records. Then she closed the lights and left her office. The electric heater was still functioning.

As she turned to leave the building, she noticed that Roland's door was slightly open. *If he is in, this is as good a time to speak with him about client deadlines,* she thought. She pushed open the door.

Roland was seated in front of his big desk, still wearing his pajamas. The desk was cluttered with art boards containing mounted color com-prehensives of various projects. He appeared to be studying each design and using markers, he was drawing variations right on top of the ren-derings. He looked up when Susan appeared at the door.

"Hi, Suzy. Come in. I thought that I heard you talking next door. I've been going over these drawings since 6 A.M. There isn't any food in the building today and it's just about lunchtime. Come down and have lunch with me."

"I don't know where we can go in your pajamas," she winked. "Are you planning to wear a bathrobe?"

"Oh! I'll be dressed in a few minutes. Come in and sit down."

Susan entered the room and walked to the desk as he quietly dressed in the bathroom and in front of his double-door wardrobe closet. His sketches were beautiful. He drew graceful curves over hard edge lines, extended some surfaces to produce more aesthetic proportions, and made the products so much more interesting than the original color renderings. *He is very talented,* she thought. *He creates beautiful things . . . but he is so sloppy.*

Fully dressed and ready to go, Roland took her arm and ushered her out of the office to the elevator. "Leave the lights on," he said. "I'll be working through the rest of the day, maybe even the night."

They entered a small luncheonette on Madison Avenue and Fifty-sixth Street and sat down at the first table that appeared to be empty. "This place gets so crowded during the week that it is standing room only. Do you ever eat here?" he asked.

"Quite rarely. The place is too busy. Whenever I do lunch in the area, I go to that sandwich shop, Au Bonne Pain, or something like that. Roland, I had a meeting this morning with Bruce and Henry."

"They seem to be doing very well," said Roland. "Are they keeping on top of things. Their job is to represent the firm. What I love, Suzy, is that they are both preppies. They went to prep schools and Ivy League colleges just like our big shot clients. Some of the clients still scare me."

"Roland, forget your personal problems. Our schedule gets screwed up often. The guys complain that they are promised a job on Monday and they are lucky to see it on Wednesday. Our clients are too big to fool with. If we make a delivery promise, we must keep it."

"I'll work on it. Peter Smith will tell you when a job should be ready for showing to a client. Then add two days. I need that time to review it. The only studio time I seem to have anymore is evenings and weekends. All day, I'm busy running a profit making business. I review purchasing, payrolls, time sheets, bank deposits, loan payments, and so much more. I feel that I am no longer an artist. Just a businessman."

When they finished lunch, they both walked toward the office. Suddenly, they heard sirens and two huge red fire trucks turned the corner and stopped in front of their building. The firefighters left their trucks and some pushed open the front door to run up the stairs while others hoisted a ladder from the truck up along the side of the building. Then they both looked up. There were flames emerging from a top floor window.

"Oh my God!" exclaimed Susan. "My office is on fire. Oh, fuck. I must have left the electric heater on and the window drapes caught fire. Let's get up there."

"No," said the police officer in front of the door. "No one can go into the building until the fire chief gives his okay.'"

Roland stood fixed in place in front of the building. He stood there immobile for several minutes. "Damn! There goes my weekend of design work. With all that smoke, the place will be a mess. Suzy, why don't you go home? I'll call a clean-up service and we'll have your office ready by Monday morning. Then I must telephone my lawyer."

"I'm sorry, Roland. I'll telephone later. Take care of yourself." She kissed him on the cheek and walked away.

"If I were an artist, I would not have this trouble," Roland said out loud.

FIFTY-THREE

ROLAND LEVY stood up from his desk, placed his hands on his hips, and slowly turned his head to look all around his office. This was more than an office. It was his home. It was his hide-away and the one place where he could be entirely alone with all his toys. The place where he once spent his most pleasant hours every day doing just what he wanted to do. The place that grew as he grew. But things had begun to change. Now, he only looked forward to his evenings and his weekends.

It was a modern room and was beautifully furnished. He was happiest during the evening hours when he was alone in this room.

He loved the lighting, all adjustable from switches and dimmers at his desk. He loved the walls, all covered with beautiful color photographs and renderings of his work. They were his concepts, further developed and coordinated by Peter Smith and the art staff, all graduates of industrial design colleges. Except for his oversized desk, the room was always clean and uncluttered. There was a small closet on one wall for visitors' clothing, which also served as a catch-all for the many items delivered or to be picked up during the day. On the wall, to the right of his desk, were two sets of beautifully paneled thirty-inch double doors. One set was locked and Roland kept the key in his desk drawer. The other one opened up to his personal dressing room. There was his toilet, his clothes closet, the sauna, and his special shower. The locked doors opened to a Murphy bed, which rolled down to provide his comfortable sleeping quarters. The only thing missing was a private kitchen, but when he wasn't dining in restaurants, he had his meals sent up to the office.

As he carefully surveyed his total living and working quarters, he felt like the chief of a major corporation, but deep down he did not believe it. He was bored with routine office work, bored with the restrictive complaints of artists, and even bored by the needless whims of clients. He was sorry for himself on one hand and happy on the other. Roland was caught in a web of his own spinning and immersed in a pool of mixed feelings.

He was interrupted by an interoffice call from Maxine Nierman. "Roland, Lester Greenberg walked in with two gentlemen. He said that they couldn't wait to see you, so the three of them are on their way to your office."

"Thank you, Maxine. Les is running a big operation now, so I guess that he has a reason to feel like a big shot. It's okay. I have the time to see him. In fact, I already hear him coming down the hall."

There was a knock on the door and without waiting for an answer, Lester entered and was accompanied by two men. "Glad to see that you are dressed, Roland," he laughed. "It's a private joke, he likes to work in his pajamas," he said turning to his two companions. "Roland, I would like you to meet my French colleagues, Mr. Pierre Antignon and Mr. Louis Lapui. They are executives with Grande Lyons Freres of Paris. They are a couple of experienced agency men. We call them Pete and Lou for short."

Both men smiled as they shook hands with Roland. "We have seen some of your company's work at Lester's office and I do not mind telling you that we were very impressed. We wanted to meet you and, if you don't mind, look around your shop. You have a rather big place here for a designer. Do you own this building?"

"Well," replied Roland, "we purchased it from the prior owner two years ago because we needed to make some major renovations. We own it, along with the bank."

"Do you have the time to show us around?" asked Pete. He was the shorter of the two, somewhat heavier, with the bearing of a man with a real purpose in mind.

"I'll do my best. Just follow me." They walked out of the office and into the studio where Roland waved at Peter Smith who was studying a model along with two other designers. He smiled and waved back, apparently too involved to break away from his discussion. Roland led them through the design and photography studios, the tech room where the large color printers and model making equipment were in use, the accounting and secretarial office, and finally to the conference room where they served themselves coffee and sat around the table to talk. Lou was the first one to speak.

"You have one of the best industrial design shops that I have seen. As an international advertising agency, we make our francs from the fifteen percent we get from the media. Often, the advertising is superb, but consumer sales are weak because of bad packaging. So, they cut the advertising program and we lose a great deal of commission. It adds up to a great loss."

"What we need," chipped in Pete, "is a company that can take a client's weak package and come up with a strong one. A great package will put any product up front with both retailers and consumers. Then, we come in with a long running advertising program."

Lester smiled. "What I like about these two gentlemen is that they are not subtle like us. They come right out with it."

"What are they coming out with? My whole business is based on the common knowledge that good packaging and well-designed products sell very well. You know! All you have to do is give us a packaged product, tell us where you sell it and to whom at what price, and the chances are that we will design a winner," Roland boasted.

Pete looked directly at him for a few seconds. Then he asked, "Would you like to sell your business?"

"It's my whole life," said Roland.

"We'll give you a whole new life," said Lou. "It's worth a lot of money to us. You can stay on as the chief and still keep the money."

"I don't know about that," said Roland. "I would have to do some serious thinking."

"Can I send an accountant down to look at your books? It is all confidential."

"What do you do then?"

"Then," said Pete, "we would offer you a great deal of money. Who knows, maybe you'll get a million dollars. You could go to Paris and live like a rich prince."

"Let me think about it. You can send your accountant down. Call me first so my accountant can be here with him. I don't know if I am interested in selling, but I would like to hear your offer."

FIFTY-FOUR

"LESTER, THIS is Roland."

"I've been waiting for your call and so have Lou and Pete. They go back to Paris in two weeks, so they have been somewhat anxious. Pete went to see another shop the other day, but Lou told me that he was very disappointed. He likes your set up! What's your decision?"

"It is a very hard one for me to make. I did speak to my accountant and he suggested that someone call him and he will set up a time when he can sit down with them in our bookkeeping office. Maxine will give you his telephone number."

"Thanks. I'll take care of it. See you at the Executives' Association luncheon on Thursday."

Roland hung up the telephone receiver and then leaned back on his chair. It was 2 P.M. He had lunched on half of a hamburger earlier and the other half was still balanced on the edge of a paper plate with a few French fried potatoes and spots of ketchup in the center. His desk was covered with time sheets, purchase orders, unsigned letters, today's mail, a large loose-leaf checkbook, and some financial reports. A wet towel at the corner of the desk was evidence of the coffee spill that occurred thirty minutes before. He held a can of Diet Coke in his left hand and started tapping on the desk with his right hand.

He mumbled intermittently to himself. Sometime his voice could be heard in the studio, but the music that continually played in the studio over-powered anything that he could say. "Clients say that I'm a good business man. I guess that means that I compulsively review everything. Somebody has to do it. When the artists and designers learned that I reviewed all time sheets, the time records and billing improved. When the accountant learned that I reviewed all in-coming payments and that I correlated them with the time records and billing, he was very impressed. Some things I just can't delegate."

He turned around in his chair and looked up at the windows in the office buildings across the street. "Does every chief executive spend his days waddling around with this stuff?" He asked himself in a loud clear voice.

The telephone interrupted his thoughts. The telephone always interrupted him when he was busy. "Roland," said Maxine, "it is Henry Marts of Mattel. He says that it is important."

"Hello, Henry. Did you like the last group of prototypes and package designs that we sent you?"

"Roland, I loved them, but we have a problem. One of our competitors has introduced a line of wheeled goods for kids from age seven to ten. Toys "R" Us loves them and they asked us to come up with a line like it . . . only entirely different. I need you to come out here and spend a day with us to make suggestions, a few drawings, an idea or two. This is just the beginning. We'll pay for your time and all expenses, of course."

"Gee, Henry, I have a desk full of paperwork."

"So do I. That's the problem with all of us. Can you delegate some of it and come on out?"

Roland was intrigued with the problem. "Sure, Henry. I'll take the early morning flight tomorrow and return on the red eye. I can do some of my paper work on the airplane."

"Maxine, ask Susan as soon as she returns to the office to come in to see me." Then he left his desk untouched and walked into the studio to see the progress on Mattel's work and to add some creative touches. When he returned to his office, he felt better and concentrated on clearing the paper work from his desk. At about 4 P.M., Susan returned and came in to his office still wearing her coat.

"Has something important cropped up while I was out drumming up some new design work?" She removed her coat and sat down on the couch.

"Two important things. First, Henry Marts wants me in California for a day. I'm flying out early tomorrow and plan to return on the red eye."

"What's the second thing? It must be more important if you hold it for last."

"Grande Lyons Freres, the French firm, wants to buy me out."

"We built this firm together," said Susan angrily. "You can't sell out."

"I'm thinking very seriously about it. I'm an artist and I want to spend my time making art, not check book markings. Suzy, I'm tired of being the boss. I would just like to paint. We'll talk about it when I return."

FIFTY-FIVE

SUSAN LIFOREST sat at a table in the elegant dining room at the National Arts Club on Gramercy Park having lunch with John Gillespie of Philip Morris. He was her oldest client and although he no longer had any direct relationship with the industrial design firm, he felt responsible for their rapid expansion. His sexual advances had been subdued and she suspected that he had found another young playmate among the many that sought his business favors. During a weak emotional period when she was furious with Roland's frenzied devotion to business, she confided in John, revealing both her love and her frustration. As a man experienced in office flirtations, he tried to sway her feelings toward him. But her affection for Roland was so strong that he accepted her friendship and earnestly tried to help her to realize her romantic dream. When she had a problem, she called John, and he somehow found a way to be helpful.

This morning, she had arrived at the office at 8:30 A.M., dressed in a new pantsuit, made-up with a warm glow to her face, and her hair floated gently to her shoulders. She was prepared to talk to Roland about her devotion to him and to the firm. Their mutual love fueled the

business and she wanted him to know that without their emotional partnership, there would be no business. But he turned her away at the door.

"Suzy, I'm up to my ears with this project from Henry Marts. My
desk is floating with sketches. I need a good part of the day to come up
with a design that I can fax to Arthur. I left notes to Peter and Maxine
not to disturb me. Can you come back later this afternoon?"

He didn't even lift his head up from his drawings. She closed his
door abruptly, went into her own office, and tried to concentrate on her
schedule of meetings, conferences, and telephone calls for that day. But
she was furious. *He wants to sell the business and he won't even talk to me
about it,* she fumed. She picked up her telephone and called John
Gillespie.

"Susan, it is nice to hear from you. Frank tells me that your firm has
been working hard with our Kraft Division. Is there anything that I can
help you with?"

"I have some real problems and a need a wise business head."

"I don't know how wise it is, but I am always ready to aid a beautiful young woman in distress. Meet me at 12:30 P.M. at the National
Arts Club. Wait for me in the front lobby. It's a quiet place for lunch."

The wait was very short. They walked up the stairs to the front
lounge and then into the bar to wait for a table. By the time the bar-
man served the two dry martinis, the table was ready and they were
ushered into the small, intimate dining room surrounded by glass-
encased cabinets of antique China. The room was dimly lit, without
windows, and was the perfect setting for her mood.

"There is a great exhibit of members' paintings in the gallery," he
said. "Do you have a few minutes after lunch? My wife has an oil landscape in the show. She was an art major at Bryn Mahr and now that she
has some time, she's gone back to painting."

"I'd love to, John, but I have a problem. You are the only one I can
turn to. Roland wants to sell the business to a French advertising con-
glomerate and I am miserable about it. He's tired of the business and
just wants to play with his paints." Her face was flushed as she blurted

it all out quickly. She held her head in her hands with her elbows on the table and she looked right at him expecting an answer that would solve everything.

He was silent for several minutes and then he said softly, "Do you feel that he loves you?"

"There is no one else. He hasn't time for anyone else . . . not even me. I just know that he loves me; I can feel it. But he is the most compulsive person that I know when it comes to his work. I just can't get him to slow down."

"Would you like me to talk to him? I still remember our first meeting when he tried to convince me that he knew more about the marketing power of packaging than anyone else at Philip Morris." He laughed. "I guess that he has learned a lot since then . . . or maybe we have."

"He is a very talented designer," said Susan. "And, he is really so sweet and caring when you get to know him. His first wife broke up with him because they drifted too far apart. But we are really devoted to each other. Only he just takes me for granted and I hate it . . . hate it!" she emphasized.

They finished lunch, spent a few minutes in the gallery, and walked down the stairs to the lobby where John asked the doorman to hail a cruising taxi. "I have a few things to do here," he said. "I'll speak to you later." She kissed him on the cheek, thanked him, and closed the door of the cab. *He is such an understanding man,* she thought. *Why doesn't he stop fooling around with young women and concentrate on his rich and talented wife?*

When Susan returned to the office, Maxine said, "He's still not communicating with anyone. I think that I'm holding up a dozen telephone calls." She went into the studio to see the progress on the Revco products. "I must call Duane Inmont today to give him a progress report."

At 4 p.m., Roland emerged from his office and gave a group of detailed sketches to Peter Smith to have color renderings produced.

"These look great," commented Peter as he assigned the job to three of his artists. "I think Mattel will love them."

As he walked back to his office to return all his missed telephone calls, he spotted Susan. "Sorry about this morning. I've been so tense with business details that I needed almost a full day to get back to design work. I feel better now and I think that Henry Marts will be quite pleased."

The phone rang in his office and he walked quickly to his desk. "John Gillespie? Thanks, Maxine, I'll speak with him. Hello John, I haven't heard your voice in a long time. I'm delighted to talk with you."

"Roland, there is a rumor floating around Madison Avenue that you are planning to sell out to foreign interests. We're all concerned."

"News travels fast. It is just in the preliminary stage. I think that I must get away from business for a while and do some painting. But I'm not sure if this is the time."

"Will Susan leave with you? You know that she has been the positive force that binds Philip Morris to your company. We'd hate to lose her."

"I haven't discussed it with Susan yet, so I don't know her feelings. In fact, I am not even sure of mine."

"She is a very devoted and highly capable woman. Together you are a great team. It would be a shame to break it up."

"Thanks, John. I'll think carefully before I make the final decision."

FIFTY-SIX

SUSAN LIFOREST sat on the worn couch in her mother's Bensonhurst apartment. She had shuddered as she walked up the one flight of stairs and sensed the odor of home cooked food. "Please," she mumbled to herself, "let it not be one of their traditional meals. I hate it." But Rebecca Levins said, "How can you come to see Father and Mother and not eat a meal with us?" They ate at the small table in the kitchen with Rebecca and Isaac asking questions about her new apartment, her job, and when she planned to marry. "You know, Sue, when you get old, you can't have children," said Isaac. "Phyllis and Jerry now have two. Little Reva is already three years old and Seymour is going on eight. Soon, God willing, we will have a bar mitzvah. But we worry about you."

Susan was silent through most of the lunch, picking on her food, eating little, and talking only to comment on the food. She was waiting for them to ask the question she dreaded and her father asked it when they were seated in the living room. "Suzy, are you still involved with your boss?" He spoke very softly, as if he was afraid to ask the question.

She looked at both of them for several minutes before she answered. *Theirs is such a good marriage,* she thought. Nearly fifty years and she did not remember ever hearing a harsh word ever spoken between them. Neither could she imagine them having sex together. She seemed so prudish and he appeared to be so timid.

"My boss? I thought that he loved me, but he's leaving the company and going to some stupid place to paint pictures. I'm so miserable." She started to sniffle and then sob softly with her hand over her face. Rebecca moved to the couch and sat down next to her.

"My little girl. Tell me about your new apartment. I understand that you worked with a famous decorator and that it is beautiful. But sixty floors up! Isn't it scary when you look out of your windows?"

Susan's face lit up. "Oh, I love to look out and see the real New York. It is so glamorous. And so many famous people live in my building. How can I go live with a guy who wants to sit alone and paint? Oh, Mom! The company is getting to be so big. I want him to stay here with me." She began to cry once more.

Isaac moved to the couch and sat on the other side of his daughter with his arm around her. The three people sat together quietly until Susan suddenly pushed their arms away and stood up.

"First, he was married. So I waited. Then he left his wife and moved to the office. I waited. He finally got a divorce. Again, I waited and waited. We work so well together. But now he wants to go away. How can I wait for him anymore?" She walked slowly around the small room as her parents continued to sit on the couch. "You must come to dinner at my apartment. I'll ask Phyllis to bring her family, too. We will only be seven and my dining room table seats ten. I have a marvelous caterer and my maid will serve. We're a family. It will be great to be together again. Let's make it for next Sunday."

She walked into the bedroom to call her limo service. "It will be about a half hour before he gets here. Would you mind if I make a few calls?" Before they could answer, she had called the office and was speaking to Bruce Brunswick about two new accounts that she asked him to follow up on. "Jack Reynolds of Merck is a doll," she said. "He promised to have us design a new blow molded bottle for their veterinary line. And Richard Ellenbogan of Brightstar Cheese wants a new logotype for his line of soy cheese products. Both are all ready to start, but we have to get them into our schedule. Discuss it with Peter Smith and I'll talk to you sometime tomorrow in the office. Bye."

She felt more relaxed after the telephone call. Walking back into the living room, she smiled at her parents and kissed them both. "I'm so lucky to have parents like you. I feel so much better now. Thank you. You helped me to deal with my feelings. I'll call you sometime during the week. I'll send a driver to pick you up on Sunday. It should be about 12 P.M. See you then. I love you."

She walked down the flight of stairs to the small lobby where the limo driver was waiting. "Hello, Charles. I'm so glad that they sent you. I want to think a little. When you get to Manhattan, drive through Central Park on the way to my apartment. It should be beautiful there today."

FIFTY-SEVEN

THE PARTY had been Maxine's idea. No one was sure whether it was intended as a farewell gesture to Roland or a welcome to the new international ownership. Probably no one cared. It was a sad occasion and a happy one—sad that Roland was leaving and happy with thoughts of expansion and salary increases as promised by the new owners.

A maintenance crew moved all the partitions during the prior evening and the top floor studio became a party room decorated with balloons and an abundance of food and drinks. A three-instrument musical group played softly from a corner of the room. The party had begun with bagels and a wide assortment of cheese at 9:30 A.M. and had mushroomed into a gourmet style buffet at 12 P.M. Gerard Denerve, the director of U.S. operations for Grand Lyons Freres, assumed the role of host. He personally shook hands with everyone, was flippant with stories, and assured all the employees of Roland Levy Industrial Design, Inc. that the ideals and the goals of the founder would continue to be followed.

"The firm will now be called," he announced from the microphone in front of the musicians, "GLF Industrial Design, USA, Inc. We were going to name it RL-GLF Industrial Design, but our directors ruled against it. We are planning to open a GLF Industrial Design London, Ltd., as soon as we establish the new name here. Letters will be sent to all the clients explaining the benefits of the new management and our pledge to continue the same high standards. We have not decided on the managing director, but for the present, Susan Liforest will be in charge of all operations and Peter Smith will be the director of design. Mr. Lester Greenberg is here with me. I would like him to tell you how easily the BBDO agency was changed to its new name, GLF Advertising, USA, Inc."

Les, in a brief talk, explained how smoothly the agency was now operating and how much their billings had increased with advertising revenues from European products being marketed in the United States. He assured them that they would soon begin packaging redesign work for many of these firms. "And remember," he added with a wink, "the only way that they will set up a London division is to promote some designers and send them oversees to start the operation."

Maxine Nierman asked, "Where is Roland? It's his party and he isn't here."

"I spoke to him this morning, Maxine. He has moved into a New York Hotel and I believe that he is getting ready to take a well-deserved vacation," he said. "He promised to drop by for lunch. Has Susan been here? I've been so busy eating and talking that I haven't seen her all morning."

The party continued until nearly 3 P.M. when the maintenance crew began to return the studio to its working order. Most of the staff left, but the designers stayed to insure that their computers and workstations were returned to their right positions. Roland Levy called at 1:30 P.M. to explain that he could not make it to the party, but that he would drop by the office the next day to say good-bye to everyone. No one had seen or heard from Susan.

"I'm worried," said Maxine to several of the women from the office staff as they were preparing to leave the party. "This is so unlike her. I must call her at home. She may be ill."

Susan's telephone answering machine gave no clues. The voice informed the caller to just leave a message and she would return the call soon. Les Greenberg had already returned to his office. Anxious to learn where she was, Maxine called Les to ask him to speak to Roland. "He's staying at the Hampshire House. I'll call him there and perhaps he will be able to tell us something. It seems unlike Susan to miss a company party. When I get some word, I'll call you back. Stay in the office."

Roland did not answer the call. Les suggested that Maxine go home and that he would continue to call both Roland and Susan. At 6 P.M., he walked to the Hampshire House and asked for Roland Levy, and to his surprise, Roland answered the hotel guest telephone. Surprised that Les had come to the hotel and more concerned when he heard that Susan had not contacted anyone all day, he asked him to wait in the lobby while he dressed.

"We had a bad day in the office a few days ago and I have not seen her since," Roland explained as they sat facing each other on a large couch in the lobby. "I had just signed the deal to sell the business to Grand Lyons Freres and was taking personal things out of my office. She was vehemently opposed to the sale in the beginning and even had John Gillespie call to try to dissuade me. Now it seems that she has thought it over and likes the idea that we will be part of an international company. She just wants me to stay on as the chief executive officer and she wants to work with me as the chief operating officer. I explained that I just could not stay another day as a corporate executive. I want to go somewhere and paint. She said that she could not go with me because this was the opportunity she had always dreamed of. She pleaded for me to stay for a few more years. Then she asked me to go with her to her new apartment. She had just moved in a few weeks ago and she wanted me to see it."

"So what happened then and where is she now?"

"I was impressed. She now lives on the sixtieth floor of a very expensive building on Eighty-sixth Street and Second Avenue. It has very dramatic views of the city. She has a huge living room, den, and bedroom with a gourmet kitchen, breakfast room, and dining room. It was lovely. She invited me to move in with her, run the company together for a few years, and then we could make more permanent plans."

"She's beautiful and smart. It sounds like a good deal to me."

"Les, you have to believe me, I would love it. I love her. But I can't spend another day running a business. I'm an artist. I must be free . . . for a little while anyway."

"So where is she now?"

"I don't know. When I told her that I had already resigned and that the French group was seeking a French manager to replace me, she became so angry that she hit me and screamed, 'For this I waited a dozen years! Get out! Get out! I hate you!' I left the apartment quickly and went to the bar at the Hampshire House to get as drunk as I could. I haven't heard from her since."

"I hope that she hasn't done anything foolish."

"No, I'm sure she hasn't. She wants the top job too badly to harm her chances. She has just gone somewhere to pout. I'm sorry about it, but I'm leaving New York in two days. I have a lot of money and my accountant, Bill Sacher, will know where I am. I promised to drop into the office tomorrow and say good-bye to all my friends and colleagues. I'm sure that Susan is fine. She is just furious with me, but she will get over it."

He shook hands with Les, thanked him for his friendship, and promised to keep in touch. As Les walked out of the hotel, Roland checked the desk for any messages and then entered the dinning room for dinner.

At 9:30 P.M., he received a telephone call from Susan.

"Ruby r, I'm sorry about what happened. Maxine called me and said that you were worried. I just couldn't go to your party. It must have been great. Those guys are big spenders. I've been at my mother's apartment for two days," she lied. "Tomorrow I will be back in the office. Maxine told me that they are giving me a bigger title."

"That's wonderful, Suzy. I know that you will be happy. I'll be in the office tomorrow to say my good-byes to everyone. I'm leaving early the next morning."

"Where are you going? Are you leaving New York for good?" Her voice was very low and she spoke the words very slowly.

"I haven't decided completely. I'm still in the planning stage. I'll see you at the office tomorrow."

FIFTY-EIGHT

THE 8 A.M. flight from New York to Los Angeles was on time. Roland had arrived by limo with only one carry-on suitcase. He had sent a large corrugated box with clothing via UPS to be picked up at their office in Palm Springs, California. Dressed in slacks, a T-shirt, and a cardigan sweater, he walked to his assigned first class seat on the airplane just minutes before take-off.

He had mixed feelings about this journey. The sheer excitement about starting a new adventure was paramount among them. He was finally going to be an artist. Sure, he had always dreamed of becoming an artist, but as a poor boy, he dreaded the poverty and the lifestyle that was prevalent in the fine arts field. Now, at age forty, fortified with a sizable bank account, he was starting out to fulfill a dream, not sure of his own talents, but eager to leave a world composed of faceless men, steel and glass buildings, and uncreative drudgery. He hated the business world and he was finally running away from it.

But he was leaving Susan, maybe even forever. His marriage had failed and now his love affair failed, too. He felt sad to be leaving his mother. To his surprise, she was happy. "I'll be fine, Ruby," she explained. "I like my apartment, I have friends, and you have been giving me more money that I need. We'll speak to each other on the telephone and you will come in to see me now and then. Maybe if I feel well, I will come to visit with you. But I'm happy here."

The airplane ride was long and tiresome. He slept for most of the flight and each time that he awoke, even for just a few minutes, the flight attendant was there with the same question. "Is there anything that I can get you, Mr. Levy?" He nodded negatively and dozed off again. At 2:30 P.M. New York time, the plane landed in Los Angeles. It was 11:30 A.M. in Los Angeles and the connecting flight to Palm Springs was scheduled for 1:00 P.M. He walked to the airport cafeteria, ordered breakfast, and then searched the magazine rack for something to read. Annoyed that nothing seemed interesting or familiar, Roland was ready to doze off in one of the chairs. Then, he heard the announcement that passengers for the American Eagle flight to Palm Springs were to take a bus at Gate 21 to board the airplane at the other side of the airport. As if in a daze, pushing his wheeled carry-on bag in front, he followed the small group of passengers and was soon strapped in his seat on the two-engine propeller airplane.

He missed Susan. He smiled when he remembered her delight on seeing the lovely green golf courses spotted intermittently over the desert landscape and the beautiful homes surrounded by palm trees and lush greenery. He had to forget her. This was to be a new life.

His rented automobile was waiting for him at the Hertz parking area and he drove off to register his arrival at the Marriott Courtyard Hotel on Tahquitz Canyon Way. The next morning he would purchase some art supplies and join the Art Center of Palm Springs.

The art world is filled with untalented followers, men and women with a deep love for art and an overpowering desire to be included among those who exhibit mature paintings. They continue to register for art classes, attend openings, and associate with artists. They comprise a relatively large group whose attendance is nurtured by most galleries and art centers. The owners of these enterprises generally welcome new comers and encourage their participation even when they demonstrate limited artistic talents. The Art Center's director was pleased to meet Roland Levy, expressed delight that he planned to live and paint in the city of Palm Springs, and she offered him the use of their studio for his first week. He was overjoyed.

Starting early the next morning on a stretched watercolor sheet mounted on a lightweight drawing board, he started to sketch a neighboring building surrounded by palm trees. Then he introduced a pale yellow wash for the sky and over painted it with cobalt blue. With sepia and yellow ochre, he washed the stone masonry of the house and finally dabbed viridian to establish the terrain. Marsha Sorkin walked over to him from time to time and was fascinated with his illustrative dexterity, his composition, and his free use of color.

"Have you been painting long?" she asked.

"No," he smiled, looked up, and said. "This is my first watercolor painting. I have been in business in New York. I want to learn to paint well."

"You do have some ability. Are you planning to register for our courses?"

"Well, I dislike group art lessons. Is there someone here who can give me private instruction? I am prepared to pay for it."

"I teach art at the College of the Desert on Wednesdays and I teach some of the group classes here on Mondays. On other days, I just help out in the gallery, do some matting and framing, and occasionally arrange the paintings for an exhibition. Would you like to work with me?"

Roland turned his head and looked up from his chair. Marsha Sorkin appeared to be close to his age, a pretty woman with soft features, brownish blonde hair that she had tied in a bun behind her head, and a lovely figure, which was partially concealed by a light green artists' smock. He looked at his painting then he raised his head and looked at her again. "If it's okay with you, let's start tomorrow."

"I'll see you here at 10 A.M. tomorrow. We'll see how well we can work together and then we'll set up a program." She walked away and busied herself with her regular duties. Roland worked on his painting until nearly 1 P.M., and then he put his things on one of the studio shelves and left for lunch. That was enough painting for one day.

He walked along Palm Canyon Drive to the Hyatt Hotel, selected a table at the outdoor grill, ordered a lunch of soup and a half sandwich, and watched the tourists as they looked at the diners hoping to spot a familiar Hollywood face. Since popular actors Charles Farrell and Ralph Bellamy started the Racquet Club as a get-away for all their Hollywood friends, show business performers have continued to come to Palm Springs for relaxation. Frank Sinatra, Bob Hope, Dinah Shore, and Sunny Bono were among the many who built permanent homes.

Roland finished lunch, walked to his automobile, and rode through the residential sections noting the white stucco and concrete block sidings on many houses, their wide expanse, and the shrubbery, trees, and fences that concealed them from casual observers. He dined at his hotel and retired early, eager to begin professional painting instruction the next morning. He arrived before Marsha, set up his paper and pallet, and was ready when she walked in.

"I can't start my day before 10 A.M.," she said. "We'll take an hour for lunch and then finish at 3 P.M. That will give us four hours, two in the morning and two in the afternoon. If this is satisfactory for you, my fee will be twelve-fifty per hour, fifty dollars for the day."

For the next three weeks, they worked together, she helping him to select the appropriate watercolor sheet, arrange the colors around his pallet, and apply the right amount of water to retain the brilliance of certain hues. At the end of the third session, he showed her a brochure describing an outdoor show of paintings on Sunday.

"If you are free, Marsha, I would like to take you. It would be fun to see the type of work that is on exhibition."

"That would be nice. I can meet you here at 10 A.M. and we can walk the few blocks to the outdoor exhibition area. Would you mind if I bring someone else along, too?"

This puzzled Roland, but he agreed to meet her and felt that she did not want to get personal with him. Who was this someone else? Was she married? Engaged? He was content to keep their relationship impersonal, if that was the way she wanted it. He was just lonely.

On Sunday morning, as Roland parked his car, there was a pretty woman with long blonde hair sitting on the bench in front of the Palm Springs Art Center. Next to her sat a little boy. Both were dressed in matching dark blue shorts with white ankle socks and white sneakers. He wore a white tee-shirt. She wore a white v-neck shirt and a short light blue jacket. *An adorable matching pair,* he thought.

As he emerged from the car and started walking toward the front door, she called out softly, "Roland, are you looking for me? The center is closed today."

The little boy jumped off the bench, ran up to Roland with an outstretched hand and asked, "Hi ya! Are you Mommy's friend?"

"This is Jerry. He's my constant companion," explained Marsha, extending her hand to Roland and smiling. "He loves art shows. We didn't think that you would mind."

"Mind? I love it," said Roland shaking both their hands, Jerry's first then Marsha's. Taking her by the arm and grasping Jerry's hand, they walked the two blocks to the art show. He smiled all the way. They both enjoyed the paintings, discussing the technique, the composition, and the color. She knew some of the exhibitors, introduced Roland as a fellow artist, and Jerry trailed along with a bag of pretzels in one hand. At 12 P.M., Roland suggested lunch and they walked to the Hyatt outdoor grill. Jerry looked tired after the first few bites of his sandwich and Marsha said that it was time that she take him home. "No, Roland, don't bother. I know the bell captain. He'll get me a taxi." She kissed him lightly on the cheek and Jerry waved good-bye.

The art lessons continued for two more weeks until Marsha said that there was little more that she could teach him about watercolor painting. "You must find a place where you can paint regularly and every few days you should sit out on the desert somewhere and paint nature. You are a very talented man."

Totally fascinated by her, curious about her family life, and anxious to see her own paintings, he asked her to have dinner with him alone at the Indian restaurant near Racquet Club Road. She said that she loved tandori chicken and that he could pick her up at 7 P.M. when Jerry went to sleep. She lived in a small California style ranch house in a condo group on Sunrise Way and Alejo Road. She was alone in the living room when he entered the house and she explained that she had a woman who came in several times a week to help her with Jerry. They drove to the restaurant in silence.

FIFTY-NINE

MARSHA SORKIN and Roland Levy began to see each other regularly. He found a small studio off Sunny Dunes Road in a former one story industrial building that someone had divided into small artists' quarters. From a large display window in front, the California sun poured into the room and at the other end, a small bathroom and an industrial sink provided some of the necessities. He purchased an air conditioner, a kitchen table with four chairs, a large steel storage cabinet, two studio easels, and two drawing desks with small swivel chairs. It was in sharp contrast to his luxurious New York office, but when he looked out of the window, he saw beautiful foliage and palm trees instead of somber office skyscrapers. He saw no reason to have a telephone.

He painted the walls a light gray color and sprayed the ceiling white. He purchased some spotlights and studio lamps and prepared a small sign for the window, "Studio. R. Levy, artist in residence." Then he planned a work schedule, not to the needs of clients, but for the sheer fun of painting any subject he desired in either oil or watercolor.

Marsha shared a sandwich lunch with him two days a week when she was at the Art Center and on the one day each week when she was free, she would come in at 10 A.M. to help him clean and straighten up the studio. They talked about Palm Springs, about artists and painting, and little by little, she told him about her life. He listened to her with a caring interest, which she felt was sincere and she refrained from asking him questions about his past. She later explained that she thought it would be too painful for him. He told her that he had been divorced for several years and that he had left his position in an industrial design firm because he was tired of the pressures of business. He neglected to include anything concerning Susan. She told him about her marriage in Chicago to a college tennis player who was hired as the tennis professional at the Palm Springs Riviera Resort on Vista Chino. At first they were very happy and they rented a small house on Tachevah Drive. Then, he started drinking with the guests and when the manager accused him of raping one of the women, the *Desert Sun* carried the story. He felt disgraced, drank heavily, and when she told him that she was pregnant, he packed a suitcase and moved out. That was nearly six years before. Her mother came to live with her for a few years to help her with the baby, but when she started working, her mother returned to Chicago.

"When I first met you at the Art Center," she explained, "you looked and acted very strange. I knew that you were running away from something and I was afraid to be involved."

■   ■   ■

Les Greenberg kept in touch with Roland by sending him the agency newsletter accompanied by some handwritten comments. When Roland left the Marriott Courtyard Hotel for a small rented apartment at the Versailles on Amado Road, he sent him a Bose Radio with the note, "One of these days, I'm coming to Palm Springs just to see how you are doing. In case you have forgotten about us working people, just turn on this radio and listen to the news." Roland brought the radio to the studio and sent Les a photograph of himself wearing a dirty smock and sneakers standing in front of his easel . . . next to the radio.

One afternoon, an airport taxi stopped in front of the studio and Les, dressed in a dark blue business suit, paid the driver and walked into the studio. It was about 2:30 P.M. on a day that Marsha was in the studio. She was preparing to leave and Roland was washing up in the bathroom.

"Hello! It says Roland Levy on the window. Is he here?" He extended his hand and introduced himself. "I am Lester Greenberg."

The man is charming, she thought. *Maybe he is a process server. Maybe Roland really is in trouble and had run away with stolen money.* She was frightened. Roland never said that someone was looking for him. She answered in a loud voice. "No! Mr. Levy is not here. I think that he left. Maybe you can find him at the Hyatt Hotel."

Hearing this loud talk through the closed door in the bathroom, Roland was curious and opened the door slightly to look out.

"Oh! If it isn't the prince of Madison Avenue. I am so delighted to see you, Les. What are you doing to Palm Springs and how long do you plan to stay?" He walked from the bathroom with his face still wet and a towel in his hand "Come, sit down at the table and let's talk. This is Marsha Sorkin, my good friend and art mentor. Marsha, Les is my old business colleague and my friend."

"Are those your paintings on the wall? I knew that you could do it. They're beautiful."

"Enough about me and my work. What are you doing in town and why didn't you telephone to let me know? We would have met you at the airport."

Les sat down in one of the chairs. "Well, I am thirsty. What do you have to drink? It was snowing in New York when I left. I'm having dinner tonight at Wally's with Henry Marts. Susan set it up. She is on top of the Mattel account and very friendly with Henry and his wife. He wants to talk about giving the agency ten million dollars of his U.S. advertising budget. He is interested in additional exposure in France and Germany and we have big staffs in both countries. Say, why don't I surprise Henry and bring you along. He will be so happy to see you. Susan says that he often talks about you."

Marsha was a little confused by the conversation and she excused herself. "I must leave," she said smiling at Lester. "It was my pleasure to meet you. You are the first New York friend of Roland's whom I have met. I do hope to see you again." She left quickly, walked out to her car, and sat for several minutes before starting it. "I wonder what Roland really did in New York."

Les sat and talked to Roland for less than an hour, bringing him up to date on some of the expansions in his agency. As he was leaving, he asked, "Do you know a man named Montana St. Martin? I understand that he owns an art gallery in Palm Springs. He is sponsoring a fortieth anniversary celebration for Raymond Loewy's design of the Avanti automobile for Studebaker. I understand that he designed the car while he was living in Palm Springs. Many industrial designers are coming here in a few weeks for a conference to pay tribute to him. I'll send you an invitation. Since you live here, you should attend." Then he added, "I'm sorry that you can't come to dinner tonight. I'll give Henry your regards."

After he left, Roland closed the studio and drove to Marsha's house. Jerry met him at the door and jumped into his arms. "Mommy said you were with a friend. Where is he?"

Roland closed the front door and walked into the living room where Marsha was standing. "Well, Dear, that New York friend was expensively dressed and do you know how expensive Wally's Turtle Restaurant is? That is where Frank Sinatra, Bob Hope, and Gerry Ford dine. What did you do in New York? Print money?" She sat down on the couch and Jerry ran to her and sat on her lap.

Roland moved to where Marsha had been standing and leaned against the wall. His relationship with Marsha had grown steadily during the past months. During the week, she was busy as a single mother taking Jerry to school, shopping, and teaching at the college and the Art Center. She spent just one day a week with Roland in the studio and a few quick lunches. But gradually on weekends, they would dine at a downtown restaurant, see a movie, and Roland would spend the night in her home. *It is about time, to fill in some of the details that are confusing to her,* Roland thought.

"When I graduated from college," he began, "I wanted to make money immediately. So I started a small artwork business on Madison Avenue specializing in industrial design. With the help of a marketing assistant, we discovered how to sell our services and my little firm grew. I actually lived in the office seven days a week. We didn't follow the traditional professional procedure of publicizing our work and waiting for clients to call. We made end runs . . . we sought business contacts from every source and then we pushed to sell our services to them. It wasn't the Madison Avenue way. We prospered. But most of my time was occupied doing office work, which I hated. When a French firm offered to buy the business, I sold it for a lot of money."

Marsha was very quiet. Finally Roland said, "Let's put on Mexican hats and have dinner at La Mancha. Wouldn't you like that Jerry?"

Jerry ran to find his hat. Marsha kissed Roland on the cheek and walked with him to the door. "I am sorry that you couldn't talk about it before." The talk for the rest of the evening was about Palm Springs, Marsha's art classes, and the new gallery opened by Montana S. Martin. Then Marsha asked, "Who is Susan?"

SIXTY

THE MONTANA St. Martin Gallery with its sculpture garden was selected as the setting to exhibit the work of America's best-known industrial designer, Raymond Loewy. Chosen as "one of the timeless buildings of the century," it seems to float above the neighboring desert and reflect the beauty of towering Mount San Jacinto, rising eleven thousand feet behind it. Located at the northern entrance to Palm Springs, on North Canyon Drive and Tramway Road, the gallery was originally designed by architect Albert Frey, who created an expansive gull-wing roof over a modern automobile service station. The only evidence today of the architect's creation is the magnificent roof.

Both Montana St. Martin and Clayton Carlson, owners and creators of this new gallery, are art curators. They placed white concrete blocks and expansive steel framed clear glass windows below the roof line, transformed the surrounded desert terrain into a somber garden, and then enclosed it all with high picket style heavy black painted steel fencing. From the openings in the fence at the parking lot, one can view the huge pottery and sculptured stonework exhibited in the garden against the majesty of the mountain beyond.

In the gallery, the Studebaker "Avanti" automobile, designed in Palm Springs forty years before by industrial designer Raymond Loewy, was on display along with renderings and photographs of many of the other famous products designed in his offices in New York and Paris. Mr. St. Martin stood behind a table near the entrance to welcome everyone as they entered the gallery and to register them for the conference.

Marsha was anxious to attend both the exhibit and the conference. "I would like to know more about industrial design," she said to Roland. "This is Saturday. We both have the time. I'll ask Rosetta to stay with Jerry and we'll have the day for ourselves." Roland wasn't too anxious, but he reasoned that no one from his old firm would be there. He accepted her invitation.

The parking lot behind the St. Martin gallery was filled, so Roland parked his car on the side of the road and he and Marsha walked toward the building, she holding his arm and he walking quite slowly.

"Roland, if you would rather not go in, we can do something else." She sensed that he was nervous. She couldn't understand why. Since he was the president of a large industrial design firm, she thought that he would enjoy meeting some of the designers who were attending the exhibition. Feeling his tension as she held his arm she asked again, "Would you prefer that we did not go in?"

Slowly, looking down at the ground, he seemed to gather his thoughts. "I guess that there is no harm in seeing the exhibition. Raymond Loewy was an idol of mine when I was young. The Avanti car was years ahead of the whole automobile industry. I just was not happy running an industrial design business. But don't get me wrong, I loved to design."

As they entered the gardens and approached the gallery, he tried to think what he would do or say if he met Susan. He had just eliminated her from his life. She had been his close companion, his lover, and the subtle force that kindled the business, enticed clients, and stimulated its rapid advancement. But she could not understand his need to create not what clients demanded, but what he felt like creating. She just did not have an artistic soul.

Life with Marsha was so different. They were both creative souls, excited about color, responsive to the relationships of line and shapes, and accepting a work of art on its merit, not its ability to motivate or produce income. Susan could never live an artist's life. She wanted more and as she acquired more, her motivation increased.

Upon entering the gallery, Montana St. Martin asked his name and then suggested that he write his name and company in a large registration book placed on a pedestal. "I'm Roland Levy. I live in Palm Springs. This is Marsha Sorkin. We are artists."

Mr. St. Martin shook his hand firmly and asked, "Are you planning to attend the conference? It starts at 1 P.M. There isn't room in the gallery, so we have rented a suitable space in the center of town on Palm Canyon Drive. Here is a picture of the building and the address. Clayton Carlson is chairing the conference and we have a number of speakers who worked for Mr. Loewy during his early years. You are Mr. Levy? I'll place your name on the attending list."

Marsha enjoyed the exhibition. She loved the renderings and thought some of the product designs were very beautiful. Roland kept looking for Susan. Satisfied that she was not in the gallery, he finished the tour and suggested to Marsha that they have lunch at 12 P.M. so they could be on time for the conference.

"How about some Chinese food? Shall we go to the Flower Drum? It's just two blocks away from the building where they will hold the conference."

Roland was still nervous during lunch and searched the tables for Susan or any other familiar face from New York. They left the restaurant at 1 P.M. and arrived at the conference facility soon after its start and the introductory remarks by Clayton Carlson. An usher handed them programs and they found seats at the rear of the room. The room was bare except for a small stage with a podium and microphone. The folding chairs were arranged in eight rows of ten seats each and most of the seats were occupied. The room was dark and a woman standing behind the podium was directing a slide projection of current product designs and corporate identification systems. Glancing at the program under the dull illumination of the exit sign, Roland noted that the first presentations were current work of industrial designers to be followed by some of the projects designed by Loewy's offices in New York, Paris, and Palm Springs. There were a few designers in attendance that had worked for Loewy during those years and their names were listed as the principal speakers. Other speakers' names were listed under the heading of "Today's Industrial Design Leaders." The room was too dark to read those names. The audience was composed chiefly of members of the Industrial Designers Society of America, most of them from California and neighboring states.

As he looked up at the slides, he heard the speaker point out that the designers in her international firm had created some of the most popular products on the market today. Roland uttered a low gasp. "Marsha, see that vacuum cleaner and that Revco trademark? I designed them both.

He sat quietly, squeezing Marsha's hand and leaning forward on his chair as the other slides were projected. Suddenly, the projections ended, the lights went on, and the speaker made a few concluding remarks. Marsha could feel Roland's anger. He stood, mumbled something about designer credit, and said in a laudable tone, "Marsha, let's leave!"

From the stage, there was a spark of excitement; the woman moved to the edge of the stage, her face seemed to light up with wide opened eyes and an ear-to-ear smile. She shouted into the microphone, "Ruby, is that you?"

She had changed. Her hair was blonde and was cut short with some strands falling over her forehead and side bangs covering her ears with just enough visible for a pair of black pearl earrings to dangle almost to her shoulder. She wore what had to be a designer created pantsuit that curved graciously with her figure and with the aid of extra high shoes, made her look taller than he remembered her. But sparkling from a finger on her left hand and visible even from his distance was a diamond ring. *Yes,* he acknowledged to himself. *It is Susan, a new Susan, as an affluent beautiful business executive.*

"Ruby! Please wait," she insisted softly, but in a determined tone. "Please, I must talk with you."

Roland continued walking toward the door, hand in hand with Marsha. When they reached the exit stairs, they both turned to wait. Susan was walking quickly toward them and following closely behind was a tall dignified looking man, Gerard Denerve, the American director of Grand Lyon Freres.

"Roland Levy! *Bonjour!*" exclaimed Gerard as he approached. Susan was first and completely ignoring Marsha's presence; she put her arms around Roland's neck and buried her head on his shoulder. "I missed you so much," she purred softly. Marsha dropped Roland's hand and moved two steps away. Gerard Denerve stood a few feet behind Susan. By this time, the next speaker was introduced and the lights were dimmed again for the slide presentation.

"Why didn't you write? Why didn't you call? Lester told me that you were out here. I wanted to see you so much. You know Gerard. I run the company now, both in the U.S. and in London." She held him closely for several minutes before he loosened her grip.

"I see that you have taken over all my work. Who does the new designs?"

"We have a large staff and retainers from many important firms. But I miss you, Ruby. Have you had your fill as an artist? Come back!"

"No, I'm through with corporate life. I'm happy as an artist here."

"Ruby! Ruby!" she sobbed and suddenly began beating him lightly on the chest with both hands. "You've spoiled all my dreams." She turned and fell into the waiting arms of Gerard Denerve. He extended his right hand to Roland, shook it firmly, smiled and turned around, leading Susan back to their seats in the darkened room.

Roland reached for Marsha's outstretched hand and together they walked down the stairs, out into the street, and along Palm Canyon Drive toward their car. Roland was silent.

"Susan is a beautiful women," Marsha finally said as they sat in the car.

"She was more beautiful then and she used her seemingly naïve charms to solicit business from some of the most hardened executives. Without her, my business would never have grown so quickly. But we had opposite goals. I was happiest designing and creating things and satisfied to just make a living doing what my talents permitted. She hung on to my coat tails and strove for wealth and power and never understood my goals. I welcomed the French buy out; she feared the loss of power. We both probably won in the end. She has evidently enticed the Frenchman and he has given her the power that she yearned for. Together, she and I were a team. We made an end run through Madison Avenue, but we arrived at two different goal posts."

He turned to Marsha, smiled lovingly, and kissed her waiting lips, tenderly holding her as tightly as he could without sitting on the gearshift box that separated their seats.

"Let's go home," he suggested softly. "Our little family is waiting."